Praise for

START AT THE END

"Emma Grey is a talented, beautiful writer, full of wit and wisdom and brilliant observations. I loved this book immensely and got a feeling that I have not had in a very long time: of not wanting it to end, of wanting to know everything."

—ROBINNE LEE, author of *The Idea of You*

"Captivating and original, this exquisitely crafted story sits in the ache of loss and gently shows us how to breathe again. Emma Grey writes as though emotion itself is her native tongue."

—ANNA JOHNSTON, author of *The Borrowed Life of Frederick Fife*

"A new novel by Emma Grey always goes to the top of my TBR list! Warm, wise, and wonderful. I could not love her books more."

—ALEXANDRA POTTER, author of *Confessions of a Forty-Something F##k Up*

"Equal parts tender, hilarious, and achingly perceptive, *Start at the End* broke my heart, and then swiftly put it back together again. I laughed, I ugly-cried, I absolutely loved it!"

—PIP DRYSDALE, author of *The Close-Up*

"Emma Grey's delicate balance of light and shade in her storytelling is nothing short of genius."

—TESS WOODS, author of *The Venice Hotel*

"*Start at the End* is devastating, hopeful, and deeply human. This book should come with a handkerchief and a tub of ice cream."

—JANE TARA, author of *Tilda Is Visible*

Praise for
PICTURES OF YOU

"With rich characters and a page-turning plot, this emotional story is one I wasn't able to put down. Grey's writing is beautiful."
—JILL SANTOPOLO, author of *The Light We Lost*

"An addictive page-turner with aching emotion and captivating characters. Weaving together themes of love and loss, seduction and control, this beautifully written novel is a must-read."
—AUDREY INGRAM, author of *The Summer We Ran*

"Emma Grey is back to break our hearts in the most wonderful way. A knockout. Five stars are simply not enough."
—KERRYN MAYNE, author of *Lenny Marks Gets Away With Murder*

"Nonstop drama and surprise[s] in this twisty tearjerker."
—*BookPage*

Praise for
THE LAST LOVE NOTE

"Why do I feel like I've been waiting all my life to read this book? What a gorgeous, charming, funny, heartrending, longing-filled triumph of a read."
—KATHERINE CENTER, author of *Hello Stranger*

"Grey's debut adult novel will break readers' hearts, taking them on an emotional ride but leaving them feeling hopeful."
—*Booklist* (starred review)

"An exquisitely heartbreaking emotional love story, packed with light, tender touches. I will be recommending this to everyone."
—PAIGE TOON, author of *Only Love Can Hurt Like This*

"Emma Grey weaves riotous romantic comedy through a journey from love to loss and back again with a raw honesty and intensity that is equaled only by her capacity to find humor and light in the darkest of moments."
—NINA D. CAMPBELL, author of *Daughters of Eve*

START AT THE END

A NOVEL

EMMA GREY

Zibby Publishing
New York

Start at the End: A Novel

 Published in the United States by Zibby Publishing, New York.

Library of Congress Control Number: 2025946335
Paperback ISBN: 978-1-968506-00-1
Hardcover ISBN: 978-1-968506-01-8
eBook ISBN: 978-1-968506-02-5

Book design by Neuwirth & Associates
Cover design by Emma Rogers
Cover art © Jane Khomi/Moment via Getty Images

www.zibbymedia.com

Printed in the United States of America

10 9 8 7 6 5 4 3 2 1

For Sebastian

May you always return to your music

the end

Well, this is an uncontested new low. My best friend has let herself into my apartment and found me passed out at the piano in my wedding dress. She shakes me gently, pain shooting to my head as I meet her compassionate gaze—shame chasing the pain, tears chasing the shame, a finished piece, the best I've ever written, taunting me on the music stand beside an empty bottle of wine.

"That was for him." I nod at the manuscript, voice raspy, throat dry from a thousand glasses of pinot gris and hours of wailing. Black and white notes blur as I stumble through the opening bars, clashing tones hurting my brain, scared I'll never get this jangled mess straight again. Not just this piece. *My life.*

"Audrey, come on. I'll make some coffee." She lifts my hands from the keyboard and pulls me from the piano stool into a hug. "I'm sure it's incredible. You're just tired."

We both know I am more than tired. Much more. I'm hungover. Devastated. Angry. *Furious*, actually—

We catch sight of ourselves in the full-length mirror: Rachael in dark jeans and a soft cream sweater, blond layers slicked into an immaculate ponytail as she props me up—face blotchy, eyes red, brown hair tumbling from a claw clip—the bride of Frankenstein. I loved the simplicity of this secondhand gown. I was convinced the black ribbon belt would elevate the ivory, as if fussing over the little details could somehow have saved us from this mess.

"All of this would have been lovely," Rach says as we slip further into a warped horror version of what was supposed to be the happiest day of my life.

Sunlight was meant to be streaming through these windows, but the curtains have been drawn for days. There should be mimosas. Strawberries. Croissants. *Hope.*

The doorbell cuts through the fantasy, and I clutch Rach's arm. "Did you call off hair and makeup?" I can't bear the idea that a duo of flawless, upbeat women may step into this wreckage. I don't have the strength to explain this turn of events to a single other person, or even to hear Rach explain on my behalf.

"It's all done," she assures me with gentle confidence as she heads to the door. My parents and Sara aren't due until after lunch. I need to sober up before I can endure even my own family reeling alongside me, reaching for some higher purpose to explain my canceled wedding, because apparently everything has to happen for a fucking reason these days.

When Rach returns moments later, she's smothered by a delivery of flowers. An explosion of pastel pink and antique cream peonies—my favorite—tied with a white ribbon. Flowers like these don't say, *Sorry your life is in bits.* They blast *Congratulations* or *Well done* or *Good luck!* I pull the card from its little white envelope. And, as the florist's handwriting comes into focus, all the oxygen whooshes from my lungs: *See you at the church. Fraser. x*

When did he order these?

Back in our other life, no doubt, before everything lurched sideways, forcing Rach to spend two straight days tearing apart our fairy tale. She assured me that handling this was an unwritten role in the bridesmaid duty statement—making the calls, canceling the bookings. *Detangling me from the future I was promised. Sweeping away the wedding when it all imploded . . .*

"All the best love stories end at the altar," I whisper as the peonies hit the wooden floor, crushed petals scattering at my feet.

In Rach's eyes, there's a flash of some boiling maelstrom of emotion that I can't pinpoint and that we simply can't entertain. She cannot break. She is the scaffolding.

Just as fast, it's gone again and she gathers herself, grasps my bare shoulders, holds me firm, and makes me look at her while she tries to bore some optimism into my brain subliminally. She is so beautiful. So competent and comforting. *So lucky that this is me and not her . . .*

"I know it seems impossible now, but this doesn't have to be the end for you," she promises, unable to disguise the waver in her voice.

I cannot take toxic positivity today. Not even from Rach, who is just trying to save me from myself. I *won't.*

"Look around us," I whisper, glancing at the bomb site of tulle and lace and the climate-scientist-sanctioned eucalyptus-leaf confetti I was so obsessed with just a week ago. "It's all over, Rach. Accept it. This is the end."

the
start

1

Three years ago

Audrey

"Just wait, you'll change your mind! You'll wake up one day and that biological clock will be *blaring*!"

It's too early on a Monday morning for this. Jill is my colleague. My age, mid-thirties, with babies three and four on the way. She bounded into the office after the ultrasound last month, marched straight over to me, and said, "We thought we'd try for one more and of course we hit the jackpot, didn't we! Twins!"

I was pretty sure I was meant to give a standing ovation. Instead I just said, "Wow! Twins! *Imagine!*" and tried very hard *not* to imagine it, because doing so would have broken me out in hives.

Mercifully, my phone vibrates now. I wave the device at Jill and point at the screen as if to convey that I have urgent business to attend to even though I'm the office manager and it's probably a reminder to reorder the firm's letterhead or finish the mandatory training.

Dear Audrey,

Thank you for sending the latest bill. On my calculations, we were overcharged $600.00 . . .

Shit. I processed the invoices in a rush last night, hurrying home to catch an online master class in advanced orchestration and acoustic sound analysis—something my boss, Peter, will neither understand nor appreciate. He aims to "delight clients." Not because he likes them. But because they fund his ski trips to Aspen, which is an expensive endeavor from Australia's capital, especially if you're forced to "drag your ungrateful family of five with you." Peter has a very low tolerance both for his children and for the variety of careless errors I seem to litter through the workplace, as my mind is frequently anywhere but on this job.

Jill darts out of the kitchen. She spends several hours a day wrangling hyperemesis gravidarum in the office toilets and the rest of her time playing phone tag with the primary school principal, strategizing about her eldest, Raphie. *He's named for the Renaissance painter*, she'd told me on my first day here in case I was confused, perhaps, that she might have named him after the Ninja Turtle. Raphie was free-range-parented until he sent Jill into a spiraling meltdown, so now he's enrolled at an exorbitantly priced Montessori school from which, on a particularly bad day last week, he managed to escape.

I flick on the kettle and read the rest of the client's message.

> I'm sure it's just an oversight, but grateful if you could follow up. Please note, I'll be on a three-month work trip from tomorrow with patchy internet access.
>
> Best,
>
> Fraser Miller

Three months? What does he do?

My mistake with Jill was divulging my secret: I don't want kids. Now she's acting like my admission was a stealth attack and has launched a relentless multi-level-marketing-like sales pitch for motherhood.

"You say you don't want them *now*," she chirped yesterday. "But you will! You're still in your twenties."

"Thirty-four," I'd clarified.

"Fertility drops off a cliff at thirty-five, Audrey . . ."

Not if I push it off first, Jill.

The water boils and I pour it into my Ruth Bader Ginsburg mug and let the tea brew while I heat my lunch and respond to the email.

Dear Fraser,

Thank you for your message. I'll check this and get straight back to you. I hope you're traveling somewhere warm.

Best,

Audrey Sullivan

I'm nothing if not an ironic mix of overqualified and administratively incompetent. Perhaps "qualified for a different job" is a better description, although I don't want to think too hard about the pieces of paper that I technically do and don't hold or the whole thing will bring on heart palpitations again.

With the response sent, I lean against the counter and shut my eyes. I've been trying to incorporate micro-meditations into my day, even though I am not that sort of person and the entire staff is foiling it. I'm half a nostril through a cycle of alternate-nostril breathing when another colleague, Brenda, materializes and starts ferreting for a tea bag and rattling through spoons just as Jill returns from her efficient performance in the bathroom and kicks off as if she'd never left. The all-day sickness detracts from her make-me-a-mother mission, so she tries to conceal it from me, which is a good thing, as I'm a sympathetic vomiter.

Spotting an accomplice, she sidles up to Tea-Bag Brenda and, in a holier-than-thou whisper—as if she's just discovered some scandalous piece of office gossip, like why the senior accountant left so abruptly (mutinous affair with the executive assistant) or who leaves the microwave in such a state (Derek)—she says, "Audrey will regret this childless-by-choice malarkey, don't you agree?"

They glare at me so intensely that I'm forced to appraise myself in their wake: tailored black pants, ordinary white business shirt, flyaway brown hair in a loose ponytail. It's not high fashion, or any fashion really, but I'm sent to the dusty basement several times a week to retrieve archival boxes full of legal documents, so—

"Is it just that you haven't met the right man?" Jill argues, through her heteronormative lens.

"The right *person*," I suggest, but her face is blank.

I can't pick this battle now. I'm freshly panicked about the fact that my friends melt at the sight of a baby while my insides *twist*. "Would you like to hold her?" mothers ask, forcing the bundle into my arms, where it assimilates with my anxiety and starts screaming. I don't know how to operate babies. I don't want to know!

Just as I'm willing the microwave to ding or my phone to illuminate with a legitimate, work-related matter that I must excuse myself to attend to instantly—paper jam, sticky-note shortage, demise of another tropical fish in the office aquarium—I seem to manifest Fraser's reply, which I scrutinize as if my life depends on it.

`Antarctica. Currently minus 57 degrees Celsius . . .`

So, about as frosty as this office.

"I blame the hormones in chicken," Jill declares, cradling her bump. Brenda, dunking her tea bag and staring into space, is probably rehashing her curriculum vitae or imagining herself on some beach in the Maldives, as I often do.

It's actually climate change, I want to argue. It's that I'm terrified of bringing a child into a future this bleak. I see myself abandoning the poor thing when I'm eighty. *Over to you, kid. Apologies for Armageddon . . .*

But I can't say that. Jill will accuse me of traumatizing her unborn twins. Instead, I nod, as if I'm seriously pondering the hormonal-chicken hypothesis and type to Fraser—a man I have never met:

```
Antarctica? Wow! Why?
p.s. Please tell me it's the penguins?
```

"It could be vaccines . . ." Jill muses, her TED Talk taking a well-worn conspiratorial turn as Brenda, finally showing proof of life, flicks her eyes at mine.

The phone in my hand stays disappointingly silent. Fraser is probably a busy man. My imagination dresses him in a dark suit and deposits him in a high-rise boardroom, lobbying about some vital piece of environmental Antarctic business. I shouldn't be fraternizing with a client without chalking up the billable time, but as Jill is now drawing "causal links" between my childlessness and what she frequently refers to in hushed tones as "feminism having gone too far," I am absolutely desperate.

```
Sorry, I don't mean to be inquisitive,
Fraser. I've just never known someone to
travel somewhere so remote. Are you a
photographer? Is it the isolation?
```

"It's just *unnatural* not to want a baby, Audrey!" Jill declares. "At church last Sunday, the pastor said—"

"Audrey, can I have a word?" Brenda interjects, finally roused from her mundanity-induced coma and hovering beside me, ready to airlift me out of Jill's one-woman war on population decline. "There's an anomaly in the weekly budget report you emailed earlier."

Is this about Fraser Miller or some fresh mistake? Either way, I rescue my lunch from the microwave and trail behind Brenda to her immaculate desk, where it becomes apparent that there is a yawning chasm between where I am now and where the exacting KPIs of Bates, Scrivener, and Daley Family Law expect me to be. It makes a refreshing change, at least, from being berated over my lack of maternal drive.

All through the conversation, I keep one eye on my phone. *Have I offended him, somehow, with the inquisition?*

Once Brenda lets me go, I type a hurried and professional follow-up while walking back to my desk.

> Fraser, my apologies for taking up your time. I'll be in touch soon re: your bill.

Tumbling into my workstation, I search "How to know if you're having a quarter-life crisis." Wait, that can't be right. I'm thirty-ish now, four threes are twelve, carry the zero—*Am I more than a third through my life already? What am I doing with it?*

And that's when a notification flashes, announcing an email from a former university classmate.

> Subject: Bit of a weird one
>
> Audrey, sorry to contact you out of the blue. Have you heard about this investigation into historic claims of academic misconduct?

I go stone cold. Everything rushes back. The confusion. The fear. The shame and guilt and defeat. Suddenly I don't care about Jill or my fertility or Brenda's spreadsheet or whatever percentage of a life crisis I was galloping toward. I can't think straight about any of it, because I'm right back at that distressing fork in the road where I so spectacularly lost my way.

I drop my phone on the desk as if it's poison, which nudges the mouse and wakes the computer, the whole exchange with Fraser Miller fluttering into the inbox like a burst of sunshine.

Thanks, Audrey. Appreciate it. And no need to apologize.

Cheers,

Fraser

(Ocean scientist. Likes penguins.)

2

Fraser

Another message arrives from Bates, Scrivener, and Daley Family Law. From the partner this time, Peter Reed. The sight of his name shoots a Pavlovian pain to my heart.

It's a shock that Maggie and I are here at all, seeing divorce lawyers, trying to steer ourselves and Parker through the wreckage without careening off this broken road, sheer drops on either side. Floundering at the wrong end of the story we began, barefoot and idealistic, beneath a hibiscus trellis on a Fijian beach nine years ago.

"It's not that I'm opposed to traditional weddings," I'd explained to Maggie back then. What I really opposed was the flamboyant version favored by her parents. They'd wanted a splashy, black-tie affair at a Sydney rooftop bar, the guest list a Who's Who of the people most likely to give us a leg up. "I just think it would be nice to exchange vows on a finite resource before climate change devours it."

"You want to start our marriage on shaky ground?"

I took her hand in mine, gazed into her beautiful, disappointed face, and used what she would later describe as my "lethal Adam Brody charm" as I said, "Not shaky ground, Maggie. Precious ground . . ."

And that had been it. No more acquiescing to her parents! She was in love with the symbolism. And with me. And I loved her. Still do love her, in changing ways that I'm fumbling to articulate, except that it's *not in the way she needs*—a fact the shared-custody consent orders attached to the lawyer's email make blaringly, heartbreakingly real.

Shared custody. I glance in the mirror at Parker's empty car seat—sun hat and coloring book flung beside it—and there's that growing band of pressure in my chest. Maggie and I have been separated for more than a year now. None of this is new. But I feel like I'll never acclimatize.

"Think of it as part-time unencumbered," my workmate advised. His own marriage is in shambles, and he doesn't have the guts to do anything about it. Unlike Maggie, who is dismantling this relationship as if it were an Olympic sport. I'm hit with a jarring memory of last week's disastrous handover. The way Parker clung to me while Maggie, with tears in her eyes, pried her gently from my arms.

Compartmentalize, Fraser. Get out of the car. I shove the phone into my jeans pocket, on a mission to collect the last few things for tomorrow's expedition, four thousand miles from the epicenter of this chaos.

"Work always comes first!" Maggie accused in Wednesday's mediation session. "Could you have chosen *anywhere* farther from us?"

Could have gone to the Arctic, I'd thought, but I'd already been chastised for using humor to deflect from our problems. I wasn't about to mansplain geography.

"I applied for the research grant eighteen months ago," I reminded her. "Our breakup wasn't on the radar then." *Not technically.* But this marriage has been on life support for years. Sometimes I wonder if our focus on Parker was an unconscious attempt to glue together frayed ends, only for the weakened connection to sever in the middle.

Inside the shopping center, a teenager slams into me,

swallowed by a giant puffer jacket as if he's the one heading south. I barely understood the various subspecies of teens when I was in high school myself, despite knowing my own confirmed place in the ecosystem: science nerd. I try not to fast-forward to this parenting phase with our daughter. She'll be drifting between two houses while *everyone else's parents* green-light vodka-fueled parties and "Schoolies" celebrations on the Gold Coast. Our biggest negotiation with her now is whether or not she can have Minecraft on her iPad.

Surely I can't be the only person in this shopping center running on empty? What's that word? *Sonder.* That idea that everyone you pass has a life as complex as your own and you're just a background extra in theirs.

It's one thing being irrelevant in the lives of strangers. Another when it's your wife. With every passing legal document, Maggie and I are shifting roles, casting each other in fewer scenes. I can't work out how to assign her a minor part, when she's been the main love interest all this time. Her playing "mother of my child" dooms us to stress fractures and jagged edges. A lifetime of papering over rifts because this can never be the clean break we really need.

My phone pings. It's her. Did you get the email about the consent orders?

Her need for certainty is driving this divorce at warp speed. We'll blink and it will all be signed off and done, everything parted and separated and settled, the three of us ensconced, no doubt, in some wretched new normal.

"Everyone finds parenting hard," my mother chimed in last night. "Your father and I slept in separate bedrooms for two years after your brother was born! Can't you give it another shot? Have some counseling? It doesn't look good . . ."

And there it was. Mum's obsession with How Things Look. *The boys are hugely successful!* I imagine she boasts. *Joshua is a renowned conductor of a symphony orchestra. Fraser's a scientist. Blissfully happy with Maggie—she's a talented psychiatrist, no less! Oh! And my grandchild! Here, let me show you the brag book . . .*

As she dished up roast vegetables and whisked the gravy, she carried on as if it had been *me* who took an axe to the marriage. "How is fracturing your family in Parker's best interest, Fraser? Why don't you fight for Maggie?"

Fight for her?

In that moment it dawned on me that my wife is right. You can't fight for something you no longer want. There's no battery left between Maggie and me. The harder we work to rewire things and the more we solder over our brokenness, the higher the risk we take that this quiet desperation will destabilize and mutate into something more explosive.

"Mum, the relationship is complete." That's how Maggie had put it. She'd said it was easier for the brain to accept than saying it was over.

"But we don't do divorce in this family!" Mum wielded the brag book as evidence, as if her precious bunch of photos could save us from years of corrosion. In frustration, I ripped it from her hands.

"You have to stop shoving this at everyone!"

"I don't!"

"Dad said you showed photos of Parker to some woman at the print store yesterday."

"She was interested, Fraser. Parker is glorious!"

"She was collating a job application," Dad added, quietly, never very keen to enter the fray.

I'm not normally so short with Mum. Or with everything. "I'm sorry we can't retrofit our story to match a perfect narrative," I said, more kindly. "I wish we could."

By the time I gather my wits at the shops, I've delivered

myself to the outdoor adventure store and seem to have paused beside a display of soft toys that Parker would love. They're all bundled up in cute little scarves and beanies and mittens, and the fact that I've gravitated here can be easily explained: I desperately miss my almost eight-year-old.

A trifle more ambiguous is why I've subconsciously bypassed all the seals and orcas and Parker's personal favorite, the polar bears, in favor of the plush penguin that has found its way into my hands.

It could be a loaded gun, the way I place it carefully back on the shelf and back away. The ink isn't dry on the divorce papers. I cannot entertain . . . *penguins* and their flirtatious associates. I'd only wreck things for some other woman while my head is still scrambled. I need to compartmentalize this, too.

"What are your three things, Daddy?" Parker asks as I dump the shopping on the dining table an hour later. We're on our regular after-school video call, and she's asking what three things I am grateful for today—a list I'm finding increasingly hard to assemble lately.

"Well, I have an incredible little girl," I start. It's how this always goes, and she giggles.

"You're going on an important trip," she reminds me. "You're fixing the world." I really should sit her down and explain that there's only so much that one scientist can manage. Our narrative—Maggie's and mine—has always been that *Daddy wouldn't just leave for several months at a time unless it was very important work.* And here I am, going away again, wrestling with familiar guilt, but it's worse now when my time with her is already halved.

"What's your third thing, Daddy?" she asks, twirling her

dark curls through her fingers. It's a self-soothing stim according to Maggie, who believes that Parker may be somewhere on the autism spectrum, something we intend to investigate properly once we're through all this family disruption.

The email exchange with Audrey Sullivan floats to mind. But how can I tell Parker the highlight of my day was a few chatty messages about financial administration with the office assistant at the firm handling our divorce?

"I saved six hundred dollars," I spin it instead. "When I get back from this trip, why don't we have a little holiday at the beach?"

And there's the iridescent little smile that I live for.

3

Audrey

"Can you see where you've gone wrong?" Peter booms, pointing at the second page of the employee agreement I skimmed when I first started work here. I feel like I'm starring in a police procedural.

I am *so* bad at boundaries. Obviously, I buried that lead during the interview for this job, given we deal in highly sensitive material, but now it looks like I'm going to bring on my own demise.

"The error was your fault," he accuses me.

"It's only six hundred dollars!" I argue. A minor issue surely, given the amount of money this place turns over. "And Fraser Miller wasn't angry about it!"

Fraser Miller was quite charming. And I'm used to dealing with an endless parade of cranky, incompatible couples citing no-fault "irretrievable breakdown." I take their coats and shuffle them into our fancy lounge while I deliver inane niceties like "Did you find a spot okay?" knowing there is *zero* parking near our office, they've probably had a blowup about it in the lift, and now they're glaring at each other, and at me like I caused it.

"Fraser Miller wasn't angry because he is a good person!" Peter says. "In fact, you couldn't have picked a nicer man to financially inconvenience!"

Usually, I go the other way. I am magnetized to the bad boys. Historically, I've selected the type of relationship that burns up like space junk reentering the earth's atmosphere in the kind of spectacular crash that makes everyone look up and say, *Ooh, did you see that? What's happened to Audrey now?*

Not that a brief email exchange over an accounting discrepancy with one of our technically-still-married clients falls into the relationship category.

"And then, instead of investigating the complaint properly or fixing it," my boss continues—unfairly, I might add, because I *was* investigating it—"you chose to flirt with our client, pressing him for details about his personal itinerary!"

Flirt with him?

He waits for me to dig myself further into this hole, and of course I oblige within seconds. I'm one of those people who crumble in the face of expectant pauses.

"He was going to Antarctica!" I argue. "Wouldn't you be intrigued?"

He smacks the desk with the contract, nostrils flaring. If he doesn't settle down, he'll bring on a medical episode and I'll have to whip out my half-baked skills from the first aid training I autopiloted through.

"It is not your role to be *intrigued*," he says, shouting. "It's your role to get the accounts right so that our valued clientele do not have to contact you in the midst of their busy and important lives—which in Dr. Miller's case involves *rescuing us from extinction*—to discuss *penguins*!"

I stifle a smile. And a crush. On Dr. Miller, obviously, not my rage-fueled boss.

"Perhaps this would be more amusing if it was your only offense," Peter suggests.

Sorry, is a SWAT team going to pop out from behind the

leather armchair and arrest me? I'd known this job would be a fiasco from Day One. My attention deficit hyperactivity disorder (self-diagnosed until I can find the doctor's referral) means I am not cut out for things like keeping on top of the filing and sending entirely accurate bills. What I *am* good at is fetching boxes of tissues when warring couples break down in the conference room. Or when I break down in the toilets, wondering if my parents ever looked at me as a baby and thought, *I hope she grows up to follow her dream of always ensuring there's enough toner in the office printer.*

Actually, knowing my parents, that's exactly where they envisaged me—rummaging through filing cabinets in my mid-thirties, inventorying the paper clips. *You want a nice, safe job, Audrey. There's too much uncertainty in the world. Just choose this one predictable thing in your life and you'll thank us.*

What they really meant was *DON'T CHOOSE MUSIC.*

Thwomp! Peter dumps a big pile of manuscript paper onto the desk, and I recoil in horror. These are very familiar lines and dots and squiggles and lyrics. My *show.*

"This was discovered on the photocopier," he says. Exhibit B. My work in progress. Not my "work work," obviously, but in my spare time I'm crafting a musical set in a divorce lawyer's office, starring an unlucky-in-love millennial receptionist—

I thought my document had failed to print. "Who found this?" I ask. Some joyless stickler for office etiquette, no doubt. Surely everyone uses the office printer for private matters every so often?

"It's not just the fraudulent use of office supplies, but the fact that you're clearly working on this theatrical masterpiece on company time."

"That's not true," I insist, jumping up, finally having an

inaccuracy to defend. "I can't think creatively in the office." *Believe me, I've tried, but the vibe at Bates, Scrivener, and Daley is lethal to the imagination.*

"Please turn to page forty-six," he demands in the type of withering tone he reserves for closing arguments.

Page forty-six? Suddenly, all feeling drains from my limbs. I know exactly why he wants me to turn to that section, and I feel like I'm in a courtroom witness box. In a panic, I try to remember the definition of slander. Or libel. Whichever applies when you unambiguously call the fictional boss at a made-up triple-barreled law firm the "Antichrist" in your show.

"This was a private document," I explain weakly. I am *horrified* that he seems to have read the whole thing in such detail, partly because it's very much a first draft and I need him to know, if he's about to boot me out, that I am better than this, creatively. I haven't even shown it to Rach or Sara yet. Gawd, my sister will have a field day when she hears this story: *Oh, Audrey—how could you? Penguins? And the Antichrist?*

I tell myself it's liberating to be unexpectedly jobless. Am I not forever dreaming that fate will force my hand and make me rely on my music to pay the rent?

Although, how am I going to accomplish that? Busk outside Woolworths? Nobody carries cash anymore. I could pick up some piano or composition students. Surely there are a whole bunch of stressed-out high school students who I could shepherd through their final exams?

Or I could do what I've been promising myself for years and pick up a casual job while I finally finish writing the show. Really work on it, properly, and pitch it to investors . . .

I go into my email one last time and set an out-of-office

message: *Audrey Sullivan is no longer employed by Bates, Scrivener, and Daley. Please contact Anne O'Rourke with any questions.*

As the sliding doors part and I escape from the glass atrium into the freedom of a meetingless midweek midafternoon, there is one final, unprofessional email that part of me regrets not taking a minute to fire off:

```
Dear Dr. Miller,
  Anne O'Rourke is a stickler for financial
accuracy, but should you find her wanting in
the Penguin Appreciation Department, here's my
personal email . . .
```

4

Fraser

"Can I steal you for a second?" a woman says, slipping her hand through the crook of my arm, disturbing me from the breather I was taking on the back balcony. I'd barely returned from my three-month trip when my colleague Zoe insisted I attend her costume party to ease back into normalcy—and now some stranger is dragging me down the steps into the courtyard garden, not that I'm putting up a fight . . .

Even after a full week with Parker (mostly spent wrestling her math homework, hosing a meltdown over the read-a-thon, then emailing with Maggie about whether or not we should be concerned that Parker seems to be scratching her arms—*is it anxiety?*), I'm still acclimatizing to "real life."

Frankly, I'm missing the singing of the ice and the creak of the ship's bow as it slices through slush, broken ice sheets roaring as they thunder into the ocean. And the boundless space I had on the research trip to get my head together. Give me the eerie silence under a dazzling aurora sky over this blast of music and lights, and this throng of people shouting to be heard while I'm forced into small talk with humans. Or with this woman. Who seems to be dressed as a cat.

She glances toward the costume party as she pushes me behind a hedge, black latex suit pressed against me as she adjusts her whiskers, champagne on her breath, and says, "I told some lecherous drunk in there that you were my fiancé."

What is happening?

"Actually, he's not some random," she confesses, falling onto a concrete seat beside us and pulling me onto it next to her. "He's my ex-boyfriend."

"Shit, really?"

"Oh, it wasn't serious! In fact, it was a giant mistake. The Everest of dating debacles—"

This sort of thing doesn't happen at the South Pole. That's why I like it. No anonymous Catwomen entwining me in their failed romantic exploits.

"I know all about mistakes," I start to say. *Where am I going with this?* I haven't been on Tinder. Nor do I see my marriage that way. That was more a case of two people getting involved before our brains had matured, dazed on the idea of love. But now I've broken Zoe's rule: *No thinking about Maggie at the party. And for God's sake, shave off that beard and make an effort, Fraser, unless you're in costume as a reclusive scientist.*

I *am* a reclusive scientist. But I did what she said. The closest thing I had to a nineties costume was a David Beckham jersey that I dug out of one of the boxes I have yet to unpack in my new rental. Maggie stayed in the house and is in the process of buying me out. *Stop thinking about her.*

"Don't worry," Catwoman reassures me. "This isn't going to snowball into one of those full-blown fake dating sagas, like in Hallmark movies and romance novels."

I wasn't worried, because I didn't know fake dating sagas existed. They sound hideous. And the way she's still got one eye on the house is unnerving. Eventually, she drags her attention from the balcony, thrusts her face uncomfortably close, inspects me in the moonlight, and says, "Have we met?"

As her features are obscured behind a shiny mask with pointed ears, it's difficult to say. "Perhaps in one of your eight other lives?" I suggest, diplomatically.

She laughs, loudly, then clamps a hand over her mouth and puts a finger to my lips as if to shush me, too, not that I have any intention of blaring our whereabouts to the alleged thug she used to date.

"Could we have met at the university?" I ask quietly, after I remove her finger. "I'm in the School of Science."

She shakes her head. "Not likely. I'm a very boring cybersecurity analyst. Currently researching international espionage, but I can't really talk about it . . ."

The woman takes self-deprecation to a new level. "You do seem quite dull," I volley, deadpan. She shrinks a little, clearly one of those brilliant people with no sense of irony. "Between the false engagement, the spy-wrangling, the whole"—I wave my hand at the costume—"cat situation."

She laughs and seems to relax, forgetting the house and turning to face Zoe's climbing roses, illuminated by a string of party lights. "I hate costumes," she admits. "This is not who I am."

Isn't that the whole point? Before I can argue, the back door bangs open and we're silenced by the heavy tread of boots on the wooden planks of the deck above us. Shadows flick through the cracks, over her face.

"Rachael!" a voice booms over the banister.

We're stock-still, then she moves closer to me as footsteps tramp down the stairs into the fenced-off courtyard that we're trapped in.

I rise to my feet before he sees us, a tattooed brick of a man who looks like he was born in a gym. His eyes narrow furiously at the sight of me, but I stand tall and straighten the glasses on my nose. Not exactly a power move. Rather a nervous habit. Unfortunately not a more intimidating one.

"Just move on, Connor!" Rachael says. From where he's standing, he might not have heard the crack in her voice, but I can. "It's been over for six months!"

Six months?

"And you've had time to get engaged?" he roars.

Exactly! I try to invent a story that explains how I've apparently met, fallen for, and proposed to this woman, not half a year after they split. But inventing stories is not in my wheelhouse. I deal in scientific fact. Perhaps it's the Beckham getup that makes me artificially confident, but I step forward and extend my hand—a civility Connor resolutely declines. Rachael is probably wondering why she picked a partner for this ruse who's conducting the altercation in the manner of Colin Firth.

"It's been a whirlwind relationship," she says, by way of explanation.

A tornado, from where I'm standing.

Connor's eyes roam over me, his hands balling into fists. "You don't look like the whirlwind type," he points out, quite fairly.

"I've been pretty gun-shy since my divorce," I admit, throwing my arm around Rachael's latex-clad waist, deciding the only way I can be remotely convincing here is if I'm honest. "We just clicked."

Five minutes ago.

He doesn't need to know I'd be the last person to rush into a premature betrothal. Not when I'm still painstakingly removing the splinters from the last one.

The sight of my hand on her waist gets his hackles up. "Mate, she's asked you to leave her alone," I hear myself say, pulling her tighter to my side. It's the first time in my life I've used the term "mate" in a threatening manner, and I'm trying to remember anything—even a single move—from my teenage tae kwon do classes.

"Did you even wait for my side of the bed to cool?" Connor pushes on. "No surprise, I guess, the way you look tonight."

I don't even know this woman, but suddenly all my hesitation gives way to anger. Fighting words, still rather Firthesque, burst forth: "That is fucking *it*."

He laughs—a high school bully picking on the science nerd behind the bike sheds—and makes his move. I push her behind me, certain I'm about to be introduced to the inside of an ambulance but ready to involve myself anyway, when he's unexpectedly brought up short by a deluge of water and what looks like hundreds of ice cubes. Having dumped them precisely on his shaved head from above, the bucket-yielding woman yells, "Leave her alone, you pathologically self-serving, insufferable twit!"

Whether he's stunned by the ice or the insult, I can't tell, but I capitalize on his confusion, grab Rachael's hand, and pull her past him as he shakes off the frozen shrapnel. We rush back upstairs, where I deposit her into a swarm of concerned friends and outraged strangers. Before we can exchange another word, she is spirited away, glancing back at me as she's pulled through the house, out the front door, and into someone's car, like a celebrity exiting a New York restaurant. She's down the street before a humiliated Connor decides to leap the fence. The whole ruckus simmers as Zoe, ever positive, attempts to reassemble the fractured vibe.

"Wow! I'm *so sorry*, Fraser," she says, cornering me in the living room once things are back on track. She's in one of those MC Hammer–inspired fluorescent parachute tracksuits that she's probably had in her wardrobe for three decades. "Thanks for your help."

"Who was she?" I ask.

Her eyes sparkle as she looks at me, thrilled at my interest. "That was Rachael McKenzie," she says. "She works for Defense. Secret Squirrel stuff that she can't talk about—"

"No, I mean ice-bucket woman." I'm describing her as if I've discovered some missing link from eight million years of human evolution.

"*Oh!* Britney Spears over there?" Zoe says, looking at her across the room. "She's hilarious. And *very* single. No crazed ex-boyfriends lurking in the wings, which is obviously an asset . . ."

This is not a dating agency. Even if it were, Zoe wouldn't have to worry about me getting tangled up with Rachael. As talented and attractive as she clearly is, guest-starring in that soap opera for five minutes was enough.

Her rescuer, though, holding court with a small group near the dining table, is all big eyes and dramatic energy, gesticulating wildly as she spins the story, admirers entranced.

"If anyone needs some hilarity in their life right now, it's *you*, Fraser," Zoe nudges. "You and Maggie were miserable for years, obviously—"

Was it that obvious? I thought we'd staged quite the convincing act of marital bliss.

"I know for a fact Maggie's on the apps." As Zoe breaks her own ban on Maggie Chat, I'm surprised at the measured way my body greets this news. Calmly, as if we're talking about an acquaintance and not my wife of nine years. Strangely, it's almost a relief to know Maggie is focused on something other than project-managing our breakup.

But *dating*? Why touch a flame when you know it's going to burn?

"It's time to get back on the horse, Fraser!"

Britney Spears pulls her audience closer with the conspiratorial body language of a practiced raconteur. "I'm not sure I have the energy . . ." My sentence drifts as I'm distracted by a peal of laughter from her fan club.

"For horses?" Zoe teases.

I snap my focus back to her. "For hilarious women."

"You don't have to marry her, Frase! Just have a chat. Win her over with your scintillating intellectualism."

This week's atmospherics lecture springs to mind. A pencil case loudly hit the floor, knocked off the desk by the hypnagogic jerk of a sleeping student, who was obviously captivated. This is a woman who breaks up fights and is besties with a spy specialist.

"I've no intention of marrying her." *Or anyone.* I'm just struggling to take my eyes off her at present—a fact Zoe has clocked. "What's her story, then?" I ask, the question and Zoe's reaction to it dislodging my equilibrium as she clasps her hands, tightens her black ponytail, and draws up a barstool, pulling me into a huddle.

"Well, we met at the conservatorium. She was brilliant. Gifted, really. Infuriatingly talented but tortured, you know, the way composers can be?"

Stuffy visions of Beethoven and Mozart are kicked aside by this backyard vigilante in the preppy skirt, shirt tied at the waist, over-the-knee socks, Doc Martens, blond wig, and wide-open smile.

"Tortured and infuriating," I parrot, playing down my enthusiasm. "Got it."

"But then something awful happened . . ." Zoe begins. "Hey!" she calls across the room, wheeling her hand in the air to encourage her over.

"Zoe, please don't—"

And what awful thing happened?

But it's too late. Ice Woman is on the move. Barreling toward me while my heart hammers the way it should have done at the earlier mention of my ex-wife's activity on the apps.

As she approaches, her face cycles through a range of emotions. Surprise. Confusion. By the time she reaches me, she seems incredulous, somehow, that I appear to be standing here at all.

I didn't realize I'd made such an impression. She'd seemed so focused on Connor and Rachael. But then she speaks, and it takes just one shaky word for her startled expression to make complete sense.

"Joshua?"

5

Audrey

“No, Audrey, this is Fraser,” Zoe corrects me, as I backtrack instantly out of the mistake. “You know, my lovely academic friend? I’m sure I’ve mentioned him . . .” *She hasn’t.* “Fraser—meet Audrey.”

Zoe shuffles us together as if she is an intimacy coordinator on a film set, while he stands here, familiar-looking brows arched into a thoughtful frown, intelligent brown eyes on mine, and it’s all I can do not to go to pieces.

This man is *so like* Joshua Miller.

And now my heart is doing unnecessary cartwheels, ahead of the inevitable, imminent attack of nervous babbling. “Sorry! My mistake. It’s just you remind me very much of someone I used to know.”

It’s not just the light brown hair and the height and build. It’s the intellectual detachment, as if he’d rather be dreaming up some brilliant idea in the recording studio. Of course, my mind has snagged on a memory of that night in the studio with Josh. The way he lit the match that blew up my life . . .

Even after all this time, I can taste that toxic cocktail of deep disappointment and fierce disagreement and *fury*—

“Josh is my brother,” Fraser explains, coolly, the information scattering anxiety through my body.

This is the brother Josh used to talk about?

"You're the science student?" I seem to be caught in a time warp. *It's been twelve years.* Joshua's brother is as much a pompous postgrad—Josh's description, not mine—as I'm still a doctoral candidate.

In fact, now that I look at him properly, Fraser isn't any sort of pompous.

"Research scientist these days," he says. "But yes."

I might have had several drinks tonight, plus the adrenaline hit of an altercation with my best friend's ex-boyfriend, but I'm clearheaded enough to take this information, tack on Joshua's last name, and come up with *ocean scientist, likes penguins.*

"*You're* Fraser Miller?" I challenge him. This is Canberra, a city notorious for everyone knowing everybody else, but I cannot believe that all along I had been "flirting," to quote the Dishonorable Peter Reed (as I now describe my former boss), with *Joshua Miller's brother.*

"You got me sacked!" I inform him, quite unfairly. A jury would dismiss the charge in minutes.

He looks rattled. "I'm sorry, do we know each other?"

Let's see. I am the woman who bungled your divorce account, along with a high-voltage situation at university with your brother, which I can't be sure, given my reaction tonight, that I'm fully over.

"You're Fraser Miller," I tell him. "You like penguins."

There's a beat of silence, while our history catches up with him.

"Audrey Sullivan?"

"I trust Anne O'Rourke sorted your bill?"

The belated professionalism is astounding, given our celebratory whereabouts. If only Tea-Bag Brenda and Hormonal-Chicken Jill could see me now . . .

"Peter fired you over that?" I can sense the injustice pumping through his body so tangibly I could almost touch it.

"To be fair, there were one or two other issues," I admit. "The usual suspects. Poor attention to detail. Mixing up appointments." *Do I really need to conduct a professional postmortem with this man?* "I wrote Peter Reed into my law-firm musical and called him the Antichrist . . ."

There's a brief glimmer of surprise, but otherwise he has a serious poker face.

"So that's how you met my brother," he says, quietly. "Through music."

Oh, I really don't think we need to get into the details of how I met his brother. It will invariably expose the whole saga of why I dropped out and quit classical music—a story that always ends in tears.

"And now you moonlight as a hit woman."

"*Yes.* I mean, not always. Not ever before, actually. But something came over me tonight and—"

"You stormed to her defense."

"I would storm to it every time. I *hate* that man! Connor is the latest in a long line who were all charm. Then it went so badly, so quickly. Now I don't trust men at all!" *Flash of Josh.* "Even penguin-loving scientists." *Too much prosecco.*

He doesn't argue, even though I've tarred him with Connor's brush, despite his unfailingly polite emails and the fact that Dishonorable Peter Reed had said I *couldn't have picked a nicer man to financially inconvenience.*

He looks like Joshua 2.0. A decade older, even though he's the younger of the two. Josh and I were never in a "meet the family" situation, but secondhand information pushes up from the murk of my memory. *Insufferably serious. Painfully aloof. Barely emerges from the lab.*

As I look at Fraser now, it's not making sense.

"I'm going to go," I announce quickly. "I suddenly feel scrambled. Not by you. Just—" *Stop. Talking!*

"Can I give you a lift?"

He doesn't know what he's asking. Or why I can't accept.

"I'll get an Uber. But thanks."

I shoot him one last glance, my brain still striving to recast his identity, awash with conflicting details. *This is definitely not Joshua. You can see it in his eyes.*

He is, however, Joshua adjacent. And given the way that man makes me feel, the sensible thing, not that I've ever done the sensible thing in my life, would be to run a million miles.

6

Fraser

Two weeks later, a packed audience floods into Llewellyn Hall as the orchestra warms up, the cacophony of notes matching my mood. Parker squirms beside me as I flick through responses to an ad that I placed for someone to help me juggle it all. Here I was thinking I was Superdad. Turns out I'm about one overseas conference away from blasting through Maggie's patience for tweaks to the custody schedule. *I also have a life, Fraser! This unpredictability makes it very difficult to move on!*

"When will we see Uncle Josh?" Parker asks, kicking the seats in excitement.

"Your uncle is the guest of honor!" Mum explains, on the other side of Parker, loudly enough that the people in front might divine the family tree and forgive the thrashing they're receiving from Parker's patent Mary Janes. "He'll be the last onstage."

"Because he's the most important?"

"Yes!"

God, it's unbearable.

Growing up, there had only ever been room on Mum's pedestal for one. I was forever trying to get her to notice me. Being made to wait when I tried to show her my latest science project or wanted to share some laboriously detailed fact about space or geology or physics. Invariably, she would be lost in Josh's music. *Right brain creativity is so fragile, Fraser. Don't interrupt. You don't understand . . .*

Ten-year-old me had wanted to understand *everything*. I'd jumped on my bike and pedaled off to the library to look up brain hemispheres. Maybe if I tried very hard, I could learn to be less logical and more imaginative, just like she wanted . . .

"Without the musicians, Uncle Josh would be staring at a wall in silence," I point out to Parker now, suddenly grateful she is an only grandchild. "Everyone's equally important."

I sense Mum's glare over the top of Parker's plaits as I despair of the applications in my inbox and flick through the glossy program for the concert in honor of "acclaimed conductor Joshua Miller's triumphant return to Canberra." It's been a succession of international awards and never-ending fanfare since he first picked up the baton, precociously gifted, as a teenager.

I love my brother. I do. I spent my whole childhood trailing behind him, trying to keep up with him and copy him and *be him*. The little brother in me is genuinely proud of his stellar career. But it's always been a complex dynamic, this competitive admiration—Josh in the spotlight, me in the lab. The edges always singed with envy, Mum square in the middle of us, brandishing the blowtorch, Dad unfailingly busying himself to avoid the confrontation that might have leveled things out.

The orchestra falls silent, the concertmaster rising to her feet to tune, before Josh appears and the performers stand, followed by the entire audience, who break from tradition, clapping wildly and cheering, as he strides to center stage—the Harry Styles of the classical scene. Only my brother would command a standing ovation before he's done anything. He's taken classical music and branded himself as some cavalier, rule-breaking, boundary-pushing, viral-reel-making genius, and his followers are mad for it, pushing him onto musical charts and lists of romantic eligibility.

As he takes a second bow, he catches sight of us near the front. Winks at Parker, who squeals at the personal attention. Smiles at our parents, his hand on his heart when he gestures at Mum. Then he locks eyes with me for a disconcerting extra second and nods. *You're here. In my audience again.*

The concert hall hushes, the orchestra motionless while Joshua gathers himself, settling everyone into a state of delicious expectation as if he's waiting for the heartbeats of everyone in this room to synchronize with his. Only once we're completely under his spell, barely breathing in fear that we'll disturb the magic, does he lift his hands.

I used to mimic these theatrics at the dinner table when we were boys, and I was sent to my room for it, repeatedly. My daughter is doing that now, hands waving fluidly in her seat, imitating her uncle. I reach across to hold her still, only to meet Mum's double standards and disapproving frown. *She's okay, Fraser. You need to relax.*

Toward the end of the second half, a flicker of movement draws my attention to the stairwell across from our aisle. She is standing there, transfixed.

This woman is no longer the ice-wielding warrior I met at Zoe's party. She looks like crystal glass. The kind he could shatter with the gentlest tap of the baton. She is translucent. Fractured, in a way that is difficult to reconcile with the sheer force of her the other day.

What did my brother do to her?

Suddenly, the music plunges. Undulating. Surging. Pace increasing, crescendo rising, and I don't need visual evidence to know he has sensed her in the wings. There's a virile athleticism in his every deliberate move as he wrings an emotional depth out of that orchestra that floors me.

And clearly impresses her. Face alight. Eyes bright. Same spell cast over Audrey that he's always cast over Mum. If I were a poet and not a scientist, I'd say he was siphoning the music directly from her soul. Some secret, vampiric alchemy, understood only by the right-brained . . .

But then he breaks her. Or so it seems by the look on her face when the music stops.

The audience, leaping to its feet, erupts into a spontaneous explosion of wild applause, save for the arts critic seated a row in front of us, who is scrawling furiously in a notebook.

My brother, savoring the moment, finally turns to face his muse, skin flushed, dark eyes flashing with exhilaration, body seemingly coursing with the thrill of having conquered the room, or one corner of it, yet again.

What he's incapable of seeing with the stage lights blasting into his face, or even without them, is the way that she crumbles. Once he succumbs to the demand for the inevitable encore, Audrey throws her weight against the swing doors and flees into the atrium. And I don't care who I'm about to disappoint or what concert etiquette I'll break; I clamber over Parker, push past my parents' knees, distract the music critic, disturb the energy of the Cult of Joshua, and steal one final backward glance at the stage.

For possibly the first time in my brother's illustrious career, he misses a beat.

And I tear out after her.

7

Audrey

In retrospect, I did not need to witness that. That shimmering burst of Joshua in his prime. Nor did I need to observe the way his genius escaped from the bottle the second he saw me—over a decade of distance dissolving instantly, exposing the uneven entanglement that I remembered.

Not much has changed. I'm still fuel for his glittering career. I let him help himself, the way he always did, and I am furious all over again.

God, Audrey. *Will you ever get over it?*

I burst out of the building, gulping the cool night air. *What was I expecting?* That I'd catch a glimpse of him and finally prove to myself that I was really through with all this? That I was over the betrayal? Or did I think he'd take one look at me and show even the tiniest spark of remorse about what he did?

Because there was none of that. Worse, he handed me the full force of everything I've lost in exchange for a public demonstration of all he has gained. So now I'm leaning against a tree, gripped by a surge of anger and anxiety and disbelief that I let it turn out like this.

"Audrey?"

My heart thumps, limbs tingling, head spinning—absurdly alert to the proximity of Miller blood.

"Please go away," I whisper. My body is spent from exposure to Josh's success, my voice betraying how much it got to me.

"Are you sure?"

There's a quiet warmth in Fraser's tone, and for one full, alarming second it feels even more dangerous than whatever just happened in that auditorium. I should not allow warmth of that nature near these exposed wounds.

"Audrey, I am not my brother," he adds, his voice low and controlled, a deep edge to the words, as if he's been forced to debunk this fact for years. I already told him I don't trust men. Not even the penguin-loving scientist kind. But despite their physical similarities, all of Josh's brainwashing, and my natural suspicion of *anyone* these days, as I turn and meet his concerned face, a jolt of truth passes between us. He is not Joshua. He's not anything like him.

I need to get out of here. I take out my phone and call Rach, though I'm not sure how to position tonight's turn of events with him standing here, listening.

It turns out I don't have to. Rach, whom I messaged on the way, confessing my imprudent lapse in judgment, dives straight in when she picks up the call, every sentence ratcheting upward and so shrieky there is no way he's not hearing it. "*Audrey!* I got your message. I cannot *believe* you went to that concert! *Have you completely lost the plot?*"

Yes, quite possibly? I can't even summon the words to explain myself. Fraser, watching me freeze, clears his throat, takes my phone, and says "Catwoman?" in a way that is so disconcertingly confident and charming and ridiculous, it knocks my anxiety sideways. "It's David Beckham, your fiancé from Zoe's party."

There's an audible gasp from Rach. "David Beckham. The younger brother?"

Yes, why not alert the man to the fact that he has been exhaustively discussed since we met, sinking from party hero to brother of nemesis? I snatch the phone back, as if by holding it, I'll will my best friend to play it cool.

Since the night at Zoe's, Rach and I have, naturally, overanalyzed this situation. She applied her considerable cyber skills to a forensic investigation, initially of Joshua's last decade, sickeningly as good as predicted, but then of Fraser himself. *That* sleuthing not only surfaced nothing remotely scandalous, but led us to a spectacular public lecture series about ocean currents and tipping icebergs and the slow burn of a warming globe, from which we both emerged with a burgeoning infatuation.

Fraser, aware of none of this (thank God!), takes my wrist and moves the phone closer to his mouth as he says in an incredibly civilized and understated manner, "Is there any chance you might meet us at the School of Music, Rachael? Audrey had a moment with my brother."

A *moment*?

Next the doors fling open and hundreds of people swarm out, led by a rollicking child who bolts straight over to us and leaps into Fraser's arms, squealing, "Daddy!"

Mayday!

I report to Rach via text.

There is a child.

She types back, unfazed, because, unlike me, she adores kids:

Joshua's or Fraser's?

The little girl is squeezing her father half to death.

Affirmative on the latter.

The child turns her heart-shaped face toward mine, dark, inquisitive eyes taking in my startled expression as she says, "Who are you?"

Now I'm not only having to interact with a small human, but being made to answer unsettling questions about myself, the only available frames of reference being a disastrous connection with this girl's uncle and whatever it is that I'm inventing here with her dad.

"Yes, who is your friend, Fraser?" an older woman asks, not in a good way, when she catches up with our party. She's trailed by an apologetic-looking gentleman with a kind and handsome face who I can only assume is Josh and Fraser's father. He smiles at me—it's Fraser's smile, not Joshua's, which means I warm to it instantly, a fact that I add to the growing list of items Rach and I will have to psychoanalyze after this horrendous social experiment is over.

"You ran out of there so quickly, Fraser, I assumed it was something important—" the mother says, losing interest the second she spots a glamorous dark-haired woman power walking across the quadrangle. She is all business. Straight hair clipped up. Immaculate everything. Confident gait. The child wriggles free of Fraser, dashes toward her, and screams, "Mummy!"

"Sorry," Fraser whispers, "in advance."

Advance of what?

Ex-wife alert, Rach. I repeat: EX-WIFE.

"Daddy's got a *friend*!" the child sings, swinging her mum's hand and raising everyone's blood pressure as she presents us through the lens of total innocence—all "met in the sandpit" vibes.

"Gosh, aren't you a busy little bee!" I exclaim, and she seems delighted by the descriptor. "I'm not a *friend*, exactly—"

Not of Daddy's, anyway.

Then, as if I weren't already overwhelmed, we look over to where, fighting off a large posse of fans, posing for selfies and signing autographs, Joshua emerges from his most recent epicenter of triumph.

Rach, who has rushed through the park from her office across Marcus Clarke Street in her stylish, espionage-esque tailored whites and beiges, turns to Fraser, winks, and says in a sultry tone, "Hello, my beloved." I'm almost envious of the way that he smiles at this, except that his mother, not clued in on the fake-fiancé joke and clearly battling to understand what fresh hell this is, glares at Rach, while his ex-wife fires daggers at us both.

Joshua, meanwhile, has ditched his clamoring devotees and is searching intently through the bustling crowd. Finally, he pushes free from the throng and locks eyes with me, and my heart thrashes. I've spent more than a decade imagining this precise encounter, replaying versions where he doesn't recognize me or hates me or sweeps straight past and ignores me. In every one of those scenarios, I never predicted this unfurling reality: Joshua Miller approaching me after a performance, charged atoms of unresolved conflict leaping between us, taking me right back to that head-spinning moment when he crushed me.

"Good to see you, Sully," he says in a low, gravelly voice as the Miller clan holds its collective breath. His hand reaches for my waist as if he wants to pull me into a hug he does *not* deserve and back into a fictional world where we're still friends. Does he really think he can fly through this interaction the way he flew through all the others—on class A charisma and my unrelenting streak of goodwill? We're not twenty-two anymore. I've stored up twelve years' worth of fury!

I pull away, ducking from the attempted embrace, unpracticed rejection playing across his features with a flash of red. Then, after I've cut the power from his confident pose, everything lands in my mind with belated clarity. This man's career soared. Mine lay stagnant. For more than a decade, I've allowed this fact to eat my potential alive, and it needs to stop. Tonight. Or I will never get my life back.

8

Fraser

This is Sully? The musician Josh was obsessed with at university? The one he described back then as his "musical soulmate," so crucial to the upward trajectory of his career that he'd kept her hidden from us throughout the whole, fiery affair? Former divorce-firm office manager Audrey Sullivan—friend of Zoe, savior of Rachael—is *Josh's Sully*?

She had disappeared back then, abruptly. That's how we really met her. Through the space she left in my brother's life. A great, cavernous hole the size of a football field into which he had plunged hard. It all fell apart just as his star was rising, pressure mounting, publicity peaking. He'd been abandoned right when he needed her most—to help usher him through the biggest break of his life.

At least, that's the story we got at the time.

Well, that's composers for you, Mum declared, fired up in his defense. The ghost of "Fickle Sully" haunted our dinner table every time Joshua experienced even the slightest setback. Performance off? *Fickle Sully.* Bad reviews? *Fickle Sully.* Medicating with various substances while leading on half of the woodwind section? *If Fickle Sully hadn't left him, he would have settled down . . .*

I'd seen enough of Josh on boys' nights out to know it was

less about "Fickle Sully" and more about "Laddish Miller," who first discovered a talent for breaking hearts in high school. The only thing ghostly about her now is just how pale she has gone in his company. Wow, he really did a number on her.

I try not to appear *too* delighted at the sight of my brother fumbling through the overdue comeuppance of a foiled embrace. Or at the fact that Audrey won't meet his gaze but will meet mine. When she does, it's an intriguing mix of deer-in-headlights panic, unbridled rage, and some sort of natural high. I can't work her out. And increasingly want to, because nothing about the woman I watched fall apart in the wings tonight aligns with a single accusation this family has flung in its twelve-year-long smear campaign.

"I'm going to be a musician one day!" Parker announces, pulling at Josh's sleeve and breaking the tension.

"Parker, you *are* a musician," he corrects her, scooping her into his arms. "I remember what you could do on the Fisher-Price xylophone as a toddler!"

My attention sweeps along a still-infuriated chorus line of Mum and Maggie and Rachael. Each has been observing the same situation, fuming for a different reason. Dad is oblivious, or pretending to be. He's the classic "bystander." Never said a bad thing about "Sully" all these years, though also never intervened in the trash-talking, and isn't that just as damaging? Finally I land on Josh, who, with my daughter in his arms, has clocked where Audrey's attention has drifted.

"Congratulations," I say, extending my hand. "That was great work."

While he accepts this professional compliment, I can see in his eyes that he's slating an inevitable heated confrontation about how it is that I fled his concert hall this evening with his former muse. It's like engaging with a charging bull.

"Do you need a lift home?" I turn and ask Audrey, ignoring my brother, knowing there was talk of a post-concert family dinner, but if we don't disperse soon, we'll hand the arts critic a salacious postscript for his article.

Rachael lights up and says on behalf of them both, "Thank you! We were bussing it home otherwise, and it looks like rain."

It doesn't look anything like rain. I can't tell if Maggie is glancing at the moon as it beams in a cloudless sky or rolling her eyes. Either way, I send her a silent plea not to overreact.

"Good to see you again," she says, dispensing hugs all round for her ex in-laws. Ordinarily she'd have attended tonight's performance, but we're still in the part of this split where we're disentangling our calendars, shaping new social identities, and trying not to confuse Parker, whose hand I hold now as I walk with them both to Maggie's car. It's a journey we take largely in silence after Parker, looking thoughtful, says, "Your new friends are really pretty, Daddy."

Maggie, probably struggling to unpack which aspects of the last ten minutes have annoyed her most, stays uncharacteristically silent. Frustrated, too, no doubt, that we're so deeply entrenched in the lore of this failed relationship that I can still read her mind.

That's the thing with divorce. You can break apart. *Implode.* Yet somehow, in the center of those crumbling ruins, a library stands, with all the knowledge the two of you ever shared.

I open the car door and help Parker into the seat the way we've done countless times. Maggie jogs to the other side, and I know it's because the belt latch sticks, each of us leaning to kiss our daughter.

It's like a dance, choreographed by subtle data that once oiled every interaction, now a bittersweet reminder that even this was not enough, that everything can tumble and split, but here the two of us stay: grandmasters in each other's lives, alert to every moving piece, watching for the tells.

"Fraser—" she begins, trapping me with a judgmental gaze over the car roof.

She's going to warn me off whatever she thinks is going on here with Audrey and Rachael. "See you at Parker's assembly tomorrow?" I say instead and she retreats, annoyed.

As they pull away, I'm hit by a wistful pang, as if Parker and I are joined by a rubber band that stretches thin in our absence and that I'm worried might snap. Equally, away from Maggie, it's as if I can breathe again—a necessary distance keeping our disjointed family afloat. It's only when the taillights disappear that I exhale and remind myself, perhaps for the hundredth time, that this is all exactly the way it needs to be.

9

Audrey

After a minor scuffle about who is sitting where, Rach pushes me into the front seat of Fraser's sensible sedan and slips into the back, beside his daughter's empty booster seat. We buckle up and wait as he gives way to Joshua, who roars off in a sleek black Mercedes, fierce energy palpable through the accelerator.

"Where are we heading?" Fraser asks, absolute Teflon to his brother's showboating. Another green flag for our list.

"Could you drop us in Dickson at mine?" Rach asks. "Audrey's staying with me."

His eyes flash at me as he pulls into the stream of traffic, but he doesn't pry into my private affairs, so naturally I take that silence and shovel into it an unnecessarily detailed explanation about my living situation.

"You might recall I was sacked," I say.

He checks his blind spot, changes lanes, and says, "Something about your sudden interest in polar marine life?"

"To be fair, Auds, you did immortalize your boss's pompous arse in song," Rach argues.

"It was *good*, too," I defend. "I was particularly fond of 'Six Minutes.' You know, the tap-dancing number about billable increments?"

As Fraser swings onto a side street, I notice the crinkles around his eyes, and for a moment I'm disproportionately proud that my comment has placed them there. Perhaps it's the former doctoral student in me, and maybe I'll forever grasp for validation from his ilk, but I am quietly thrilled at the idea that I might have said something clever enough to amuse him.

"Anyway, my theatrics in the office have brought my rental situation undone," I explain. "It's fine, though." *It really isn't.* "I'm sure Rach's couch is just temporary."

She has said I can stay as long as I like, but she's in a tiny one-bedroom apartment and there's only so long I can couch-surf without scuffing the friendship.

Fraser inches his window down and clears his throat. Then he's honked at from behind for missing a green light, and we're all forced to wait out another cycle at the intersection.

"Everything okay there, driver?" Rach asks from the back.

"It's just . . ." He glances at me, unsure. "I'm currently sifting through a disenchanting bunch of applications for someone to take my spare room and help with Parker."

Is he suggesting—

"I should have admitted I was out of my depth months ago. Just couldn't bring myself to have to navigate around my own kitchen with someone I don't know."

"GO!" Rach yells as the lights change, and Fraser and I all but leap from our seats.

"But you don't know *me*," I remind him. *Not really.*

"Nonsense, Audrey." Driving off, he seems to regain control of both the traffic and his composure. "You saved my life at Zoe's party. One more second with Rachael's ruffian of an ex-boyfriend and he'd have gone for a knockout blow."

There is no way this man would be volunteering to involve me in his domestic affairs if he'd seen Rach and me at her place last week, scoffing Pringles and wine, surrounded by piles of my worldly belongings and huddled over her laptop, forty minutes through his presentation on "Advances in Oceanographic Data Assimilation Techniques" from some Toronto climate conference he headlined eighteen months ago. I'd nearly searched him on LinkedIn before she reminded me he might have a member account that shows who's stalked his page.

"I don't think renting a room from you would be a very good idea," the logical part of me declares. My unemployed self argues that house-sharing, rather than renting a whole place, would ease my financial quandary, and the musician in me is thrilled. But I'm meant to be running miles from this man, am I not?

"Speaking of Connor, I'm thinking of rejoining Tinder," Rach announces. It's an outright lie designed to push me out of my comfort zone and into Fraser's spare bedroom. She's never been on Tinder. With all her cybersecurity expertise, she doesn't trust the apps. "Things are getting a bit cramped in Dickson. Of course, you could always move in with your sister," she suggests.

No, I could not.

They're moving me around like a chess piece, and I can't help feeling woefully behind. Career at a standstill. No partner. No home. No kids, not that I want those, and—*Oh! That's my perfect out!* "The thing is, I'm really not great with children," I admit. "I mean, your daughter seems delightful, but I'd be a bad influence, so—"

Waiting patiently now on Northbourne Avenue, he turns to me and says, "A bad influence how? All the classical music and kick-arse heroism at parties?"

This man seems to be laboring under the mistaken impression that I am a far more interesting version of myself than I really am; nevertheless, I'm positively flushed at the compliment.

"I am a failed musician," I confess. "And a failed office manager. Honestly, the least reliable kind of flatmate."

"You haven't failed. Day jobs don't foil raw talent. They just make it harder to squeeze it all in." His tone is professorial and authoritative, and as he accelerates across the intersection, I realize there's something experienced and steadying about him. Then he gives me an electric jolt as he looks sideways and adds, "I remember the way Josh used to talk about you."

I squeeze the seat belt tight and restrain myself from fishing for details, helped by the car's side mirror being tilted at such an angle that I catch the reproach on Rach's face. It used to feel like a drug, the way Josh talked about my music. The endless quest for extrinsic validation was always my undoing. It's why I am "temporarily unmoored," as Rach kindly puts it. And to think I was once the subject of a music journalist's headline: "Girl Most Likely: Meet the Teen Composing Sensation Taking the Contemporary Classical World by Storm."

Where has that girl gone? Why am I messing around writing The Office *meets* Wicked*? Musical theater?* Josh and the rest of my classical cohort would be appalled. But there I go again, measuring my choices by what other people think. It's hard when everyone else—Fraser, his brother, his ex-wife, Rach, even Hormonal-Chicken Jill—managed to get their act together while I squandered my twenties in a zigzagging haze of failed dreams and self-doubt, botching things so badly that I am currently living on someone's *couch*.

I rub my chest, willing myself not to hyperventilate. I can't keep living like this—on the run from my own potential.

"Sometimes you just need a hard reset," Fraser says, oblivious to my spiraling, delivering exactly the antidote to it.

Was it only an hour ago that I vowed, rather dramatically, to steer clear of Miller blood? I said I couldn't let this warmth near these wounds. This man is inextricably linked to the person I blame for my now being light-years behind my peers. Not only that, but I'm pretty sure Fraser's ex-wife loathes me. *Oh, God. It would be an unmitigated disaster . . .*

My phone illuminates with a text from my back seat wingwoman:

A hard reset from Fraser Miller sounds utterly delectable.

I let out a nervous laugh, and before he can ask me what's funny, I pull down the window and stick my head out, letting cold air blast onto my face and hopefully blow some sense into my brain.

"It's this driveway here," Rach says as we pull into the residential street behind the Australian Broadcasting Corporation studios a few minutes later. "Thanks for the lift!" She's up and out of the car and halfway to the secure entrance of her apartment building before I can so much as fumble for my handbag in the footwell.

"Wow. Is she an Olympic sprinter?" he inquires, dryly.

There's a beat or two of silence, during which I become aware that I am supposed to be following my best friend out of this car. I unlatch my belt, which seems to retract in slow motion, as if conspiring to delay my departure.

"Cards on the table, Audrey," Fraser says, a moment later. "My ex-wife and I lost our heads the other day and bought Parker a puppy. We thought it might smooth the handovers if she went with her between households. Of course, in our desperation to make life easier, we did the opposite. The little devil has taken to blocking my exit from the house and feigning injuries whenever I put shoes on. I can't bear the guilt!"

I coach myself to stay immune from this puppy sorcery. "Cute story, Fraser, but how do I fit into your dog's separation anxiety problem?"

"Oh, Betty isn't a problem. She's adorable!" he explains. "Parker named her. Some sort of Swiftie reference." Then his smile fades as he says, "As much as my brother irritates the hell out of me—"

"And out of me—"

There's a flicker of surprise, as if he hadn't expected me to pile on. "I think my daughter has inherited her uncle's gift. She won't leave the piano alone. He wasn't kidding about that xylophone. She's pretty extraordinary. I know all parents say that—"

"If she's anything like her uncle, she needs careful nurturing," I cut in. "Who's teaching her?"

He rubs his forehead, as if soothing a sore spot. "She's almost entirely self-taught. The kind of kid who refuses instruction. She's already burnt through three teachers who couldn't keep up."

"I've met kids like this before." I don't divulge that I *was* one. "Sometimes they have more music in their little fingers than their teachers have in their whole bodies."

When I look into Fraser's face, it's not that of a world-class scientist on top of his game. It's that of a parent without wings trying to show his child how to fly. His genius lies elsewhere. I know that from all my snooping. If Parker is half as talented as her uncle and Fraser isn't musical himself, he must be wildly out of his depth.

This is like that moment when there's a medical emergency and they ask if there's a doctor on board. Except *I* am the doctor. Or I would be, if I'd finished my PhD . . .

"Audrey—"

"It takes someone with experience to handle a Miller prodigy," I blurt out. *Experience I can't deny that I have, despite the way it all ended.*

His brown eyes are alight in some jumble of fear and hope that my inner romantic could very easily latch on to and run away with, and I have to remind myself this is not about me at all. It's about his daughter.

"It wouldn't have to be forever," he suggests, and I imagine an atom-sized objection floating between us, before it quickly evaporates.

When I don't answer, he stares at the dashboard, lips tight. "Sorry. I'm not usually this impulsive." I can see how excruciating it is for him to ask for help. "She's miserable in after-school care. Apparently it's attended by her nemesis. I don't know that she's strictly being bullied, but she's certainly—"

"Different?" *I remember this.* "I was the classical music geek at school. Lunchtimes holed up in the music room, avoiding people who didn't understand why I was playing an imaginary keyboard on my desk in algebra, like a freak . . ."

The memory lashes the air before I can censor myself. I'd pushed from my mind how isolating it was, being obsessed with something conventionally "uncool," trying to keep a lid on the passion as it leaked through the cracks. The thought of that little girl who rushed into his arms feeling just as lost as I did makes the car seem hot, and I peel off my sweater.

Fraser flicks the key in the ignition to let the air-conditioning flow.

"It might look miserable sometimes," I add, wanting to soften my admission in case it worries him, "but you don't hear the music in our heads. The soundtrack we carry everywhere we go. I actually don't know how people survive the world without it. It's hallucinogenic, in the very best way . . ."

There's that passion again, still bubbling through as my voice rises in pitch and volume, threatening to expose me again. *Too weird. Too much.*

But he breaks into a smile and leans toward me, elbow on the center console. "I try to get home from work as early as I can. But I can't rearrange the teaching timetable. It's got a hundred moving parts. I hadn't realized how much easier this all was when I was married."

Is that regret? It's definitely guilt.

"You know, Fraser, I don't have kids, but sometimes I think you can measure a good parent by the hours they lie awake at night. What are you meant to do? Quit your job? Leave humankind in the lurch?"

He laughs. "You seem to have an inflated view of my work."

I would beg to differ, citing the illustrious biography Rach and I studied on his university web page, but I can hardly admit that. It's irrelevant now, anyway. I already know I'll say yes. Obviously. I can't let Parker struggle the way I did. She needs to know the way she feels about music is normal. Maybe I'll heal my inner child? At least, that's what her mother would probably say. *God. What will his ex make of this plan?*

"Seriously, if you were to consider this even for a short while, I figure by the time you pay me for rent and I pay you for music lessons and childcare and dog-minding, you'd be ahead. And the rest of the time would be yours. Maybe you'd have space to finish the musical?"

Is he aware how persuasive this is?

"Surely it needs a duet about penguins?"

It does need that. He's barely suggested the idea, and I'm hearing their tapping feet in the chorus. I take him in, sitting here under the streetlights, shadows from the trees playing across his face—domestically vulnerable, acting legitimately interested in my show and offering a temporary solution to my leading logistical problem.

"I'd thought about asking Josh to give Parker a few lessons," he adds, leading the elephant carefully into the room. He checks my response. "You didn't abandon him when he got the gig on that first album, did you?"

Is that the story Josh gave them?

The injustice of it all surges under Fraser's inquisitive gaze, and he says, "None of it ever added up. I knew at the time he'd have thrown even his girlfriend under the bus, if—"

"No, it wasn't like that," I interrupt, placing my hand on his arm for emphasis. "I mean, the bus, yes. He *flung* me under it. But it was only ever a creative partnership between us."

I could unpack exactly how things were between Josh Miller and me for days, but why would I pollute this conversation with that? Fraser is dangling a sanctuary and the space to compose. Fraser, who worries about his daughter and writes charming emails and says nice, encouraging things about my show.

Rach messages again.

> If you won't move in with him,
> Audrey, I will!

My heart flies. If I were playing this true to form, I'd reject the offer on the grounds of needing to make it through this unfortunate blip independently. I would self-sabotage, but with my head held high. That's what I've always done. And where has it got me? Deferring to others' success. Sweeping up the dropped pieces of my own life after it smashes to the floor. This is exactly the reason my classical career crashed—because I've never known how to put myself first.

"All right, Professor Miller," I concede, expecting a panic

attack at the spontaneity of this decision but finding my nervous system surprisingly calm. "What sort of dog is Betty?"

Three days later, I'm dragging a heavy suitcase from my trunk and channeling Julie Andrews paused at the gates of the von Trapp mansion—or Fraser's Braddon town house, in my case—complete with guitar. He has only one child, but for all I know about how to interact with her, he might as well have the full complement of seven.

"You met this guy when?" my sister, Sara, squawks into the phone when I call to report my temporary change of address. "And you're already moving in?"

"It's not like *that*! He's got a spare room. We have a mutual friend!" It's as if I'm chanting these facts to myself as I ring the doorbell. "Oh, and I went to uni with his brother." The less said about that, the better. If Sara finds out exactly who Fraser's brother is, she will go through the roof.

Sara is a data analyst. She deals in risk. Ever since my final year of school, when our parents—both in the army—were posted away and left Sara in charge of me, she has watched my rudderless path through life with her heart in her mouth. "Keep me on the phone, Audrey! People can still be brutally attacked by the brothers of people they went to uni with!" she points out loudly, on speaker, just as Fraser flings open the door and the phone falls from my shoulder, where it was cradled, into one of the bags I'm carrying.

He seems less concerned about my sister's accusation and more perplexed by the amount of baggage I've brought, between what I've dragged onto his doorstep already and the volume of possessions still bursting out of my illegally parked car. My main problem, meanwhile, is the way golden hour sunlight filters through his light brown floppy fringe, studious glasses perched on his nose, tie loosened, shirtsleeves rolled up as if he's not long home from the office and I've interrupted him making dinner in front of the evening news. This is the sort of gentle, humble person I'd usually stand beside in the lunchtime rush at a sandwich bar and not even notice. *Why am I nervous?*

It's the responsible-looking ones you have to watch, Sara would explain. To be fair, she warns me off every sort of man. *Nobody would pick him as a potential heartbreaker in a lineup, Audrey. He's an underdog. Keep your wits about you!*

"Is this still okay?" I ask. Part of me wants him to turn me around and say, *Actually, Audrey, I've come to my senses. This is, in fact, ludicrous!*

Instead, he reaches for the biggest suitcase and pulls it, and me, toward the threshold and further into his life, saying, "Let me help you."

He holds open the door, and I try to squeeze past with my assortment of plastic bags, including an extra-large orange one bulging with the laundry I didn't do in the frantic pack-up. Attempting to hoick everything in while he stands there, we're jammed close, sandwiched by the plastic bag in a not-entirely-unfortunate turn of events, during which I can't help but inhale the woodsy, masculine scent of his aftershave as it goes straight to my head and triggers the apologies to run away with me. "Sorry, Fraser. I'll just squeeze through. Oh, *hello*!" My face is thrust right up into his rather startled one as we're wedged even tighter by the force of my belongings. "Breathe!" I encourage him. "*Push!*"

Why am I carrying on like a midwife coaxing a laboring mother through the ring of fire?

Then I'm catapulted into the hall, bag exploding on impact,

and my unmentionables, as my mother would describe them, tumble out of it and onto the pristine floor.

"What a muddle!" I exclaim, now apparently channeling the narrator from the Thomas the Tank Engine series, because it would be far too big an ask for me to converse normally. "Thought we'd have to call the fire brigade to dislodge us!" I barrel on. *Stop making a thing of it!*

He's still standing there, my suitcase in his hand, staring at the impact site. And at me. Listening to my sister, whose muffled voice is persisting from inside the bag. Perhaps he's trying to work out what he has suggested here, and whether it's too late to redact his offer.

"I really appreciate this," I gush, scooping out my phone, ending the call, and trying to stuff my things back into the bag, which, having split in half, has now retired.

"You won't even know I'm here!" I overpromise, staggering up from the floor.

"In the same way that a hurricane might pass me by?"

Please don't be witty, too!

Following him upstairs, I say, "You look like the sort of landlord who'd have a full disaster plan printed in a binder on the coffee table." Now I have a mental picture of him in a bright red hard hat, which he would ably carry off, in a delicious mix of white-collar worker and emergency hero.

He shows me into a furnished bedroom with leafy views across Haig Park. Then, having deposited my suitcase on the bed, he steps back, lingering in the doorway. I zip open my bag, aware of him leaning against the frame, feet crossed at the ankles in that unintentionally confident way that invites easy conversation, while I start flinging everything into the piles I should have attended to before I moved. A rogue stiletto, destined for donation, plants itself in the pot beside him, monstera fronds waving as if a storm is going through.

He bends down and retrieves the shoe, so now he's standing there, holding it, looking at me in the manner of Prince Charming as he says, "You don't strike me as someone who'd be easy to marshal in an emergency. You seem more like the threat itself."

I meet the amused sparkle in his eyes and am struggling to articulate a clever response when he tosses my shoe aside, checks his watch, and in a completely understated, humble, and matter-of-fact tone says "I've got a BBC interview with the British secretary of state for the environment at eight."

Oh, yes. I'd momentarily forgotten I'd shacked up with one of the world's leading experts in changing ocean currents. In an attempt to mitigate any rogue fangirling, I plaster on a neutral expression, as if it's normal for people in my circle to utter such sentences, and mumble, "Of course. Yes. That's—" *Vitally important? Enthralling? Extraordinary?*

"Shall I heat up some soup?" he asks when I'm unable to complete my sentence. It's like being socked in the face with one glorious suggestion after another. "Do you like red or white wine?"

I'm sure I can't even remember!

"Throw me your keys," he adds. "Don't want you to get towed."

So now he'll put a roof over my head, rescue my car, pour me a drink, and serve me dinner before doing his absolute best to salvage the planet before bedtime. And there, unavoidably, trots a piece of my heart in his direction. Already.

10

Fraser

"Don't let Parker get attached!" Maggie had warned that first week, over an emergency coffee to "strategize" the apparently wild development of my having uncharacteristically blurted an invitation for Josh's "Sully," *of all people*, to become my part-time nanny, dog minder, music teacher, and roommate, even temporarily. She could never abide the label "fickle" (*It's outrageous internal misogyny from your mother, Fraser*), but that was before Audrey was quasi-parenting her child, and she went into panic mode, reminding me in no uncertain terms of the holy trinity: "Parker needs stability and certainty and predictability."

Was she always this rigid?

"It's *for* Parker," I'd explained. "You remember the demands of my work. And Audrey understands her, musically."

Parker had been delighted from the start. *Daddy's pretty friend* from Uncle Josh's concert moving into her house? Once the two of them gravitated to the piano together, I had no hope of de-escalating the budding attachment, no matter how nervous it made Maggie. And now, several weeks in, my house is *alive* with music, all the time, whether Parker is home or not.

When she's not working through an increasingly complex classical repertoire, Parker has been teaching herself pop songs—on a specific mission to learn the entirety of Taylor Swift's discography. I catch Audrey in the doorway now, in jeans and a bulky bottle-green cardigan, nursing a hot cup of tea and listening, her face bright with interest.

"May I join you?" she asks at the end of Parker's emotional rendition of "All Too Well."

Parker launches into the piece again—she has the hyperfocus you'd expect from a neurodivergent child—and shuffles along the piano stool, making room. Audrey sits beside her, pulls her brown hair up out of the way, and places her hands on the keyboard, effortlessly turning Parker's piece into a duet, mashing it with "Champagne Problems." I know that's the song because, as a single dad, I've made it my business to study all things Taylor Swift, keen to stay relevant in Parker's life.

Up until now, they've only listened to each other play. So I'm astonished at how seamless this first go is. The way they anticipate each other's every move, as if they're a seasoned duo, their first duet soaring.

Forget Maggie's instruction not to let Parker get attached. Audrey is bonding with our daughter in a language Maggie and I don't speak. If this is what it was like between Audrey and Josh, it's no wonder their reunion seemed so charged. Nobody can touch a shared passion like this. It's poetry.

When they finish the piece, Parker is wide-eyed. She's never experienced this sense of being met exactly where she is, only to be so expertly lifted higher.

"Should we mix 'Enchanted' with 'So High School'?" Audrey asks before glancing at me and smiling. My daughter has stars in her eyes. It's as if Taylor Swift herself has moved into our house and taken a seat beside her at the piano.

The whole scene chokes me up when I realize this is the first time in years that I've felt liberated to truly enjoy my child.

Watching her play, I've always felt this pride. Excitement for her. Hope that she'll cherish this love for the activity she adores and that it will soothe her through all the hardest parts of her life.

Watching Audrey and Parker together, there is nothing but music.

It's a sharp contrast to the tension that permeated my and Maggie's moments with Parker, which is not a fair comparison, of course. Audrey and I haven't been through the split of the finances. We haven't spent years nursing each other through stressful work deadlines or interest rate rises or viruses. There hasn't been time to build up a loathing of the way the other stacks the dishwasher or reverses into a parking lot. This isn't that sort of relationship, which puts it at a distinct advantage from the start.

I tell myself not to conflate the two, the way I've been ordering myself, ever since the night she moved in, not to think about her in the next bedroom. This is nothing more than the short-term, mutually beneficial rental solution we negotiated. No matter how comfortable it's all becoming.

No sooner do I allow myself this glimmer of contentment than it's chased by that familiar pang in my chest. The one I routinely ignore, because I am the parent here. A single one, at that. I cannot afford to feel anything less than strong and stable.

Parker looks at Audrey and says, "'Cruel Summer' and 'Love Story'?"

Audrey catches my eye. *Look at me! Hitting it off with your daughter when I said I'm not good with kids!*

"Why not, Parker? What's the worst that could happen?" she says.

They throw themselves at the goal, stumbling and laughing through the duet until the melodies slot into place and float through our house, and I catch a starstruck expression on Parker's face that I fear is mirrored on my own.

The worst that could happen? We're only a few weeks in and that's already becoming obvious.

Parker and I could get used to this. Worse, we could fall in love with this woman.

She could pull her life together.

And she'd leave.

11

Audrey

"Are you *sure* we're not going to distract you?" I ask Fraser for the second time, several months after I've moved in. He's sitting at the kitchen table in jeans and a long-sleeved white tee, settled in for a night of grading, a glass of red wine and a pile of student papers beside his laptop.

He considers me over the frames of his glasses. "It's a book club, Audrey. How riotous could it get?"

But other than Rach, he hasn't met my friends. He has no idea how nervous I am about hosting the Bookies here, worried the event will devolve into a soft launch of the dashingly eligible man with whom I have been secretly and temporarily living and I'll never hear the end of it.

They know that I'm house-sharing for a while, but I left out the bit about living with science's answer to Anthony Bridgerton. Two nights ago, after Parker went to bed, we had a meandering late-night conversation about Shakespeare, standing beside his bookshelves. I can barely recall a word of it, because he reached behind me at one stage and produced a volume of sonnets, his face so close I couldn't tell if I was intoxicated from the wine on my own lips or his, or by the string of articulate sentences flowing from his mouth while I fell further under his spell.

I've kept him a secret because I'm in real trouble here. Madly applying for jobs I don't want so I can liberate myself from this accommodation-of-convenience arrangement while my heart is still vaguely intact.

He's newly divorced, Sara would point out. *Statistically, you'll only ever be the rebound.*

Technically, even that's getting ahead of things, casting myself as the lead in his potential rebound fling when he hasn't made a single move in my direction. It's all academic. And unrequited. And endless tossing and turning in the next bedroom . . . *imagining . . . wondering . . .* and having him look at me like that over his bloody glasses (*why* does my stomach flip?) as if he can read my mind!

Sure enough, as the first three book club members bustle through the front door minutes later, arms bursting with bottles of alcohol and wheels of cheese, they make their way into the kitchen and are silenced by the unexpected sight of my handsome housemate.

"Fraser, meet the Bookies. This is April and Clair and Jess . . ."

They're quite simply gobsmacked.

"This is Fraser." *How do I explain him?* "My, um—"

All four of them turn to me now, very keen for this explanation, and I have to restrain myself from babbling all sorts of nonsense into the growing pause: *He's my flatmate. And my ex-musical-soulmate's younger brother. A former client from that job where I was sacked—you know, over the Antichrist and whatnot? Oh, also, briefly, Rach's fake fiancé . . .*

I don't end up saying any of that, because, watching me struggle, he gets up from the table and places his hand fleetingly, but significantly, on the small of my back as he steps past me, unburdens my friends of their provisions, and says, "Audrey's told me all about you."

The three of them are like those open-mouthed clowns in sideshow alley, heads turning in unison from him to me. April, dressed per usual to the nines in tailored black pants, boots, a crisp white shirt, a black vest, and a deep red Windsor knot at her throat, steps toward him with her CEO energy, pulls him into a hearty and unexpected hug, and proclaims, "She's told us *scandalously little* about you!"

That's when he offers everyone a drink, because I appear to have lost all my social graces. I'm still back at the part where he touched me, skin alight from the gentle pressure of his fingertips through my dress. There he is, pouring cabernet sauvignon and making small talk with the Bookies while I wrangle visions of Shakespeare and candlelight and being properly backed up against his bookshelves next time, while he—

There's a sound at the door before Rach breezes into the kitchen, all flowing blond hair in a cloud of sky-blue linen, and says, "Fabulous! You've all met!" Then she sweeps me aside and whispers, hopefully not loudly enough for anyone else's hearing, "Why do you look like you've just had sex?"

What?

Fraser passes me a glass of wine, his fingers brushing mine as he tilts his head and looks into my face. Probably because I've become nonverbal. And apparently look like I've been ravished by the merest touch of his hand.

The rest of them prattle on about pâté and crackers and the outcome of Clair's job interview and whether or not we should get tickets to the Canberra Writers Festival while, for just a few moments, I let myself pretend this is more than it is.

That he is mine.

That this is our house.

That Parker, upstairs, is the stepdaughter I never knew I wanted.

April says something funny that I miss and taps glasses with Fraser, and his warm laughter fills the kitchen. It's such an easy rapport, as if we've all been friends for years.

Aren't left-brained geniuses meant to be socially awkward? I didn't know they liked sonnets. And they have no business looking the way Fraser does, arms crossed, leaning against the counter with the relaxed countenance of a person who doesn't have a rambunctious Cavoodle to train and eighty assignments to grade.

Oh, God.

I'm drowning.

Rach is all empathy when I dare look at her, knowing it's written across my face. Fraser is oblivious, absorbed in his post-divorce co-parenting, doing his BBC interviews, saving the world . . . And here I am right in front of him, brakes failing, tumbling headfirst into every element of what was only ever supposed to be a temporary reset.

During that first book club, I made a plan. I would stay out of his way. Get *any* job and get out of his house. It wasn't a new plan, by any means. More a reversion to plan A, before I'd inadvertently signed up for the bonus broken-heart package. "This is just so in line with your past behavior, Audrey," Rach accused.

"Ever since university—since *Josh*—you've run full tilt from anything good," she pointed out. "We all have that one guy who hung us out to dry and left the country—*yes, literally in your case*. But that was years ago! Take a *risk*."

"I did take a risk! Remember Teddy?"

"The understudy?" Rach had nicknamed him that. My one long-term boyfriend among the duds. "He was *lovely*. Husband material. But no—you were waiting for some conveniently fictitious, even more remarkable leading man . . ."

And now, seven job applications, countless swoon-worthy, over-the-spectacles glances, and six weeks after that book club, I'm acutely conscious of Fraser's proximity. Our socked feet are up on the coffee table and we're in pajamas, sharing a block of chocolate and watching a movie about the apocalypse with the lights off. So technically, I'm not so much staying out of Fraser's way as flinging myself straight into it.

"You're the type to watch plane crash films during flights, aren't you?" he says, breaking off a piece of rum and raisin and passing the packet.

I take my feet off the table and pull my legs up underneath me. "Oh, I'm obsessed with disaster flicks! *Contagion*, *Geostorm*, *Twisters* . . . give me a race against time and a brilliant scientist and—"

He is a brilliant scientist. What am I doing, showing my hand?

"And what is it about the imminent threat to life that you find particularly soothing?" he asks, tactfully ignoring my slip.

I have to think about that. "Probably that their lives are more of a mess than mine."

"Come on, your life isn't that bad, is it?" He delivers this with a nudge of his elbow that repositions us closer—a situation neither of us bothers to address. The reshuffle leaves me leaning into the swimmer's biceps and cyclist's quadriceps that he's been assembling ahead of a summer triathlon, like the overachiever that he is.

"Please," I reply. "I'm in my mid-thirties, after a series of unappealing jobs and even less appealing boyfriends, I'm renting a single bedroom—"

"Technically you have the run of almost the entire house. I mean, look at you. Look at *this* room alone."

We cast our eyes at the shopping bags strewn across the doorway, my coat over the back of the armchair, shoes flung haphazardly in the hall. I've really made myself quite at home in the last few months, and he's such an organized person. The kind who washes dishes as he cooks and keeps his tax spreadsheet current.

I open my mouth to apologize, but he says, "You were inspired to write a song. I get it."

Does he really, though? Josh always did. We'd go whole weekends in dizzying episodes of wild creative flow, barely keeping our heads above water as human beings. We couldn't eat. We wouldn't sleep . . .

"Fraser, do you ever get struck by some brilliant scientific hypothesis and you're terrified you'll lose the idea before you can capture it? Or are you all type A and have to do your filing first?"

He takes my wrist and twists my hand palm up, as though he's giving me something to hold, and I'm surprised at the unexpected touch. "Sometimes it feels like sand, slipping through my fingers," he says, trailing a finger across my palm. "But it's invisible. I know it's there. I can feel the weight of it. But I can't see it. Or understand it yet. It's this intangible, frustrating, exciting, excruciating possibility, and it's almost unbearable not to *know*, one way or the other . . ."

I try not to shiver as my gaze travels from Fraser's invisible idea in my hand, up his torso, to the academic aesthetic of glasses and messy hair. It settles on brown eyes that search my face with a question that I badly want him to articulate as I reach and smooth the frown lines on his forehead, just briefly. So many huge thoughts in that brain. Such massive problems that it's trying to solve. *Does he have any idea how attractive that is?*

"You're a trip hazard, Sullivan," he observes, removing my hand from his face.

Not "Sully." *Sullivan.* A grown-up, elegant, proper version of my surname that thrills me as it seems to shift us one tiny step closer.

"Maybe you need to take more risks?" I reply.

The dare leaves my mouth and seems to spark in his eyes, closing the space between us, nerve endings alight where our hands are still touching. I have visions of him taking my instruction literally. Pushing me back on the couch and kissing me just as the tsunami crashes into the city on the screen, skyscrapers crumbling while he picks me up and grants me access to the last off-limits room in his house.

"What's stopping you?" he says, pulling me from the fantasy with serious eyes. *Am I supposed to make the first move?*

"Stopping me from what?" I ask, the weighted words falling into a half whisper.

"Why aren't you chasing music the way you want to?"

Oh!

He's reversed us out of the flirtation zone and turned career coach. I remove my hand from underneath his.

"Probably fear," I hear myself say before I can properly editorialize a response. "Everything else is just an excuse."

I don't know what it is about Fraser—what magic hold he has over me—but for once I haven't dished up my default answer. I always blame "the situation" or the way I was wronged, rarely taking any responsibility myself.

"Someone stole my music," I divulge, slipping back into familiar territory. "The major composition I'd been working on for my PhD."

He reaches for the remote, shuts off the television, then turns on the table lamp beside him and looks at me the way Rach does when I'm about to spill the tea. Except she acts like she's Parker's age on Christmas morning. Fraser is patient and distinguished, as if we're about to apply academic rigor to my past.

"I was so young. So ill-equipped . . ." Shame catches in my throat as I falter through this. Failure. Rage. The poisonous cocktail that I force myself to swallow every time my memory dishes this up. "And here I am, further from my dream career than ever. I associate classical piano with my piece, and that piece with ditching my PhD, and pulling out of the doctorate with running away, and running away with failure. Whenever I hear it, and the way he claimed it and mangled it and—"

Fraser's chestnut eyes darken, muscles tensing in his jaw. "What exactly did he do?"

My heart rails against the déjà vu. An almost identical conversation on a different couch more than a decade ago. Youthful vulnerability rushing through my veins, seeping through flushed skin on my face as I dared make the accusation.

Sully, I'll keep your secret safe . . .

If I'm trembling now it's in quiet rage. My secret was never safe once I exposed it to Josh. It was ablaze in his hands. I'd assumed the buckets he promised were filled with water. I thought he'd extinguish it, not accelerate it . . .

"What's scaring you?" Fraser asks, reading the agony on my face.

I'm terrified my secret will wedge itself here, between us.

I'm afraid of how messy this is. That his brother's blistering betrayal will make me bolt from this room in coltish fear that this conversation will go as badly as the other one did.

And then I will lose this. I will lose *him*. An outcome I'm increasingly certain would devastate me, not just professionally this time, and that's the part that scares me most . . .

"I'm afraid history will repeat itself," I say, blinking back tears, rising to my feet. "And that I won't survive it twice."

12

Fraser

It's two in the morning and I've been staring at my bedroom ceiling for hours.

Did my brother steal her music?

It's unconscionable. Illegal. A criminal offense, according to the internet search I've just completed, attracting hundreds of thousands in fines and imprisonment, depending on the severity. And I am fucking infuriated.

I know how this process works in the sciences. Is it similar in the arts? Harder to prove, perhaps. I'll need to look into it—

Except she hasn't asked for my help. She's barely told me anything about it. Clammed up almost the moment she raised it, only to come out all emotionally brittle, the way she dissolved that night in Joshua's audience. *Like he'd broken her heart?* Presumably protecting him despite his crime . . .

I groan and sit on the side of my bed, elbows on my knees, head in my hands.

God, what a mess this has become.

I'd walked in yesterday to find Audrey and Parker on the lounge with the puppy, Betty, watching YouTube clips of various women composers, adding new favorites to a Spotify playlist. I hadn't thought it possible that someone could convince my child there's more than one woman in the world who's making music right now. But there she was, propped against Audrey's shoulder, fangirling over Whitwell and Wallen and Wolfe instead of Swift.

I'm really not great with children, Audrey had warned before we began. *I'd be a bad influence . . .* The reality is I'm pacing the floor now, wondering how we ever survived without her, terrified of the day she announces she's leaving because she's freshly employed in some reliable job she'll hate, because she can't quite trust herself to risk music.

As I tread quietly down the stairs, I run my hand along the rail to avoid flicking on the light and waking her. Of course, as I reach the landing, it's clogged with her clothes, despite the coat hook being only a foot away, so I hang the jacket and drape the scarf, only for the faded hint of her perfume to catch my breath.

It's the darkness. If you can't see, your other senses are heightened. Why else would I be at the foot of the stairs at two in the morning, tormenting myself with her scent?

In the kitchen, I fill the kettle and think back to the insinuation Maggie flung at me last week, which I fiercely denied. *Either you're interested in this woman or not, but either way be careful. Parker has had enough disruption already.*

Audrey is not a disruption. Over the last few months, she's become the edge. So much more than a flatmate. *Less than what? My partner? Parker's surrogate stepmum?*

"All I'm saying is that everyone could do with some certainty," Maggie said. She included herself in that, I think. And my sleepless night is doing no favors for the counterargument I made: that there is nothing going on here, because Audrey's interests lie elsewhere. I saw that at the concert, no matter how platonic their history might have been.

Minutes later, the kettle clicks, but so does the light switch. Audrey appears in soft pink short pajamas, pulling the panels of some flimsy cardigan tight across her chest, and I have to focus on the rising steam in an attempt to clear my thoughts.

When I look back, she's regarding my non-professorial attire of flannel pants and white sleeveless shirt and perhaps my uncharacteristic state of deep confusion at the kitchen counter.

"Nearly fell over your coat," I tell her. "I hung it up."

She smiles. "Why don't you write that into your rule book?"

"You never read the rule book."

There's a beat of silence.

"Tea?" I offer.

"Toast," she requests.

"Cinnamon?"

"I haven't had that since I was a kid, Fraser! *Yes!*"

"Audrey, can we talk?" The suggestion fights its way out of my mouth and through all this small talk before I can think straight.

She drops bread into the toaster, then picks up my watch, which I left on the table. "It's two in the morning."

We stand still for a minute—she's all bedhead and smudged mascara, and I get a flash of the unmovable evening skincare routine Maggie always insisted on, even if we were in the middle of something else.

Like this.

Audrey is not just the edge in my daughter's life, I realize. She's the edge in mine. The reason my mood shifts when I leave the university and remember I'm coming home not to a house with tension you could slice through, but to the sound of some new piece she can't wait to play for me. It's like that even if I have to step through a minefield of her belongings, strewn across the floor because she had the idea for the piece on the light rail and burst into the house in a creative flurry.

She moves to the counter beside me now and reaches across me for the plates. There's that scent again, softer now, as if she left the rest on her sheets. As she stretches for the crockery, the cardigan slips from her shoulder and I fight an urge to graze my lips across her skin, lift her onto this counter, and wrap her legs around me—

"It wasn't Joshua," she says, breaking the fantasy with a clunk.

"Pardon?"

"He wasn't the one. If that's what's been keeping you awake tonight."

As I look at her now, up this close and innocently concerned about my insomnia, she can be assured my brother is the last thing on my mind.

The toast pops up and she grabs it, spreads it with butter, shakes on the cinnamon sugar, and offers me a bite that I can barely swallow, before leading me to the table for the small-hours reckoning I'd proposed, hijacking it in her opening sentence.

"Josh didn't steal my music," she says, sipping her tea. "My PhD supervisor did that. Your brother was just the accomplice."

13

Audrey

I'm going to tell Fraser this story if only to distract us from the mood in this kitchen, because I swear I'm imagining bedroom eyes.

"My professor's argument, as is *so* often the case when you're a man, and a woman has a hot idea, was that he thought of it first. He showed me samples of his unpublished work and claimed it was me who had lifted *his* ideas."

He arches an eyebrow.

"I wrote the music, Fraser. Every single note of it. I brought it to him, the DNA of it fully formed."

The accusation marinates and I focus on the tick, tick, tick of Fraser's watch on the table between us. It pushes time forward dispassionately, carrying me further and further from the incident that derailed me, every soft flick of the hand another wasted second. How quickly it adds up. Minutes. Hours. *Years, in this case—*

Fraser's arms are crossed on the table, the rest of the toast untouched, body poised for a brawl, despite the absence of an opponent. "What happened next?"

That's the question that has haunted me. The one that's kept me awake not just tonight but for years. Because what I did next was open an enormous void of inaction into which I should have poured the fight. I should have stood up for myself. I should have ripped my music from his thieving hands and raised academic hell.

"He included my piece in his bestselling solo piano album, passed it off as his own, and gave zero credit to me. The album won an ARIA. It all feels very William Shakespeare and Emilia Bassano. Not that I'm saying my music was in that league . . ."

"Plagiarism is a criminal offense, Audrey. You know it can involve prison time?"

I get a flash of Professor Ridges in solitary confinement. Guards passing inedible slop through iron bars, while he's entirely deprived of music. That would be punishment enough for him. Of course, in reality he'd probably know the judge—he had that sort of network. He'd evade punishment altogether, or end up in some state-of-the-art detention center where he'd be the hero, offering free music therapy classes for fellow inmates and discovering some protégé. He'd be like the Martha Stewart of the music world.

"Are you with me?" Fraser is saying when I finally come to.

Am I with him how?

"I was fantasizing about Professor Ridges and Martha Stewart."

The way he ignores this statement, as if it's a completely normal thing to have said, suggests he can handle even the quirkiest parts of me. The aspects former boyfriends used to criticize and try to change. *He is not your boyfriend, Audrey!*

"Did you report this at the time?"

Now I'm really off my toast.

There is no way through this part without involving Joshua, and I can sense my face rearranging itself, searching for the expression that says, *Don't take this personally, Fraser, but your brother's a dick.*

"It's not too late," he goes on, before I can articulate it. "At the very least you could sue him for royalties, but the man should lose his job."

"That's what Joshua said," I cut in. "When I first confided in him."

Fraser sits back and runs both hands through his hair, a long, slow breath rising out of his chest. I know he's angry, but, wow, he has no idea that the action, in that sleeveless shirt and those pajama pants, makes him look like a billboard model.

"Josh and I had been partnered for a film score assignment," I forge on. "So we got to know each other pretty well. You know how intense he can be. There wasn't a piece of mine that he didn't know so intimately he might as well have written it himself. I mean, if anyone had been in a position to steal my work, it would have been him—"

Fraser is looking at me like I'm a first-year student whose various great-aunts' deaths are mystifyingly on the same timeline as assignment deadlines. Or like I'm the vice-chancellor after the announcement of a departmental funding cut.

"Anyway, Josh worked with Ridges as a grad student. He promised to help me confront him—"

"Ridges? Wasn't he Josh's mentor?"

I'm glad he's putting this together himself. I won't have to spell out every part of it.

"Let me guess. Instead of helping you plead your case, Josh gave Ridges a heads-up?"

"By the time I confronted Ridges, he'd got the university legal team involved. He'd fabricated this whole body of supporting evidence showing he'd had the idea first. He completely gaslit me."

"So they ambushed you." He hangs his head as if he were the one who did it, taking a collateral hit.

"Your brother was just so ambitious, and he went in with the right intentions—"

"Oh, I can imagine," Fraser says, darkly. "He would have gone in all heroic, guns blazing, then jettisoned you and his morals at the first whiff of a career break. What did Ridges offer him?"

The biggest opportunity of his life.

"He recommended him for that position with the Vienna Philharmonic."

He stares at me. "Fuck, Audrey. How are you not enraged?"

Not enraged? It's nearly consumed me! "I've been furious with Josh since the day it happened. You saw that!"

"When?"

"At the concert!"

He stares at me, anger forced aside by confusion. "I thought—"

I watch as his mind seems to recalibrate the way that he'd always read this. He proceeds quietly. "I thought he loved you. We all thought that. He all but said it. After you left, he was a mess."

A laugh bursts out of me. "You'd be a mess, too, if you were riddled with that much guilt."

His brows knit, the way they do when he's talking about rising sea levels or warming temperatures. "What was that in the wings at his concert? That . . . *longing*?"

"Oh, that was definitely longing. For the career I'd given up. Look, Fraser, it's true that I've never met someone as professionally compatible as Josh. Whenever I write something, even now, it kills me that I can't show him—like when you forget for a second that someone is dead and you want to call them to share your news? All that bad behavior can't erase the infuriating fact that he's just so fucking clever, musically. We were clever together. And he destroyed that. But what you saw at the concert was pure fury at him for letting me down. And fury at myself."

"Why at yourself?"

"Because instead of getting up and moving on, instead of fighting back, I stayed where they left me. I used to listen to Ridges' version of my piece on repeat. I couldn't get it into my brain that he had taken it and made it a hit on the classical charts. He didn't just steal it. He stripped the emotion, *wildly* ruining it. I was young and naïve and a chronic people pleaser. I convinced myself I'd imagined the plagiarism. Maybe he'd come up with it after all? Perhaps, as he said, I just wasn't talented enough to have written something like this. And my place wasn't on the stage. It was in the audience . . ."

Fraser's chair drags along the wooden floor as he pushes it back. I've watched this man wait on hold with an airline over lost luggage. I've seen him handle a meeting with the chief finance officer at the university when his research grant application fell through the cracks and cost him an important opportunity. I hear him on the phone with Maggie most weeks, working through disagreements in parenting style. His blood pressure never rises a blip.

But he is not like that now. This is a caged animal, muscles flexing, blood boiling, as he rises and paces the room, processing all that Ridges and Joshua did to me.

"Do we need to see a lawyer?" he asks, taking a pragmatic turn. "Surely you weren't the only one he did this to."

"When did this become your problem?"

He seems taken aback and stands still. "Sorry. I didn't mean to barge into this. I just feel . . . partly responsible somehow."

"You're not your brother, Fraser. You said so yourself. Lawyers are expensive. I've been tempted to confront Ridges again in person, now that I'm older. See if the threat of legal action is enough? Demand to know why he *butchered* my piece . . ."

He smiles for the first time tonight, swings the chair in front of me again, and sits on it. "Maybe don't use the term 'butchered' in your defense. Stick to the crime itself and not a creative critique? Focus on high-level strategy."

"Which would be what, hypothetically? A public apology? A redaction of the album? Payment of some kind?"

I'm back into the mind-blowing mess of imagining the way it would all implode, knowing the collapse would take me, too. I am a woman. I'd be the troublemaker. This is an adored teacher and revered composer. He got away with this because he could, and I let our power imbalance intimidate me right from the start.

"I'm scared if I stir this up, it will push me even further from my path. You've only seen a fraction of what I can do, because this has been holding me back for years. You asked what I was afraid of?"

He nods.

"I'm scared I'll never find that creative part of myself that feels like fireworks. The part that Josh knew, before it all exploded. We've been living together for months, and you've barely met the real me, Fraser—"

We lock gazes for a long moment in the stillness. Then, without breaking eye contact, he reaches for the chair I'm sitting on, grabs the wooden seat between my legs, and in one strong, fluid motion, pulls it and me across the floor and between his thighs. Seconds tick in the shocked silence, hearts hammering as the time that seemed to push me away from my past starts pulling me toward him instead, an electric rush of sparks and yearning and hope.

"What did you say?" he half whispers, leaning forward,

forehead touching mine while an alchemy of florals and cedar and sage and cinnamon swirls between us.

"We barely know each other," I repeat, his hand gripping harder on the chair between my legs, which are trembling now. None of this is what I had imagined. If it had felt dangerous having his gentle warmth near my wounds, now that the urgent heat of his obvious desire is this close to mine, I can barely take it.

"Allow me to reintroduce myself, Audrey Sullivan," he says, voice low, chest rising and falling as he waits for my word. This is a hundred times hotter than I thought a science nerd could orchestrate, and my pulse is thundering now, the seconds blaring, every nerve ending screaming at his proximity.

"Is this some sort of elevated, articulate request for consent?" I ask, my breath quickening.

Dark eyes flash as they meet mine. "Is it approved?"

My lips brush his mouth in a kiss that starts gently and deepens quickly into the promise of something confident and assured. He lets go of the chair, hands traveling to my waist before he scoops me across his lap, scaffolding me as he *dismantles* me—my anchored past, all the bad dates and failed relationships trying to hold me back from this bliss until the rope snaps and I'm drifting, untethered, into a rapid new current.

It's all soft touches and firm intention, as if he's never done this before and done it a thousand times. Cinnamon between our lips, fingers cradling my neck, thumb at the thrashing pulse beneath my ear, he whispers a redundant "May I?" as fabric falls from my shoulder and he plants a line of kisses that feel like they're being scorched onto my skin.

He may. Anything. Everything. All thought leaves my brain as my senses take over, back arching, hips sliding toward his, body angling to give him everything. Then, as the mess of my life collapses, long-forgotten music surges into my brain, clamoring for air as he touches me.

"It was the second you dumped that ice at the party," he whispers between fevered kisses, one hand threaded through my hair, the other at my hip, under my top.

I drag up his sleeveless shirt, palms trailing over the sculpted muscles of his chest, as I pull it over his head and off his shoulders onto the floor. "It was your keynote address in Toronto for me . . ."

He pulls us apart, laughing.

"What, you think you're the only one who's good at research?" I challenge him.

And that's it.

In this moment, in his eyes, I am his match. It's all music in my mind—his body and mine, sounds and colors I couldn't speak into words if I tried.

When we finally break apart, we're left with just our ragged breaths and the reliable ticking of Fraser's watch. That, and the inevitable future that rolls out spectacularly in our path like a carpet.

the
middle

14

Fraser

"You and Audrey should take the tickets," I tell Maggie. There's a strict two-tickets-per-family policy at Parker's scholarship concert, which presents the three of us with an awkward problem. "She's spent the last six months preparing Parker for this. I've heard nearly every practice. You two should go."

Maggie and I are at a playground with Parker, having "family time." Her theory is that if we do this now, it will normalize shared birthdays and Christmases and Parker's wedding and the grandchildren's naming ceremonies. But now that I've mentioned Audrey, she looks like she's at an awards ceremony, camera zoomed on her face while another nominee's name is announced as the winner.

Parker is at the top of a zip line, waving at us. *Nothing to see here. Just Mum and Dad about to rip through another swing of the split-family gauntlet.*

"Can't Audrey get a ticket herself as the piano teacher?"

"Come on, Maggie. You know she's more than that."

She shoots me the expression she's been wearing since the moment I delivered the certainty she was craving: *You were right, Mags. There* is *something there . . .*

Perhaps I shouldn't have understated things, but I was still reeling. Swept into a relationship without my usual full battery of controlled tests and a thoroughly examined hypothesis.

“It’s serious,” I tell Maggie. What it is, is a chaotic, out-of-character, electric, tumbling free fall, and I need to restrain that joy during this conversation.

“Serious?” Maggie parrots, as if she’s lost her own vocabulary and can only recycle mine. I watch as she grapples with the idea that her ex-husband might have a second chance at romantic happiness and that it’s not the flash in the pan she predicted. “Fraser, it takes you *ages* to fall in love.”

We stare at each other, her statement cocooned from the noise of the playground while the truth lands.

It’s true that our relationship was more of a slow burn, a cautious start. But Audrey makes me rush to the water’s edge. I don’t care about doing this right or waiting for a sensible amount of time to elapse before I plunge toward her. I want her to crash into my life. I want her to rip up all the stones I paved so carefully and change the landscape of everything.

“Mummy! Daddy! Look!”

We smile and clap and yell “Great job, Parks!” hoping she won’t tumble off the monkey bars and break her wrists before the concert. I wouldn’t say this to Maggie, given psychology is generally her turf, but after Audrey found an article about the link between playground bravery and performance risks, part of our daughter’s rapid musical development has been the result of the two of them dangling from tree branches and diving from swim platforms while I keep my eyes shut.

Maggie’s inner authoritarian was always going to be threatened by the concept of another woman making micro-decisions about Parker’s life. *Does she have permission to watch a PG-rated movie in class? Is she tall enough for the roller coaster?*

She’s ready to call Parker down, but I reach for her arm and pull her back.

"If you just spent some time with Audrey—"

She looks at me, annoyed, as if this divorce hadn't been her idea and she hadn't brought this outcome upon herself. As if it had been me who'd sat *her* down unexpectedly that rainy Sunday afternoon and said, *This isn't working anymore, is it? Don't we both deserve more?*

"I know this isn't easy, Mags—"

"It seems pretty straightforward for you!"

Straightforward? She flung me from our nine-year marriage! It was lonely and devastating and heart-wrenching—

"Sorry, Fraser," she says, pinning dark hair nervously behind her ear. "I didn't mean that. Maybe you're right. Audrey and I should take the tickets."

It's as if we're defusing a bomb.

"Just wait until *I* meet someone and you're the one facing the prospect of some strange adult sharing your daughter's life," she suggests.

"I hope you do. I want you to be happy."

She nods.

"And then we can rise above ourselves the way I'm sure we can now if we just stay focused on the right thing. Look at our daughter." Parker is running toward us, beaming. "Isn't she worth it?"

The three of them—Parker, Maggie, and Audrey—burst through the door late on Friday night, Parker elated.

"Daddy, I won!"

She's brandishing a trophy, a certificate, and a letter of offer awarding her a semester's tuition at the music school. It's reminiscent of so many nights from my childhood when we'd all tumble in after another of Joshua's wins and I'd think, *There he goes! My incredible brother!*

But this is my incredible child, flanked by the woman who brought her into the world and the one who is mothering her creativity, and for just these five seconds, at least, it feels like we are *doing* it. We're making this work.

Parker rushes straight to the piano, and Maggie's smile is radiant. "I have to hand it to you," she says to Audrey. "What you've done with her is extraordinary."

Have we crossed some magical threshold of marital dysfunction and turned ourselves into one of those gold-threaded Japanese vases, crafted from our brokenness?

"Parker, I'm heading off now!" Maggie calls. "Come and say goodbye."

She drags her finger up the keyboard in an enthusiastic glissando, jumps up from the piano, runs over, and gives Maggie a hug before dashing upstairs to her bedroom.

"Always so busy, Bee!" Audrey says, using the nickname Parker loves, though it gets under Maggie's skin. As settled as she has become with our new arrangements, our daughter still avoids this doorstep goodbye. It's why we generally do the handover via the bookends of a school day.

I reach for the door handle. "Wait," Audrey says, glancing upstairs. "Something's not right with Parker." Her voice is low, brow furrowed. "I heard it in her piece."

Maggie recoils at the very suggestion. "She was unbelievable tonight. She swept the whole thing. I don't think she needs extra pressure, Audrey. I know what you musicians can be like, but she is nine years old—"

Audrey stands her ground. "I'm not pushing her. I wouldn't. She *was* amazing and she deserved to win. But there was something off about her performance."

"I'm sorry, were we at the same event? She brought the house down. I was moved to tears!"

Audrey, trembling, is rattled at having raised this, but she won't back down. "Technically, it was flawless. But her dynamic range was limited. Emotionally, it fell a bit flat and that's what worries me."

Both women turn to me, expecting me to mediate.

"Could it be nerves?" I ask, pushing down an inconvenient thought that "emotional flatness" can be hereditary.

Audrey shakes her head. "Nerves only elevate her."

Maggie is staring at Audrey. Grappling, perhaps, with the fact that this piece of parenting intel is being dropped by the woman in the room who is *not* certified by the Royal Australian and New Zealand College of Psychiatrists.

"I can't say I've noticed anything," I begin, even though it feels like I'm betraying Audrey. "But, Maggie, Audrey is exceptionally gifted. She hears things we don't."

I'm met with a silent "thank you" in Audrey's eyes.

"All I'm saying is that I think we should watch her," she says. "Something is missing in her music."

"Please fill out this questionnaire," Dr. Kumar says, three days later, handing me a sheet of paper with a range of scenarios asking how I've felt over the last month. If something is wrong with Parker, this is no time for paternal heroics.

Maybe it's a midlife crisis. I read that midlife is late thirties, statistically speaking. Maybe it's existential dread. Overexposure to climate crises at work? Burnout?

How often did you feel tired for no reason? the question reads.

There's always a reason. I can't think of the last time I got an uninterrupted night's sleep. Even at nine, if Parker is with us, she inevitably crawls into our bed, and if she's with Maggie, I wake up anyway, listening for footsteps.

How often did you feel nervous? So nervous nothing could calm you down?

I tick *none of the time.* I'm not anxious.

How often did you feel hopeless?

This test isn't nuanced enough. Of course I've felt hopeless. I have a child with some sort of problem and a job that exposes the threat of human extinction . . .

How often were you so sad nothing could cheer you up?

I undo a button at my neck. Until this moment I'd thought this appointment was a waste of time. An overreaction, in response to all the men's health advertisements in bus shelters and on the back of restroom doors. I have a fascinating job. A beautiful daughter. An amazing new partner. Even things with Maggie have settled down. I should be on top of the world!

Should be on top of the world . . . Dad said that to me once. University entrance scores were out. I'd been thrilled with 98.85 until they pointed out that, two years earlier, Josh had scored 99.00. *And majoring in music, Fraser, where it's harder to scale up.*

My whole childhood had been an effort in scaling up against my brother, striving to impress Mum, in particular, never quite making it no matter how well I did. Every prize. Each scholarship. None of them ever quite as good as whatever Josh pulled off, and I wonder if that's where this all began.

How often have I been so sad nothing would cheer me up? My hand shakes as I mark the applicable box, knowing this one answer will unlock a "mental health plan" and psychology appointments and medication. And having to burden Audrey with this, right in the dizzying thrill of our "honeymoon period."

You never have to struggle alone, I reassured Parker the other night. Is the advice the same for an adult male? Because even as I hand the paper back and the doctor tallies up the score, and despite how enlightened I pretend to be on this stuff, even before the official diagnosis is handed down, I'm already making a mental list of all the people I am not going to tell.

15

Audrey

"Fraser was right." Rach and I are on one of our regular walks around Lake Burley Griffin, sipping coffee we bought from a little truck near the National Library and kicking our feet through the crunch of leaves. I just *have* to confide in her. "Ridges didn't only steal my music. It happened to several of us—all women, of course. He's *still* teaching—"

My best friend has been training for this fight for twelve years. Blond hair scraped into a ponytail. Camouflage-themed running gear. She has elite take-on-the-world vibes. Assassin-like, whenever we talk about this.

"My classmates are determined to take him down. And you know me. I am so nonconfrontational I forced down an extra-spicy vindaloo last night when I'd actually ordered mild massaman, and I can barely taste this coffee anymore. They added me to a group chat and I'm already losing sleep."

She frowns. "Wouldn't taking down Ridges inevitably expose Joshua?" She can tell by the look on my face that this is exactly my problem. "Not that he doesn't deserve everything he gets," she adds. "I despise that man on your behalf."

Even now, after everything he did, her words hit me in conflicting ways. He was once my closest friend. That's why the betrayal stung so exquisitely. As recently as a year ago, it would have been why I would have walked away from this.

But those stakes have been raised. "I worry about the blast radius," I admit. "I've barely got a foothold in that family, and this would burn the house down. I can't lose him."

"I sincerely hope you mean Fraser," she says.

"Of course I mean Fraser! You know their mum always called me Fickle Sully? They think it was *me* who wrecked things with Josh. Imagine the story they'd concoct about me infiltrating the family a second time, through the other brother, and blowing it all up again. I know this sounds dramatic, but I *would not survive* without that man."

Rach, who is the last person to throw herself into a public display of affection, hugs me, her body charged. "Fraser would be on your side, you know," she whispers. "He always is. He adores you."

"So why would I sabotage that? How can I threaten Parker's uncle?"

"Josh did this to himself."

"Do you think the group could manage this coup without my direct involvement? They could use my piece as evidence. But I could stay all aloof and 'no comment' about it and make myself look like some sort of martyr to the Millers. *We were wrong about Fickle Sully. Turns out she actually sacrificed her career for Joshua's . . .*"

Rach pulls out of the hug. "Are you even listening to yourself?" Her brain is ticking over. The same brain that tackles cyber espionage, so I'm hoping it's about to deliver some ingenious solution.

"Okay, hear me out," she begins. "What if you reach out to Josh?"

She can't be serious. "Confiding in Josh is how I got here! Oh, God, this conversation is making me anxious. Let's talk about something else. Let's have a deep dive into your trainwreck date with Tin-Foil-Hat Timothy from Tinder," I suggest.

"I thought you refused to be on the apps?"

She grimaces. "A momentary lapse," she explains. "Worse than expected. Never going back. But listen, maybe Josh has changed?"

"You'd have more luck changing Timothy's opinion on the moon landing," I reply. "Josh *has* changed. He's fed on his own success, and now he's an even more narcissistic version of the person who threw me to the wolves at the outset. There's no scenario in which I involve him that ends with me and Fraser in a better place."

I step out of the way of a speeding electric scooter, coffee spilling on my shirt, and I try to mop it up with my sleeve as Rach shouts one of her trademark grandmotherly insults at the offending rider: "This is a shared zone, you incompetent ninny!" She looks back at me and says, "Reporting these wretches could grant you back the credit for the best piece of music you ever wrote. The publicity alone would open opportunities. Your career could blow up!"

Do I want it to? I've been playing it safe for so many years, the idea of taking off now makes me queasy.

"I don't mind my plan B," I reply. Word soon spread at Parker's school about how well she was doing with our lessons, and I picked up a bunch of other students. I teach at home while Fraser is at the university. It leaves me with flexibility to write my own stuff and share the creative process with Parker. She and I are writing a surprise piece for Fraser's upcoming fortieth, and this bond with her is the magic in my life. "It mightn't be the big, glossy, international composing career I was tracking toward at twenty, but I'm pretty happy."

It isn't that yet, Fraser reminds me. He has infinite faith in my capacity to take the long way around.

"You *don't mind it*. You're *pretty happy*. You were so ambitious, once. I worry this won't be enough for you."

Rach voices my internal angst with a best friend's accuracy. But I'm looking for the least worst outcome here. Right now, Fraser and Parker matter more than my professional life does.

She tosses her coffee cup into a bin. "Promise me you'll talk to Fraser before you decide? It's his brother, after all. And you're his partner."

Yes. *Why would I ever force him to choose?*

"Audrey, can we talk?" he asks, two hours later.

Has he got wind of this already?

"Don't panic, it's not about us!"

Now he's unlocked a new fear. This man is heaven. We can't entertain any we-need-to-talk-level issues. Everything is going far too well. He leads me to the swing seat on the back balcony, in the kind of filtered afternoon sunlight that should invite happy conversations about books and films and holiday plans and how this is the best relationship of both of our lives. Not whatever dire news he's about to drop.

"It's about me," he says, a calm expression attempting to fight its way onto his grave face.

A trap door opens beneath me, trying to suck me through. *What's wrong with Fraser? Is he sick? Trouble at work?*

"I went to the doctor today—"

Oh, God! Blood rushes from my heart. I am *stricken* at the idea that he's unwell.

"I think it's just pressure from work," he says, brown eyes wary, as if this is the most naked admission of his life. "She's suggested I take some time off and given me something to help. Mentally. An antidepressant, Audrey. For moderate depression."

He reveals every part of the statement as though it's a mini chapter, edging us toward the denouement. I hold the silence that follows as if it is sacred. Brain spinning. We can work with this. He's not dying. *Why would he be?* Oh, this is a relief. Not that he's struggling, obviously, but—

"It's not because I'm not happy with you," he says, even though the thought had never entered my mind. I look at him, all off-duty academic in jeans and boots and a steel-blue knit sweater, earnest expression imploring me to believe we are safe, despite this storm.

I place a reassuring hand on his arm. "Of course it's not that. I'm so sorry you've been struggling. You should have told me."

He pulls me tight against his chest and kisses the top of my head, while I listen to his steady heartbeat. This man is strong. He'll wrestle this, particularly now that he's involving me in it. Nevertheless my mind is hit with a barrage of news stories and social media posts, always with long lists of helplines beneath them, and I squeeze my eyes shut to try to banish the mental pictures.

"I worry there'll be ramifications if it gets around at work," he confides. "You know: *Fraser isn't coping. Should we rethink that promotion to full professor?*"

I sit upright again. "That would be discrimination, obviously. Half your department is probably medicated for one thing or another. I was, too, once, back when—" I stop short. "The point is, I can empathize. Don't ever hold this in, Fraser. We just need to keep talking."

"Wasn't that the gig I signed up for?" he reminds me. "We tell each other everything?" His fingers touch the side of my face as he draws me into a slow kiss. The kind that feels like mental telepathy, as if every brush of the lips is a conversation. *I adore you. We'll get through this.*

I think of the group chat about Ridges and the conversation

with Rach about Josh, and the idea of finally righting ownership of that piece of music and igniting my career.

"Of course we tell each other everything," I promise him, stuffing down those secrets.

Almost everything.

16

Fraser

"Morning, Frase," Rachael says, flicking blond hair out of her face, arms laden with an impressive double-decker masterpiece that she's fashioned with fondant crotchets and quavers and keyboards and guitars for Parker's tenth birthday. The cake is her birthday gift, by prior arrangement with Maggie, who was only too delighted not to have to outsource this to a local patisserie as usual.

I sweep the balloons aside and help Rachael set it carefully on the dining table just as my parents arrive, Mum glaring at the cake or, more accurately, at Audrey's best friend's involvement in the whole thing, as Parker comes racing down the stairs on a video call with Josh in Europe.

"Grandma and Pop should have my gift," he tells her. "Sorry I couldn't be there, Parks." He'd originally promised to tee up a work visit that would coincide with her birthday. But "something came up." Perhaps an acute dose of guilt, now that Audrey's back in the picture.

When she hears his voice on the phone, there's a flicker of surprise on her face. I can't pretend I don't notice the frowns that she and Rachael exchange. When Parker opens her uncle's present, a professional conductor's baton from the gift shop at Juilliard, Audrey scurries into the kitchen, immediately followed by Rachael—not before she taps me on the arm and says, "Don't worry. It's not what you think."

What does she think I'm thinking? Is she worried I can't handle anything else? According to my bank account, our family is single-handedly propping up the psychology industry of Canberra.

It's taken hard work over several weeks, but between the cognitive behavioral therapy, the drugs, and some practical strategies, I seem to have wrenched myself out of immediate danger. Maggie and I have been taking Parker to a play-based psychologist in the city who confirmed Maggie's suspicion of neurodiversity and referred us to a pediatric psychiatrist for a battery of tests, several diagnoses, and the addition of a stimulant that seems to be vastly improving the way Parker navigates everyday life.

I'm about to follow Audrey and Rachael into the kitchen when the last of the guests pile in. Audrey's sister, Sara, the more introverted of the two, with darker hair and a permanently anxious expression hidden behind tortoiseshell frames. Behind her, Maggie, along with ten-year-old Rose—Parker's new and only friend—and Rose's father, Kurt. Maggie gave them a lift. They've been having frequent playdates and even have a day trip planned to Batemans Bay.

"Fraser," Kurt says, striding across the room to shake my hand. "You don't mind if I stay?"

Rose has been here several times. But from the bright look on my former wife's face, I suspect Kurt's presence at this party might be for other reasons. At *that* thought, my heart skips a beat. Just the one. On behalf of my younger self and the expectations that life derailed, despite all the greenery flourishing in our charred landscape.

"Maggie!" Mum says, arms outstretched. *Will she ever get*

over my divorce? I'm almost grateful Audrey is holed up in the kitchen having some sort of Josh-related debrief with Rachael and isn't privy to this return-of-the-prodigal-daughter-in-law performance.

"Parker, take off your sweater! You're too hot!" I say as she rushes past with Rose. I press the button on the air-con, cooling the house since she completely ignores me, as if teen rebellion has set in three years early.

And now the smoke alarm is going off! That'll be Audrey, who is many incredible things, but not a competent chef. She'll have set something on fire again . . .

17

Audrey

"You *have* to tell Fraser," Rach urges me, waving a tea towel ineffectively at the smoke detector while I retrieve the charred remains of sausage rolls from the oven and drop them onto the side of the sink, burning my finger. "It's not fair."

She means it's not fair on me: *You deserve a sparkling career, Audrey. Just like Josh.* But with ruined food, a burnt finger, and the alarm still blaring, I can't think about it. I run the tap and wrench open the kitchen window as Fraser appears, takes the towel from Rach, waves it aggressively from his taller height, and shuts off the noise. Then he pulls my hand from the stream of water to inspect the burn, frowning.

"Sorry," I say, despairing at the sausage rolls. "I'll run out and get some more from the shops, shall I?"

"Audrey, there are exactly two children at this party," he says, using an oven mitt to pick up the hot tray and dump twenty-four mini sausage rolls into the bin. "I really don't think we need to worry."

Is he annoyed?

He rubs his forehead in a way that is unlikely to be about burnt party food as Rach makes a graceful exit from the kitchen with a tray of dips.

"Is everything okay?" he asks once we're alone.

This is his daughter's party. His parents are in the next room. It's not the time or place to alert him that his brother's reputation is at risk.

"Josh's call upset you," he continues. "You're acting weirder than usual about him. He's avoiding family events. And now I've walked in on your conversation with Rach about needing to tell me something? What's going on?"

I flop onto a chair. I'll admit it looks bad. Even then, he's handling it calmly. Classic Fraser. But he's got it all wrong. "I've been trying to protect you," I explain.

"From what?"

Fraser's fierce integrity is never going to let this go. "From any potential family fallout about the university case. You were right. My professor didn't only steal from me. My peers are building a case to lodge an official complaint, and they want me involved in the formal investigation."

He nods approvingly, and his enthusiasm makes my stomach plunge.

"Even if Josh *could* be kept out of it somehow, I don't know if I could stand the scandal," I admit. "Something like this would be all over the media. It's the kind of niche crime producers pounce on for TV dramas. All those shows about people stealing others' identities, inventing fake personalities, fake illnesses . . . Wouldn't a lauded professor and composer stealing music from his female students be a true crime hit?"

The party hums in the background as deep eyes promise all the time in the world for us to work through this. But I just want to bolt from it. Still.

"How long have you been carrying all of this?" he asks.

"A few months?"

He sighs.

"Rach knew," I assure him.

"And what's her position on it?"

I don't look at him. He and Rach are always on the same page and he knows it.

"I don't think we need this extra stress," I argue. "What if they start digging and find out that Joshua knew? What if it comes out that he was bribed to keep it quiet?"

"Then he'd deserve the fallout."

He'd really see his brother tumble? "Fraser, he's one of the most respected conductors in the world. I could tear his career to shreds."

"The way he shredded yours?"

He is *burning* with outrage. It should be galvanizing . . .

"You heard him on the phone with Parker," I point out. "She idolizes him. Why would I risk her relationship with him? And with you? I mean, think about her . . ."

"I *am* thinking about her," he answers gruffly. "What if someone did this to her one day? What if she wrote a piece and someone pilfered it and made money off it and used the ensuing awards and accolades to fuel the next decade of his own career, leaving hers in the dust? Somehow I don't think you'd stand idly by and let him do it. Not if it was Parker. Even if her uncle knew."

Just listening to the scenario makes me sick. I would protect her at all costs. I'd ride in on some white horse and fight for her intellectual property and *never* let some guy wield his power over her. I would *never* let her compromise her own success . . .

"I'd have her back," I admit, stomach churning horribly. "Of course I would."

He pulls me into a long hug, leaving me to join dots that reveal a picture I can no longer ignore. And when we look up, Rach is in the doorway, empty tray in hand, eyes misted.

"It's cake time," she announces, ditching the tray, tightening her perfect ponytail, smoothing her dress. My best friend has "drawn a hard line on romance." She's going to "focus entirely on her career." But every so often, when we're watching a romantic comedy or she visits her loved-up grandparents or catches me and Fraser in one of these intimate moments where he is just so *there for me* in a way that must make her feel so starkly on her own, her expression clouds, and she comes off a little wistful.

Fraser must notice it, too. He rises from the table, takes me by the hand, and scoops Rach in, pushing us into the living room for "Happy Birthday."

He is the one on the white horse. At any hint that one of us needs help, he is there. And I can barely make it through the song without my voice cracking.

18

Fraser

"It might seem like we're moving through life in a linear way," I explain while we're at our favorite restaurant a few weeks later. "But there's a theory that everything is happening concurrently. The past and present and future exist all at once—each dimension equally as real as the other."

Audrey glances up from the menu. "Fraser, I love you. But what the hell are you talking about?"

I laugh. "It's this philosophy of time called eternalism. Time doesn't *pass*. It just *is*."

"So you're telling me right now, somewhere, we're being born and we're already dead? Did you have the gnocchi last time? Was it spicy?"

"You wouldn't like it. And yes, that's the idea."

A waiter approaches. "We need a couple more minutes," Audrey says, leaning across and adding, "That's if minutes even exist. According to you, I'm already eating what I am about to order, even though it hasn't yet been cooked."

"You're about to order it, you're eating it, and you finished it decades ago."

"But this is what I always say about destiny!" she replies, putting the menu down. "Imagine we do have free will, but at the same time we've already made all of our decisions. We've done it all, and that's why it feels so fated."

I love it when we do this. Swap ideas. Her music. My science. This kind of philosophical wandering. There's something deeply bonding about the vulnerability of questioning things aloud. Of being beginners in each other's worlds.

"Fraser, are you saying that we are six years old in one part of the universe, we're here tonight, and we're ninety-six somewhere else?"

I reach for her hand. "I'm saying we're on a date in this Italian restaurant, and we've been married fifty years."

A hush seems to suck in all of time.

"Have we?" she asks, chestnut flecks shining in her eyes.

I didn't mean to ask. Not in this specific moment. We just dashed out for a spontaneous meal. She's in a simple black sundress, straps tied at the shoulders, hair twisted in a casual knot on her head. *Would she have wanted this to have been better planned? And for me to produce a ring?*

As I meet her wide eyes, an inevitable future seems to reveal itself, rushing and tumbling all the way back to this red-and-white-checkered tablecloth, candlelight flickering across her face—the answer to a question I haven't yet voiced already in her eyes.

"Will you?" I ask her, heart thumping.

"I already have," she replies instantly, reaching across the table with both hands. "Isn't that how this works?"

I'm hit by a calming certainty that this is exactly what we're meant to do. This is the future we already have, not creating itself but unveiling itself. As our waiter returns, Audrey beams at him. "We're getting married!" she announces. "Shall we have champagne?"

Then she smiles at me. "Fraser, I will *burst* if I have to keep this quiet! Can I at least call Sara and Rach?"

All I can do is stare at her, heart racing. It's not a sense of events getting away from us, or that we're rushing things or that I didn't think this through. It's that in every corner of time, across every decade, at every age we'll ever be, *I can't believe this woman is already mine.*

If I could marry Audrey without telling my family, I would. As perfect as the gentle falling into the inevitability of this engagement has been, three days later, I'm nervous about breaking the news. I've gone on ahead, without her, and I find my parents on their front veranda. In the Miller family, it's best to navigate information of this magnitude in private.

"This isn't a subconscious attempt to one-up your brother, is it, Fraser?" Mum says, right out of the gate. "How does Maggie feel?"

"Maggie is fine. Parker, more important, is thrilled. She's already practicing to be the flower girl."

I took Maggie out for coffee yesterday. There's a certain grief associated with moving on, even when Maggie chose to end things. This feels like the final piece of evidence that we failed.

"She's good for Parker," she conceded, back ramrod straight. "And she's good for you, too, Fraser. You seem happy."

I wouldn't say so to her, of course, but this relationship feels like the big bang in my world. The later-in-life origin moment, despite all that came before it.

"I think it's wonderful," Dad says now. "You deserve each other." He squeezes my shoulder the way he used to when I was a kid, eyes misting.

"Oh, here he is!" Delight spreads across Mum's face as my brother pulls aggressively into the driveway, classical music blaring from his sleek vehicle, a show as always.

She can't bustle fast enough down the steps to his car.

"Fraser's marrying Fickle Sully," she announces, before he can even extract himself.

He kills the engine, gets out, slams the door, and kisses Mum on the cheek. "You should stop calling her that," he says sullenly.

Then he locks darkened eyes with me over Mum's shoulder and says, "Congratulations."

The attention on my news is fleeting. As they walk up the steps, he brightens and says, "You're looking at the music and artistic director of the New York Philharmonic!" And he punches the air.

While our parents bask in this development, I'm thrown to another part of the eternal timeline. A younger Audrey confiding in him about the plagiarism. His promise to help. The call he made to prioritize himself instead, every notch he's carved on his career belt since falling into line like dominoes at her expense, right up to this fresh coup in the States.

Mum throws herself into his arms the way she ought to have thrown herself into mine. Josh is the squeaky wheel. He's the brittle one. *You're not like him, Fraser. You're logical and sensible and strong. I never have to worry about you.* It's the fallacy that has driven this lifelong orchestration of hushed tones and special allowances that I'm contemplating when she hits us with "I assume you have a wedding-related question to ask your brother?"

The suggestion is delivered into charged silence, while the two of us stand on the porch like chastised schoolboys, all torn shirts and scrapes and bruises, being forced to make up after a fight.

Is she envisaging matching suits and a reception speech?

"I'll compose something," Josh says. "She can walk down the aisle to it."

If anyone's writing music for this ceremony, it will be Audrey. Or Parker. Or they'll cowrite.

Mum glares at me and tosses her head at Josh, because it's my role, apparently, to smooth the way for him. She cannot possibly be insinuating that Josh still cares. Or that he ever cared for Audrey the way that I do. She still doesn't know he betrayed her—Audrey won't let me set the record straight. All my parents saw was the way he acted out when she left. As if they'd been in a proper relationship and he'd loved her. Not used her to get ahead.

She pulls me into a corner after he goes inside with Dad. "You keep insisting it was only ever professional between the two of them, but, Fraser, when have you known 'colleagues' to have that sort of chemistry? This New York job is another important step. We can't have him falling to pieces at yet another critical moment in his career!"

It's followed in my head by a familiar echo. *You're like your father, Fraser. Solid. Uncomplicated. Josh is fragile. You know he battles depression . . .*

I didn't tell her at seventeen and I'm not telling her at thirty-nine.

"Are you asking me not to marry her, Mum?" I'm not serious, but the way her eyes light up, I feel compelled to add, "That's rhetorical, by the way. Of course I'm bloody marrying her!"

She recoils. "*Language*, for goodness' sake! I just want both my boys settled and happy."

I could educate her with stories from around the time Josh was hanging out with Audrey. All the bars I extracted him from. All the women I had to help get home when he'd had enough of them. Josh doesn't *care.* He isn't capable of loving anything but his own career. People are dispensable. Audrey particularly.

Music bursts from inside the house. Some modern classical thing I've never heard. On he goes, climbing higher, and suddenly I am *sick* of pandering to my "fragile" brother over this. Audrey's still worried about the ramifications for me and Parker if Josh gets mixed up in the plagiarism case, while the one thing holding her back from chasing the recognition and success she deserves is offending my family.

I scoop up my keys and wallet.

This suddenly feels urgent. Audrey knows I have her back, but she still doesn't have her own. The higher the volume on my brother's music, the clearer it is that my incredible wife-to-be needs to put her demons to bed, take the extraordinary step of putting herself first for once, and unleash those creative fireworks she's promised.

19

Audrey

"It's been almost three years since those penguin emails," I say, arguing with Sara, who's reeling at the unexpected sight of the diamond ring on my left hand. We bought it from an antiques store the day after Fraser accidentally proposed. She's shocked by the news that we're getting married in five weeks.

Sara's always been hysterical, while I habitually underreact. As teenagers, I'd be cliff-diving and she'd forever swim between flags. Now she chairs boards and intermittently fasts and has a proper retirement fund. Just *once* in all her forty-three years has Sara ever been so careless as to fall in love. *It could derail me, Audrey!*

"But why the hurry?" she asks. "Is this a shotgun wedding?"

"It's not the 1950s!"

"But are you pregnant?"

"Is it so hard to grasp that we're just in love?"

She knows Fraser. Apparently it's not hard to grasp that part. She can't get over this idea that I would do something so seemingly spontaneous and hectic. "He didn't even mean to propose, Audrey!"

"Fraser and I have been living together since before the start—we're in our late thirties. People get married at first sight on TV!"

"Hardly something to emulate!" she says. "You're still in the honeymoon period."

"Statistically, we're beyond that."

"Don't make this level of commitment until the gloss has worn off!"

"The gloss isn't *going* to wear off," I protest, even though I know it's almost inevitable that our combustible attraction might dim over time. "Grandma Sullivan told me her heart still skipped a beat when she saw Grandpa well into their eighties! And they married after *three months*."

"Because he was going off to war! Seriously, Audrey. Remember all those explosive couples at the law firm?"

She's just scared. Getting accidentally engaged during an ordinary dinner is the complete opposite of the kind of thing she herself would do, and she can't force the concept into her brain.

"We all adore him, of course," she concedes. "But you haven't let his faults surface. You still think he's perfect. It's like he was made in a lab."

My brain sets to work, trying to cough up any of Fraser's annoying traits just to satisfy her, but it backfires.

"He restacks the dishwasher after I've done it," I argue.

"That's not a fault, Audrey. I've seen the way you stack dishwashers."

"He dog-ears the pages of books!"

"He reads actual books."

"Listen, why don't *you* marry him if you're determined to defend him?"

She changes gears. "It's just you've been hurt so many times . . ."

"I hurt *myself* all those times," I explain. One mega betrayal at university saw me smack every attempt at a close connection since. *Don't let them in. Men invariably let you down.*

Until now, when Fraser elevates every aspect of my existence.

"Maybe it's that you have been hurt too little," I suggest. "Only once! And it scared you off everyone, forever. It's me who worries about *you*. It's hard to see you lonely."

She gets the same look in her eyes that she always does when I raise Phoebe. The one woman to break her heart. She was twenty-two and an entirely different person back then. Intoxicatingly in love, which led to burns so deep she never recovered.

"I'm not *you*," I remind her. "Fraser isn't Phoebe. We're not in our twenties . . ."

Sara's now silent. *Have I gone too far?*

"Look, is this a house of cards? Maybe? But there are never guarantees. I'm going into this with my heart open and my eyes wide. I'm not walking away from the best thing that's ever happened to me on the off chance that something goes wrong."

The next month passes in a whirlwind of phone calls and bookings, finding my dress, organizing catering and flowers and invitations. Parker and I rambled for hours near Googong, where her friend Rose lives, collecting fallen eucalyptus leaves in soft greens and pinks and grays and using a hole punch to make baskets of environmentally friendly confetti.

It's the Thursday before the big day when I miss the first call. And the second. I'm on the first official video chat with the final complement of the Plagiarism Task Force, as the seventeen of us have dramatically labeled ourselves.

"Shouldn't I join in after the wedding?" I asked Fraser a few days ago, while we were finalizing the honeymoon arrangements. We've booked a few days down at the beachside haven of Mollymook, at a famous clifftop hotel called Bannisters, a place I've longed to visit for years.

But it had taken weeks for the group to align our schedules, and it was just an introductory call to get the ball rolling—nevertheless I was still trying to slide out of it. "This has held you captive for more than a decade," he reminded me. "It's an hour out of your day."

"He was so clever the way he did it," Maya says, black hair fixed with a pencil on top of her head. "If you listen to the art song he wrote for the opening of that new concert hall in Brisbane, it's like he's lifted aspects of my opening stanza, but before that takes hold, he's introduced several bars clearly inspired by Belle's piece. *Is he joking?* Did he think we wouldn't stitch this all together?"

To be fair, stitching this together has taken us years. He very nearly did get away with it and still might.

"Why didn't we?" Annie asks.

"Because he never took enough of any of our stuff—except Audrey's—for us to really question it. In retrospect, I don't think he's put together a single idea of his own. Ever. He's like the Wizard of Oz. All bluff, no actual power."

My phone is vibrating on the table beside me. Hopefully they'll leave a voicemail, because this situation is fascinating and infuriating. Fraser was right—the idea of us coming together like this and getting justice and closure . . . *and my dream back* . . . is the most stimulating, enticing, exciting, terrifying situation I've ever found myself in. It's almost exciting enough to distract me from the wedding dress and veil hanging in the doorway beyond the laptop, as if the two experiences—finding my voice at last and officially connecting my life with the man I love—are on some wildly thrilling mutual trajectory.

"We'll only get one shot at this," I say. "He can have no warning or time to prepare." I shiver, thinking about how my last attempt was foiled. And by whom.

"Yes! A concerted attack! All the evidence in one place, so it's impossible to disprove," Belle agrees, enthusiastically. "Password-protected folder in the cloud? Everyone uploads original compositions beside his, along with a detailed note analyzing the specific aspects that he's taken and any other evidence we can find? Assignment notes? Feedback? Early development of the pieces if you still have those?"

"And then we should take this to a lawyer," Annie suggests. "Agreed?"

Agreed.

Our path set, the conversation shifts into a more general chat about what everyone is up to these days, which plays out like a catalog of all the paths I didn't take. The more they divulge, the angrier with myself I become. I'm proud of my teaching. I enjoy it. I'm good at it. But when I hear what they've accomplished—not just playing and writing classical music but getting it produced or performed at elite levels—all I can think is that I am the only one who gave up. *Was I so crushed by Josh's betrayal I let it swamp everything?*

"What about you, Audrey?" one of them asks, when the question can be avoided no longer. I don't answer immediately, distracted by the missed calls, all of which I now notice are from school, along with a text saying Parker isn't well. *Please, God, don't let it be gastro! We have a wedding on Saturday!*

"Yes! You were always the superstar in our cohort. I can't find you anywhere online . . ." someone is saying as I join the video call from my phone and grab my bag and keys.

Shame creeps through my veins at her words, until my body is on fire with it. *They can't find me anywhere because I quit. I let this one thing beat me. I've stayed small. I'm weak . . .*

Just as I'm scrambling for words I can *actually* say, I miss another call.

"I'm sorry," I say to my classmates. "My stepdaughter's school is calling me. I'll have to rush—"

I'm out the door and in the car and pulling into traffic within the minute, carrying a foreboding sense of dread. *Something always goes wrong at weddings, doesn't it? Isn't it meant to be good luck?*

"We'll message you," Annie says. *I shouldn't be on a video call while driving.* "Thanks for coming on board, Audrey. You're amazing!"

Hardly . . .

I end the call and immediately another fills the screen. I hit the green button.

"Is this Audrey Sullivan?" a woman asks.

"Yes, who is this?"

"My name is Abbey," she says. "I'm with the ACT Ambulance Service. One of our teams is just leaving the school in Ainslie on the way to Canberra Hospital. There's been an incident . . ."

My stomach falls through the floor. *Why is a paramedic calling me from Parker's school?* The message said she was unwell. Not that it was an "incident." *Did she hit her head?* She may not technically be my child. I'm not listed on her birth certificate and I'm third in the parental pecking order, so why are they calling me? But I've become a mother figure in all the ways that count.

I am weak with fear. *Is this punishment for all the times I said I never wanted children?* I was allergic to the whole idea. But Parker crashed into my heart like nobody ever has, not even her father, and the idea that something serious might have happened to her just *impales* me.

I blurt out "I'm on my way" and end the call, flooring the accelerator, instinct telling me if I'd let the paramedic finish her sentence, I wouldn't be able to drive at all.

On the way to the hospital, heart in my mouth, I undergo a tectonic shift. This is what parenting feels like. This rush of love. This panic. This sense of wanting to swap with her, to hook myself up to her and siphon the pain out of every cell . . . *All those years* I've wasted, agonizing that I'd never measure up for a child. Telling myself I couldn't handle this. Actively repelling the idea. And now this one shocking moment has shaken the full-fledged mother out of me, despite myself.

But what if it's too late?

20

Fraser

We're an hour into another insufferable faculty meeting when a sharp rap on the boardroom door is followed by my colleague, Keith—an unpleasant and officious man at the best of times—phone in his hand, looking harassed.

He scans the room. Somehow I already know he's looking for me. I've been overcome with what I can only describe as an inexplicable urge to slam the brakes on time and stop whatever is about to unfold.

"Fraser," he says, waving me over urgently, manhandling me into the corridor. "I'm sorry. I think the office missed several calls from your daughter's school. It doesn't sound good."

He passes me the phone as if it's a poisoned chalice. There's more humanity in these few seconds than he's demonstrated in the full six years that we've worked together, which must be a very, very bad sign.

"My name is Abbey," a voice says. "I'm with the ACT Ambulance Service . . ."

And by the time Keith has rushed me to his car and driven like mad through the roadworks on Commonwealth Avenue Bridge, flown through two red lights, and dropped me at the entrance to Emergency, all I catch is the blur of blue scrubs as she is whisked from the ambulance through swinging doors.

Someone has clambered on top, pumping her chest as she disappears from sight, and I'm restrained, helplessly, every molecule wanting to leave my body and trade places while they work on her . . .

Audrey

I didn't let the paramedic finish. Perhaps on some primal, instinctive, awful level, I *knew*. The incident didn't happen inside the school . . . with Parker. It happened to Fraser as he belted there. *Because they couldn't reach me . . .*

Fraser

It should be me in that OR. The school had tried me several times. It's *my* daughter she was rushing toward . . .

Audrey

"Are you his wife?"

Yes. Almost.

Fraser

"Does she have any allergies?"

Not to medication.

Audrey

"Medications?"

Antidepressants.

Fraser

I got her sacked once. Over penguins.

Audrey

It was the way he looked at me, over his glasses . . .

Fraser

We're alive here and we're dead somewhere else along the timeline.

Audrey

"We're losing him." It hits so hard, so sharp, so deep, so loud I can't survive it. I'm desperate, *desperate*, for this to be the other way around.

Fraser

A bolt of agony shoots along the length of the corridor, slicing me in half, along with time and space, opening some new black hole into which we're all imploding . . .

Audrey

. . . tumbling. Can't catch my breath. There's not enough oxygen on this earth for two. Is it me losing my life here? *Is it?* Or is it Fraser losing his?

Fraser

And she is beside me. Passing through this corridor. Passing through my life, in some inexplicable transformation that my atheist mind will forever fight to unravel as she slips into some parallel world, where this nightmare isn't mine at all.

It's hers.

the

end

21

Audrey

Nobody tells you about the weightlessness of loss.

Isn't it Fraser who is supposed to be having the out-of-body experience? Why does it feel like it's me floating near the ceiling of this hospital room with a bird's-eye view of my crisis?

From this angle, it doesn't even resemble panic. He looks asleep on the bed while I just stand there, staring at him, the way a parent watches over a slumbering child.

No urgency. No rush. Nothing to be thought or said or done. Just me. Detached from him. From everything. An actor frozen onstage in the last moments of the final scene before the lights go down.

If I float farther out from this epicenter, I see we are the only two motionless figures in the tableau. Beyond the stillness of our bubble, the hospital bursts with chaotic energy, on fire with the emergency of life. Desperate attempts to salvage the air in people's lungs, to extend the beats in their hearts and give them moments, hours . . . *years.*

Don't they realize how transient it all is? How fragile? How close everyone is to where we are? This cliff from which people just *slip.*

But then, BAM. I'm sucked back into my body in a rush, blood coursing through veins, heart splintering into minuscule pieces that shatter and evaporate, and I realize there is nothing calm about this picture at all. I am not standing here, watching him silently. I am *screaming*. Lunging at him. Lunging at *us*. Shaking his lifeless form, clutching his shoulders, pulling him into my chest while I yell at him to stay here.

"Don't you *dare* do this, Fraser!"

I am trapped. Trapped between an all-encompassing, desperate wish to be dead and the natural urge to fight to the surface. To burst through these suffocating depths and *claw* at my life.

The violence of this is going to kill me . . .

Somewhere, in the near hyperventilation, I draw a breath.

And on that breath, his scent.

I kiss his cheek, salt on my tongue from my own gushing tears, which have sprung from the future somehow. From all the missing moments from the fifty years that he promised.

"Don't do this." I whisper this time. "*Please*, Fraser. I'm begging you."

His silence horrifies me. *Gaping silence.*

"FRASER!" I shout. "Wake UP."

There isn't enough hope in the world to turn this around. He won't move. He is not here. I am yelling, redundantly, at just the unresponsive shape of him—nothing left inside it for me to reach.

Gradually, his lack of life stills me, until a flimsy acceptance starts to land and I ease his shoulders, slowly, back down on the bed, my head coming to rest on the bruised chest that they pounded relentlessly between the impact and the moment they checked the clock and called it. So brutal. It must hurt.

No.

I am the one hurting. It's *my* chest that feels like it's received hundreds of compressions. My heart that aches with five thousand futile attempts to bring him back.

And now I'm backtracking to the decision I made not to have children. The pieces of him that I could have had now and don't. The alternative future that I would bargain for now, because if we'd gone down that path, or any different path, every moment of today would have been different. This is what happens when a thousand innocent, inconsequential actions end up shattering it all, the week of our wedding—when the flowering of everything, so much joy and light and *life* to come . . . is *dashed.*

Never in my life have I felt so desperately alone. While he is so perfectly still. So serene and untortured. So *safe* from this unbearable agony.

22

Fraser

"Isn't it incredible," she said to me once over dinner, "I have access to the same twelve notes as Mozart or the Beatles or Madonna or Adele but if I arrange them my way, I can create something no human has ever heard! It's not just the order of the notes, Fraser, it's the spaces in between. It's the sounds I leave out. It's the pace and rhythm and volume and color and the way you can take dots and squiggles and make them lift off the page like alchemy."

"You know you would have been burnt at the stake?" I replied. Really, I was basking in the rapturous way she spoke about her creativity. She didn't just hear music. She saw it and tasted it. It was always a full-blown synesthetic explosion of sensory stimulation that I envied.

And now there is no rise and fall of her chest. No explosion of color and sound and light in her mind. No sweet and sour. No spice. No crescendos and diminuendos. No spaces in between . . .

It's nothing *but* space. It's all silence.

The lost potential is so crushing I can barely breathe. Not just the potential between us and Parker, for our family's future. *Her* potential. Her whole *life*.

There's no coming back to music now. *Not for one single note.* And now I'm angry at the impostor syndrome. The self-doubt. The consuming fear that means all that unwritten music has died inside her. We've lost pieces that were never played, and the world will always be less colorful. And I am *furious* at my brother and Ridges for what they took from her.

"I can't survive this," I hear myself whisper. I won't make it. Depression has slammed into a wall of grief that has crashed in to overpower me. This loss is incompatible with life. It will see me out. Worse, *I want it to.* This feels like the last few frantic, desperate beats of my heart before it turns to stone and I have no choice but to join her.

My phone beeps with a message. Parker. She's with Maggie, who rushed to the school when I called her earlier. She doesn't really know that there was an accident. We've been able to shield Parker from Audrey's fate.

Daddy, are you coming after work? What is happening?

My heart thuds at the innocence. What's happening is that my need to be here for my daughter is at war with a stronger longing not to be here at all. I've never known such miserable purgatory . . .

"You're in shock," someone says, in pink scrubs. "The way you're feeling is normal. You *will* survive this, Fraser."

I can think of nothing worse than surviving this.

From somewhere I find the courage to ask this next thing. "Did she suffer?"

What I mean is, did she suffer at the end? I know she was in pain earlier. I'll never forget the inhuman wailing I heard over the phone at the scene until they could sedate her.

"She's not suffering now," she says.

I'm gripped by an intense longing to twist fate and swap places with Audrey. Women are built to withstand pain.

I want it to be me who is dead. Me who is no longer suffering.

Selfishly, I want Audrey to be here with this nurse, hearing this news in reverse. I wish it were *her* being forced to pick up her phone and call Parker and say the impossible words: Daddy's gone. *Because what use will I be to Parker, like this?*

Audrey would push through this misery to the other side and into the future I know she would embrace. She would drag herself through these initial steps of agony and make all the music she held back.

She would appreciate that life is short. I'm certain she would. All I know is that it's unbearable. And all I can think about is how this would all unfold if that mess of missed calls from the school had landed the other way.

If this whole thing were the other way around . . .

23

Audrey

Rach envelopes me the second I step into the hospital foyer, and we're adrift. As if we're twenty again, with no clue how to handle life. Back then, we thought we knew everything. We bluffed our way through study stress and romantic calamities like endearing heroines in Richard Curtis rom-coms.

There is no bluffing now. We're free-climbing on the edge of an abyss. No safety gear. No ropes. Clinging to rocks by our fingernails, petrified of the height and the dark and the cold.

It would be so easy to let go. So tempting to unfurl my fingertips and fall. I'd black out before I even hit the ground. It would be *merciful.* All I want is for Fraser to climb up behind me, wrap his arms around me, and guide me to safety, one tentative footstep at a time. But he isn't showing up.

"How is this possible?" Rach demands, her voice fractured, shaking in my arms. She never cries. She is always strong. Always calm. She doesn't overreact or get hysterical or do things she'll later regret. Her brand is chilled. Professional. Serene. So when she lets go of me and bends over as if this physically hurts, I realize we are in huge trouble.

For a few seconds I can only look at her, the emotion locked inside me, churning, gathering steam, searching for a broken fissure from which to explode.

Finally, she grasps at some strength, drags herself upright, blue eyes determined, and pulls me toward her again, whispering, "I'm sorry, Audrey. Sorry. *Sorry.*"

Her body straightens in my arms. "I'm just so broken for you," she explains.

We can't debrief any further, because Clair and April arrive on the scene with Jess. Collectively horrified.

"This is a fucking *nightmare*!" April says, squeezing me hard, her language sending an elderly couple nearby scampering.

At the sight of my bridesmaids, I'm freshly crushed by the timing of this tragedy, which we can't even keep private while I digest the shock, or sixty people will show up at the church on Saturday expecting a wedding instead of a funeral.

"Come on, we're taking you home," Clair announces. "You need a nice cup of tea."

"Or something stronger if you wish? You won't be left alone for a *second*," April assures me, flicking dark curls confidently from her forehead.

A kernel of instinct tells me the stronger beverage is somehow the wrong move, and a quiet night with Rach is probably more sensible, but when I look to her for backup, she seems to have collapsed in on herself again. The concept has already taken flight anyway, and April, Jess, and Clair will hear nothing of my tackling this unfolding catastrophe untethered. It's an echo of all the times some man broke one of our hearts and we'd obliterate the crisis as a team. Often with tequila.

But I don't want to obliterate Fraser. I'm scared I'll forget this happened, only for the shock to hit just as hard again in the morning. We're not in our twenties anymore. We have sensible jobs and responsibilities and mortgages.

Oh, God!

Fresh panic descends, shock and grief shoved sideways for a

second by a mental picture of the balance we owe on our town house.

"I'll have to sell the house," I say, feeling sick. It's another layer of terrifying on top of everything else.

Rach shakes her head. "Don't think about logistics now. We'll sort it out."

No offense to Rach, who has been beside me through every failure, but we've never "sorted out" something of this magnitude before.

Can losing your almost husband technically be construed as failure? And am I going to be trapped in this torment of calling him my "almost husband" for the rest of my life? We were so close to earning those titles. He's my husband in every way. I feel as much of a widow as someone with the piece of paper I would have held in my hands two days from now, if only I'd picked up that phone call before he did.

Except, if I had . . . who's to say I wouldn't have been the one? Wouldn't it be him here in this foyer, staring at dashed wedding plans and panicking?

No. Fraser doesn't panic.

Didn't.

Past tense.

What is *wrong* with me? Why am I even playing God in my mind, twisting the outcome, flipping our misfortunes? Why am I thinking about money and semantics when it's been a mere hour since he died?

"Slow down!"

I think it's me who says this, but it could have been April. She places an arm around my shoulders and says, "Seriously. Slow down. We will get you through this."

I have a flash of Fraser on that bed. "He only looked like he was asleep," I say, panic strangling me. "I have to go back!"

What if I made this up? What if I called them all in unnecessarily, and they left meetings and kids, in Jess's case, and a date in Clair's, and my fiancé is about to bring the car around and ask what on earth I'm playing at: *I knew you had a wild imagination, Audrey, but this is preposterous!*

I grip Rach's hand. "I don't think he's dead," I assure her, more confident about this than I've ever been about anything. He can't be. "They made a mistake. He was unconscious. Can you check? I have visions of them burying him alive. I can't do this to him!"

They exchange glances. I've seen this look before. The time I gave serial cheater Declan Maxwell a third chance. The day I dropped out of the Con. Every decision I made on that Contiki tour after Declan's final, deal-breaking fling with my second cousin.

"Sweetheart," Jess says, flicking long red hair over her shoulder. I hate it when anyone calls me that. Even one of my best friends. "You're in shock, which is why it doesn't seem real. It's okay that you don't want to believe it yet . . ."

Will there be a time when I *do* want to believe it?

"Will they give him a blanket?" The nonsense words that are coming out of my brain now. But I imagine him becoming colder by the second and then being . . . Ugh, I see him being *refrigerated*, and I simply cannot bear the idea of him not being wrapped in something warm. I've watched enough episodes of *CSI* to know that he won't be. They will cover him in a sheet or put him in a bag and reserve the blankets for people who really need them. People with oxygen in their lungs and blood pumping through arteries. People with thoughts and emotions. And a future.

"We can drop off a special one if you like?" Rach assures me.

I don't even understand where we would deliver it. But my

heart skips a beat at the desperate chance of seeing him one last time. Of checking, again, for the miracle my brain won't allow me to abandon.

24

Fraser

I scroll through the contacts in my phone, shuffling between two numbers, imagining each woman responding to my call, reluctant to inflict this misery either way.

Maggie knows there was an accident. She had to leave work to collect Parker when the school called to break the news. It's our week to have her. *My week*. But, of course, she'll have her for as long as we need. *As long as I need.*

My brain won't accept the truth, sentences spluttering as it corrects entrenched pronouns, outdated by events. It's been "us." It's been "ours." "Me" and "my" and "mine" try to force their way into sentences, unnaturally, and it's breaking my brain.

I need to tell Parker what's happened. Parker, who, last night, was flitting about the house in a flower girl dress, twirling and dancing after her final fitting with the dressmaker.

My hand is shaking, holding my phone. Or is it my phone vibrating in my hand? Hard to tell. The world itself feels like it's rattling. I glance at the screen.

It's Rachael.

My heart drops through the floor. This will *wreck* her.

I hit the green button and lift the phone to my ear, only to sense worry in her voice already. News travels fast. *Who told her? Maggie?*

"Fraser," she gushes. "Audrey's left me on read! She's not answering calls. I've got this horrible sense . . . Oh, God. I can't breathe. Has something happened?"

It's me who can't breathe. Can't confirm what she already seems to know, information gleaned from that sixth-sense bond they claimed, which I always tried to debunk with logic and reason. *How can I destroy this woman?*

"Rachael, she's—" Can't say it. Don't need to.

There's an aching pause between us that swallows their whole friendship. A giant void into which all their memories and future plans are vacuumed.

"Where are you?" she asks, after the longest silence engulfs us, the life having been sucked out of her voice, the way I can hear it's been sucked out of mine.

Rachael now lives in an apartment in the award-winning Nishi Building, overlooking Lake Burley Griffin. She bought it because she can glimpse both the sunrise and the sunset from the balcony. Audrey called her a "look at the sky" person. Rach would make the three of us visit Mount Stromlo Observatory for the astronomy open nights and go stargazing along country roads outside Canberra. I guess all of that is over now.

I've been to the apartment countless times before. Most recently last Friday night, when Audrey and I picked up Thai takeaway from a restaurant on London Circuit and the three of us ate it on Rachael's balcony with a bottle of red before catching a comedy night at the theater. Tonight, I've arrived empty-handed. Arms hanging loose at my sides, nothing to offer but a barbarous story about how both of our lives have been bayoneted by this tragedy.

As I wait to have Rachael buzz me in, it's as if Audrey is

standing here, right beside me, just as she was less than a week ago. *That staircase is as good as half the sculptures in the National Gallery*, she said, running her fingers along the wood. I can almost smell her perfume—impossible, of course—as I touch the timber plank where she did.

The elevator doors open and Rachael appears, pale with shock, in a pale green dress—shoes kicked off. It's the bare feet in the foyer of the apartment building that gets me. That's more Audrey's style—she didn't stand on ceremony. Rachael does *not* gallivant anywhere half dressed. Let alone looking this fractured. This *lost*.

She steps out of the elevator into the foyer and into the blank space between us, where Audrey should be. Into silence, which should be filled with her voice. She was our conduit. She meant everything to both of us, and this feels all wrong, us being here without her as we hover beside the backlit staircase she loved, scattered timber up the walls, united in our loss.

I don't know how many minutes go by before I say, "It happened outside Parker's school. A distracted parent behind the wheel. She was crossing the road . . ."

Rachael looks like she hasn't cried. As if it's all trapped inside her. But this is what she's like. Stoic. She's not a crier.

"What about Parker?"

Instant anxiety slams into every cell. I would do anything to save my child from this torture. She was so young when Maggie and I divorced, and we did such a stellar job cushioning her through that. Now we'll have to break her all over again.

"I told Maggie I need time to pull myself together. She'll handle it tonight and we'll tell her tomorrow."

Rachael nods. "Makes sense. But, Fraser, it's okay to fall apart, even in front of your child." Ironically, she's all business herself. "You should come up," she announces, pressing the call button for the lift. "You should not be alone."

I think she means that she shouldn't be.

The doors open and I am expected to follow her in. She calls the seventeenth floor and, as the elevator lifts, she looks at me, wretched expression on her face, a fresh formality carved between us by Audrey's absence, and says, "We are not going on the balcony tonight."

25

Audrey

When my friends and I crash through the door at home, I fling off the worst day of my life: keys, purse, shoes, earrings . . . and stride to our bedroom. I rip apart my shirt, buttons flung to all corners as I barge into the bathroom, flicking the shower tap.

I toss the shirt into the bin. I can't ever wear it again. It's the shirt Fraser complimented me on as he left the house this morning. The last shirt he saw me wearing. The shirt I wore as he took his final breath. My clothes are strangling me. I tear everything off, needing to be naked with my grief, and toss it all in a pile. I want to set fire to it, a bonfire of trauma that will spread and burn my whole life to the ground.

In the shower, the water attacks my sensitive skin the way it does when you're feverish. My pain receptors are screaming. But I'm not sick. A thunderstorm of anguish has me weeping at first, my tears barely discernible from the hot water dripping onto my face, until I crash against the shower tiles, sobbing.

How could Fraser—kind, funny, loving, vital Fraser, who was so *alive* this morning—possibly not be coming home tonight? Or any night, ever again. Fraser, with whom I had intended to see out the rest of my life. How can he just not *exist*?

I'm shaking now. It's not shock. It's fear. Because the idea of struggling through this without him is inconceivable. I need him here to help me through losing him . . . *I must be losing my mind as well.*

"Audrey?" It's Jess, calling from just outside the bathroom. "You okay in there?"

"Yes," I call back, voice cracking. There's something terribly isolating about the shower. I shut off the tap and reach for a towel. Drying myself feels like an exhausting ordeal, as if every ounce of my energy is already accounted for, absorbed in the hideous task of processing exactly what has happened.

"Here," she says, passing an enormous glass of white wine through a crack in the bathroom door.

Surely I can make it through the shower without alcohol? Nonetheless, I take the glass from her since she's gone to the trouble of carrying it upstairs. I swallow three mouthfuls, set it down on the vanity, and stare at myself in the mirror, steam swirling around me like it's my spirit, escaped from my body, refusing to reenter somewhere so dangerous and unstable. *Threatening to join him?* God, it's as if I'm already drunk!

On the countertop, beside my toothbrush and his, is a smaller purple one. At the sight of it, the heart-wrenching loss I've been wrestling lights a spot fire that ignites a far more serious blaze. Parker, the stepchild I love so acutely, has lost her father. Rachael had called Maggie, who'd suggested we give Parker one more sleep before breaking this to her.

I imagine Fraser, wherever he is, trying desperately to reach us and help. Circling us. Going to Parker first, as he should. That's his job as a father: to protect his baby. It must be killing him that he can't. Killing him, though he is already dead—what a nonsensical thought. I gulp more wine. And more. Veins already tingling with the alcohol as it tries valiantly to ease the unsoothable.

What if I lose contact with Parker? What if circumstances

change and Maggie moves her away? Maggie and Fraser agreed that neither would take jobs in other cities until Parker was at least eighteen, even though both parents' professional skills were so eminently transferrable. But now Maggie is free. *What legal rights will I have? Any?*

I take another sip, rack my brain, and think back to the custody battles we used to handle at the firm. Had I known I'd need this information in the future, after I'd fallen for, almost married, and lost the client I was flirting with over penguins, perhaps I'd have paid more attention.

Draining the glass alarmingly quickly, I pull on pajamas, brush past the wedding dress I can't look at on a hanger in the doorway, and pad downstairs to face the others, head spinning. My friends are crowded around the kitchen counter in a worried huddle, having some sort of emergency congress in hushed tones. They stop talking when I appear in the doorway, empty glass in hand.

Clair flicks on the kettle.

I glance at the wine bottle, and April, reading my mind, twists the screw top and splashes liquid liberally into the glass, as if placating me this way has been medically ordered.

Not enough grapes exist to make the gallons of wine required to anesthetize this crisis. We migrate to the living room and Clair, already in all black, with matching long black hair and a red streak, plonks the bottle on the coffee table while we let the situation simmer in stunned silence.

"Right. We're going to help you through every step of this," April declares, pushing up her sleeves, ready to start work on my calamity, reiterating the catchphrase they laid out in the hospital foyer. Rach nods but can't seem to trust herself to speak.

"This cataclysm will be conquered by your friendship circle plus tea and chocolate and sauvignon blanc," Clair says, as if it is remotely possible to scale it using any of these items.

"I can't just drink this away," I argue, weakly, taking another sip, as Rach places a large glass of water in front of me. "I don't think that's how it works." I *wish* it were. It would be so much easier if I could just be sloshed for the foreseeable . . . if I could let a torrent of alcohol carry me through this, surfing the pain right through to the end, wherever I wash up. I've only ever drunk out of *want*. Not *need*. "I should stop here, before I end up in rehab . . ."

"Don't be so dramatic, Auds! You've had two glasses. Not two bottles!" Jess says.

I feel like I could *easily* polish off two bottles. The two glasses, mixed with trauma and grief, appear to have set off some new chemical reaction in my brain.

Surely it's okay to numb this agony just for one night? Tomorrow, I will attack grief with exercise and early nights and mindfulness and sufficient hydration. Maybe I'll do this so well, I'll be the poster girl for healthy grieving.

I have to be.

Or I suspect losing Fraser is going to kill me.

It's probably an hour and a half later when I realize, in horror, that Rachael told Maggie I would call Fraser's family. It would have been a helpful promise to have remembered before the shock really hit and we ran out of wine and April switched us to Baileys. I should have accepted Maggie's offer to do it. They love her.

I am in no state to arrive on their doorstep, so I call his parents' landline. I don't know anyone else who still has one. In any case, it rings out several times before I quit. Relieved. I can face them tomorrow.

"I don't want to do this," I mumble. My friends think I'm talking about doing my life without Fraser, so there's a fresh and enthusiastic round of *You won't be alone, we'll be beside you, Audrey.* But really it's that I'm texting Josh.

Can you come over? It's impotent.

The message whooshes off. "*Fuck!* I wrote 'impotent'!" I say, through blurred vision.

"Who's impotent?" April inquires, pouring more liquid into her glass.

"Josh."

"Josh is *impotent*?" Jess repeats, heartily. "That explains a lot—"

"No, it's autocorrect. *God!*"

I-m-p-o-r-t-a-n-t.

He's seen the message. No response. I can't just text straight out that his brother died. But he's not going to reply unless I drop some sort of attention-grabbing bombshell:

It's about Fraser.

Still nothing.

The wedding is off.

"You know, if Josh hadn't done what he did, you wouldn't have been on that Zoom and missed those calls, and you'd have arrived at the school before Fraser and he would still be alive, so really it's all Josh's fault," Clair rambles—an observation I'm sure she'll regret voicing aloud in the morning.

In my intoxicated state, I don't want to start piecing together whose fault this is, particularly as somewhere in the spinning inside my brain is an awful thought that Clair's logic could equally apply to me, somehow. *If I'd fixed this years ago . . .*

"It's the butterfly effect," I mumble instead. "Eternalism?"

They look at me blankly.

"You know, all time exists now? Fraser'll explain it—"

My sentence backfires, the explosion firing straight in the heart. Fraser won't be explaining anything. How is it possible I have forgotten that he is gone, right in the middle of a conversation about his death?

"I think I'm having a nervous breakdown," I admit. Rach comes and sits beside me, arm around my shoulders, and takes the glass from my hand.

"It's not that," she assures me. "It's shock. And wine. And cream liqueur, unfortunately. You're going to be so unwell tomorrow, I'm afraid."

By the time Joshua arrives, I am barely able to stagger to the door. I fling it open and there he is, in jeans and a leather jacket, an older, edgier version of his brother, looking the opposite of impotent, and now I'm in tears at the resemblance.

"What did Fraser do?" he asks, his temper frayed. "Where is he?"

"He didn't do anything." I didn't expect him to be so angry.

"Why is the wedding off? You having second thoughts, Sully?" He looks at me more closely. "Are you . . . *hammered*?"

It might be the alcohol, but as he shifts his weight and crosses his arms, I imagine a glimmer of hope flashing in his dark eyes.

"I have to tell you something, Josh. It's not good." *Understatement of the year.*

His fixed stare penetrates my skin the way it always did. I'm hot and flustered and exceedingly nauseated all of a sudden because this is a million times harder than it was the last time I sat him down for a confessional.

Clair's argument spins around my head like I'm on the Gravitron. *If Josh hadn't done what he did . . . It's all his fault . . .*

"It's all your fault!" I accuse him, and he flinches. "I missed a phone call that meant Fraser had to leave work to pick up Parker instead, and some distracted parent in a four-wheel drive swung across the pedestrian crossing without looking and—"

I can't say it. I don't have to, judging by the expression on his face and the way he's unfurling his crossed arms, drawing me across the threshold outside, and holding my hair back while I hurl into the front garden. A minute passes while I pull myself together, rage bubbling up.

"You helped Ridges steal my music! There were others, Josh, and while I was meeting with them earlier today, I missed the call."

Somehow, despite my shock and grief and drunkenness and the compounded anger of many years, I realize I've just told Josh his brother died and his career might crash, all at once. I throw up again and, when I'm done and he's passed me his handkerchief, he pulls me gently to his chest—a place I do not want to be. His firm hand supports the back of my dizzy head while I focus on his heartbeat as it thuds through his shirt. It stirs vague memories of wild university parties, and how he was there for me like this before.

I hate this. And need it. And desperately wish Fraser were holding me.

"Sully," Josh whispers after an eternity. "I'm so incredibly sorry. About everything."

26

Fraser

> Parker's at Mum's. I'm outside your place with food. Where are you?

It's been hours since we formulated our strategy after I messaged Maggie with: She's gone. Don't tell Parker yet. I'll call you later.

Since that text, this death has swallowed me whole. Rachael, too. We have been sitting on opposite ends of her living room couch now for over an hour, in silence.

"Can I get you a whiskey or something?" she says at last, making no move.

I stare ahead. "I don't think so, Rach."

I don't know where the warning bells are coming from, but the way I feel, as though I could die from this anguish, tells me one whiskey would turn into two and then four . . . and then years.

I pass Rach my phone with Maggie's message on the screen. "I don't know how to reply," I confess.

She reads the text, glances at me, gives me the phone back, and says, "I wouldn't mention me."

Rachael and Audrey used to psychoanalyze Maggie and concocted some theory that she tolerated Audrey but mistrusted

Rachael, ever since her joke that I was her "beloved" outside the concert the night they all met.

"Do you think we could go for a walk?" I ask, light changing through the window, summer sun sinking toward the Brindabella mountains to our west, streaky clouds promising the kind of glorious sunset I know Rachael loves. "Seeing the sun go down on Audrey's final day feels important."

Rach's stoic expression collapses, and as she moves off the sofa, I grab her hand. I can sense the energy it's taking for her to stay strong for my sake, and she doesn't need to. "I'm so sorry you've lost her, too."

She doesn't speak. Just gives me a small smile and goes to put on shoes, while I return to my phone, and to Maggie.

> I'm not home yet. Will be later. Thanks for food. Can I pick it up in the morning?

She calls me immediately. "Fraser, I need to know you're okay."

The sound of Maggie's voice, so normal and familiar and . . . *alive*, seems to ground me in the fresh hell of my reality. I can see her, perched on the edge of the gray sofa we bought together during the Boxing Day sales several years ago. The one we watched Netflix on and argued on and broke up on.

Unspoken guilt hangs in the gulf between us. About today. About how Audrey died. If either of us had made a different choice this afternoon, if one of us had picked up that call and gone to the school instead . . . if we'd arrived there in her place like we should have, since Parker is ours . . .

"It was one of those freak accidents," I say, uttering words you hear on the news. Not out of your own mouth, about your meant-to-be wife.

Is anything like this ever really an accident? Audrey always believed our heartbeats were numbered, that our deaths were set down in some cosmic script that couldn't be edited, no matter how much we tried to interfere with it. It's how she made sense of things when she lost someone. *It was always going to be this way,* she would say. *This was their inevitable story.*

But everything about losing her in this chaotic turn of events is wrong. My body burns for that whiskey. Instead, I pour myself a glass of water and listen for Maggie's voice. Not the psychiatrist. Not my ex-wife. Just a fellow human being, caught in life's stranglehold.

It should have been me. I should be dead. I'm seeing spots. Everything is seizing up and shutting down, as if I'm barely clinging to this world myself.

"Just breathe, Fraser." I know she's issuing the instruction to us both. That voice, the one I've fallen in and out of love with over the years, feels like an island, as she pulls me from this storm. There's a level of compassion in her tone that we lost toward the end. Somehow, despite everything we've been through, the intimacy we once shared and that we lost still has sufficient power left to cradle this interaction.

"Are you safe?" she asks, just as Rachael reappears in running shoes, pulling her hair into a ponytail. Maggie knows about the depression. We've never had any secrets, particularly when we share custody of Parker. It's a salient question. All I've thought about for the last two hours is how and when I could end this unbearable pain.

I watch as Rachael fishes one of those pocket packs of tissues out of her handbag and waves it at me as if to say, *We've got this.*

Am I safe?

"I will be. Thanks for the call, Maggie. I'll see you tomorrow." *And we will break this to Parker.*

■ ■ ■

Rachael and I make it to the other side of the Acton Peninsula, near the National Museum of Australia, about five minutes before the sun kisses the horizon. We're the only ones here, as if the world knows we need space for what feels like a sacred moment of goodbye. When the sun makes its bed of pink and red and purple above the mountains and drops slowly out of sight, the grief cascades through my body, weakening me with every passing realization of all that we've lost. Every plan we made. All the unmet dreams. The travels. The simple nights at home with beans on toast. The midnight conversations in each other's arms under the covers. All the ways we would have helped each other through every challenge and parented Parker together in this patchwork family.

The sky erupts in ever more dazzling oranges and deep reds, then fades as twilight creeps in and the evening star appears. And I am cracked open by a violent flash flood of despair that carves valleys to depths I didn't know existed. This agony will tear me inside out, every nerve exposed until I'm so frayed, my skin so raw from pain, I'm scared that Rachael will touch me in comfort and I'll just . . . *combust.*

And when equally violent sobs erupt, I can barely tell if they are mine or hers—our grief entwined as darkness descends and the one we love grows even more silent, while the two of us just fall and fall and fall . . .

"I need to see Sara," I explain as we amble back. I can't bear the thought of breaking the news that she's lost her sister, sentencing her, or perhaps me, to making an awful call to their parents, whose bags were already packed to fly from Queensland to Canberra tomorrow for Saturday's wedding. It all happened so fast this afternoon. I'd called Sara on the way to the hospital, but she hadn't picked up.

"We should go now," Rachael says. "Before it gets too late."

Before long, we've driven over and we're standing at Sara's door, not far from Rachael's place, in Turner.

Rachael's mouth is moving. Somehow mine won't. All I hear is static.

And as the information lands and Sara's face splinters, I can barely witness her distress. It's unfathomable, losing a sibling. The rest of us share only scenes. Sisters appear in every chapter, from the opening sentence to the very last page.

So do brothers.

I turn this around in my mind, imagining Audrey telling Josh if it were me. *What would his face have done?* And now I'm down a mental path where I call him tonight and tell him what's happened here, needing his support, having him smash back a serve of Main Character grief that I cannot be expected to help him through. I can barely hold myself up.

Rachael sweeps Sara into a hug, and we promise to meet her tomorrow and do whatever it is that grieving families do the day after their person has died, when there's meant to be an imminent wedding.

Before Rachael turns on the engine, I say, "The logical thing is to keep the booking in the church. Everyone's got it in their calendar. Food is booked. We could have a memorial for Audrey now and a smaller event next week at the crematorium, family only. And you, obviously."

Rachael stares at me, and it's unclear if she's horrified, impressed, or relieved.

"Just compartmentalizing," I explain. But that reminds me of that plush toy penguin I saw the day Audrey and I first emailed.

And somehow the memory of that almost undoes me.

27

Audrey

It's my wedding day, and I'm standing in my ivory dress, the peonies Fraser sent me crushed at my feet. At some point, probably around two in the morning or about eight glasses in—whichever way you want to measure it—I thought it would help the creative process if I tried it on.

The satin felt so sleek and cool against my skin. I tied the ribbon belt around my waist and watched the crystals sparkle in the mirror under the halogen lights. Then I sat at that piano, took the piece I'd been writing for his fortieth, and finished it. My best work, because he was in every single note. Lyrical, because we were together through it all.

I pass the card to Rach, flopping beside her. *See you at the church.*

She reads it and almost dissolves.

"Oh, God!" I say, palm shooting straight to my forehead in distress. I reach for my phone and check the messages I sent last night.

Yes! Here it is. Sent at four thirty a.m.

> This is for the service. Keep your fucking hands off it. But tell me what you think.

Attached to the message was a voice recording of me playing the piece, punctuated by my sobs and sniffs, which Rach and I listen to now.

"Maybe they're onto something when they say to 'write drunk' . . ." I say in the silence after it's finished. "I can't believe I sent this to Josh."

"If you had to drunk-text him anything, at least it was a masterpiece," she argues, wiping her eyes, my music having finally broken through her tightly wound emotional defenses. "I think it's a perfect tribute to the love of my best friend's life."

The words catch on her breath, and in the air, and we stare at each other, as if we're absorbed in a mental flashback of this love story from beginning to end. From those very first emails in the office, and that moment in Zoe's back garden at the party. The way Fraser had stepped forward, facing Connor—a fight he would have comprehensively lost, which made it all the more attractive that he tried—moments before I intervened with that bucket of ice and caught his eye.

"Told you a hard reset from Fraser Miller would be utterly delectable," she says, nudging my leg with hers, summarizing our entire relationship in one line, confirming that she'd been right all along. She *always* knows what's best for me, and she'd called this, right from the start.

Fraser Miller was perfect.

28

Fraser

Parker sits between Maggie and me, swinging her legs under the pew in her flower girl dress, holding our hands, bringing them so close that our knuckles brush, as if she's trying to stitch us back together as a family. So now, in addition to grieving Audrey, I'm swallowing guilt that Maggie and I weren't able to keep *this* together. Not even for our child. She has ten years and two traumas in her life, and I'm worried there'll *always* be something missing from her music.

"Dad?" she said at the unexpected sight of me in her mother's kitchen yesterday. Broad smile. Arms flung around my neck. Hopeful expression, as if we were about to spring a surprise trip to Disneyland and that's why we swapped custody on Thursday night.

"I'm so sorry, my darling," Maggie said after we broke the news. She was stroking Parker's head, cradling her to her chest, but looking over her, directly at me, addressing us both. "I know how much you loved her."

Now, as Sara and I are called up to speak, I untangle my hand from Parker's, pull out the folded paper from my suit jacket, and glance at Rachael, ashen-faced and sitting with the

Bookies across the aisle. Everyone is dressed colorfully, as requested. There are flowers up the aisle, preordered and paid for weeks ago. It feels as though somewhere across time, in this very church, there is an alternate version of reality where we're all deep in celebration right now, and I'm kissing the bride.

I stand beside Sara at the lectern. Sara, whose military parents are disintegrating in the front row. *You should not have to bury a child.* Sara, who warned her sister that bad things happen and was always advocating restraint and caution and keeping hope in check to avoid exactly the kind of mass devastation on show here today, and who has been unexpectedly proven right.

"I hope I didn't hold her back," she says, moments later. "Audrey always dreamed big. If she tripped, I thought, *Slow down*. If she fell, I thought, *I told you so.*

"If my sister's wings were clipped . . . if my reluctance ever caused her to pause or wait or retreat, then I deeply regret that now that she's lost the opportunity to fall or fail and the chance to rise. And, Fraser—"

She turns to face me.

"I'm glad she didn't listen to me when she was running like gangbusters toward you, because you were the best thing that ever happened to her. You and Parker. Loving her was worth losing her."

Was it? From where I'm standing, this pain is impossible.

When it's my turn, it occurs to me I've delivered plenty of conference papers in my career. Hundreds of lectures. I'm completely confident and comfortable before an audience. Of course, standing at the lectern at your fiancée's funeral is another matter, as is staring out and seeing Parker's frozen gaze, instead of students or scientists—though there are plenty of those here today as well.

"I first met Audrey at a mutual friend's party," I explain. "She was introduced as somewhat of a tortured artist. Once we were together, I realized how talented she was and how prolific she could be. I could see where she was headed and how far she could go . . ."

I glance at Josh, sitting beside our parents, steely gaze fixed on the pew in front of him. My throat constricts, but I need to choke the rest of this out.

"Music stopped for me the day she died. I don't know how I'm ever going to listen to it again, except I know what it meant to her. I know how deeply it ran in her veins—the way it runs in my brother's veins and my daughter's. The idea that we might stop searching for the music that lit up her life, because she's gone, would break her."

All you can hear now is the sound of people taking out tissues or stifling coughs and tears as Audrey's own composition swirls. Josh finally looks up from his seat now and locks eyes with me. *Are we thinking the same thing?* How much further she could have gone, if . . .

My throat burns. As I return to my seat, I know she would have suggested we play something else. Something by Chopin or Brahms or Schumann. She'd think the partially written piece she'd been composing for my birthday with Parker wasn't good enough. Wasn't *finished*. She always blamed the stalling of her career on what happened at university, but I think what held her back was the perfectionism. The fear of criticism. If she'd been able to cut herself loose from that stuff, there's no telling how far she'd have flung herself.

My parents and Josh meet me at the church door. Mum has spent the time since Audrey died rewriting history. *We're just so devastated, Fraser. I'm sure you'd have been very happy.* She notices Maggie standing on the gravel path outside the church now and tries to disguise the subtle hope in her expression. "How kind Maggie has been, standing beside you through this tragedy . . ."

Joshua nudges our mother along, then shakes my hand, cool and aloof. He's flying back to New York in the morning. I don't know what my almost wife's death might have done to him, except that he looks haunted. Face drawn. Eyes hollow. And I wonder again how truly platonic it was, from his end.

"We're adopting you and Parker," Rachael says, hugging me on her way out of the church. "The Bookies. All of us."

I should have known the rest of Audrey's friends would storm in behind her.

"But you only read rom-coms," I reply as Jess catches up and joins the conversation. I'm hoping dry humor will guard against my losing it. "I'm more into golden-age detective fiction."

"How dare you!" Jess says, in an orange dress, with uncontrollable flames of red hair and gigantic sunglasses barely hiding her blotchy cheeks. "We read an array of literary fiction!" Her breath catches in her throat, humor no longer enough to carry the grief through this doorstep interaction as she drops the attempt at levity and hugs me, muscles clenching around our loss. "I'm so desperately sorry, Frase. We all adored her."

This loss has ripped her friends apart. "Let me know if you want to go for a walk this week? Or anything," Rach suggests as the queue sweeps her along and everyone's offers of help pile up. *Coffee. Dinner. Golf. Lasagna. A distracting film? Beach house on the coast—no need to rent it, Fraser, stay as long as you like.*

Every idea is thoughtful and appreciated. Nothing touches the sides.

■ ■ ■

The night after the funeral, I face a disjointed new rhythm. With Parker asleep, I have hours to fill, staring at a silent piano until I have to endure another night in the empty bed.

I'm outside, Rachael texts, at nearly nine o'clock. Dropping off a quiche.

When I unlatch the door, she is standing there holding a dish covered in a tea towel, looking unusually disheveled, no makeup, blond hair tumbling out of a low ponytail, face gray, eyes glistening.

"Here," she says, holding it out like an offering, looking like she needs to come in.

I take it from her with one hand and guide her in with the other. When I kick the door closed, she just *buckles*. She was a rock at the funeral, smoothing social interactions, making introductions, ensuring everyone felt included and cared for and loved. And all the while she was imploding.

"Have you eaten?" I ask, knowing the answer already. She looks like she hasn't eaten since Thursday. "Come on."

I lead her to the kitchen, sit her at my table, and place the quiche on the counter while I cut a slice. She watches, without protest, as I find a plate and cutlery, pull out the leftover salad from the fridge—an offering from another well-wisher—and deliberately pick out all the richest bits, the darkest red tomatoes, the brightest slices of pepper.

After zapping the quiche in the microwave, I check it's not too hot and place it in front of her. She doesn't move, even when I push the plate closer. It's like I'm coaxing an animal to eat that's just wound up in a refuge.

"Have some. Just a little bit. Keep your strength up." Even as I'm saying it, I realize she's well beyond having any strength to conserve. I edge my chair close to hers, pick up the fork, carve off a small piece, and hold it out to her.

She stares at me as if she is locked into her own body. Delayed shock. That's what this is. Shock, exhaustion, and the deferred impact of the enormous loss of the best friend she's ever had. She looks at me, blue eyes grateful, as her lips part and she takes the food and chews it like she's being force-fed.

We repeat this process, in silence, until she's taken the fork from me and eaten half the slice and a cherry tomato. Then, without speaking, she lays her head on my shoulder and makes no sound while her tears seep through my shirt and I try to fathom how the two of us have ended up together in such an unholy tragedy.

29

Audrey

Weeks pass through the window of anxiety.

"I don't know where I stand with anything," I tell Mum on the phone, wishing for the millionth time that they lived closer. "I've lost control of everything!" Parker, Maggie, my house, Fraser's estate, my work. Rach. Even Josh. I feel like I've flatlined. Woken up in this half world, where nothing looks right and everything that's still standing could evaporate.

I don't tell her I'm constantly shaking. Or what might be causing it.

"Should I book a flight?" she asks, my pain absorbed and reflected in her voice. "I could be there late this afternoon?"

Late this afternoon! I have a hot flash. *Surely I'm too young for hot flashes?* It would be just like the gods of fate to take my almost husband and exchange him for perimenopause. Or maybe it's that I'm hot and flustered at the idea of someone, even Mum, interrupting my increasingly disturbing private evening routine.

"You could stay with Sara?" I suggest, hopefully. Her guest bedroom is set up for visitors. Mine resembles Vesuvius, mid-eruption.

"Hardly! Your sister runs her household with more military precision than your father and me. It's *you* who needs the support."

"I just . . . I feel like I need space, Mum." Even through the lie, it's hurting my heart that I need her this much, yet I'm pushing her away. "I feel like I'm the worst widow in the world." *And the worst daughter. And the worst friend.* "Everyone else is doing everything, even this, better than me."

"I need a more reliable job," I confess to Rach an hour later, crying into a cup of strong black coffee that I hope might resurrect me after another bad night of self-medication. "Maggie and I met with lawyers about the estate. It's so complicated, my brain hurts even thinking about it, but part of Parker's inheritance needs to come from Fraser's share of the house. I'll have to sell it."

"Move in with me," she says immediately. After a series of promotions, she's recently upgraded to an executive apartment near the lake. "Till you're back on your feet."

The concept of being "back on my feet" seems so far removed from reality I can't understand how she's even entertaining it. And I would move in with her, except . . . *God. This is bad.* The idea of trying to get through an evening "normally" in front of Rachael sets off a panic attack. It's not like Rach doesn't appreciate a nice wine. It's just she doesn't use copious quantities of it to knock out her life every night the way I have been now for *weeks*. I can't sleep without it. I have visions of leaving my nonexistent new job at five o'clock, calling in at the club for a couple of drinks on the way home, hiding bottles in my car, drinking after she's asleep . . . *What is wrong with me? Pushing away my inner circle over this?*

"I might have to!" I tell her, knowing she's right. It's okay. This is not a permanent dependence. Just a temporary leaning, sequestered in my grief bunker while I get through these initial chapters of my nightmare. Doesn't everyone who has just lost someone grasp at whatever survival tool is within reach? I could stop if I wanted to. *I just don't want to.*

"I'm going to sell the piano," I announce.

She gasps. "Audrey, no. Fraser told you that was yours."

"Parker doesn't stay over now. Her piano is at Maggie's house. The school said I can use theirs to see out the term for my students instead of teaching at home. It won't fit if I move in with you—" *And there's just no point.* "Oh, and I've withdrawn from the plagiarism case."

Haunted by Clair's drunken words about Josh—that it was his fault I was on that Zoom and that Fraser is dead—I just can't bear to face it anymore. The butterfly effect might be true, but was it Josh's one injustice or my fifteen years of holding on to it that caused me to be on the call that day? My brain has been wrestling with it, exhausted by it, concluding that, accident or not, my career choices are interlaced with Fraser's death. The end result is I can't do this anymore. Classical music. I am traumatized by it.

"Even if I wanted to write something, my mind is locked. I can't even hear music in my head. I'm walking away from it."

Walking away from the piano. An unbearable new layer of loss.

"But you can't breathe without music, Audrey. You're the same as Parker . . ."

I *wish* I were the same as Parker. Maggie said she is pouring herself into it, wrestling with her grief through the keyboard. That's the way I imagined I would carry myself through, too. I glance at last night's empty bottles peeking out of the recycling bin near the fridge and shudder.

Rach realizes she's losing the battle and drops it. "Can I help you with the house stuff?" she asks. "I can speak to agents. Coordinate repairs, cleaners, packers. You know Jess is obsessed with interior styling. It won't be overwhelming if you let us project-manage it."

All the project management in the world wouldn't stop this from being overwhelming. But she's right. I can't handle this on my own. I can't handle anything at the moment, and I'm sure I am privately barreling toward either a medical or a psychological crisis, rehab, or all three, so I say yes.

It's two nights later when I drag in from a walk to the local grocery store—messy bun, stretched gray cardigan, track pants, UGGs—and find Joshua sitting on my doorstep.

The sight alarms me at first. I think for a millisecond that he is Fraser. He doesn't see me straightaway, his head bowed, deep in thought, probably listening to some symphony in his brain. When he realizes I'm there, he greets me with his usual stern expression, and I have a jolt of regret that our once close association has landed in such a wasteland.

"Sully," he says, quietly. "How are you?"

How does he think I am? Tired of this already, I dump my shopping bag on the step and sit beside him.

"Oh, you know. Just returned from my evening frolic," I inform him. "A little cavort through the fresh food section is the highlight of my day." My shopping bag tips over then, and out of it rolls a large and traitorous bag of potato chips.

"I've come to buy a piano," he explains.

I'm going to throttle Rachael.

"You're moving to the Upper East Side," I say. To his credit, he delayed the start date of his new contract to be here for Parker in the immediate aftermath of Fraser's death.

"Greenwich Village, actually. But I'm keeping my apartment here."

"An apartment that presumably already has a full-size grand? What do you want with a midrange student upright?"

"I've got a spare wall. I like decorating."

"With pianos?"

He shrugs. For the first time since Fraser died, there's a flicker of amusement. But it doesn't last.

"Audrey, you'll regret selling it."

Here we go.

"Then don't buy it."

"Consider it long-term rent."

"And then you'll hand it back when I come to my senses, right? Josh, I don't need you to rescue the piano." *Or me.*

He looks at me. Bores into me, really. Hitches this idea to what little hope I have left that I will ever return to music and pulls on it until the tension snaps. "I'm not being entirely selfless," he says. "You composed Fraser's funeral piece on that instrument. It could be worth a fortune one day."

And that's it. One tiny breadcrumb of praise and years fall away. The professional part of me flashes back, craving his feedback, basking in the glow of having impressed someone with his indisputable talent.

"I don't need your money," I say, swatting those feelings aside, even though I do desperately need the money. "But I might need somewhere to store it."

He reaches for the railing and pulls himself to his feet, then offers his hand to haul me up. I find myself a step above him, eye to eye, as he says, "Respectfully, my brother left you without his affairs in order, and you look—" His eyes roam over my permanently wrecked, hungover appearance. "I suspect you do need the money."

This *burns.* Not just the part about my floundering financially or looking the way I do, but the insinuation that Fraser didn't think to look after me. "It's been a long time since you treated me respectfully," I say—an accusation it's impossible to refute.

He passes me my shopping bag, frowning at the sound of bottles clinking, and I fumble for my keys. "Thanks for your concern about the piano—"

He grabs my arm and speaks in a low voice. "I said I was sorry, Sully—"

I spin to face him, shaking him off. "You said you were sorry for my loss."

That's what he meant that night. *Wasn't it?* I'd been far too plastered to read between any lines.

For a few seconds, we lock eyes and I'm twenty-two again, swept into his orbit.

No. Not *into* the orbit. Just near it, like those asteroids they report in the news that have near misses with Earth but ultimately fly past with no risk of human extinction.

I fear I am already addicted to something that's very bad for me and am fully capable of spiraling without this man's expert assistance. His praise fulfills a need in me, but I am not so desperate for self-annihilation that I can't step back from this particular ledge now, before I lose my grip.

"Please just forget it, Joshua. And forget me." He falls back a step. "I can't look at you without thinking of Fraser, and to be honest, it's completely unbearable. Just go and dominate New York like you know you want to."

30

Fraser

There is a frightening crossroads, a few months in, when I realize Parker is the only thing keeping me alive.

I don't know how safety is measured. How close to the edge I need to be standing, technically, before the risk is sufficiently elevated for everyone to panic. Isn't it normal, when the love of your life leaves, to imagine being dead, too? Who wouldn't want an easy end to this?

Parker, though, stops me. She doesn't know the responsibility she's carrying. The way my mind is using her, forcing an imaginary version of her to collapse in despair and struggle to exist without me. Convincing me to stay, because she needs me. *How could I even think of doing this?* It's that thought that drags me back, every time.

There's a knock at my office door, and when I look up, I'm surprised to see Maggie, who hasn't visited my workplace in years. Even when we were married, we rarely encroached on each other's professional turf. So of course, I immediately panic that something has happened to our daughter.

"It's you I'm worried about," she explains, glancing fruitlessly for somewhere to sit down.

The room is bursting with books and journals and piles of essays and manuscripts. I've got lists of things I haven't done.

Lecture notes I need to file. Book chapters to write. Conference papers to edit. Reference reports for former students' jobs or current students' scholarship applications. Reports for the university administration. Two years' worth of taxes . . .

Something about Maggie standing here in the eye of the physical manifestation of my inner turmoil—her perfect hair and makeup, her pressed suit, her patent leather heels, and the shocked expression on her face—makes it clear how far I've slipped. No longer able to hide that sinking grief has met rising depression and I'm barely clinging on.

"I'm a bit behind," I admit. *On everything.*

She balances her Oroton bag on a pile of books I keep meaning to donate and steps over sixty essays I've printed, despite the significant guilt I felt for wasting paper. I can't seem to focus while reading on a screen the way my Gen Z colleagues do. Then, in the midst of this mess, she walks up to me with no ceremony whatsoever and puts her arms around me.

"You are not safe, Fraser." This time it is not a question. It's an educated observation. And I am far too exhausted to keep up the pretenses. It's easier just to admit it, because she didn't ask; she just told me how it is, and she is right. *Am I meant to ask her for help now?*

"Here's what we're going to do . . ." she says, before I can.

An hour later, we're in the waiting room at the doctor's. The receptionist, who's known us since before Parker was born, seems enthralled by our presence. Probably wondering why the two of us are here as a team, without our child, knowing as she does that our accounts are now separate.

"Fraser. Maggie." Dr. Kumar welcomes us into the room we've sat in together ever since we first found double lines on that pregnancy test. We've been here with baby Parker on our laps, checking for ear infections or getting needles or asking if it was normal that she hadn't rolled over yet or that she hated tummy time. "How can I help?"

Maggie lets me do the talking. A rarity for us in this setting. But she is a solid presence beside me, and I've never, even throughout our marriage, felt like the two of us were more united.

"There are a number of ways we can tackle this," Dr. Kumar explains, once I've outlined the sleepless nights, the overwhelm at work, *the thoughts*. "I'm going to increase your dosage of sertraline and add another medication to help you sleep at night. I'm recommending some leave from work. Just a few weeks to help you catch your breath. And here's a referral to a new psychologist who's just moved to the area. These are just first steps. There's much more we can do. It's not unusual for the lines to blur between grief and depression. How you're feeling and what you're tackling is very much to be expected with trauma like yours."

Trauma like mine? It hadn't occurred to me that our family deserved that label, but Dr. Kumar is right. Of course that's what we've been through. A violent, accidental, sudden loss. *What else would you call it?*

Maggie's hand takes mine, just briefly, and squeezes it. A tacit *You are not alone* and a reminder that, despite all the time I spend questioning what went wrong and grappling to understand her point of view, there was a lot that was always right. She is a good person. She has a kind heart. We have a long history and an even longer future together, and even if our shared parenting wasn't a factor in our continued presence in each other's lives, at times like this, I realize I'd hope we could be friends.

31

Audrey

When I wake up, I don't know where I am. I can feel someone shaking my shoulder and calling my name.

"Parker?"

"Audrey! Wake up."

It's not Parker. It's a louder voice and it's angry.

"Wake up, Audrey. Come on. Sit up."

I risk opening my eyes. Crushing pain shuts them again. Crushing pain and the sight of Fraser's ex-wife standing over me like a fire-breathing dragon.

My mouth is parched. Throat burning. Someone across the room knocks a wine bottle onto another one, and the sound of the glass clanging feels like the thundering of an earthquake. *Or is this an actual earthquake?* Everything is spinning.

"Sorry!" It's Parker's voice. She must have knocked the bottles. "I had to call Mum. I was scared."

Oh, shit. Things are starting to come into view. I struggle to sit up. World off its axis. And finally I open my eyes and take in the scene.

The living room looks like it's in late-stage atrophy. The same piles of washing are on the couch, just continually recycled from there. Glasses on the table, not just last night's. Takeaway food containers. It resembles the quintessential scene in a movie when the person has gone through some breakup or personal tragedy and is discovered at rock bottom. Except I'm hitting rock bottom in front of the last two people in the world who should be seeing it.

"Parker, pack your bag, please," Maggie says. Parker starts crying across the room, pulling at the cuffs of her sleeves the way she always does lately. In the back of my mind, I have a terrible suspicion I know why, but I can't think about that right now, and the fact that I can't think about something so important tells me all I need to know about how dire this situation has become.

"I'm so sorry!" she reiterates, and I realize she means she's sorry for calling her mother in. She thinks I'm in trouble. I *am* in trouble. What have I *done*?

"Maggie—" I want to apologize. Explain myself. Explain how it is that she trusted me to take care of her daughter last night because we have *such a special bond*, and I repaid that trust with *this*.

"Don't even start, Audrey. I'm furious."

She deserves to be. How have I possibly sunk so low that I've prioritized knocking myself unconscious with wine over the safety of a *child*?

Our daughter is thumping about in the bedroom upstairs. Maggie's daughter. *Fraser's daughter*. His precious child. This is the kind of neglect that has kids taken away from families. Although I don't have that sort of arrangement. She'd been begging for a sleepover for weeks, and Maggie finally relented. She hadn't wanted to "confuse" Parker by setting an expectation of some sort of shared parenting continuation now that Fraser is gone, and I abused the opportunity. *Because I can't go one single night*.

Maggie picks up the bottles. She tosses them into the recycling bin in the kitchen and comes back for the glasses.

"Is it just alcohol?" she asks, casting a glance around the room for evidence of anything else.

"Yes," I assure her. Yes. Although there's no "just" about it. This roaring tidal wave has engulfed me, and I am powerless against it. I can't outrun it. Every morning I promise myself it will never happen again; every night it does. I know people drink, some every day, but they stop at one glass or two. *I don't know how.*

"I want you to have a shower," Maggie says. "I'm going to drop Parker at school—" I check the clock on the wall, and my head pounds anew at the idea that it's now midmorning and she's so late. "Then I am canceling my appointments for the day and coming back here."

I don't know what she means, but I accept my fate. I feel like I deserve to be arrested, but that might just be my hungover confusion catastrophizing the situation.

"Would you like me to call your sister or Rachael?" she asks.

A precision bolt of fear hits. "Neither!"

I can't bear to have my closest people see how far I've plummeted. I've mastered the art of hiding it. If I see people in the evenings, I pre-drink. I carry vodka in my purse and gulp it in toilet cubicles. I never agree to wine by the bottle to share. Can't bear the excruciating wait while they get through a glass in a sedate and classy manner. When they talk, I hear nothing but the blinding noise of alcohol as I monitor how much is left, resenting their slowness, veins screaming for it.

But I'm careful. If I drink too quickly or have too much, I know they'll step in and stop me. After every night out, I await the dreaded *We need to talk*. Dreaded not because I'll have to give up drinking. But because alcohol will choose itself over my friends.

And if I suspect they're concerned, I throw in the wild card of a "sober" evening, guzzling mineral water or lemonade while holding off drinking until I'm back home, alone. Then I make up for it. Late into the night, I drink enough for all of us. Those nights are the worst.

"It's the only way I can sleep without him," I confess to Maggie. I picture her, in her immaculate home, efficiently working through her problems, sleeping like a baby. Or like a proper adult, more to the point. One who hasn't lost her way so badly, so humiliatingly, that she's had to be parented by a ten-year-old.

"We're going to go to the doctor," she informs me. "There's medication that can help. There are programs."

"Please don't tell anyone," I say, begging her. "I've lost everything else that matters, now presumably including access to your daughter, and I understand why. I do. I can't lose my dignity."

Is there anything less dignified than begging to hold on to your already obliterated dignity? That ship has not only sailed, but circumnavigated the globe. This is me, pleading with my almost husband's ex-wife—the woman with *everything* together, always—to keep my darkest secret.

"I will help you, Audrey, and I will keep your secret. But you can't have unsupervised time with Parker anymore. I'm sorry."

Before I can process this missile—a direct strike to the heart—Parker comes back into the room, uniform on, backpack over her shoulder, tears streaming down her face as she runs over to me, launching into a hug as if she's trying to apologize for exposing me. Or perhaps she knows this is goodbye.

"I've ruined everything," she says, voice shaking. "I'm so sorry! This is all my fault."

Now my heart splinters.

"How could this possibly be your fault?" I ask. "You did the right thing, calling Mum when you were worried."

Then she looks at both of us, a replica of her mother—dark hair in a neat ponytail tied with a gold ribbon, backpack falling to the floor beside her feet, chest heaving, despair written all over her innocent face, as she says, “No! It’s my fault you’re like this. Because it’s my fault Daddy is dead!”

I have never sobered up so fast. Maggie and I scoop Parker up as if she’s a baby bird fallen from the nest.

“Darling, it wasn’t your fault that Daddy died. How could it be?” Maggie says, the worry furrowed deep into her face.

“I went to sick bay. They tried to call Audrey a couple of times, then you.” Her voice breaks. “Then Daddy.”

I have been over this scene in my brain a thousand times, but I don’t think I ever quite imagined this little girl inside that school while the accident unfolded, teachers trying to shield her from the frantic efforts to save him outside . . . Ugh, I can’t bear it.

“You weren’t feeling well,” I tell her. “You can’t help that.”

Her little face falls in an emotion I’d recognize a mile off. Guilt.

“Hailey Pearce said I was going to marry the piano,” she confesses, hands wringing, more sleeve pulling. “They think I’m weird because I love classical music. And then someone saw you at my scholarship concert and said I have two mums, and I told them, *So what if I do?* And they teased me about that.”

The room is spinning. I am inwardly imploring Maggie to take the lead here, because I can barely keep myself upright.

“Was that before or after you went onstage that night?” Maggie asks, glancing at me.

“Before,” Parker confirms. “I tried so hard with my pieces.”

She did. So hard that striving to get it right flatlined the emotion, just as I’d said.

Silent apology is written across Maggie’s face. She’s sorry for doubting me back then. Something *had* been missing from Parker's music, and Maggie hadn't wanted to face it. Even though we'd got her help since, she'd been suffering through all of this alone, until it got to be too much and she faked an illness and asked to be picked up from school early . . .

Such a normal, innocent, deadly chain of events that we have followed through to this new low, today. Me letting them both down. Maggie furious. Parker distraught. At ten thirty on a weekday morning.

I glance at the clock again. An hour and a half until noon. We have a broken child. A fractured family. Enormous problems. Yet my addicted brain prioritizes just one thought as it blazes through this mess to the surface.

Still too early for a glass.

32

Fraser

"I'm sorry, have I forgotten something?" I ask Rachael as she bustles into my home, kicks off her shoes, dumps her briefcase on the end of my kitchen table, and opens the Uber Eats app. I don't recall inviting her over.

"Welcome to the inaugural meeting of the Every Other Monday Night Club," she announces, smiling proudly at her brainchild. I had a conversation with her on the phone last night about the brutal 168-hour gaps between Parker's appointed weeks with me, and how hard it has been to adjust to the silence. I'm on my third box of the increased dose of antidepressants, and the world in general is feeling kinder, but the loneliness in Parker's absence hits me fresh every fortnight. *Maybe I need a hobby or something,* I said on the phone.

"Every second Monday?" I ask her. "For how long?"

"As long as it takes. What do you feel like? Chinese?"

She makes an executive decision, ordering two dishes and some spring rolls. Then, waiting for the food to be delivered, she flits around the house, humanizing it.

"*Never* use the overhead lights, Fraser. I'm serious," she lectures, turning on lamps, lighting candles, straightening cushions. She almost presses the power button on the speaker, but glances at me, reads the expression on my face, and decides against it.

"One day you'll handle music again," she promises. "That's when we'll know you're really—"

"Over her?" The idea ignites a flash of indignation. But I've forgotten for a second whom I'm talking to. Audrey's best friend. Someone who stops fussing with the cushions and looks at me, shocked that I would put such words in her mouth.

"I meant if you can learn to love music again, that will be a good sign," she clarifies.

It will be a fairy tale.

"I saw a reel on Instagram about how micro joys are the way we survive macro grief," she says. "Micro joys, Fraser. You and I should chase them."

A few weeks ago, in that doctor's office with Maggie, I would have written off this advice. Now, well medicated, with weekly psych appointments, daily exercise, and better sleep, I might not be leaping ecstatically through life, but I'm able to lift my head and look around again. And tonight, with the overhead lights switched off and with candles flickering and the promise of warm food and good company—I let myself have a moment of contentment.

It prompts me to go to the sideboard and pull out the top drawer. Inside is a rectangular box from a jeweler's. I take it out and turn to look at her, suddenly nervous. "Rach, I've been waiting for the right moment to give you this."

She looks at the box in my hand before blue eyes flick back to mine, confused. "What is it?"

I open the lid and lift out the silver chain, from which hangs a delicate blue teardrop sapphire. "This was meant to be a wedding present," I explain. "She'd want you to have it."

She's stunned at first, eyes smarting with tears as I coax her to turn around and face the hall mirror so I can place it around her neck. "Are you sure this shouldn't go to Sara?" she asks, touching the gemstone as it rests on her breastbone, meeting my gaze in the reflection. "Or Parker?"

"Matches your eyes."

She's still unconvinced.

"I gave Sara the family heirlooms Audrey had, minus a couple of special things we agreed to give to Parker eventually. Rach, I really want you to have this. Think of it as a thank-you gift from Audrey for everything you've done for us."

Before she can respond, there's a knock at the door. The delivery driver must be early, and Rachael jumps up to answer it. When she returns, it's with an odd expression that makes sense when Maggie and Parker trail in after her.

"She left her PE bag," Maggie explains, inspecting the cozy transformation of the place she left with Parker just an hour ago. It's as if Cinderella's fairy godmother has swept through.

Rach follows her gaze to the candles burning on the coffee table and says, "I thought he needed a bit of hygge."

Maggie bristles. "Did you?"

Something about this frosty interaction is giving me déjà vu, which of course is when the actual delivery driver arrives, handing over a plastic bag.

"Are there fortune cookies?" asks Parker, leaping at it.

Nobody stops her, but I wish we had when she breaks open both of them and reads, "Dad, you have an exciting opportunity ahead! And, Rach, don't be afraid of competition!" The twin destinies scrape up against the fictional love story lingering in Maggie's imagination, which is not helped when Parker, ditching the fortune cookies, pounces at the sapphire around Rachael's neck, squeals in delight, and says, "*You gave it to her!*"

It's not like that, I want to argue as Maggie sweeps up Parker's bag and bustles her back out the door after another round of hugs, saying, "Don't let it get cold."

"Too late for that," Rach says softly when the door shuts. Her opinion of Maggie isn't one she's arrived at independently. It comes with years of conditioning from Audrey, having sided protectively with her best friend through all the angst early on in the blended family relationship.

"I think it's the type A professional thing," I say, wanting to defend my former wife. "Maggie's very ambitious. She likes to be the most intelligent woman in the room. She's very clever. But you're obviously—"

She's obviously what? I look at her, standing beside me in leggings and a gym top, locked briefcase on the table beside us probably containing some sort of vitally important national security paperwork. And I remember joking about her being dull in her cat costume at the party years ago. She's obviously not that.

Suddenly, I don't want her to misread Maggie. "You know she helped me when I hit rock bottom," I explain. "Saved me, probably."

Rach looks up, midway through dishing some rice into a bowl.

"She came to my office, saw how bad things were, and took me to our GP. I think she was worried about the impact on Parker if I couldn't get my act together."

"She was," Rach replies. "She called me about it."

Maggie called *Rachael*? She never said.

"I think it's good that you have her." She passes me a bowl of food and flops on the floor beside the couch. "But I don't think she appreciated the hygge."

I choke on my dim sum.

"She's more of an overhead lights sort of person," she adds in all seriousness, undeterred by my coughing fit.

I look at her, relaxed on the floor beside my coffee table. Legs crossed, hair up, somehow managing both chopsticks and the artful rearranging of a stack of books for aesthetic impact. When she's happy with the styling, she catches me watching her from the sofa, smiles brightly, and performs a little bow with a dramatic flourish.

Micro joys are the way we survive macro grief, she said.

I don't know. I think the secret is borrowing a best friend from your late fiancée.

33

Audrey

"The worst part is, I've been hiding it," I said to Maggie's GP the day she got me an emergency appointment. "My friends think I'm recovering from the shock and the trauma and the loss. I'm back in a job, not one I like, but still. I'm socializing, exercising—I mean, it's a full-time activity looking as under control as I do. But it's an act. Every bit of it."

"Look, here are the details of a local group," the doctor said, passing me a flyer. "I know it's hard to show up the first time, but I'm certain it will be helpful for you."

Walking out of the practice with a script for a drug to curb cravings, I looked at the information in my hand. I knew if I didn't do this immediately, I would push it aside for months, and who knew how bad I'd be by then. *Or if I'll even be alive.*

So I stood on the path outside the building and called the number. And ended the call. Called it again. Hung up. Third time around, I allowed a woman to pick up.

"It's been six months," I explained. "I just can't seem to get past it."

"Of course! You'd be most welcome." Even her voice was comforting. "It's just a small group at the moment. About eight people. Come on Tuesday?"

Eight people. Each struggling as much as I was. *Do they have any idea how much their existence means to me?*

That was two months, five million bottles, countless regrettable text messages, and an immeasurable swath of dropped obligations ago.

I wanted to get better. I did. I just didn't want to do it without drinking.

In the end, having gone to extraordinary lengths to hide the worst of this from Rach, I opened up to her about how truly bad things had become. "Whatever you're imagining, it's a million times worse. Maggie took me to her doctor—"

"Maggie?" She was affronted. Of course she was. And I get it. I'd trusted Fraser's ex-wife, with whom little love has ever been lost, over her. My best friend since university. Addiction had taken another swing of its axe.

"I couldn't bear to disappoint you, Rach."

She looked at me across the café table, devastated.

"It's this *giant problem* swallowing everything," I explained. "It's me. Not you. And the only reason Maggie knows about it is because I did a horrible thing. I made a huge mistake, and she discovered it."

She leaned forward.

I could hardly dare admit this, I was so humiliated. "Rach, I got blackout drunk the one night she let me have Parker for a sleepover. I'm talking almost completely unconscious. Parker couldn't wake me and called her mum. She was two hours late for school, and even then I couldn't wait for them to leave, because I was that jittery, I needed something to take the edge off . . ."

She sat back then. Flummoxed. "How have I missed this? What kind of friend am I?"

"No! I'm a master at hiding it. Or I was. Oh, God, and there's this whole other story about Parker. I'm worried sick. She blames *herself* for Fraser's death. All this time that I've been drinking myself to oblivion, I've been pushing away this awful, swirling instinct that she's struggling with something even worse than what she's already told Maggie and me. And now I'm not allowed to see her, and Maggie wouldn't listen to the ramblings of a drunk woman anyway. So I don't know what to do."

She poured me a huge glass of water while I tried to fend off the anxiety attack. What I really needed was a huge glass of wine. Alcohol dampens the nervous system. *How did she think I'd made it through eight months without him?*

Rach reached across the table then and took my hands in hers. "I think the best way to help Parker is to help yourself, Audrey. And the best way to help yourself is to let me back in . . ."

So now we're parked outside the center in Rach's car and I'm shaking. I'm scared. Terrified, even. "These people are about to confiscate the one thing that makes my life survivable," I explain, making good on this afternoon's commitment to be honest with her. "There'll be no protection from this horror."

I can't possibly go in! *Why would I torture myself?* Give me this messy half-life and the permanent fog of semiconsciousness over burning exposure to the full force of life without him.

I'm desperate for her to throw the car in reverse, when a montage of the life I'm trying to preserve here presents itself: chaotic nights, fractured sleep, endless covering up, and backsliding across every critical area as time folds and shrinks and I slip further from the woman I was. The woman he loved.

Forever telling myself I'll "start tomorrow": more water, better food, earlier bedtime . . . that meaningless mantra that always goes nowhere.

It's my fault you're like this, Parker had said. Remembering that, I unlatch the seat belt.

I. Have. Lost. His. Child.

All time exists now, Audrey. You are thirty-seven, sitting in this car outside the meeting. And you are forty . . .

But I can't see forty! Can't make any version of the timeline stretch, which throws me into a deeper panic.

"The night he died I had a premonition that, if I wasn't careful, his death was going to kill me." *And here I am, eight months on, weapon in my hand.*

"I'm not going to let that happen," Rach says, as she leans across and pushes open my car door.

I get out and walk toward the building before I can talk myself out of this. Inside, the waiting area is full of public health brochures and posters about loneliness and breastfeeding and sexual health—finally a problem of no concern to my present monastic lifestyle. The group meets in a room down a carpeted corridor. To get to it, I'm forced to walk past one labeled *Mums & Bubs.* My gut clenches with that confusing cocktail of loss and fear, laced with endless sadness that, even though I'd made my decision, the choice was terminally ripped from me when Fraser died. *Triggers everywhere.*

When I arrive, there's a motley gathering. A couple of people around my age, some older. One shockingly young. People in business suits. Jeans. A gorgeous woman in a floral dress with puffed sleeves and a pixie cut. People checking phones. Someone stirring a cup of instant coffee from the table in the corner. Laughing. Chatting. Talking about football scores and politics and grandkids.

Normal people, all of them. Carrying on as if this is a social occasion. And then there's me.

"I'm Audrey." My voice is shaking minutes later as the meeting begins, heart pounding, skin tingling, as I'm metaphorically stabbed by the fork in this road. *Lapsed musician. Reluctant admin officer. Widow. Ostracized stepmum. Veritable wreck.* "And I'm an alcoholic."

Everyone was right. Admitting it was hard but also a relief. The undeniable fact is that somewhere, in the space between that first glass in the shower the night he died and arriving at this community center, I have become miserably, intensely, and what feels like irrevocably dependent on alcohol.

I can still see Jess passing that wine through the bathroom door. Still hear the flimsy objection in my mind. *Surely I can make it through the shower without alcohol*... Fast-forward to tonight, and there's barely a minute of any day that I'm not strategizing my next sip.

I'm embarrassed to say I thought alcoholics were people who sidled up to a bar all day, or I pictured a reclusive writer, tucked away in some attic, brilliant words lubricated by red wine or whiskey. At absolutely no point did I see myself—an administrative officer from a nice family, with a beautiful late almost husband and a precious stepdaughter—just as dependent as anyone else.

But I have to admit that I am. I just said so in there. And the sky did not fall.

"Audrey?" It's a woman from the group, Ali, about my age, trailing me out. "Well done."

"Thanks?" The people pleaser inside me is giddy at the praise until I remember I'm being congratulated for admitting I have an addiction. *Doesn't that make me a failure?*

"It's not easy to do what you did tonight. How are you going to celebrate?"

Champagne? It's as if the two notions are married at the hip.

"Er . . . I hadn't thought it through." Not in any palatable way that I could explain to this woman. And I guess that's why she's asking.

"Would you like to grab a bite?"

I imagine perusing a menu, looking for nonalcoholic options to accompany the meal. It's been so long since I've had dinner out without wine—most nights my dinner *is* wine—I can't even imagine what the point would be. It would feel like half an experience.

Wow. Every unfolding idea illuminates just how far down this pit I have crashed.

"I should probably just go home and have an early night," I say, only for the two bottles of chilled wine in my fridge to spring to mind. Yes. *And I was still considering going to the bottle shop?* I wouldn't have drunk all of that in one night. *Would I?* But if my supply gets too low, I feel anxious. Now I'm wondering how I allowed it to spiral this far without admitting to myself that I have a problem. And when I started referring to it as my "supply."

"It would be really positive if you could go through this night, after your first meeting, sober," Ali says.

I agree. It would be. The idea of failing so fast is almost as worrisome as the concept of no wine. It would unleash a massive tumbling into an abyss from which I couldn't claw my way out. *Is this the "slippery slope" everyone talks about, or has that been overtaken by events?*

"The way you'll feel in the morning will be worth it," Ali adds. "I'd be happy to keep you company." I'm meant to call Rach for a lift, but maybe I should spend some time with someone who really gets this, from experience.

"I've got two bottles of wine at home," I blurt out. I don't mean for it to sound like an invitation. If it was, two bottles for two people wouldn't be enough. "It's not far from here, and I know we just met, but would you come with me and hold me accountable while I tip them down the sink? I'll cook you dinner?"

She takes my arm the way characters do in Enid Blyton novels when they're about to skip to the store and purchase cakes and sweets. Except what we're doing is the opposite of Enid Blyton. It's dark. It's terrifying. I can feel myself sweating and shaking at the mere thought of trying to get through even one evening without that magical softening of the edges.

"It's just tonight," Ali assures me.

It *isn't* just tonight, but I can see why tonight is all that we have to handle right now.

"Audrey, you can still have a beautiful life," she promises as she unlocks her car. "This is the start. Not the end."

the start (again)

34

Three years later

Audrey

"This is why they say not to make major decisions!"

Even the torrential rain pounding on my Jeep's soft-top won't drown out the *I told you so* in Sara's voice.

"You're not meant to make major decisions in the *first* year," I remind her. "Pretty sure I'm off the leash in the third."

"But what made you think you could reverse a camper without crashing into anything?"

"It wasn't *anything*." Gallows humor has always been my go-to when things are dire. "It was a RAM truck bigger than Miss Bennet!"

Miss Bennet is my vintage camper trailer, bought on a whim from Facebook Marketplace. She belongs to the broad-spectrum whim that also saw me quit the public service job that I had been trundling along with quite nicely and sell almost everything I own without consulting my hypercautious older sibling, hence the latest in her lifelong lecture series.

"How did the owner take it?" she probes, nervously.

I glance at the obnoxious gunmetal-gray travel trailer towering beside me. It's one of those off-road behemoths, built to conquer raging rivers in the wilderness. *Outback Viper* is emblazoned threateningly along the side in bloodred lightning font.

"I'm sure he'll be reasonable?" Really, I'm certain of nothing of the sort. I catch sight of my own camper in the mirror—the type you'd hire out as an Instagram prop for weddings. A delicate little thing in white and Tiffany blue.

"What are the precise coordinates of this campground?" Sara demands. "Drop a pin!"

Just as I'm cursing the hat trick of bad luck that led me to become Sara's opposite in every way—fiscally irresponsible, wildly romantic, hopeless at parking—the behemoth's door flings wide open, spilling golden light through sheets of rain.

The Viper presents himself. A villainous silhouette in black jeans and a plain T-shirt, with unkempt dark hair and tattoos—definitely capable of digging the hole he might need to bury whoever dented his truck. *Why couldn't I have crashed into the vehicle of some bespectacled computer nerd?*

I watch as he processes the news that Miss Bennet's rear is wedged tight against the nose of his prize rig. "He looks furious," I whisper to Sara. At least, *I* would be furious if this situation were reversed. "He's coming over."

I end the call and throw my phone into the center console as I try to scramble my face into something approachable and apologetic, something that says both *Mea culpa* and *Please don't murder me.* "I'm so sorry!" I gush, clambering out of the Jeep and into the rain. "I'm new to this."

I mean that I'm new to reversing caravans. In truth, I'm new to a lot more than that, but this guy doesn't need a play-by-play of the whole saga of the last three years. *Stick to the crisis at hand.*

He ignores me, walks to the back, gives both my camper trailer and his truck a powerful shove, and gets on his haunches to assess the damage. I trot behind, peer over his shoulder, and, in the manner of a panel-beating apprentice, say, "Any closer and the two vehicles would have successfully cycled through the entire welding process."

It goes down like a lead balloon. He glares at me over his shoulder, then, concluding his assessment of the vehicles, he rises to his full impressive height and begins to scrutinize me: wet clumps of toffee-brown hair stuck to freckled skin, thread-bare T-shirt rapidly soaking through, and frayed denim shorts. I seem to be dressed like a teenager and can blame only the incoming perimenopausal crisis Sara has monitored in recent months with the meticulous fascination of a meteorologist tracking an offshore storm surge.

"Obviously, I'll pay for the repairs," I promise, hoping I sound more mature than I look. The Viper frowns and pulls me out of the rain under the protection of his heavy-duty awning, critical gaze settling on the bright yellow thrifted Wellington boots on my feet.

"How do you drive in those?" he asks, deep voice surprisingly warm in the chilly air.

Is it a rhetorical question? We have the evidence right here of how I drive in them.

But as I try to think of an answer, he takes a giant step across the A-frame of my trailer, walks around the Wrangler, and opens the passenger door. "Get in," he instructs, nodding at the driver's side as if his senses have taken leave. Surely it would be irresponsible to let my negligent driving loose on the rest of the South Coast holidaymakers ensconced for the night at Pretty Beach?

I've had a casual flirtation with my own death ever since I lost Fraser. It's nothing serious. I just occasionally glance its way. But getting in the car with this stranger, facing potential danger for real, it hits me that perhaps I'm not in so much of a rush. Maybe I don't want to die just yet. Certainly not on the eve of my fortieth birthday. Not when everyone has promised that, after emerging from such a stormy few years, life is about to begin again.

The magnificent realization that I don't want to be murdered by this man and its birthday-eve timing is so intoxicating that I allow it to seep in, rain pelting on my skin as I glance skyward just for a second, eyes shut, gratitude beaming, and breathe in this newfound, invigorating desire to endure . . .

"Is this some sort of incantation to the gods?" the Viper asks when I look back at him, rain soaking his T-shirt as he waits for me. "What are you *doing*?"

"Wouldn't it be better if *you* parked it?" I suggest. He looks like the practical sort of man upon whom my epiphany would be lost. "I'll take copious notes."

He ignores me and swings into the passenger seat as we fall into a stalemate, sizing each other up through the windscreen while I stand in the mud, illuminated by the Jeep's headlights, wipers mirroring my indecision as they flick relentlessly back and forth until he holds up his hands, questioning the delay. It's only a brilliant flash of lightning and an almost instantaneous clap of thunder that hurry me to the driver's door. But I find it jammed. *Another broken thing in my life.*

"It only works from the inside," I yell, tapping the glass and nodding at the latch while I rub my arms in the cold and have an unwanted flash of Fraser and the unruffled, scientific way that he would have handled this. But I can't think about him now. This is my Fresh Start. I didn't stagger to my feet, pull myself through a drunken apocalypse, and *do the work* (when there was just so much of it to do) only for him to barge to front of mind and interfere with the fight-or-flight response when I need it most.

The Viper leans across the driver's seat, pulls the door handle, and surveys me through the car window with exasperated dark blue eyes. I get in and slam the door, shivering. For a few seconds we stare at each other, cocooned in the relative warmth of the Jeep, rain pouring on the vinyl roof. Actually, it's not just pouring, I notice. It's leaking straight through!

"Sorry," I say, reaching between his muscular thighs and wrenching open the glove box. A roll of gaffer tape tumbles out, along with a bunch of papers, which flitter into his lap. Top of the pile is the very last document I want this man, or anyone, including me, to see. The death certificate. I snatch it before he can register what it is, fold it in half, and shove it down the side of my seat, instantly remorseful. It feels like I'm shoving Fraser down there with chewing gum wrappers and the receipt for the sump gasket. *Out of sight, out of mind?* How ironic when, even three years later, he is the permanent backdrop to every scene . . .

The man hands me the tape with the demeanor of a surgical assistant. I stretch a length from the roll and bite it off with my teeth, then stick it to the roof where the rain is getting in, heart pounding with the exertion of holding myself and my car—and my life—together in this moment because *everything* is going wrong.

"Let's get this parked," he says, in a softer tone. Unexpected kindness will wreck me. But when I turn the key and the car pairs again with my phone, my Broadway playlist springs to life, belting the soundtrack from *Wicked* and detracting from the defenses I intended to mount about my careful, undistracted driving. I shut it off with a flourish.

"I'm writing a musical!" *Trying to, anyway.* "That was research."

How is this helping?

I hope he doesn't ask me the topic of my show. I'll have to explain how it is that I'm qualified to write *Widowed: The Musical* and that it's funnier than it sounds—like that menopause production that was a global smash. It's not a conversation we should enter with my foot on the accelerator.

"Seat belt," he commands, nodding at my body.

"But we're barely going anywhere."

"From where I'm sitting," he says, "we seem to be in an accident hotspot." At least he's acknowledging it was an accident. Perhaps he's not going to bury me in a ditch after all.

I'm busy weighing my risk of botching this again and making the whole thing worse when he sighs and reaches over me, grabs the belt buckle, and pulls it gently across my shoulder and chest, clicking the lap sash into the slot at my hip. It's been so long since a man has been this familiar with me, it feels like one of those overly romantic slow-motion scenes in those South Korean rom-coms I've become obsessed with, and I tell myself not to fall for these antics. Not with him. Or at all. I can't afford to. *Be Sara!*

"Now, inch the car forward," he instructs as I let go of the handbrake, press the accelerator, and wish I hadn't shut off Elphaba, because all we're listening to now is the hideous sound of vintage metal scraping just-off-the-assembly-line chrome. I move us safely forward a couple of meters and brake.

"Throw it in reverse," he says, stretching his arm behind the back of my seat, twisting his body so he can check the rearview. I've barely recovered from the intimacy of this maneuver before his other hand closes over mine on the steering wheel, his fingers wrapping tight as I attempt not to dissolve in his grasp.

"Every move you make is counterintuitive," he explains quietly as he concentrates, gently turning the wheel. "Slow and steady will give you more control . . ."

There is no personal space. None. We're so close, I'm able to monitor a single raindrop as it falls from his brown hair and runs down his jaw and through the maze of stubble on his chin, disappearing into the hollow at his neck. And now the windows are fogging up! My eyes flick back to his, and I find him transfixed by the extent to which I am not paying attention to the right thing. He's probably wondering if I even have a license.

"The most important thing is to focus," he says.

Well. "Is it my fault the poster boy for off-road adventure is whispering instructions that sound like RV-related ASMR?"

His brows rise.

"You know, pleasing sounds that give you a brain orgasm—"

WHY use that word with the handsome stranger, Audrey? Gawd!

"I know what ASMR is . . ." he says. There's a beat of silence before he clears his throat and adds, "I meant 'Defying Gravity.'"

O-oh!

"Now turn around and look where you're going!"

I'm still reeling from his impressive show tune knowledge as he squeezes my hand tighter on the wheel, the gentle pressure of his arm nudging the back of my seat as we hold our collective breath and reverse Miss Bennet as a duo. Eventually our choreography brings my little vehicle nestled safely in beside his enormous Viper, and I turn off the engine and unleash my belt in a flash.

"Go forward again," he says, letting go of my hand and facing straight ahead.

"But it's fine here, isn't it?"

"If you can park it independently in this weather, you can park it anywhere."

I don't care. It's late. It's dark. I'm exhausted from a long drive and an even longer three years, and I don't need a driving lesson *now*.

"Come on. I might not be around tomorrow," he says.

I find myself disproportionately disappointed by this news. Are we trauma bonding? No, this is a minor mishap. Barely a scratch in the scheme of things. I'm just hungry and light-headed and haven't so much as hugged a strange man in more than thirty-six months, so my libido has clearly gone haywire at the slightest touch.

Next, I'm driving forward, reversing again, and slowly but surely getting the job done perfectly! So I go straight in for an unreciprocated high-five—enthusiasm incommensurable with our circumstances, apparently. I won't mention the expensive towing course Sara recommended, or the fact that I'd redirected that budget into Etsy, ordering Miss Bennet a blue-and-white-striped cloth awning from which I plan to dangle fairy lights.

He wrenches on the brake and says, "I assume you're insured?"

"Oh, yes!" I'm proud to show some competence at last. "Administration is my superpower! *Thanks, Ritalin.*" He stares at me while I blunder on, oversharing my psychiatric diagnosis in the adrenaline comedown. "I quit my job last month. My reference says I'm particularly talented at Excel, which, had you met me five or six years ago, you honestly wouldn't believe!"

The man can at least mark himself safe from being flirted with by the unemployed spreadsheet whiz who has run up several thousand dollars' worth of damage to his vehicle. There's a flash of that first email exchange with Fraser about the six-hundred-dollar mistake at the law firm, and I blink my eyes, attempting to banish it.

"All right, Peter Drucker," he says. "Give me ten minutes, grab your paperwork, come next door, and we'll sort it out."

"Siri, who is Peter Drucker?" I ask as soon as he gets out and walks between our vehicles, stripping his wet shirt over his head on his way up the steps, treating me and my derelict libido to a preview of his torso as the door slams shut. The image burns itself into my brain while I sift through the glove box again for my paperwork and Siri says, "Peter Drucker was the father of modern management and administration."

I stop shuffling and catch sight of myself in the mirror. Between the bedraggled hair, smudged mascara, and having just been compared to a dead twentieth-century management theorist, my confidence is in free fall.

I feel around in the back seat for something dry to change into. Anything. My hand finds yesterday's shirt—not ideal, but any port in a storm—and as I begin to strip the wet one off, there's a loud rap on the car window. *Oh my God!*

Pulling down the glass, I glare at him while clutching the top against my chest. "Do you mind?"

"The amenities block is closed," he informs me, seemingly not a bit interested in my state of undress. "Flooded from earlier."

My gaze travels to the brick building, yellow hazard tape draped across the entryway reflected in a giant puddle of muddy water.

"Camping seemed more glamorous on Pinterest," I mutter, remembering all the times I told Fraser I didn't care for it. But that's the point of this. To do things *differently*.

"Bring a change of clothes and use my shower if you like."

He can't be serious.

I might have blown up my entire life, sold my things, resigned, and stormed out during my family's anti-camping intervention, but I'm not entirely reckless. Not in a million *years* will I be scurrying next door with my insurance policy and my toiletries case, kicking off my yellow Wellingtons, and taking a shower in the Viper's lair.

35

Fraser

The Bookies have made themselves comfortable in my living room, the way they've done almost every Thursday night for the past three years since the first gathering Audrey missed. They almost never read the book these days. I'm convinced they're just posing as a book club to offer guerrilla grief support—and it's been a master class in friendship that would have knocked Audrey's socks off.

"White or red?" I ask Rachael.

The conversation has drifted to dating apps, and specifically why I am not on them. I'm not ready for this. Rachael knows I'm not. But instead of helping me by changing the subject, she nods toward the bottle of cabernet sauvignon, blond hair tumbling over her shoulders, unreadable blue eyes refusing to meet mine as she proffers her glass.

"Come on, Fraser," Jess says, next to her. "She'd want this for you."

Want it? Audrey would be the ringleader! But that's beside the point if I don't want this for myself.

"It's too early," I argue, the familiar excuse practically threadbare. "For Parker."

Thirteen is difficult at the best of times. We've become such a fierce little duo in the wake of our loss, I can't imagine a strange woman tramping through our delicate ecosystem—even with our best interests at heart.

"Nonsense!" Jess declares. "Nothing's going to tear down what you've built here."

She was the one who raised the idea of the Bookies taking Parker out for high tea and starting a motherly group chat about incoming puberty. *In case she's with you and not Maggie when it happens, Fraser.*

Everyone assumes because you're the dad that you'll blunder through it. "She'd love high tea," I agreed, "but I've packed period undies in her schoolbag since Year Five."

"Period undies?" Jess replied, seemingly astonished that I—a *man*—was au fait with the cutting edge of the feminine hygiene industry, ignoring the fact that, as a single dad, knowing this stuff is right there in the job description. "Who *are* you?" she added, laughing. "Menstruation Man?"

"Parker only needs to know about your love life if it gets serious," she says now. "Let go a little, Fraser. We're worried about you."

They're acting like I haven't met a woman since Audrey died. In truth, there seems to be something counterintuitively magnetic about my situation. Perhaps it's the tragedy of it all. The champion status I seem to earn just from doing basic parenting stuff as a solo dad. Period undies. School lunches. Cake stalls. I'm particularly proud of my working diorama of the life cycle of water for Year Seven Human Society and Its Environment. But magically, all this ordinary work makes me into some sort of romantic unicorn. Except with the Bookies, who know me best.

"We need him to seem nice and normal," April decides, calling this crisis meeting to order, commandeering the laptop and speaking as if I'm not in the room. She's a freelance journalist and the designated writer in the group, and I watch helplessly as she interlaces her fingers, stretches her arms, and cracks her knuckles as if she's limbering up to write the Great Australian Novel.

"Am I not normal?" I question as I pass the cheese platter, complete with baked Brie drizzled in warm honey and my signature guacamole with sweet chili sauce.

She scoops some cheese onto a cracker and swallows it, brown eyes fluttering shut in delight. "Actually, you're not normal, Fraser—this Brie is supernaturally good—but what I mean is that men are so weird online! We need you to be yourself! No pictures with fish." She glares at me as if I'm posing with a barramundi this very second, instead of with hors d'oeuvres and the contents of my cellar. "Now, what are your interests, apart from avoiding life?"

Surviving. Raising a child. Keeping my job.

"Put down rock climbing!" Jess says, wild red hair flying as she leans over April's shoulder. "You did that recently, didn't you? Something flashed past on Instagram—"

"It was an indoor rock-climbing party for Parker's school friend," I clarify. "I sat in the café and wrote a brief for the annual report."

She frowns. "That's not attractive, Fraser."

"Noted."

"Weren't there any mums you could have bonded with?"

"They were deconstructing *Bridgerton*," I explain. "I was out of my depth."

"But that would have been *perfect*! This is exactly what's missing from your life!"

"What, more period drama?" I chuckle at my joke, but the architects of my future love life seem to have lost their collective sense of humor.

"Put down that he's saving the world . . ." Rachael suggests, deadpan, after a swig of wine. The irony in her tone flies over the others' heads, but not over mine. She reaches for this week's abandoned novel and flicks through the pages like she's speed-reading for the literary discussion she wishes they'd switch to. I need to remember she was Audrey's friend first.

"You *are* saving the world!" Jess agrees.

"Analyzing data?" I counter. "It's not that sexy—"

"Rubbish! You're science's answer to James Bond!" Jess taps April on the arm and nods so she'll capture that.

"I map emulators of climate models—"

But they have glazed over. April raises a hand to stop me elaborating. "Some heroes wear lab coats," she explains. "Can we call you a 'climate warrior'?"

Make it stop.

I don't even own a lab coat, but far be it for me to ruin their galloping fantasy. "Why don't you put down 'still sleeps with partner's ashes on the bedside table'?"

Rachael finally looks at me, and I offer a tight, empathetic smile.

Of course, Maggie will never get on board with these shenanigans. She organizes her personal life around our agreed timetable. The older Parker gets, the tighter Maggie holds her. I can't see her opening her schedule for extra nights' custody while I search the dating landscape for potential stepmothers and work my way diligently through Bumble.

"I'm only free every second week," I argue.

"We'll babysit!" the group choruses as someone pops another cork.

I take in Audrey's posse: shoes off, hair down, each in various stages of recline between the furniture and the floor, as if they're life models for a Baroque artist's Roman banquet. "You think prospective partners will find this appealing? Four women at mine getting sloshed while we're out on dates?"

I collect an empty platter and follow Rachael into the kitchen.

"Midnight talks! Must love books!" Clair calls from the other room as if this is bingo night at the local club. "She might want to join the Bookies. What else are we looking for in a woman, specifically?"

"They sound like late-in-life lesbians interviewing for a new sister wife," I observe, and Rachael almost cracks a smile. "You okay with all of this, Rach?" *I know she's not.*

She and Audrey are from one of those "Wind Beneath My Wings" friendships. It's why, three years ago, when Audrey died and people closed ranks around our immediate family circle, I knew instinctively to pull Rachael across the line with us. She has been an impeccable friend, but often at her own expense—bolting into the role of carer while she was still bleeding out from her wounds.

"It's your life," she says now, propping herself against the counter and playing with Audrey's sapphire pendant, sparkling under the kitchen lights. "The whole thing is a waste of time, isn't it?"

Our eyes meet uncomfortably. She knows I've tried. And that it's Audrey I'm endlessly searching for and even the Bookies couldn't sub someone in who'd have a hope of measuring up. She will play along with this doomed matchmaking scheme. She'll accommodate it because the others are so into it, but the truth is, somewhere in the last three years, my damaged heart has made Rachael McKenzie weary.

"Funny. Clever. Artistic?" Clair is still listing off desirable attributes as we return to the next room.

"Musical?" I add before I can think, glancing at the closed lid of Audrey's piano, wondering why I'd do this to myself. Apart from the incessant blaring of Taylor Swift, I've gone full Captain von Trapp here, unable to tolerate reminders of her talent. The guilt still stings when I think of the digital keyboard and headphones I gave Parker for Christmas. A compromise. She could follow in her stepmum's footsteps. I could make it through the day unscathed, without the sound of music destroying me.

April frowns at the laptop. "You can be compatible with more than one person, you know, Fraser. You don't need this woman to be Audrey's clone."

Rachael sighs, as if April has raised one last point in a corporate meeting that should have ended an hour ago.

"Outdoorsy or no?" Jess scrunches her face as she analyzes me, still in my gray trousers and white shirt after a long day in the office. "What about camping? Aren't you heading off to the beach tomorrow?"

They know I love camping. Audrey loathed it and would never come. Couldn't take the piano in the tent. I was forever trying to nudge her out of that particular comfort zone and into a future in which we might one day ditch our jobs, hitch a trailer, and just *go*. She'd never have done it, but I'm always sad we missed the chance.

Jess, April, and Clair are sparkly-eyed and high on the romance of the idea. "Starry nights, campfires, moonlit walks on the beach!" Clair gushes.

Mosquitoes, sunburn . . . I imagine Audrey arguing.

"Put 'camping' down," I suggest reluctantly.

36

Audrey

With my insurance papers stuffed into my shirt, I rush through the rain and knock on the RV's metal door.

"It's open!" he calls, and I reach for the handle and hoist myself into another realm. The trailer is palatial. Cinema seating, ducted heating, mood lighting, surround sound. Premium everything. And it's *so warm*.

I think of the stash of adhesive toe warmers in my car and the solar-operated lantern from Kmart, just as my eyes are drawn to the kitchen counter, upon which sits a bottle of wine in a metal ice bucket and two long-stemmed glasses.

My heart gallops. Blood vessels alert. *Still.*

Condensation clings to the bucket where ice meets heat, and the olive-green glass of the bottle beckons me into a habitual free fall. Once again, I step back from the edge. Breathing. Mantras. The distraction, in this case, of an immensely attractive man . . .

Whatever he thinks he's doing with this come-hither little tableau, it's not happening. I pull the paperwork from my top and serve it to him, officiously, to make the point that I have signed up for the business transaction. Not the seduction experience.

"Take a seat?" he suggests, examining me more closely in

the proper light, while I try to resist the apology slipping from the tip of my tongue about the first impression I must be making.

"Thanks for the offer, but I won't stay," I explain, waving at the wine. "Not that the idea isn't enticing after the day I've had." I don't know what my sober mouth thinks it's talking about.

He glances at the ice bucket and back at me, thoughtfully.

"I wasn't driving under the influence, if that's what you're imagining," I blurt out. I have done many regrettable things around alcohol, but never that.

"Actually, I've got someone coming over shortly," he explains, gently detangling my awkward assumption, onto which I seem to have piled an unnecessary suggestion that I committed a crime. He rakes a hand through freshly washed dark hair, and only now do I note the change of clothes. The different jeans. The dry shirt. The scent of cedarwood cologne and the sound of water still dripping in the shower cubicle, which, in my defense, he invited me to use just minutes ago.

"Anyway, what's the next step?" I ask him, summoning my inner Mr. Drucker.

"I thought you were the admin genius?"

I seem to have overstated my prowess. "This is my first car accident," I say, truthfully.

Looking as though he finds this fact very difficult to swallow, he flicks through my insurance policy. "Okay, Hepburn," he says, although my resemblance to *that* Audrey is unfortunately nil. "We need to swap details and call our insurers." He slides his own papers across the table with an impressively tattooed hand and says, "I'm Beau."

As in French for "handsome"? And "boyfriend." It's a softer name than I'd expected for such a rugged-looking specimen of a man, and I'm lecturing myself to drop this bilingual nonsense and pull myself together, when he passes me his phone and says, "Mind if we swap numbers in case there's anything to discuss?"

Of course! I rammed his car and owe him thousands in insurance money. He probably thinks I'm a flight risk! "Should we cut our thumbs and make a blood oath?" I joke.

He looks at me, horrified. "I don't think it's necessary for us to exchange bodily fluids, Audrey. Do you?"

Try as I might, I *cannot* stem the blush that rises furiously to my cheeks. Thankfully I'm saved by a knock at his door, followed by the swanning in of a woman in a slip of material that looks like it cost $400, her wet skin glistening as she shakes rainwater off long platinum hair like an Afghan hound.

I don't know about Beau, but I'm mesmerized. She beams at him before she clocks me and my rescue-dog-from-the-pound aesthetic and says, "Sorry, did I mix up the time?"

Are we on some sort of roster? My head goes into a full-blown David Attenborough narration as the woman glides past me, scented like a field of wildflowers, plants a soft kiss on Beau's cheek, and then wipes lipstick from his face afterward with a perfectly manicured thumb.

The amenities block is out of order, I want to point out. *This top hasn't been washed, and the other was saturated after I crashed into Beau's truck.* Thankfully I say none of that and just stand here looking starstruck.

"I'm Harlow," she says, in an appropriately silken voice, taking my unexpected presence in stride. I've gone all ungainly in her presence, as if I can't work out how to stand.

"Audrey parked next door," Beau explains. *Is this the most interesting observation he can muster?* I'd almost rather the embarrassment of the full dramatic story. I wait for him to deliver a punch line about my parking, but he doesn't.

Perhaps he's saving it for later, when they unpack the scenario in bed. *It was pouring. She was in those ridiculous yellow Wellingtons, blaring Cynthia Erivo* . . . Although, surely they have better things to whisper about across their pillows than my footwear.

"Well! You seem to have everything in hand here," I tell them. I've gone full site-supervisor-wrapping-up-a-visiting-inspection. "Beau, I'll make that call in the morning. And thanks for, you know—" I can't articulate the list—we'd be here all night.

He waves his hand as if it's a mere trifle that he didn't explode at my wanton destruction. His guest lifts the bottle from the ice and de-corks the wine with the skill of a sommelier, the pop firing an explosion of full-body muscle memory straight through my body.

This is not her first rodeo in the lair, I can tell. It's also my signal to leave.

Extricating myself from their love nest, I trudge into the wet night, back to my leaky car and decades-old little camper, sans ambient light and music and heat and the kind of heady testosterone that I didn't know I missed so much. *Heady testosterone.* Not a term paired with my beautiful, gentle Fraser, as a rule. Not by people who knew him only as a quiet academic. Behind closed doors, though, when it was just the two of us . . . *that man and all the ways he knew me!*

I'd imagined this moment for ages: my first night on the road. I'd envisaged a campfire under the stars and fairy lights in the window. I was meant to see out my old life—the last day of my thirties—and usher in my fortieth outside my comfort zone, with some sort of sunset clearing ritual. Burning what I want to let go. Journaling dreams. Opening my heart.

But instead I head a little way up the park and into the

shrubs with a toilet paper roll, then tramp back, lock myself in the camper, and use my phone's flashlight to find something dry and warm to sleep in.

The light goes out before I can. Battery drained. So all I can do is feel my way into the bed, pull the blankets up around me, and listen to the rain on the tin roof, deciding tomorrow will be easier. Sunnier. Less accident-prone.

This whole decade will be better. It has to be.

I'm not sure what wakes me first: the squawking magpies or the smell of bacon and eggs sizzling outside my window. Wrapping myself in a blanket, I open the door to see my neighbor illuminated by crisp sunlight, tongs in hand.

"Happy birthday, Hepburn," he says as I emerge, sloth-like. He's in gray sweatpants, a thin black hoodie pushed up to the elbows, showcasing the tattoo of an incomplete nautical compass on his forearm.

What's that about, then? The thrill of the unknown?

He mistakes the concentration on my face as confusion. "Your birth date's on the insurance papers," he says. "Couldn't help but notice it's a significant one."

I hadn't expected this attention. Color rushes to my cheeks as I wonder, fleetingly, if I'm older or younger than Beau. Older, I'm sure. And then I realize, with a jolt, that I'm also older than Fraser ever was. He hadn't made it to forty. My heart plummets at the idea of overtaking him, as if he's taken a tumble in a race and I haven't stopped to help him up because then we'll both lose . . .

The sight of this stranger standing here, frying up a full English on the first milestone birthday I've been dreading without Fraser, leaves me breathless and prickly hot. I throw off the blanket, and it bunches around my legs as I kick it back into the camper and step barefoot onto cooling grass, damp with dew.

"You okay?" Beau asks, turning the sausages. "You're not vegetarian?"

I don't even know where to begin or how to explain the swirl of emotions here, but whether or not I consume meat is the very least of our challenges.

"Is this all for me?" I glance at the eggs and mushrooms, then up at his RV, expecting the Hound to bound out of it any second, fresh-faced and resplendent with beachy bed hair, shrouded in afterglow.

"Depends how hungry you are," he replies, nodding at the trailer and adding, "Harlow didn't stay."

"Ah." I try to decode that statement and how, if at all, it applies to me personally, while engineering an air of casual disinterest, as if the idea of the two of them rolling around on his premium foam mattress, discussing my galoshes, had never occurred to me, just as a council truck rumbles into the park and stops near the shower block. Two workers in high-vis vests amble out of it and promptly go on a smoke break.

"Listen, why don't you grab a shower in my RV while I cook?" Beau suggests, frowning at their lack of urgency. "There's fresh coffee ready to go in the machine. Just hit the start button."

My eyes drift from the mud that is still caked on my ankles to the scrapes of white paint on his truck. In broad daylight, the damage makes my stomach churn, and I walk over and inspect the back of Miss Bennet, who fared even worse.

"Don't worry about that," he says, waving the tongs at the dents. "I reckon I can fix it. You won't even notice."

"I must say this is all . . . very good of you," I admit. Either it's good of him or he's grooming me for one of the many spurious outcomes on my sister's comprehensive list of ways that I could die during this "midlife camping crisis." Although, if that was his plan, why would he have texted a photo of his driver's license late last night, which I expeditiously forwarded to Sara, as instructed, *In case I need to show the police, Audrey.*

"It's really not that bad," he says, nodding at the truck. "As long as nobody gets hurt."

Fraser used to say that. And then he got hurt, while my own pain snowballed into eight months of whiteout shock. A tumbling, alcohol-fueled, antigravity avalanche through which I could barely see nor stand until it cleared into the white-hot precision pain of sobriety. No more smoke or mirrors. Unadulterated agony, from which it has taken nearly two and a half years to painstakingly claw myself here.

That's what this trip is all about. Feeling something *good.* Breaking the inertia and making progress in this plot twist of a life I've been handed.

"Do you mind if I charge my phone?" I ask, wishing I'd charged the solar power pack before I left home. Maybe I'll take up the offer of a few minutes locked inside Beau's mansion of an RV to get my head together. "I left my sister hanging last night, and she thinks you're a murderer."

His rich laugh sails across the camping ground as I retreat to collect my things. And myself. Sara would see breakfast with this man as the equivalent of my teenage cliff-diving. She's spent forty years exactly today dragging me to solid ground, pulling me from rocks and rips—forever alert to undercurrents I always ignore. When I first mentioned his *Ocean scientist, Likes penguins* sign-off, she took one look at my face and warned me about the "dangerous sparkle" in my eyes. My greatest worry now is that she'll never have to concern herself with that sparkle again.

Beau is heaping shredded potato onto the barbecue when I reemerge. I don't tell him I skipped dinner in all the kerfuffle last night, but I steal a strip of cooked bacon on my way past, making my vigorous appetite evident.

Once I'm under the hot water, availing myself of his ocean-scented shower gel and inhaling the steam, I'm overcome by a wild sense of wonder.

How did I get here?

Here, in this strange man's trailer, on the morning of my fortieth birthday, when I should be with Fraser, who would be showering *with* me until the water ran cold.

Birthdays mess with my head. They convince me the butterfly effect is real—that every tiny step we've ever taken, every decision we've made, every conversation we've ever had, has brought us to this specific moment in time.

That line of thought inevitably leads me straight back to the day I lost him. And *how* I lost him. Wondering—if either of us had flapped our proverbial wings just a fraction of a second earlier or later, if we'd uttered one more word, or even taken a slightly longer breath—whether everything might have been different . . .

37

Fraser

“Is there Wi-Fi?” Parker whines as I turn into the secluded Pretty Beach campground on Friday morning. “It’s saying I don’t have service. Have you got service, Dad? *DAD.* I’ll lose my streaks!”

I’ll lose my mind.

Her panic makes me want to ban screens altogether, but I can never seem to follow through. I’ve allowed far more time online than Audrey would have, a fact that has me wrestling with the intrusive thought, *She’d have done this better than me.* There were never enough hours to implement all the offline activities on Audrey’s list. After she died and the ideas dropped off, I’m sad to say I let the internet step admirably into the breach—something I’m paying for now.

The campground is quiet. Plumbing issues, according to the sign at the entrance, although the council truck is here. I park and drag out the canvas tent bag, dumping it on wet grass. Parker takes the mallet and bag of pegs and sets her phone on the ground, where it strives for TikTok like one of NASA’s deep-space tracking dishes in the hills beyond Canberra, searching for intelligent life. Occasionally she bangs a peg with the mallet, between obsessively refreshing the screen.

“Just don’t hammer the phone,” I say, the pun flying directly over her head.

The guy opposite our site gets it and chuckles. He's cooking breakfast beside one of those enormous state-of-the-art travel trailers. Parker fires up the portable speaker and starts blasting *The Life of a Showgirl* into the unwilling ears of everyone on the South Coast. "Headphones!" I yell over the music, switching the speaker off as I wave at our neighbor. "Sorry!"

"Personal best!" she yells a few minutes later, high-fiving me. Despite distractions, we've set up the tent in record time, and I want to file this moment and remember it in three years when she's sixteen and being dragged from weekend parties for an offline camping trip with Dad that will "ruin her life."

I play these mind games, envisioning the future, positioning it on the timeline I described the night I proposed.

We're on a date in this Italian restaurant, and we've been married fifty years.

I shouldn't have been so optimistic. We wouldn't have fifty years. We wouldn't even make the wedding. But even now, in a coastal campground she never would have agreed to visit, I feel the whisper of Audrey's energy. We were so close, I'm convinced there are moments, like this, when time implodes, stardust glitters, and her particles dance back to life in the fireworks of our existence.

"Dad, are we done? Can I explore?" Parker asks, snapping me from a cascade of memories and back to the wet grass, broken amenities, and lack of service.

"Just stay inside the campground, okay? Don't go on the beach."

The same comforting thought that keeps Audrey alive in my mind taunts me with an imagined future where bad things happen again. What if it's just an illusion of free will, as Audrey suggested? What if the scripts of our lives are set and we're actors running prepared lines that feel improvised but aren't, because everything that's going to happen already has? It's thoughts like this that make the endless battle to balance risk and safety with a teenager feel even more fraught, and I'm dreading the push and pull, the older she gets and the more I need to let her go.

I watch my once-inquisitive child wander across the grounds, oblivious to a kangaroo and her joey, who observe her from the mist in the nearby bushland. She holds the phone aloft in a fruitless search for a rogue bar of service, and I lament the future direction of human evolution. Staying offline this weekend is fine by me. Somehow, probably just to appease Audrey's friends, I got the guts to publish a vastly edited version of the pile of insufferable cringe that the literature think tank concocted last night in my living room. It was a dating profile brought to the single women of the internet by best intentions and Brown Brothers vintage 2022. And now I can't bear to look at the app.

"You've got a happy camper there," our neighbor says as he turns sausages on the hot plate. Tattooed, with dark stubble on his square jaw, he looks like a walking advertisement for the Shoalhaven coastline.

"You didn't hear the angst over the internet on the way in."

He laughs and I walk over and shake hands. "I'm Fraser."

"Beau."

"Impressive tourer," I say, nodding at his trailer.

He glances at it, then slides a spatula under some hash browns. "Home for a few weeks while I'm based here for a project."

Something stirs in my chest. I used to have stints working away from home, too. It feels like another life, researching ocean currents in Antarctica, flung far from the routine of the university, deep in focus, doing work that made me feel alive. I would never say this to Parker—and if I had to choose, she would win—but as a single dad now bound to desk research and teaching, there are moments, usually when we've bickered about bedtime or homework or boundaries, that I pine a little for the freedom I exchanged for parenting.

"What sort of project bases you here?" I ask Beau as he moves around his elaborate outdoor kitchen with the relaxed confidence of a TV chef.

"Screenwriting."

He delivers this news nonchalantly, as if he'd answered *senior executive in the Australian Public Service*, which, two hours from the capital, is the more likely response.

Then he reaches for two plates and some cutlery and says, "I do a bit of directing. We've got a film shoot coming up on the coast."

Somehow, I think the Bookies would find this far more appealing than the data guy with the nonexistent lab coat. The absurd thought pops into my head that perhaps Beau and I are rivals on the apps. Next, I've cast imaginary women swiping left on the analyst with the phone-addicted teen. Right for the tattooed writer-director.

Will you get a grip, Fraser Miller! I imagine Audrey urging from some overlapping fold in time. *Don't undersell yourself! You were everything. Always. Right from that very first email exchange . . .*

38

Audrey

April drops a screenshot into the group chat, the ping waking me on my second morning of trailer life. It's some guy's dating profile.

He says, "I don't want kids but yours are fine." It stings a bit. Not the part about his not wanting kids. The fact that April is emphasizing it, as though not wanting children is the hill I'll die on.

I sit up and shove my feet into hot-pink Crocs. The council has removed the tape from across the shower block, and all is quiet on the Viper front, so I grab my toothbrush.

My bar is higher than doesn't want kids, I type while I walk. This new, deliberately transient life, disconnected from any expectation of my future direction, is all about running toward what feels good. Not away from things that don't.

That guy has been on the same app for three years, Clair replies, and I roll my eyes. I once did an experiment where I had a totally blank profile. No profile pic. Just my age and a fifty-kilometer radius from Canberra. He sent me a message and said how fascinating he found me.

Ha!

But you are fascinating, Rachael assures Clair as I set my toiletries down on the counter in the shower block.

Yeah, in that I am a woman with a pulse and it wouldn't take a full tank of fuel to meet up with me.

I squeeze some toothpaste, pausing to type, If you must know, I met a guy Thursday night. Obviously, I didn't *meet* Beau in quite the way I'm implying, but that doesn't mean I can't borrow a little from the truth to get my friends to ease off. The chat evolves immediately into a video call, and I'm staring at four shocked faces as they watch me brush my teeth.

"What do you mean you met someone!" Jess almost screeches. I rapidly reduce the volume on my phone and spit the toothpaste into the basin. *Is it really that astonishing?*

"What if he's roaming about outside the toilets, listening?" I whisper loudly. "Although, if he's roaming outside campground toilets, that would be very weird. Possibly borderline criminal—"

"It's just typical of you to meet someone and immediately cast him as a criminal, Audrey!" Rach says.

"He's criminally attractive, if that helps?"

Clair's eyes are wide as saucers. "But *how* did you meet him?"

I don't know why they sound so shocked. "Oh, you know. The usual way?" I brush my hair and pull it into a ponytail. "I caused thousands of dollars' worth of damage to his property, then he cooked me birthday sausages."

"Is that some euphemism the cool kids are using?" April knows full well I do not now nor have I ever belonged to that demographic.

"Anyway, I'm pretty sure he's in some sort of thing with a model named Harlow."

The quartet stares at me, then says, in perfect unison, "A *model*?"

"Yes, a model. Is it so hard to believe a criminally attractive man with a model girlfriend would have cooked me breakfast?" There's silence. "Don't answer that. Of course he noticed me. My camper and his truck became one flesh—"

We're interrupted by Rach's baby, Jasper, who has no sense of dramatic timing, crying from his crib. "Do not say another word!" she demands as she pops to the next room and fetches him, scrambling to unhook her maternity bra and latch him on so we can return to the business at hand. "This baby never *sleeps*!"

"Aw, he needs the aunties there!" I declare. My past self would be astonished to know I am self-appointed auntie-in-chief. Being Rach's birthing partner, and missing Parker so much, something shifted in my opinion of other people's babies. Perhaps it's inevitable when your best friend becomes a sole parent via IVF and you spend enough time in a rocking chair at two or three in the morning, just you, the baby, and your thoughts.

"Is this her?" April drops another screenshot into the chat. I know she's good at online sleuthing, but this must be some sort of record. There is Harlow's arty black-and-white headshot, platinum hair falling over her shoulders in long, gentle waves, big eyes staring down the barrel of the camera, slight curl to the lips. Professional, beautiful, yet still perfectly attainable for someone like Beau.

"That's her! The Viper's evening guest. To be honest, she's even more glamorous when she's damp—"

"You met the boyfriend of *Harlow Sinclair*?" April follows up, chestnut eyes sparkling. She is off and away with this whole state of affairs.

"Who is the Viper?" Jess asks.

"Who is Harlow Sinclair? What's she famous for?" I can't keep up with my own rapidly developing situation.

"She's not just a model! She's a film star! She's in an upcoming movie they're shooting in Tathra!"

"How do you know all this, April?" I don't know why I'm so surprised. She's connected to all of Instagram, somehow.

"How do you *not* know? Her rumored relationship with that hot screenwriter is all over the internet! You know the one. He was a writer on that buzzy, Oscar-nominated movie last year. Historical film. What was it?"

I have no idea what she's going on about, except the bit about the screenwriter being hot—a rumor I am fully qualified to corroborate. I wish I'd never mentioned it, though, and that I'd paid as much attention to his insurance papers as he had paid to mine, because I barely know a thing about him.

I zip my toiletries bag and exit the block, only to find the man himself walking toward me in nothing but a pair of black running shorts, towel slung over one shoulder, tattooed chest glistening in the early-morning sunlight. I can't tell if he's glistening from sweat, salt water, or the powers of my overactive imagination, but exactly how we arrived here is irrelevant. The impact is glorious.

"Audrey! Tell us you didn't meet *Beau Davenport*?" April practically shouts from my phone. I might as well have tethered it to a high-voltage speaker and blasted it through the entire campsite.

"I have to go!" I tell them, but what I really mean is I have to expire, instantly, from mortification. There is no way he didn't overhear his name. All I can do is stand here helplessly as he dries his dark hair and rubs the towel across his chest under what seems to be my intense micromanagement.

"I haven't been googling you," I blurt out, even though he hasn't asked. *No, it's worse. My friends and I have been gossiping about you in the toilets like we're in Year Nine.*

He laughs. "That's a relief. Google is not kind."

I'll be the judge of that once April sends the dossier she'll be preparing forensically as we speak.

"I was actually just using you as an excuse to stop my friends from matchmaking," I explain. It sounded more sensible in my head. "They sent me some man's profile this morning, and he looks like a cannibal."

Whatever Beau expected to come out of my mouth, it clearly wasn't either of these points.

"Met many cannibals?"

"He likes war games. You know, with the figurines?"

He checks that his smart watch has logged his exercise and says, "Good to know I rate higher than a war-gaming cannibal."

He has misunderstood. He is not being rated. He's not even in the running! And I am not throwing myself at him, despite appearances. If I was really looking, it would be for someone without the capacity to drag me into the social pages, where I'd only flounder from one faux pas to the next, garbled interviews and wardrobe malfunctions propelling us toward the inevitable public breakup, because I'm just not cut out for the spotlight.

"My friend April tells me you're a screenwriter?" I'm going to kill her. She knows I can't stay silent with such fascinating information.

He's bent over, drying his legs now, allowing me to study the muscles rippling across his bare back as if I am cramming for an anatomy exam. When he straightens and flicks the towel over his shoulder, he says, "I'm sorry, do I know April?"

How to explain her?

Before I can answer, he motions toward our vans. "Hepburn, do you want to grab a coffee in town? Breakfast, maybe?"

Is this? . . . Is he asking me on a date? No, don't be comical, Audrey! The man probably has his own IMDb page.

"I've got writer's block and a deadline," he admits, with a quick glance at my pajamas and Crocs, then back to my face, which I'm beginning to wish had something applied to it other than SPF 50 and a startled expression. "And there's something about you . . ."

39

Fraser

“Come on, Parks,” I say, shaking the tent from the outside. “The day’s getting away from us!”

There’s a muffled “Leave me alone, bro” that heralds our official arrival at the Teenage Years.

I zip open the tent door. “Do you want breakfast?”

She rolls over. “Dad, I don’t feel good.” She’s lying on the air mattress, half in and half out of her sleeping bag, in the fetal position, clutching her stomach.

“Are you going to be sick?”

“No, it just hurts.”

“What sort of hurt?”

“I’m literally *dying*.”

“You’re figuratively dying. Is it a sharp pain on the lower-right side?”

Please say no! I really don’t want to be contending with a burst appendix in a tent.

“Stop asking,” she says, groaning as she sits up. She’s very pale. I put my hand to her forehead. No temperature.

She staggers up, shoving her feet into a pair of sneakers, and heads to the amenities block while I run through a mental checklist of everything she’s eaten in the last twenty-four hours. She’s gone a long while. Finally I head over, too, hover near the door, and call out, “Parks? You okay in there?”

"No-o."

Her voice is teary now, and small. Eventually she comes back out but won't look at me. In fact, she just stands there, arms crossed, looking totally lost.

"Did you pack the things?" she asks.

It takes me a moment to catch on. "Oh, God. Parker. I'm sorry. I didn't." She folds over, stricken, and I don't let her see how it guts me. *Audrey wouldn't have let this happen!*

"It's going to be absolutely fine," I reassure her. "I'll head to the supermarket."

She looks like she has no idea how to handle this in the interim.

"Fold up some toilet paper," I advise.

"I have!" She rolls her eyes.

"Do you want me to call Mum?"

She shakes her head, trying not to cry, allowing me to pull her into a hug, during which I seem to revisit every single age she's ever been and all the ages she will be. This milestone is evidence that time thunders forward, whether we're ready or not. "I miss Audrey," she says into my chest, rendering this into one of *those* moments, where grief attaches itself to the cells of a normal experience like a virus, because the person *should be here*—the situation only magnifying their absence.

"I miss her, too," I admit, heart lurching. "I'm sorry she's not here to help."

"I feel like I'll turn around and she'll be standing there," she says quietly. "I literally just felt like that in there." She motions toward the shower block.

Of course Audrey would be there for this.

"Don't tell my colleagues"—I squeeze her tight and say this more softly—"but I think the best thing we can do is allow ourselves to be comforted by that feeling, even if science can't explain it."

My brain won't compute this phenomenon at all—that sudden, strong sense of someone's presence. I've been tempted to discuss it with the neuroscientists at work but haven't been brave enough. I need to keep my job! Surely there's some logical, scientific explanation involving our desperate hope for connection or our clutching denial. That desire to believe they never leave us, even years later, because a part of us won't ever accept they're really gone.

"Listen, why don't I leave you with my phone, since I've got a signal. You can stay in the tent, relax on TikTok. I'll pop to the shops and be back in twenty minutes with everything you need. Including chocolate. How does that sound?"

When I'm back with an armful of options, I can hear Parker in the tent laughing. I fling open the door like Superman throwing his cape over his shoulder and ceremoniously toss the items I've foraged onto the air mattress.

"Pads," I announce. "Tampons. Liners. Overnight pads with wings. Period undies. Period cup, some sort of wipes, some kind of deodorant, this special wash stuff, naproxen, hot-water bottle, heat patches, milk chocolate, hazelnut chocolate, caramel chocolate . . ."

"Wow, Parker!" *Is that Rachael's voice coming from my phone?* "If it isn't Menstruation Man returned from a triumphant quest!"

Parker bursts into fits of laughter. "Dad, how many uteruses do you think I have?"

"Is that Rach?"

"Yes, I called her. She's coming to visit!"

Here?

I take the phone out of her hands. Sure enough, Rach lights

up the screen, luxuriating in bed in her Canberra apartment, sun streaming through the window, long blond hair splayed across the pillow. She doesn't look like she's in a rush to go anywhere.

"What's going on?" I ask her, backing out of the tent. "Hang on. Parks—do you need Rach for any of this, or are you all right?"

"I'm fine," she says. *She's fine.* My child—getting on with the business of being *grown up*, suddenly.

I carry the phone over to a picnic table. "Sorry she called you so early."

"Are you kidding? I'm thrilled she did. It's a big thing. And she misses Audrey." There's a moment of silence, the way there often is when one of us mentions her. We don't pause deliberately. We're not lowering the flags to half-mast and going all ceremonial on ourselves. The sound of her name just catches us off guard sometimes, even when it comes from our own lips, and snowplows the day sideways a little.

Parker emerges from the tent, selected products from my haul bundled into the towel she's hugging to her chest. I salute her as she walks past, as if farewelling her to the front, and Rachael smiles.

"By the way, Dad," Parker calls. "Your phone was going *off* with Bumble notifications. Gross!"

Oh, God. I forgot about that.

"This one woman messaged you three times! And then Uncle Josh called. He wants to visit me at my summer music school."

"But he's in New York."

"He said he's coming home for something important."

My muscles brace as if he's already here, my body preparing to spend his visit avoiding conflict.

"Look, Frase, if it's okay with you, I thought I'd book a room tonight in a motel near the campground," Rachael says, drawing my attention back to the phone in my hand. "Spend the weekend with Parks? Also, I've got some news I want to discuss with you."

"Are you *really* on Bumble?" Parker calls, still backing away toward the showers.

"What news?" I ask Rach.

"Like, dating *actual women*?"

Speaking of actual women, Rachael rolls onto her side in the white tank top she's slept in, head propped in her hand, bed hair tumbling across her face. *Fuck, is she going for dating wingwoman or contestant?*

"Because, Dad, if you want to meet someone," Parker shouts back, dragging my attention away from the phone, an increasingly difficult challenge, "it's okay with us!"

Us?

I look back at Rachael as she swings her legs over the side of the bed and sits up. "She and I had a long chat, the executive summary of which is that we agreed it's time for you to move forward. I told her I want you to be happy."

40

Audrey

It's like being in the school cafeteria with the popular boy. I'm pretty certain the café's teenage employee is just as clueless as I am about who Beau is exactly, but he's got the presence of being *someone*, and she is blushing furiously just taking his coffee order.

"S-Sorry, was that one or two shots?" she asks him, flustered. "I know you already said—"

"No trouble at all," he reassures her, with patience that seems off-script for the model-dating, Oscar-nominated, social-pages-inhabiting big deal of a person I've built up in my mind. "Two shots, thanks. Didn't sleep well."

She notes this down and underlines it as he returns his attention to me. *Am I the cause of his lack of sleep?*

"Writer's block," he reminds me. Of course! What am I doing, casting *myself* as the cause of his insomnia?

"What are you stuck on, exactly?" I've stepped into my professional self, as if I'm his script adviser and this is an emergency meeting to help shape his narrative arc.

"This is going to sound worse than it is," he begins, and I find myself leaning forward, glued to his incoming confession. He pauses and smiles, skin crinkling around his eyes behind his sunglasses, as he says, "Should I wait while you get out a tape recorder?"

I sit back, bolt upright. "Sorry!" I blurt. "I'm just . . . also in a creative industry." It's a gross exaggeration, but "professional empathy" is a better excuse than unbridled nosiness.

"A creative industry that relies heavily on spreadsheets?"

Oh, lord, I need to steer this back to him and why he's stuck, in case he asks me for evidence of career success I can't produce.

"Tell you my story later," I promise, wondering exactly what I'm intending to share, and buying the time to invent it.

He exhales like an athlete calming his nerves at the start of a sprint. "So there was a woman . . ."

Of course there was. I all but bang my fist on the table like a gavel, case closed.

"Let's just say I allowed *write what you know* to get out of hand. It was fine while things were going well, but then we fell apart, she got lawyers involved, the project crashed, and to cut a very long, very fraught, very expensive story short, I need to come up with an entirely new character for the female lead in my movie in the next seven days or my reputation in the industry will be shot."

He breathes again, trapped words exorcised.

"I see," I say. I very much don't see, and need much more information, but at this point I am most definitely riveted.

"I told you mine. Now you tell me yours," he challenges me, his penetrating dark blue eyes fixed on mine, as if we're at a press conference and there will be no further comment about his situation.

"Do you have any ideas?" I barge on with the tenacity of a good journalist, ignoring his demand. "Anything at all? Seven days seems impossible!"

The coffee appears, and he stares at it the way a fortune teller might focus on a cup, as if he's trying to divine a fresh plotline from the swirls of froth. Steam curls gently into the strong lines of his face, and the whole visage just *smolders.* If I'm not careful, I will slip into some sort of hypnosis . . .

"Nothing that's working," he admits. He looks up from his coffee with a disarming level of vulnerability for someone with his track record of success. It sends me into a momentary panic. *If it's this hard for him at this advanced point in his career, then when, if ever, does it get easier?*

"In my case, it feels even worse than writer's block," I begin, his candor breaking me open. "Not that I'm trivializing what you're going through—gosh, it sounds like *hell.* I just mean, oh, God. This is such a complicated story . . ."

Now it's him leaning forward, arms crossed on the table, intense gaze inviting me to gift him the part of my history that I rarely disclose. *Could he really be this interested?* I sense the story bubbling to the surface and rushing toward him in a burst of uncharacteristic frankness.

"Something bad happened to me early in my career. A professor did something to me—"

I falter, the way I always falter telling this tale, and Beau reaches across the table. I try not to allow it to thrill me as much as it clearly does when he places both his hands over mine, his grasp warm and firm and certain, while I instruct myself not to get carried away, because he's literally just explained that he's heartbroken.

"Sorry, Audrey. I didn't mean to intrude . . . You don't have to tell me unless you want to."

Oh, I want to. "It's not the way it sounds. He took something from me, but it wasn't . . . that."

He looks relieved, lets go of my hands, eases back, and slowly stirs his coffee, the metal spoon tinkling against the ceramic cup, steam still rising cinematically in the morning sunlight.

"You're really not a viper at all, are you?" I say before I can stop myself.

He laughs. "Not that I'm aware of."

"Your trailer. Outback Viper?"

He shrugs. "Oh, it's not mine. The production company rented it so I could, quote, 'sort out my shit.' They thought I'd have a clearer head here than in my Sydney high-rise." He glances at me. "Fewer distractions."

Now I'm picturing him and a parade of alluring A-listers on some plush designer lounge, city lights twinkling across the harbor through floor-to-ceiling windows. It's not my world. Not anywhere near it. Perhaps that's why it's so easy to open up? Because there's a part of this that doesn't feel real.

"What did the professor take from you?" he asks, serious eyes considering me through dark lashes.

"He was one of those charismatic lecturers. Fortyish, attractive, clever. He had all the students in his thrall, including me. You know the type?"

He *is* the type. Look at the easy way he's extracting my secrets—information that, apart from Fraser and Rach and Sara, I've kept from my closest friends. I haven't talked about this for so long, and it's not how it started that makes it so difficult. It's how it ended. And when. And I don't care how many tricks he tries to entrance me with—I'm not prepared to tell him about the day Fraser died. Not on day two.

"It was that edgy rock-star vibe, you know? Except he wasn't a rock musician. He was one of the most respected classical composers in the country. Still is. And my composition teacher."

"What was your degree?"

"This was during my doctorate."

"Wow, so it's Dr. Sullivan, is it?"

Academic failure rises up my esophagus like bile, and I look at him and want to run from this. "You're not going to put this in one of your screenplays, are you?" I say, suddenly overcome with my usual problem: I don't trust people.

He crosses his heart and holds my gaze steady. I haven't seen anyone do that since the primary school playground, and it's extraordinarily attractive on a grown screenwriter as he sits across from you, in absolutely no hurry, while you gather your skeletons.

"Anyway, after this incident—let's call it academic thievery—I lost my confidence. He stole my intellectual property. My faith in people. And in myself." I'm awkward now. "Sorry, this sounds so dramatic—"

"No, it doesn't," Beau says, quickly. "We pour so much of ourselves into what we make. If someone stole even a line or two from me, I'd be furious. I'd storm in and steal it right back!"

Joshua energy. Pre-betrayal. I'm momentarily thrown.

"What happened then?"

"I gave up for a while . . ." *A decade, give or take.* "I was twenty-two. He convinced me I wasn't talented enough to have written what I did. Turned the whole thing around in meticulous detail and accused *me* of stealing ideas from him. He told me a creative path was too hard. And that I was too thin-skinned to cope with the knocks. He planted so much doubt and made me so scared of the ramifications for my career that he effectively silenced me. I thought I was going crazy."

"Classic professional gaslighting."

I don't tell him the worst bit. That it wasn't a spontaneous response from Ridges. It had been calculated. He'd prepared for days. And the reason he even had that opportunity was because I had been double-crossed by the one friend who could have truly backed me up. The one who'd been there in the room when I wrote the piece, watching as the notes fell out of my head. And who'd said they were brilliant.

"I'm afraid to say that he only stole one piece of work, and I allowed it all to snowball in my mind until I might as well have given him everything. All the unwritten music. All the power. I walked away from him. And from classical music . . ."

"And from yourself?" he asks, after a pause.

I look straight at him. "I completely lost my way."

Lost my way? Is this my new euphemism for what happened when the plagiarism kick-started a nightmare that blew up everything? It did more than silence the music. The timing of my eventual response took Fraser down with it. And then it all but destroyed me.

"Lost your way and turned up here," he says. "With musical theater blaring in your car. You said you're writing a show?"

I might as well put everything out on the table. "That's not going well, either . . ."

He laughs. "What a pair! Why do we torture ourselves? Maybe we should get reliable jobs, where we don't—"

"No," I interrupt, quite forcefully. "I've done that. And as scary as all of this is, not trying this when you want to so badly is even harder."

We choose this. Nobody is standing over us, gun to head, forcing us to do this work while relentless questions swirl in an endless crisis of confidence: *Is this any good? Will anyone like it? Will their opinions crush it? Crush me? Am I making anyone care?*

"I'm forty," I go on. "The age my professor was when it happened. But so far behind."

He shrugs. "Pfft! Behind whom? Haven't you seen all those inspirational stories about late bloomers? What's your musical about?"

I've gone clammy, the way I always do when people ask. Because the answer is invariably much bigger than the simple question they think they've raised.

It's about being widowed. *Just say it.* But as soon as I even think about that, a montage of memories pushes forward, of all the times I've tried to break this news gently in the past. People physically reeling, as if assaulted by my situation. The awkward silences. All the platitudes when, desperate to ease the horrendous pressure hanging between us, they say the least helpful things of all.

At least he didn't suffer . . . At least it was quick, Audrey. That must be comforting?

Not having a chance to say goodbye? The ending of it all, just *instantly. Where's the comfort in that?*

Beau is watching me closely, waiting patiently for my brain to step through all of this and make my announcement.

"The working title is *Widowed: The Musical.*"

I stare him down, daring him to panic. Expecting him to pull out his wallet, place some cash on the table, and make an excuse to get away from this. Away from me and all my broken pieces.

You have to be strong to deal with the story of my life. Unflappable, once we face the inevitable *How did it happen?* And the even worse *How did you cope?* When I share those answers, it's like I'm stripping off my clothes, each awful piece of information exposing yet another layer, until there's nothing left but bare skin and open wounds and the gnawing guilt that I'll never shake, because what sort of person would I be if I forgave myself?

People can't be near the naked truth. What if the ice I'm standing on cracks, and they fall through, too? So I run the safer mantra: *I'm fine. It's fine. We're all fine.*

But it turns out I don't have to say any of that now, because Beau simply looks at me, calmly, still leaning forward, striking eyes compassionate and deeply engaged. There's no sign of flight. He isn't trying to reassemble me or distract me. He doesn't seem to know *we might fall.*

He simply says, "I'm sorry, Hepburn," in a tone that is warm and real and strong, accompanied by body language that suggests he is not going anywhere. "I really am. That's fucked."

41

Fraser

In the four hours that it's taken Rachael to pack her bags and drive here, I've thought of little else but the way she looked on that video call and the fact that she has news.

She was withdrawn with the Bookies the other night, and it's not like her to bolt to the beach on a whim. If she must experience the ocean, it's from the balcony of a five-star hotel. Rachael is pro-planning. She is anti-sand.

"Where's Parks?" she asks, fidgeting with an uncharacteristically messy blond bun, her car parked beside our tent in the campground. She's in blue jeans, a white T-shirt, and sneakers, which, on anyone else, would look like a normal weekend outfit, thrown on before running out the door. Rachael is not the run-out-the-door type. She's not even wearing earrings. The whole situation is an unsettling glitch in the matrix.

I nod toward the playground, where Parker has struck up a conversation with another kid. They've been in each other's pockets since breakfast, going back and forth on the swings, liberated from the shackles of online connection and back in the real world. With the morning's momentous developments, I'm glad to see the childish exuberance intact.

"Did you really come all this way just to see her?" I ask, hands in my pockets, body on edge.

She lifts up her sunglasses. Even then, I can't read her. "I remember the day I got my first period. I would not have wanted it to happen in a tent."

"You never want anything to happen in a tent," I argue. "But thank you."

"The long drive was probably good for me, too, Frase. I needed to clear my head."

Clear it of what?

"There's a café up the road?" Tea brewed over the campfire isn't going to cut it. She'll need a latte.

"Does Parker want to come?"

"I mean, if you want to debrief about your problems with a thirteen-year-old—"

She laughs. "They're not really *problems* . . . More of a crossroads."

No good can come from an announcement of a crossroads that couldn't wait until our regular Monday-night dinner back home.

Parker runs over when she sees Rachael, and throws herself into her arms for a long hug.

"You came!"

"I said I would! Might even go for a walk on the beach with you later!"

"But you hate beaches!" Parker's eyes are wide. She knows Rach as well as I do.

"Always willing to make an exception for you two." This is delivered with a pointed glance in my direction. *Are too many exceptions being made?* "Come with us to the café, Parks? Or do you want to stay with your friend?"

"Bring me a milkshake?"

As she runs off, Rachael and I start off on foot, sunlight filtered through towering eucalypts as we saunter along the road.

Her hand flies to my arm when she spots a pair of king parrots, red feathers glistening, and we stand still while she watches them and I watch her. Trying to shake a foreboding sense of unwanted, incoming change.

When we reach the wooden shack converted into a popular coffee spot, she orders her latte, but can't face food, apparently. *Another warning bell.* She puts her keys and her phone down on the empty third seat, and I watch the subtle shift in her expression. *Audrey should be sitting there.*

I have been so constantly aware of Audrey's glaring absence from this party of three, I seem to have missed our comfortable slide into a duo. The shape of us felt wrong without her. "You marry one of us, you marry both of us," they once joked. It was like having a live-in sister-in-law at times. No, not a sister-in-law exactly. Not any sort of sister, now that I'm really looking at Rachael.

The thought ignites but barely has time to lift off before she slams me with "Frase, you know I've been wanting a baby?"

Is that it? The baby thing. A million questions jostle in my head.

"I've booked an appointment with a fertility doctor," she barrels on.

Right. That Rachael wants a baby is not a surprise. Audrey had let it slip during one of our rolling conversations about her own decision on this front. I think she was checking that I hadn't descended into the resentment she always feared, despite the reassurance I always gave her.

"So you're really going to do this?" I ask now. It would make sense of a lot of things. Her having been withdrawn. The weird looks. The crossroads.

She's shaking with nerves.

"I'm forty," she says. "I'm almost out of time. Could already be out of it. I can't wait any longer for everything else to fall into place."

The *everything else* burrows under my skin like a fresh splinter.

Audrey and I once set up Rachael with a colleague of mine, Michael, a nuclear physicist—loves neatness and cats and galleries, hates being outside. He found her clever and interesting, and she said he was fascinating and kind. Everything had aligned, on paper. But she always found a way to call things off with a man before they became too serious.

"Do you need my help?" I say without thinking. *What am I even suggesting?*

She swallows a mouthful of latte, scalding herself, and splutters, "No, Fraser. That's not why I'm here."

The idea, just seconds old, is pierced now by a shard of disappointment. "Parenting is hard. We could make a good team?" *We already do. With Parker.*

She rolls her eyes. "You don't just jump into a lifelong parenting commitment with someone over a hot beverage."

"I'm not just *someone*!" The argument presents itself before I can stop it. "Am I?"

"I appreciate the offer, but I don't want to have your baby, my friend." She places her hand on my arm briefly. "It's cleaner this way."

Cleaner? I must look injured, because she adds, "It's nothing personal, Frase. You know I adore you. But I need a complete change."

My heart really kicks off now, more than it did at the idea of suddenly becoming a dad again. Something tells me the baby is just the beginning of whatever Rachael's working up to here.

"I had a chat with Parker about this on the phone this

morning. You two are doing okay now, aren't you?" She blows gently on her latte to cool it. And to avoid eye contact. "I mean, you don't need me around as much now. Not like the early days?"

I'm hit with a big serve of regret. "Have you been staying around for us? Have we been holding you back from something?"

She shakes her head. "No! It's not that. I just feel like you two have become my family. It's been amazing and wonderful, and I don't regret a moment of it, but spending so much time with you and Audrey, and then with you and Parker since she died, has become a bit of a . . . placeholder in my life."

My toasted sandwich is delivered but now sits unwanted on the plate as I try to calibrate her words. I understand the concept of the placeholder. I can see why she feels that way. *But hasn't this been so much more than that?*

I run a mental reel of it all. After we lost Audrey, Rachael swooped in to support us. Events we would have had to endure on our own, she endured with us. But hadn't that support shifted over time into a friendship that had grown in its own right? The kind of friendship that would have evolved naturally, even if Audrey had never been in the picture.

Looking at her across from me, earnestly discussing her next steps, I realize with a jolt that this woman is not in any way a "placeholder" for me. She is my closest person. She's the closest thing Parker has to a mother figure when she's with me—I mean, look what happened this morning with the period drama. The fact is, I'm searching for the right words to define exactly what Rachael McKenzie has become in our lives . . . In mine, in particular. And it's terrifying.

"I'm scared if I don't detach myself and chase my own little family, I might miss out altogether," she confesses.

Detach herself? Why does this feel like grief?

We'd wondered once before if our convenient little arrangement was soaking up opportunities for us both to meet other people. But we barely gave lip service to the problem. Neither of us made a single move to change anything. We were too comfortable. Perhaps we kept each other safe.

The same conversation now cuts straight through me. I try to imagine her with a family of her own. I can see her with children—I've always seen that and wanted it for her. And with some amorphous man who'd be their father . . . Though suddenly, the latter isn't settling so palatably.

"Are you going to eat that?" she asks, pointing at the sandwich. I shake my head, and she picks up a triangle and bites into it, steam escaping, cheese dripping, which she wipes from her mouth with the napkin I pass her on autopilot. *I thought she wasn't hungry?* Perhaps getting all of this off her chest is bringing back her appetite.

"I'm thinking of moving," she suddenly says.

"Cities?"

"Countries."

Am I being dragged out in a rip?

"Maybe Ireland?"

"Ireland?"

"You know, green fields, Guinness—"

Can't see it. "But you hate beer. You hate . . . fields."

And I hate the mental picture I now have of her and some brawny Irish poet, traipsing the moors until rain forces them into some cozy pub for a pint and a glass of red. She'd be all rosy-cheeked and *alive* . . .

The opposite of how she looks now, I realize. Trapped. Tired. Pale.

Have I done this to her?

"I have relatives in Ireland, Fraser. An elderly aunt, for starters . . ."

She's never mentioned Irish relations. "Is this the same elderly aunt related to my recalcitrant students? The one who keeps dying every time they have an overdue assignment?"

She laughs and pulls out her phone, scrolling through the photo app. "Here. Evidence. This is my great-aunt Aisling on my dad's side."

I take the phone and find myself staring at a gray-haired, wiry little woman with Rachael's blue eyes, swallowed by a floral-printed, doily-covered armchair. She looks about a hundred and fifty.

"The distance could be good for you, too, Frase," she suggests as I pass the phone back. And I know she is wrong.

Audrey would tell her to go. She'd fill out her passport application and research house swaps. She'd pack her bags and drive her to the airport, where she'd cling to her and cry and then push her into the queue for the security screening and tell her to have a wildly brilliant, exciting, *incredible life.*

Because that's what you do when you love someone, isn't it? You suck it up if they want to sever themselves from you and follow a different path. You prioritize their happiness above your own and kick your convenience to the curb because they mean so much to you that all you want is to see them fly.

When you love someone. When you really love them—

Shit.

"Frase? What do you think?"

You let them go.

42

Audrey

"Hepburn, I'm taking my writer's block on a road trip to one of my film settings today," Beau announces. "If you're not frantically busy"—he glances at the novel in my hand as evidence that I am not—"why don't you come with me?"

It's obvious I've been idling through the first weekend of my open-ended sabbatical. Having just woken up, I rack my brain for plausible reasons why getting in Beau Davenport's dented Ram and tearing up and down the highway is not going to work for me today. But I'm coming up short.

He's in jeans and a white sleeveless shirt, pegging his washed clothes on a line under his trailer's awning. The sleeveless shirt bunched at his waist, rises and falls as he pegs his clothes, revealing washboard abs that pull me smartly to full consciousness.

"Is this your completed OOTD?" I ask, pretend-yawning to disguise how fascinated I am.

"My what?"

"Outfit of the Day," I explain, translating the acronym and wondering how someone as cool as him wouldn't have already known it.

He sends me a Jonathan Bailey circa *Wicked* smolder and replies, "I'm sorry, does this offend you?"

Ha! My eyes help themselves to a rove over it, just for

accuracy's sake, before I shrug and stammer out, "Of course not. Wear whatever you like. And yes to the road trip, I guess. Why not gallivant who knows where with a perfect stranger?"

"Come on, we told each other our secrets yesterday," he reminds me, pulling off the sleeveless shirt and swapping it with a dry one from the line. "We're not *really* strangers anymore, are we?"

He told me he had writer's block and admitted to some scandal with an actress. I told him my show title, implying the love of my life died. Our secrets aren't equally weighted. "You can tell me more about your musical in the car," he adds, and I wonder if he means the show or the torturous story behind it.

"There's really not much to tell," I say. It's best to manage expectations, if we're talking shop. This is an Oscar-nominated screenwriter, according to April. You can't fudge the creative update, or he'd see right through it.

Nodding at the straps of my swimsuit under my top, he says, "Save the swim for Tathra? We can have lunch at the pub on the hill."

"You know, most people just go to grief counseling," he observes as we hit the highway and turn south. "You wrote a show."

I tap a quick message to Rach: "Heading south to Tathra with Beau. Will check in." As nice as he appears, *someone* should know my whereabouts.

"Obviously a musical wasn't my first thought," I say, tossing the phone into my bag. "It's not like I was hit with inspiration for lyrics in the hospital." Looking back, starting the show right there might have been healthier. "The night he died, my friends rescued me with wine and shots. I know Baileys is not the drink you think of in a crisis, but—"

"The effects are fast?"

Practically lethal in the quantities they dished up. Alcohol caused the propulsive eradication of thoughts I couldn't face. Of fresh memories I wanted to unsee. And that one last, unspoken goodbye, the lack of which haunts me to this day.

"What I really wanted to do . . . should have done . . . was sit at the piano. You'd get this, as a writer. Every thought had to be expelled through my fingers on the keyboard. The music I made that week! I've never been able to replicate the depth of it. It was as if I bent time."

He focuses on the road, giving me the floor.

"That group of friends isn't particularly musical. I think they thought I was properly losing it."

"No, the opposite," he says, getting it instantly. It's such a relief.

"Before Fraser died, I'd half composed a piece for his fortieth. The rest of it came out of me in a fully formed rush, after absolutely no sleep. I played it at his funeral. You know those times when you're completely in the zone and the creativity doesn't feel like it's coming from you, it's coming—"

"Through you."

Yes! It's been years since I've spoken to someone on this same wavelength; it's as disconcerting as it is hugely welcome. "There was something about that music, having straddled both his life and his death. It's the best thing I've ever done."

He turns the stereo off, easing back on the accelerator as if to prolong this journey and make more space for the conversation. "Do you ever wonder if what you're making already exists in the future?" he asks. "You're just pulling it into your present reality?"

This theory slots seamlessly with Fraser's; it almost feels as if Beau is delivering a message from him. I rub the goose bumps on my arms. But if the idea is true, that means there either is or isn't a whole body of music existing now in my future. I shiver at the notion that there might not be any, that I might stagger on like this forever and never really write again in a way that I'm proud of—the headline-making, knocking-it-out-of-the-park stuff I *know* I can do if I just reach for it again.

"Play it for me?" he says.

"Fraser's song?"

The request triggers a shock wave of stage fright.

"It's really not a road trip kind of thing." I can't taint it, having it play over the drum of the engine, while we pass semitrailers and gray nomads and road signs that say *Wrong Way Go Back* and *Road Works Speed Limits Enforced.*

"I had a complaint once from a neighbor. A note slipped under the door of my apartment after I'd been playing it on loop at top volume, sobbing. All I'd wanted to do was *roar* the music, bloodletting my agony through the notes. Do you know what I mean?"

His eyes are firmly fixed on the road as he nods.

"The note was in all caps," I tell him. "STOP THAT FUCKING RACKET."

Beau lifts his foot from the pedal instantly, as if he's been personally assaulted by my neighbor's ruthless insult. Next, he's swinging off the highway onto a side road covered in thick shrubs. He takes a sharp right, down a dirt track that the truck gobbles in a way that thrills my inner adrenaline junkie, but I've got Sara's voice in my head, concerned about our sudden change of direction. I clutch the door handle and say, "You're not a murderer after all, are you?"

"Trust me." He is focused on the bumpy four-wheel-drive track until eventually we arrive in a deserted dirt car park at a headland overlooking the ocean, the truck coming to a stop in a cloud of dust that clears over a breathtaking vista of endless blue. I imagine we can almost see all the way to New Zealand.

"How did you know this was here?" I ask, unclasping the seat belt's latch and leaning forward.

"Scouted every lookout up and down the coast for a film scene."

Ah, that's right.

"I don't mean to brag, Hepburn, but this vehicle has nineteen speakers."

He passes the auxiliary cable while the ocean crashes on the rocks beneath us and I look into his steady, patient gaze. I've never heard Fraser's piece outside my own living room and in the chapel at his funeral, or while playing it hundreds of times through headphones at a volume so loud it's probably damaged my hearing. I recorded two versions. The one I sent to Josh, drunk, the night I wrote it, and a more refined example for posterity, which I tried to record sober. The former has my heart.

My fingers shake as I plug in my phone and fumble to the private SoundCloud account, hovering over the play button while Beau waits patiently for me to summon the courage I need to share this. At the funeral, I was desperate for the tune to sink deep into everyone's heart so they'd get it: *Can you feel it? This is what he meant to me!*

Do I need Beau to understand that, too? To see how deeply I have loved. To know what I'm capable of in this department. Emotionally? Musically?

It's not just about Fraser. It's that half terror, half thrill of handing someone an example of what you can do and who you are as an artist.

He seems to take my uncertainty and instinctively understand that this would be easier if we weren't trapped inside a small space. He dials the volume to max on the stereo, opens his door, walks to the front of the truck, gives me a hint of a smile, then pushes himself up on the bonnet, swinging to face the ocean.

I stare at his broad back and shoulders through the windscreen. I don't even know this man, but without looking back at my phone, I press play, pulse racing.

The usually soft introductory bars belt through his speakers and grow into the first three lines as I listen to the familiar melody, in an unfamiliar way. Beau tilts forward and rests his elbows on his knees as I open my door.

When I reach the front of the truck, I realize he's not staring at the waves at all. He has his eyes shut, listening. Salt spray whips my skin, and strands of hair blow wildly across my face as I push myself up beside him. Fraser's piece soars while the bonnet vibrates with the music beneath us, the wind carrying the notes, scattering them, like ashes, from this cliff.

I place my palms flat on the warm metal of the hood, the rhythm pumping into me and through me like a thumping heartbeat, working up to the crescendo I know is coming, the one that always makes me want to scream, though I never have. You can't let yourself go like that in a city apartment. You'd have the authorities on your doorstep.

It's like Beau isn't even here. Suddenly I've kicked off my shoes. I'm pushing myself to my feet, standing on the bonnet now, barefoot, music thundering through my soles, coursing up my legs and through my body, dress flapping against my thighs, hair flying, trapped grief surging, unleashing, while I sense the noise raging through me . . . up, up, up . . . and finally belting out of my mouth in a scream that doesn't sound like my own, and will never be too much, or too loud, because we're a match now—the wild ocean and me.

And suddenly there's no music left. Nothing to hear. Nothing left to voice.

Just the waves again. And me standing on the hood of Beau

Davenport's truck on a clifftop while he sits calmly at my feet, as if he wouldn't have directed this scene in any other way.

Eventually I sit again. I draw my knees to my chest and hug them. I desperately want to explain what just happened, but can't find the words. I mean, who just stands up on someone's car bonnet, screeching into the void?

I turn to face him. "Beau—"

He puts a hand on my knee, briefly, to silence me, before he looks back out to sea, at a storm brewing on the horizon. There's a long pause, during which every cell in my body seems to tingle and vibrate the way they used to with alcohol, now with the powerful charge of three years of emotional release.

Eventually he turns to me and clears his throat. Blue eyes glisten as he says, in a voice that aches with a disarming blend of compassion and admiration, "No notes, Hepburn. Not a single one."

An hour later, the hot sand of Tathra beach stretches before us. Another cliff towers above the historic wharf, the cove fringed by a national park buzzing with cicadas, as we place our towels in a shady spot under the trees near the surf club.

"This is exactly how I imagined my midlife crisis would unfold," I say, smiling. At least I'd imagined as far as the sun and the sand . . . I hadn't ventured to the hot screenwriter taking his shirt off in front of me, which is frankly as breathtaking as the ancient wilderness framing the scene behind him.

"You're hardly middle-aged," he argues.

"And how old are you, then?" I counter, fascinated to know.

He holds my gaze for a second, on the verge of telling the truth. Then, eyes glinting, says, "I'm not middle-aged, either."

I can see that. The whole beach can see it. The man is clearly *in his prime*.

"Come on, Beau, you know my age."

"And you know mine. It's on the paperwork we exchanged."

I pull my dress over my head, if only to snap myself out of blatantly staring at the elaborate tattoo of a magnificent lion roaring across half his chest.

"Courage?" I ask, nodding at it, as soon as I've freed myself from the collar of my dress, which has scraped through my hair and wrecked my ponytail. *This wouldn't happen to Harlow.*

"Sorry?"

"The lion. Does it represent courage?"

"Something like that," he replies after a beat, turning to face the ocean, but not before I notice the name "Lucinda" buried in the lion's mane. Is she the woman he's had to write out of his screenplay? Or another woman? *I'll have to check April's notes.*

My navy one-piece is the most boring article of swimwear on this beach, beside all the neon orange and hot pink and with kids dashing around in frilly florals with big plastic floaties. Normally I'd be self-conscious in swimwear in front of someone like Beau, but in truth I felt far more exposed screaming at the ocean, standing on top of his car, having some sort of existential spiritual reckoning. Perhaps I'd been screaming for Fraser, as if the song I wrote for him was an over-the-waves siren call, tempting him back to me through a glitch in time.

But he didn't come, of course. He never does. "Beau, thank you for facilitating that, um, that—"

"Exorcism?"

Yes! That's what it felt like. Not a "calling in" of Fraser at all. An expulsion of something else. Grief? No, *trauma*. Trauma from the way it happened. My role in it. The fact that it was my fault. The guilt I've been carrying that I could have prevented

Fraser's death if I hadn't been on that Zoom. If I'd been braver, earlier.

As raw as it was, the experience on the hood of Beau's truck had felt like an epic, cinematic eleven-o'clock number—that sweeping, show-stopping song that comes late in the second act of a musical, where the protagonist has some sort of life-altering personal revelation.

"The exorcism was all you," he says. "I've never seen nor heard anything like it."

I must look worried, because he tilts his head and looks directly into my face to ensure I'm paying attention and adds, "It blew me away."

He starts walking toward the water, but I'm still wired from the way the music pumped through me and how it felt to expel that scream. I run after him and pull his arm. "You know this area. I thought I read that there was somewhere near here where you can cliff-dive." He seems taken aback, but I point at the lion on his chest. "Courage, remember?"

"*Courage*, Hepburn. Not stupidity."

We stare each other down, and I watch in real time as his expression cycles through disbelief and worry, landing on excitement. "Cliff-jumping. In middle age? It's unseemly."

I hoot at this and push his tattooed shoulder playfully.

"Right," he says, taking my hand and marching us back toward our towels, which he scoops up before we head back to his car. Moments later, he starts the engine, revving it. His arm is on the back of my seat while he reverses, the same as it was in my Jeep the other night, and I'm staring at him, thrilled by this sudden adventure, until he catches my eye: "Second thoughts?"

"No!" I say emphatically, smiling broadly as he screeches out of the car park and drives up through the hilltop village, and toward Kianinny Bay. If we live to tell this story, Sara will kill me. But after the sensitive way he listened to my music, I don't feel so compelled to update her as to my whereabouts anymore.

Once we're parked, it's only a short walk to the cliffs and suddenly my bravery is wavering, the swell rolling, ocean heaving, white foam bubbling in the dark blue depths.

"After you," Beau says, on the edge of the rock.

"Goodness," I respond. "You go." It's as if we've collided at the door of a Michelin-starred restaurant and we're dancing through the interaction with two sets of excellent manners.

A larger wave crashes in the water beneath us. "*Fortiores una*," Beau says, pointing at another tattoo on his shoulder.

"I only did a term of Latin in Year Seven—"

"Stronger as one," he translates as he takes my hand, pulls me toward the edge of the cliff, and then right over it. We plunge into the ocean below, hitting the water hard and sinking beneath it in a thrilling burst of freezing cold, shrouded in the bubbles we've made, his grip on my hand tightening as we kick toward the light and burst through the surface just as another wave crests over us. He pulls me tighter against him, until we surface into the brilliant midday light.

"That was *incredible*!" I yell, face to the sun, smile to the sky.

We power to the edge, clamber out onto some rocks and back up to our starting point, and jump off twice more, each time more sure of ourselves. It's exhilarating.

Finally, we tire of the climb and bask on the warm rocks below, ocean breeze on wet skin, spent from all the exertion.

"You must miss your husband," he says as water crashes, seagulls swooping overhead. He is propped on one elbow now, casting a shadow across my face and a halo around his own, all sculpted muscles and tattoos and brooding, brilliant writer vibes, and I'm sure Fraser would forgive me—*nay*, expect me—to be distracted from the question.

"I do miss him," I answer, at last, wrestling as always with the semantics, knowing the timing of Fraser's death was the greatest tragedy of all and not wanting to elicit even more pity from this man by explaining that we were just a whisper away from walking down the aisle. "At first, I thought I'd never be able to breathe again, let alone . . ." I swallow down whatever I was going to say, because I'm convinced it involved the rapidly developing crush I'm fighting here.

"Let alone what?" he asks gently, the corner of his mouth threatening a lopsided smile. It's that gentleness that gets me, juxtaposed as it is with the gloriously rugged *everything else* . . . and my eyes sweep over his face, dark hair still dripping with salt water, blue eyes intent and compassionate as I lie here, powerless to extract myself. *And why on earth would I want to?*

"Beau, this is . . ." *Magical? Temporary? Why am I attempting to label it?*

The way he's looking at me morphs from what I can describe only as hopeful, verging into wants-to-kiss-me territory, and then into a flash of worry, brows knitted. Perhaps he is concerned about the state of my heart? He saw the depth of its bruises on the other clifftop. Perhaps it's not me he's worried about at all, but him, and the danger of getting tangled up in any way with another woman after the last scandal. Or maybe I'm just getting this all wrong because—look at him. *Who am I kidding?*

"Is there something about clifftops that brings out the best in you?" he asks.

I prop myself on my elbows, squinting into the sun.

"The music," he suggests, tilting his head and smiling. "The adventure. Throwing your heart out over one, flinging your body off another. The general audacity of it all."

Something about the word "audacity" trips a wire in my brain. It's been so long, years, since I've felt bold. But when I think about what I've pushed through, what I've survived—things I've told Beau already and things I haven't trusted him with yet—maybe the audacity has crept up and overtaken me. You think you've come a certain distance but find that you're further ahead than it seemed.

I plunge us into the silent exchange of a long gaze, during which another sort of audacity springs to mind. It would be so easy to take the lead here. To close the gap, trace the lion on his chest, and reel him toward me, teasing him closer until he pushes me back onto the hard surface of the rock we're lying on like this is a scene from one of his films . . .

But just as I'm tempted to do that, right when I feel my body tilt toward his, my knee rising and making contact with his thigh, there's a loud bang from a wave hitting rocks, and a threatening wall of water suddenly crashes overhead and onto us as the rock becomes terrifyingly slippery and the wave engulfs us in white foam.

I reach for something to hold. But I'm on my back, the power of the sea threatening to pull me in. I feel myself slipping, until Beau throws his weight across my body, anchoring us as he grasps a ridge in the rock with one hand, his other arm around my waist, sheltering me from the surge. As the water drains away, every ounce of the audacity he'd so admired just seconds ago seems to rush out of my body and I soften into the hard lines of his, my face against his chest, his heart thundering.

He eases off me and helps me sit up, and we shake the water from ourselves. Finally we look at each other, stunned. As dangerous as that was, I feel sixteen right now. A light, carefree age I never thought a widow could access again. It must be magic.

"Is that how you'd have directed it?" I ask. "For your movie?"

His smile is strained as I catch him glance at my lips. "More or less," he admits, blue eyes flashing back to mine with an unmistakable edge of desire.

Twenty minutes later, we fall into the Tathra pub, physically worn out, sunburnt, and thirsty. There's a table for two near a window, and he suggests I nab it while he orders our meals at the counter before the kitchen closes after lunch.

"What can I get you? Beer? Wine? Something stronger?"

"Lemonade," I answer firmly, and because I know how this goes and want to head off at the pass the inevitable negotiations, I add, "I don't drink."

"Lemonade," he repeats. "And the burger?"

I nod. Usually by now we've entered into a debate over my avoidance of alcohol: *I can't tempt you with bubbles? What about a cocktail? Espresso martini?* I have to say, *No, thanks, just a soft drink*, while the entire venue seems to fall into silence, because this—the not drinking—is positively un-Australian. People can't make it work in their heads.

"Do you mind if I have a beer?" Beau asks, doubling back to check, having seemingly thought of the question halfway to the bar.

"Go ahead! Just stay under the limit unless you want me driving your truck home, and we know how that goes . . ."

He shudders and laughs aloud as he heads back to order, and I watch his effect on the room. The way people turn. The smiles on the faces of the bar staff when he greets them with some invisible aura, all of them falling under his easy spell, as if he is the movie's star, not its architect. And when he turns and locks eyes with me again, beer in one hand, lemonade in the other, and smiles, I realize this man is stirring some long-forgotten, grief-trodden part of me. And I don't just mean the libido he shook to life on Day One.

Surely it's okay for a forty-year-old to entertain a distracting little infatuation during her birthday week, even if Beau Davenport ordinarily attracts models like Harlow and presumably Tattoo Lucinda and all the other glamorous women he's been spotted with in the social pages April has been sending me. It's a grief version of those "safe crushes" teenage girls harbor on pop stars and film idols. The ones that let them experiment with love without risking any real heartbreak. *What might it be like if I fell in love, post-Fraser?*

He crosses the room, places the drink in my hand, sits down, and waits for me to clink glasses. Then he takes a large sip of beer, puts the glass on the table, leans in, crosses his arms, and looks at me as if Harlow and Lucinda are in the rearview mirror.

"Audrey," he says, picking up the pub's branded coaster and tapping it on the table while he chooses his words, before setting it down flat and meeting my gaze. "I can't get your music out of my head."

43

Fraser

It takes Rachael and Parker about five minutes to cook up a scheme that we drive an hour away to hike Pigeon House Mountain.

Parker and I love hiking. Rachael prefers an air-conditioned gym but appears to be undergoing a personality transformation, and after her bombshell Ireland announcement, this feels like one of our family "lasts."

And that, there, is the problem. This feels exactly like a family.

The whole car ride, the two of them prattle on about TV shows I've never seen, podcasts, and viral reels on social media, and it occurs to me that Rachael speaks fluent "teen." Or perhaps it's that she speaks fluent "Parker"—that fluency having crept up on me, along with so many other things, it seems.

"You know this one, Dad!" Parker says, playing a snippet from a song on her phone, which has apparently inspired some weird viral dance.

"No?"

"How can you not? It's everywhere!"

"I don't listen to the top forty."

"Parker, your father doesn't listen to the top four thousand. You should have seen him the night the three of us met! Absolutely no idea who either me or Audrey was dressed as—"

"Tell me the story again!" Parker says, delighted. "Especially the bit about the ice bucket!"

Rachael smiles, the memory no doubt sinking in of when her best friend came to her rescue. She and I have talked about this before, about how helpless we've always felt that we couldn't rescue Audrey right back when she needed it.

"Well, the party was nineties themed—" she begins, swiveling in the passenger seat so she can look at Parker while she recounts the evening.

"As in the late nineteen hundreds? So you were all, like, wearing antique clothes?"

"*Gosh*, Parker. Yes. Last century. And let's go with the term 'retro' rather than 'antique,' shall we?" Rach says, indignantly.

"Technically the industry term is 'vintage,'" I add. "For anything thirty-plus years old."

Rachael thumps me on the arm. "Anyway, your stepmum went as Britney Spears. You know, '. . . Baby One More Time'?"

There's a blank look from the back seat.

"'Oops! . . . I Did It Again'?"

"Did what again?" Parker asks.

"No, that's a song title. Anyway, your dad was as clueless as you are about who she was—"

"But you were alive last century, Dad."

"Parker, will you stop referring to the nineties as if we're talking about the Middle Ages?" I order her, laughing.

"You *are* middle-aged. The Bookies think you're having a midlife crisis!"

Rachael laughs off this suggestion and forges on. "Audrey was dressed as Britney. Your dad as David Beckham."

"Oh my GOD. Why were you dressed as Brooklyn Beckham's *dad*? He's *ancient*."

Rachael and I explode now.

"Who did you go as, Rach?" she asks.

"Catwoman," I reply, confident I've got this one right, at least.

"Victoria Adams," Rachael says, frowning at me.

"Who the fuck is Victoria Adams?" I ask, forgetting for a second that Parker is in the car. I am thoroughly confused. "I thought you were Catwoman. Or the only thing you had hanging in your wardrobe happened to be a latex catsuit . . ."

We exchange a look that seems to convey my thoughts about said outfit.

"Fraser, you are *hopeless*," she accuses me. "I was Victoria Adams, circa the 'Say You'll Be There' music video? *Please* tell me you've heard of the Spice Girls?"

"Wait!" Parker says, sitting bolt upright and then leaning forward from the middle back seat. She grabs both of our shoulders as if she has finally pieced all this together, like the chief inspector in a murder mystery. "Dad went as Brooklyn Beckham's dad, and you went as his *mum*? You two basically went to this party as a married couple!"

She lets us both go, falls back, and rolls around laughing. "It's like you fell in love with the wrong pop star, Dad!"

This is endlessly amusing, apparently.

"Parker, your dad is a brilliant man, but this level of pop culture complexity is well beyond him."

Rach touches me on the arm as I swing onto the turnoff to the mountain trail. "To give you credit, Frase, that was a good line. Remember the one about my eight other lives?"

It hadn't got a rise on the night. What with my ineptitude over the brewing brawl with Connor, my woeful lack of cultural knowledge, and ice and water raining down from the deck overhead, I'm amazed she even recalls it.

■ ■ ■

According to the hiking notes online, the final climb to the summit involves a series of steep metal ladders bolted to the side of vertical rock faces. If your legs haven't already given out, your nerve might, and there are warnings to avoid the ladders if you're anxious. Parker scurries straight up the first one without even taking a breather after our punishing climb.

"After you, Mrs. Beckham," I say when Rach and I have caught our breath and had some water.

She shakes her head and takes another swig from the drink bottle. "I think I'll wait here—you two go ahead."

"Oh, Rach, you can't give up now!" Parker begs from above. "Please come with us!"

Rach is the fittest out of the three of us, but I forgot she has a thing with heights. Audrey used to talk about the time they had to be relocated when they'd inadvertently purchased the nosebleed seats at a concert in one of Sydney's Darling Harbour theaters.

"You don't have to," I tell her before looking up the ladder and calling out, "Don't pressure people to do things they don't want to do!"

Rachael glances upward, squinting and shielding her eyes from the sun, then back at Parker. And at me. "I could go a little way up? Just give this first ladder a try?"

It's probably part of her newfound resolve to extend herself. The fertility treatment. Emigrating. Settling down in some picture-postcard cottage with a rugged Irishman and his good craic, delivered with the kind of irresistible lilting accent that leave the rest of us—

Where am I being left, here, precisely?

"Dad will help," Parker says, scurrying up the second ladder. "I'll get the content for TikTok."

"Please don't, Parks!" Rach begs, turning me around so she can stash her drink bottle in my backpack.

She takes the first few steps up the ladder, and I watch from the ground. So far, so good, as she makes it to the first landing. I follow her up and wait while she tackles the next one, watching as she slows her pace, hands gripping the railings tight.

"You're fine," I call from below. "One step at a time."

She's gone quiet. Then she makes the mistake of glancing down, and I see her press herself forward on the ladder, both feet on one rung, frozen.

"Fraser," she says, her tone urgent. I step up behind her, two rungs at a time, until I reach her lower legs.

"You're okay. Take a step down."

She shakes her head, and I pull myself up until my feet are planted a rung below, my body right behind hers.

"*Come on*, Rach!" Parker shouts from well above.

"Just ignore her," I say, calmly. "There's no rush."

She's shaking, and I'm trying to work out the best strategy to help her back, when I feel her foot lift up as she reaches slightly higher with one hand. *God.* Here I was trying to get her down.

"That's it," I say, and she pulls herself up, her body rigid with fear while I shadow her.

It takes a full five minutes to ascend the next eight steps, and by now we're being chased by a boisterous family with young kids, whooping and squealing below us. Reaching the next landing, Rachael runs her hands along the rail as if she can't see, pushing herself into the corner, facing the rock wall, and not the increasingly sweeping views toward the coast and the hinterland, letting the family past. Parker is long gone now and hopefully behaving herself at the summit.

I don't want to point this out, but the higher we go, the harder it will be to clamber back down. I've got visions of

Rachael having a mental health crisis at the top and having to be helicoptered out.

“Talk to me, Fraser,” she says, determined progress being made as we set off toward the next landing. I’m right behind her, wrapped around her, more proud of her than I can articulate for even attempting this.

“I think I’ve been taking you for granted for years,” I blurt out.

I’m sure she meant for me to deliver some lighthearted, distracting banter and not a hard-hitting personal revelation. It’s just, if she’s going to cling to the side of a rock face and stare down her fears, maybe I should as well.

In any case, she’s not moving now. She’s got a viselike grip on the upper rung, as a coastal breeze whips around us, wisps of blond hair teasing my face.

“We’re almost there.” I bring a steady hand to her waist, palm resting on the soft Lycra at her hip. “We’re closer than you think.”

There’s another gust of the sea breeze, and I’m overwhelmed by the dueling scents of sunscreen and salt and eucalyptus and that perfume she always wears, that I *always* like, until it’s me who feels unsteady, and I have to release her hip and take the railing again.

“Don’t let go,” she whispers, moving her body back into mine, and I instinctively press forward to secure her between me and the ladder.

She doesn’t see how hard I swallow as I place my hand back on her waist and shut my eyes for a second as we push upward together. We’ve held each other through the detonation of losing Audrey. We’ve seen each other at our best and worst. But what she’s oblivious to is the fact that her turning up here and flinging her crossroads in my path has brought me to a crossroads of my own. It’s me with the vertigo. Suddenly, deeply, and in a time-sensitive, potentially life-altering way, everything I haven't dared feel about this woman has rushed forward. I can't tell her now, because what if we both let go and fall? But I am even more afraid than she is.

44

Audrey

I've woken before dawn to a bad case of sunburn from yesterday's antics on the cliff, but I barely notice the pain, because for the first time since Fraser's funeral, music is exploding, properly, in my brain. It's an almost overpowering synesthesia of lights, colors, textures, and tones. Emotions I can't articulate transform into notes, clustering in phrases, rising and falling as temperatures fluctuate kaleidoscopically in my mind's eye, and ear, as if I'm on some powerful hallucinogenic drug.

I'm hungry to capture it all. To pluck it from the sky. Save it in audio recordings. Scramble it onto the pages of the notation paper that has tortured me, blank, for so long. I am breathless with the return of this. Overwhelmed by the prolific intensity. Terrified it will stop.

Swinging my legs over the side of the bed, I hold my head in my hands and check the sounds are still there, scared to move in case I trip a wire and the creative onslaught evaporates. I haven't had a rush like this since Fraser's piece burst onto the page, so I reach for my phone and the portable keyboard, my laptop and the headphones, paper and pen, Miss Bennet instantly transformed from holiday camper to remote recording studio.

This is how it used to feel with Josh. This *grappling*. Scared of dropping ideas. Frantic for every last note. I thought he and I had brought out each other's best. Thought my music needed his. I never imagined that I'd be sitting here cross-legged on the bed of my tiny vintage camper, sand on the floor, waves crashing on Pretty Beach—a world away from his glittering New York stages—with this blast of music that won't stop. Because I won't ever let it. Because it is *mine*. Yesterday's cliffside unleashing of pent-up emotion liberated everything—and now there's years' worth of silence to fill.

By midmorning, I've ripped the headphones off. Sunburnt skin is shouting louder than the music, spaghetti straps slicing through to my bones. I try to ignore it. Fraser would be so relieved by this breakthrough. This is everything he wanted for me. This, and the courage to take what I write now and actually *do* something with it. To risk the constructive criticism I'm so scared of, always fearful someone will steal it or tamper with it and I'll lose it.

Josh flashes to mind. I still crave his approval but have to stop myself from sending him samples. He's been in New York for three years and I've seen him three times, when he comes home for Christmas with his family and I get invited over—not to the Christmas meal itself, of course, but something on the twenty-third so I can spend supervised time with Parker. I can't contact her without running it by Maggie first. *We don't want to confuse her,* she explained, even though my sudden disappearance from her life will have driven fresh cuts into her much bigger loss, and I'm left following her music online—listening to her grow up from a distance.

Thinking of her, another whole tranche of melodies falls into my brain. I need to get this down, but my red raw skin is blaring.

I set the laptop down and fish around in my belongings for the body cream. *How can I have lost it in a space so tiny?*

Fuck, I haven't got time for this. I fling open the door and am greeted by the sublime sight of Beau, in black swim trunks, washing his trailer. Why isn't he sunburnt? Is his skin protected by the tattoos? *Don't be absurd . . .*

"Wow," he says, turning around, dropping the sponge into the bucket, and wiping wet hands on his shorts. "Look at you."

"I know, ugh . . ." I pull at the pajama top and run a hand through messy hair. I must be a picture!

"Look at your eyes," he clarifies. And I can feel what he's seeing. This spark. This afterglow from composing and knowing what I'm writing is *good*, even in its first-cut, straight-from-brain-to-paper form.

These are the fireworks I promised Fraser. He never saw the expression I can feel on my face right now. One I haven't felt since my undergraduate degree, pre-fallout. This is the revival of my real, creative self having taken the long way around, as he always said I would, his faith in me stretching well beyond his death, until I've finally caught up with it, too.

"And look at that sunburn," Beau observes, wincing at the sight.

"Do you have any aloe vera? I can't find mine."

He goes inside, returning moments later with a tube of cream.

"Thanks! Toss it here," I suggest, preparing to catch it.

Instead he flicks the plastic lid as he wanders over, squirting lotion into his hand. "Turn around," he commands when he meets me at the step of my camper.

"It's okay. I'll do it—"

"Are you a contortionist?" He waits for me to capitulate, knowing I will, as reaching the raw skin on my back is impossible.

"Wow, how did we let this happen?" he asks, fingers slipping gently under my straps, edging them off my shoulders carefully.

"Well, I am a middle-aged woman, give or take. It was probably on me not to be this careless."

I shut my eyes, inhaling sharply as cool lotion hits hot skin, and I lift my hair from my neck as his fingers brush my shoulders. He steps closer, pulling the fabric away from my back, dipping his hand underneath it, tracing the outline of my swimsuit until I have to grip both sides of my camper's doorway. Scorched skin, desperate for this touch, floods my brain with a swirl of conflicting sensory signals, and my heart throbs, head spinning—quite certain he's rubbed aloe vera onto the skin of so many women it's probably tabloid-magazine canon by now, hopelessly convinced, nonetheless, that it was never quite like this. As if he is inside my head, extinguishing a trail of sunburn that lights a new blaze.

"Over your writer's block, then?" He knows exactly what he's doing, spinning me gently by the hip, resting a hand flat on the metal of my camper as he leans against it, satisfied smile in his eyes.

I seem to be over *every* sort of block, if he must know. The man has set me on fire in every conceivable way. Creatively. Emotionally. Physically. And now the sounds blasting through my mind are urgent. They're hopeful. The melody so fresh, so unexpected, and my desire to capture it so intense, I'm almost scared of it as visions flash of the way our legs touched on that rock face yesterday. How it thrilled me and scared me to tumble toward him like that . . .

"I've had an idea," I announce.

"You look like you've been ravished by ideas."

I adjust my straps and fidget with my top and my hair, trying to straighten up, attempting not to dwell too long on the word "ravished," as uttered from those particular lips.

"Don't do that," he says, nodding at my hair, taking my hand,

and leading me off my step, into the space between our vehicles. "Frenzied creativity suits you."

I suspect it would also suit him. I imagine him deep in concentration, perhaps with a pair of reading glasses and a strong black coffee steaming in a mug beside him while he writes. If he's this attractive *not writing*, I can't begin to envisage the impact of Beau Davenport with a laptop, impressive thoughts tumbling into a document while he writes some award-worthy script.

"I want to help you with your screenplay," I announce, not just because I really want to see him in that state. I'm eager to shift the conversation away from me and how frazzled I look, and onto him and how genuinely I want to help.

He smiles. "Oh, yes? How would you do that?"

"Come with me to Canberra," I say. Confidence has overcome me in some sort of delirious, post-creative high, convincing me it's worth asking the eligible screenwriter, who seems to divide his time between high-rise Sydney and L.A., if he would like to tag along on a trip to the nation's capital.

"What's in Canberra apart from the prime minister?"

"A rehearsal room at the School of Music, for starters," I explain. "I'm hiring one to use the piano for a few days."

He tosses some kindling and a couple of big blocks of wood into a rusty metal drum for tonight's fire before he looks over, catches me staring, and says, "Where do I fit in?"

My brain produces an instant collage of all the ways . . .

"Bring your story," I say, preventing that train of thought from going any further. "Tell it to me and I'll set it to music. I don't mean officially—I'm sure you'll have already locked in a composer for the actual film—"

"Harlow and I had another email from him this morning, asking if there were any content concepts we could send through yet."

Harlow? "I thought she was an actor."

"She is, but she's also shadowing me in the writers' room. She wants to move in that direction. I guess I'm mentoring her, unofficially. In return, she's been helping out with some of the project-management stuff, emails and so on, *while you're off being creatively brilliant, Beau*, she said. I haven't been entirely open with her about how dire things have been on that front."

His frustration is palpable, standing here, arms folded across his chest.

"Yesterday I was just as stuck as you," I remind him, leading us to the camping chairs. "All it took was for you to let me play my piece in a new place, and that changed everything."

"You had a bigger story stopping you," he says. "I don't have the same excuses."

"Being somewhere different could help, though. Showing a new person. Staying here hasn't worked for you, has it?"

"Why waste your time on my stuff?"

I pull my chair right in front of his and lean in so close he edges back in his seat, away from the wild composer. "You don't understand. I'm not on a deadline. Nobody's waiting on me. Right now, I don't care *what* I write. As long as it's new. If you tell me the plot of your movie, that will be just another creative stimulus for me. *You* won't use the music, but I might. And when we put your words and my music together, maybe we'll find this elusive female lead that you're searching for."

The waves crash on the nearby beach and we stare at each other.

"I started a piece this morning, inspired by that moment on the cliff."

He tilts his head. "Which one?"

I meant the one standing on the hood of his truck, but now I'm thinking of the one on that rock, water gushing over us while he was on top of me. The way he never took his eyes off me, as if the whole ocean could come at us and we wouldn't move. The way his thigh had felt against mine, pushed into the hard surface of that rock, hot sun, cold water, delicious anticipation. Now I shake off a shiver, which he catches. I know he does, because he's covering a smile.

"I want to play it for you on a real piano," I say, slightly breathless. *Why does it feel like I'm undressing in front of him?*

He considers me carefully. "What are you telling me, Hepburn? I'm your muse?"

This line he delivers deadpan, but with a sparkle in his eyes that unleashes the butterflies inside me that are never far from the surface around him. *Something* has crashed through the barrier that has kept me from my music all this time.

"Maybe you are," I venture, scared to assign him a role this critical when our acquaintance is so new and both of us are creatively fragile. I've been here once before, with disastrous consequences.

He leans forward now, too, pulling on both arms of my camping chair, tipping it toward him. Like that time Fraser wrenched my chair across the floor . . .

My heart quickens at the idea of just how unexpectedly far I have come in three years, and how unexpectedly far I might potentially let myself go. "You might be my muse," I repeat as I reach out and brace myself on his shoulders. "But more importantly, maybe I'm yours."

45

Fraser

"You don't have to stay," Maggie instructs, having enrolled Parker in the summer music school, which I'm convinced is meant to be exposure therapy for me. She's conveniently ignoring the end-of-program concert we'll be subjected to and which she knows I'll attend, because I would never let Parker down like that. "Just drop her off and collect her. What are you going to do otherwise? Take her to the office?"

"Hardly. I'm still recovering from that time she dropped a piece of scientific-grade glass worth two thousand dollars."

Maggie hadn't been amused then, and she's not amused now. "This is Parker's first love. You can avoid music in your own life, but you can't keep pushing it out of hers. It isn't fair."

I hate it when she's right. In any case, it takes three attempts to dig Parker out of bed for her first day, and *can I possibly drop her off on the corner and not come in, and have I ever considered an electric car?* They're even less likely to draw attention when I drop her places, as they're practically silent. *When did this start?*

I swing the car into a spot. "Sorry for the excruciating reality of having to sign you in, Parks."

She grunts, gets out, pulls at her clothes awkwardly, and drags her feet. Is there anything less appealing than walking into a school-holiday program at thirteen, with your dad, where you know nobody? Sometimes I wonder if Maggie gets her at all.

During the sign-in palaver, they check my details against the information Maggie provided and usher Parker into a big room with all the others. She graces me with a small goodbye nod, and I attempt to extract myself without causing any DEFCON-level teen humiliation—not before stopping at a pop-up coffee kiosk to grab a takeaway muffin, and of course, because this is Canberra, I run into a colleague from the School of Geology and end up in a half-hour debate about earth science, which thankfully Parker doesn't witness, because what could be more mortifying than your father consuming a bakery item in public?

Eventually, I break away and walk down the corridor toward the exit, past a series of small practice rooms—each a hive of activity. Clarinet scales in one room, brass ensemble in the next. Every room stirring vivid associations with Audrey until it's a dizzying array of memories and a pointed reminder of all she has lost. And I'm at the door to Llewellyn Hall now, almost at the exact spot where I saw her looking crushed in the stairwell during Josh's concert, while he went and smashed it out of the park. *God, how I wanted to protect her from him that night.*

So now it's me, exposed to all this, needing the protection, even though I've worked so hard. Tackled the loss and the parenting, the depression and the endless decisions about moving through it all and moving forward. Except for this one thing. Music. *How can something this beautiful be my nemesis?*

There's only one more room to push past, and I focus on the sunlight streaming into the distant foyer as if I'm underwater, rising to the surface, holding my breath. But before I can make it past, I am entangled in familiar melodic lines.

Audrey's song. The final one she was writing, which we played, half finished, at her funeral.

I step forward and place my forehead flat against the door, eyes shut, the melody seeping through the wood into this corridor, into my soul, tangling around raw grief and the memory of the heat and the pulsing of cicadas and the whirring of ceiling fans at the crematorium.

The pianist crashes through the peak of the crescendo, beyond what I remember. Memories dislodge, splintering like ice smashing into the ocean as I realize it's not exactly Audrey's piece. It's different now.

My eyes jolt open again and I step back from the door, lifting my hand as if I've touched fire. Of course it's not her piece. How could it be, when the music died inside her? *I must be more messed up than I thought.*

When I turn, intending to run, I slam into someone blocking the corridor. It takes a second for my brain to catch up and for my heart to plunge.

He heard that piece, too. I know he's recognized it as hers. I can see that he's equally baffled. But it's only when our eyes meet and I see familiar pain reflected in my brother's eyes that something else is finally confirmed, too. He loved her once. Even if it was always unrequited.

46

Audrey

The further into Fraser's song that I play, the closer to him I feel. When I try very hard to imagine it, it's as though he's just outside this rehearsal room, listening to me play the way that he used to. As long as I keep the music going, I sense him there. Worried that if I stop, I'll break our bond, he'll be gone again, and it will be my fault. It's always my fault when I lose him.

The old voicemail message taunts me. *Audrey, it's Faith Jones from the front office at school. We've got Parker in sick bay. She said you're on pickup today, but never mind. I'll try her dad . . .*

My fingers slip onto the wrong keys.

Never mind?

I could write an entire piece based on that crushing voicemail alone. It's tattooed in my brain, the number of times I've played it, obsessively, wishing I could reverse time, hear the message, call, and say, *No, don't phone Fraser! He's at work. I'll be there in five!*

And then we wouldn't be here.

The final tone reverberates off the acoustics of the rehearsal room, and it falls silent and empty. I've lost him now. I can't keep even his spirit close, even when he tries.

Then, in this silence—that empty space between the end of

one piece and the start of another—I realize part of me is listening for the latch on the door, imagining Beau pushing it open, entering the room with the coffee he's gone to fetch.

Once I picture that, my body and my music ignite at the idea of impressing him. Perhaps because of the flashy industry he works in, or maybe because, so far, he's the only one who knows I'm composing again, and he's someone who intimately understands what an enormous deal it is to share a first draft. So he is safe.

I touch the keyboard, fingers depressing the keys so softly the sound is barely audible, just a whisper of what's possible. This next step, the idea of improvising right in front of him—nothing formed or developed or polished—is more intimate again, as if the muse itself is stripped bare, mind exposed, distance closed.

And now I am all over the keyboard, exploring some sort of mash-up of Fraser's piece and a new one—melodies at counterpoint, harmonies mingling in a way that shouldn't even work . . .

Just as I reach the climax, I hear the door open behind me, my heart pounding at the idea of him hearing this moment of a piece so precious and personal as it expands into something new, every part of me alight with the promise of this unfamiliar connection.

"Did you hear that?" I ask, on fire with the sense of possibility, a sparkle in my voice that I haven't heard in years.

"I did," someone says from the doorway, silencing that sparkle instantly. "And you're still extraordinary, Sully."

I spin around, my eyes smarting with tears. For an exhilarating moment—because the mind plays tricks and they're so similar in looks and because, just seconds ago, I'd convinced myself Fraser was listening outside this door—my entire being seems to lurch forward, relief washing through me that it was all some terrible mistake. Seconds later, that same heart has to scream to a halt, brakes to the floor, as I hydroplane toward Josh.

I cannot have him in this room, saying nice things about my music. Can't bear the thrill of Josh Miller's compliments. Not after all this time. This man's professional opinion was, after all, my first addiction.

"I thought you were in New York."

The Manhattan chic is evident. Charcoal shirt. Dark suit pants. Flash of excitement and opportunity in his eye.

"Back for a couple of weeks for work," he explains. "And to see Parker. She's here at the music school, as you'd know. I assume that's why you're here?"

My stomach sinks again. *Parker is here?* I can't be near her—*or* her uncle, for that matter. Maggie doesn't allow it unless she's present, too, despite the long stretch of time that has elapsed, sober, since that woeful episode at my place.

"How's everything going with her?" Josh asks. "Maggie tries to keep me updated."

There was a time when I could have told Joshua anything. How do I explain that I don't really know how Parker is doing? That the relationship we so desperately wanted disintegrated. That I haven't been teaching her piano and that our contact is so heartbreakingly infrequent that, in reality, I lost them both?

"Sully, are you okay?" Dark eyes roam across my face, scanning for fractures. Ironic, when some of my fractures are his.

I am not remotely okay when it comes to his niece. And he has lost the right to ask.

He steps toward the piano, and I'm served an inconvenient mental carousel filled with all the times we spent sitting together at one just like it. I'm ninety-nine percent convinced I need him out of here. But that one percent—the part of me he'll always have a hold over, creatively—just wants to play him something first. Beau will be back any second. Josh is the one part of my university story that I haven't shared. And the whole point of being here is about *reclaiming* my music—something that's difficult to do around a person who was intimately involved in its disappearance.

"How long are you going to punish me?" he asks, reading my body language and stopping several feet away.

"Punish *you*? That's rich."

His posture sinks. "You know you're my biggest regret."

If this man takes one step closer, he'll tramp on the fragile flame that I've finally coaxed to life from the ashes of the career he torched. And I will be *furious*.

"You did this to yourself, Josh. You destroyed us. I can't ever play for you with my guard down, and I'll never trust you around my music."

"You sent me Fraser's song the minute you finished it."

"I was *drunk*. I was completely out of control." *Why am I admitting this?*

"For some reason that's comforting." He rubs his forehead as though it's aching from years of this feud. "Alcohol is a truth serum."

For a long moment, I stare at that fact. He doesn't know the depths of my dependency. The choke hold alcohol had over me. The way it subdued me. Dismembered me. Thrashed me in the shallows in its crocodile death roll until it swallowed my relationship with Parker whole.

"For me it was a numbing serum, but I don't need it anymore. And, Josh, where I am with my music right now—after spending so long thinking that I had blown my one opportunity to really make something of myself—*I can't be near you*."

■ ■ ■

By the time Beau returns fifteen minutes later, I've just about pulled myself together. Frankly, it's a relief to have someone else's problem to focus on as he leans against the curve of the piano and I look up at him from the stool.

"Right, Mr. Davenport. Tell me where you're stuck," I say, calling this experiment, and the morning, and my life, to order—trying, unsuccessfully so far, to shake Josh's energy from the room.

It's as if Beau is configuring the problem in his mind, assembling it into a set of palatable key messages that he's nervous to drop, before he takes a breath and launches it at me: "The problem is that what she and I had was explosive. So the tension between the protagonists was off the charts. She was the sort of woman who lit up the sky and burnt out on impact. Dangerous, impulsive, electric . . ."

Four sentences into his speech and I'm sorry I asked. It's an eruption of information I wasn't prepared for. I'm one part enthralled, nine parts screamingly envious of the sort of woman who could light up Beau's sky and his film script so devastatingly that he's had to go all scorched earth on it in her wake.

"Audrey?"

My face is hot. I've gone straight to a place of schoolgirl inferiority, comparing myself to the iridescent cheerleader who has stolen my crush's heart while I'm in the library alone over lunch.

"I don't have to change the plot too much," he explains, unaware that my head has fallen off. "It's the character. Every attempt I've made to change her has only watered her down. No one is going to fall in love with someone I can't rouse any interest in myself, as the writer. I need to start from scratch."

Right.

"So someone equally explosive? Or a whole other energy?"

Please say the latter. Say you want someone broken and messy, with cracks and flaws, who'll smash into your car and stand on the bonnet of it and scream the place down.

Intense blue eyes search my face for answers before he says, "The character I had just *worked*."

He looks as despondent as I feel. I can't tell if he's maudlin about the loss of the character or the woman who inspired her, but I say, "Tell me more?" Because I am clearly a masochist.

"Can't," he replies. "I signed a nondisclosure agreement. Can't talk about her. Can't write about her . . ."

"Can't get over her?" The question lopes into the room, echoing off the acoustic panels, followed by a loaded beat of silence during which our eyes meet and I almost forget how to breathe.

It stops him short. "I am over her," he says quietly.

He does not *seem* over her.

My hands go ahead and fill the awkward silence that follows with a few chords on the piano. The chords are not going anywhere. They don't mean anything. They're just noise, trying to jostle the uncomfortable truth into the corner, out of our sight.

"Does the character change the story?" I ask.

"Characters always drive the story. The strong ones can survive any plot twist we throw at them."

My fingers return to their comfort zone. The final lines of Fraser's piece. The part of the sheet music with the strong double bars and two dots—the "repeat" sign that's sent me back over the same minor-key section over and over again . . .

But it won't now; the music pulls me from the old reprise through this unexpected bridge into a major key and a bright new melody that shouldn't work but does.

Beau's expression shifts as he listens, attuned to the changes, the music lifting us through some invisible transition, experimenting, improvising—

"I heard something once about loss," he says. "That the hole it leaves in your life never disappears, but your life expands around it, like this. New music mingles with the old. The central melody is still there . . . It's just bigger. It has to be. Or you wouldn't be alive."

I haven't been.

I've been in purgatory since Fraser died. Stuck thinking my chance at life had been irreparably stolen from me, too. Trying to preserve what we had. Worried any steps forward would taint his memory. Certain that our experience was so incredible and unique, there could never be a situation that would make it worth risking my heart again. Never a person worth risking that for. I've gripped onto this so hard. Thought it was keeping me safe when it was suffocating me. And here I am, daring to play different music for the first time in *years* and—

"What's going through your mind right now?" Beau asks. "Because what you've just played was exquisite."

Was I playing? I didn't even hear it.

He holds out his phone, and I get up from the piano. It's a video he's just taken, capturing music I don't even remember. It's like having an out-of-body experience, watching this. "How did you know to record that?"

"The look on your face," he explains as I pass the phone back.

This is creative intimacy.

Actually, this is intimacy, full stop. Maybe not the scorching-hot, light-up-the-sky stuff he's used to. It's not dazzling, in the way he described. But quiet power is still power, isn't it?

"Maybe you don't need lightning bolts with this new character. Not every woman has to be dangerous," I suggest.

He pauses. "Not every woman has to be dangerous in the same way." Blue eyes flash on some stormy, far-off horizon. We're no longer talking about the fiery woman his character was based on. We're talking about someone else, and something much deeper.

"Are you thinking about Lucinda?" I ask, and he snaps his attention back to me, confused. He is ruffled now, cool Viper mask dissolving, ruptured heart on display. I think he's trying to work out how I've read his mind.

"Come on, Beau," I say, stepping closer to him. "No secrets here anymore. Now it's the look on *your* face. I don't mean to pry. It's just, she's the only woman emblazoned across your chest. She clearly means a lot to you. Nobody else is, well . . ." I glance at his shirt. "Inscribed on your body."

"Have you conducted an inventory?" he asks.

Yes.

"No! I just thought maybe she's the answer to your writer's block. All the others are with you in *Who? Weekly*. She's written on you. Permanently."

"Physical inventories plus homework reading? You're turning into quite a fangirl, Hepburn."

Yes. I am. And now I'm burning with embarrassment, my mind going haywire in its attempt to shake off and lighten this line of discussion, for some reason landing on the *deranged* clapback: "Struggling not to take my bra off and throw it at you as we speak!"

He laughs. "Is that so?"

Of course it isn't! My cheeks are on fire. "April forwarded the article, and several others, about you and Harlow, and you and the actress I can only assume is the woman behind this movie script derailment. And about you and Lucinda. April is the real fangirl. She has an encyclopedic knowledge . . ."

"And what conclusions has she drawn?"

I can see this conversation going very badly.

"She thinks you're obviously . . ." *Smoking hot, I think were her exact words. His eyes, Audrey. Those pecs!* "Talented. She said your last movie was nominated for Best Original Screenplay."

"I cowrote it," he clarifies.

"I remember. With a writer named—"

He's caught in the headlights now. "Lucinda Taylor."

"To whom you were engaged, according to April. And who inspired you to get inked." *Why am I interrogating him?*

"The ink was permanent," he clarifies. "The engagement was not."

I try not to look too thrilled, rearranging my face into *supportive muse mode.*

"What's with the inquisition, anyway?" Frown lines furrow around his eyes as he leans in to the curve of the piano, arms crossed on the lid. He needs to workshop this obstacle before it tears his project apart.

Swallowing, I push back the stool and rise to my feet. "Perhaps your current block is because you're writing without your former partner, with whom you enjoyed great success, and you're scared you can't replicate that success without her?"

The room catches this and holds it for a beat. "Where did you read that?"

I round the piano as he straightens and turns to face me. "Here," I say, brushing the side of his face, restraining myself from threading my fingers through his hair and pulling him toward me. I'm so nervous, it's as if I've summoned the nerve to touch a lion itself.

I want to erase his doubt. I want to smooth the pain of the breakup and the creative fear and wait with him while he finds his confidence again. "When your rebound relationship with the actress imploded, you let it take the screenplay down with it . . ."

My voice drops now, as if I'm afraid to suggest the next part. "And if you give up now, you won't be tested. You'll always be the screenwriter who was nominated for an Oscar. You'll never know what proportion of the accolades were Lucinda's and which were yours."

He stares at me, dark eyes flashing, the room charged with a heady mix of shock and daring and truth and resistance . . . and a tsunami of sexual tension, at least from where I am standing, watching Beau Davenport crack open.

He is all raw intensity—looking as likely to sweep out of the room as he is to sweep me into his arms. And suddenly, if it's going to be the latter, I need him to know about more than just my messy grief story and the failed music career. I need him to know how low it all pushed me and what I lost because of my actions.

He's scanning my face as all of this plays across my brain. *Or is he mapping it ahead of kissing me?* Yes, now he's taking a step closer, dark eyes devouring me as he reaches for my hand. I don't think I've ever wanted anything, or *anyone*, more.

"Beau, wait," I whisper, letting go and putting my hand on his chest as he leans toward me. If this isn't going to be just some random event, if there's even the smallest possibility it could head somewhere deeper, I need him to hear exactly how far I fell. "I'm an alcoholic," I stammer into the charged air between us, entirely out of context, killing what was left of the mood. "That is, I have alcohol use disorder. You're not meant to say 'alcoholic' these days—too stigmatizing. You're meant to use person-first language—" *Getting off track, Audrey!*

I take a breath and refocus on him. "Eight hundred and

fifty-two days sober. I lost Fraser's child from my life because of it. She's here, actually, at a music school. I'm not supposed to see her without her mother present. And the reason I know this is because Fraser's brother—my original muse and vice versa, who is meant to be in New York and who was involved in the plagiarism case—was here, in this room, half an hour ago, before I kicked him out of my life again—"

The admissions gush out of me, one after another, as if my subconscious mind is attempting to lope several steps closer to Beau via the exposing of every single secret in one massive information dump. If I share my deepest, ugliest truths, perhaps he will, too? Except, now I'm worried all of this will push him further away. He's certainly paused the kiss. And as my hand drops from his chest, he steps back, considering me carefully from arm's length.

"I know about the alcohol," he replies, unexpectedly, his voice calmer and softer. "Not the timing and details, obviously . . ."

"How?"

"*Your* face, when I didn't press you about your choice of drink in Tathra. The sheer relief that this wouldn't become a battle."

"Am I that easy to read?" I've been an expert at hiding this. It terrifies me that he just saw it, straightaway. And it intrigues me that he didn't run then.

"I'm a writer. I notice details." He waits for me to make eye contact again, and when I do, my whole body feels flushed with the nakedness of this admission. "I'm very impressed, Hepburn."

Impressed? Shouldn't he be shocked or disappointed?

"There's nothing attractive about recovering from addiction," I confess. "It's a painful, ugly, shameful, messy—"

"There is, actually," he interrupts. "I mean, here I am, mucking around with a small creative problem, and there you are, being a bloody superhero." He looks me up and down. *Really* looks at me, in a way that makes me feel even more undressed, as though he can see through my skin, observing every sinew and nerve ending.

"It's not something I tell people," I admit. "I'm scared that between this and the death stuff and the creative angst and the whole soap opera I've just outlined—"

"What, you'll be too interesting?"

That is not where I was going.

"You're right about Lucinda," he says, interrupting my inner thoughts and taking a seat on the piano stool now, backward, resting his elbows on his knees. "I'm scared I'm not up to it without her. It's easier to avoid it, then run out of time."

"Failure on your terms, right? I've spent the last eighteen years proving this methodology, with a perfect success rate."

He smiles at me from the stool. Reaches for my hand, pulls me over, and stands me in front of him, between his knees, looking up at me. "Thank you for telling me all of that."

He hasn't let go.

"I trust you," I find myself admitting. I *must* trust him, given all the information I've disclosed.

"We met on Thursday, Audrey. It's now Monday."

"Are you saying I shouldn't?"

There's a bolt between us. Lightning attraction, breath quickening. This is Beau Davenport: Hollywood darling, wildcard entrant in *People* magazine's sexiest man alive, person who'll let me unleash the terrors of my heart and who will stay, even after I guide him through a tour of the very worst parts of me . . .

He breaks our eye contact and exhales slowly, looking worried.

I let go of his hand and step back, skin prickling. “Please tell me I can trust you.”

He was entirely discreet about the actress when I asked. But with her he signed an NDA. We have no such legal scaffolding. Just our word. And I’ve told him everything about me that counts.

“You can trust me,” he says, unable to meet my eyes, pain spreading across his face, his energy pulling away from mine already. “But you’ve read the tabloids.”

What’s that supposed to mean?

“Audrey, sorry. I just need a minute.”

47

Fraser

"Who's in the room?" Joshua asks me once the piano falls quiet.

How do I answer that? We both look like we've seen a ghost. It sounded like Audrey, until it didn't . . .

"It's got to be Parker," he says, matter-of-factly.

Is he jet-lagged?

"How could it be, Josh? She's thirteen. That was really advanced."

He stares at me for a second, trying to work out my point. "She *is* really advanced. You've heard her! How do you think she got into this gifted program?"

"She's in Year Seven. That piece was composed by someone who almost got through her doctorate." *The less said about that, the better.*

"And the transition into the new section is glorious," my brother says. "You should be soaring."

He pushes past me, knocks lightly on the door, then opens it a little, peeks in, and quickly throws it open all the way. "Thought I heard my favorite niece!"

She leaps off the piano stool and rushes over to him, throwing her arms around his neck while I compute the exponential development of her talent, and the fact that I've missed it.

"Uncle Josh! I didn't know you were here yet!"

"Would I miss a chance to hear you perform?"

I should be soaring.

He's right. I can't believe that was Parker playing. The realization of what my unresolved grief has been pushing away punches me in the gut.

"Can I play you something?" she begs her uncle, face shining. She's always longed for his feedback, ever since he introduced her to the piano when she was tiny. She glances at me. "You don't have to stay, Dad."

All this time, she's been making allowances like this while I've been extinguishing the stars in her eyes. It's been three years of turning music off, of hitting mute and leaving rooms. Three years of jogging only to podcasts and audiobooks, of driving listening to talk-back radio, and of leaving events before the DJ kicks off. Three years of *Parker, can you play that somewhere else?* Of buying two concert tickets, psyching myself up to go, and then giving the other one to Maggie.

As my brother stands close to the piano and she double-checks he's listening, I realize it's been three years of missing out not just on music. Missing out on Parker. Time that I've lost sharing the one thing she loves more than anything else in the world and, worse, the outlet she's used to bring herself through the loss of her stepmum.

Josh catches me floundering. I thought I'd done so well. I manage my mental health like a pro. I take the medication, go to counseling. *Why can't I handle this?* The sight of my gifted daughter in her element.

Just as I'm about to walk out, he pulls me beside him while she plays, throwing his arm around me the way he used to do when we were boys and I fell off the equipment at the playground, or when I was tormented by the neighborhood bullies. After years of frostiness between us, this touch of humanity hits almost as hard as the notes she's playing.

This music sounds like Audrey. It sounds like everything

I've missed with Parker. It sounds like bad parenting and cowardice and makes it desperately clear that unless I can conquer this grief, I'm going to lose my daughter, too.

"I am shutting out my own child," I admit to Josh once Parker has packed up and gone to a tutorial. "Denying the part of her that connects her to Audrey, because they were kindred spirits on this."

He knows that feeling. I wait for him to remind me he was Audrey's kindred spirit first.

"Give yourself a break," he says, instead. "You're parenting through a horrible situation, and look at her. She is a fantastic, talented kid. You know, I'm envious of you. You got the family I always wanted."

Has he been paying attention?

I glare at him. "You're aware my first marriage ended in divorce and the second in death? What can you possibly find to envy here?"

"Apart from your amazing kid?"

"Apart from that."

He looks at me closely. Vulnerably, actually. We haven't had a conversation like this in so long I can't remember the last one. Maybe never. "I've only been properly in love once," he admits. "It all went wrong and hurt so badly, I never allowed myself to get that close to a woman again. You think I'm happy in New York? You see me connected with singers and actresses and Broadway stars—"

I actually don't keep up with the New York social scene or his apparently leading role in it, but that's not the point.

"I've never been more lonely." He checks how I'm taking all of this and adds, "You know I lost her twice."

I'm not getting into an argument with Josh about Audrey and which one of us hurts more.

"It all goes wrong for you, and you go back for more. You're a fucking romantic, Fraser. I bet you're still capable of falling in love, even after the worst has happened, third time around. You've gone through all of this, and you'll still end up married fifty years."

That jolts me. "That's what I promised Audrey. Fifty years."

For the first time since her death, a revised timeline presents itself. No. Not *revised*, exactly. The same timeline. Revised expectations. Maybe my time with Audrey, which had felt so bright and promising, was always intended to be just this short, dazzling slice.

"You didn't get fifty years with her," Josh is saying. "But you still could. With someone else . . ."

I loathe *Everything happens for a reason*. I loathe *God's will* and *She's at peace now*. The people who speak like that have never had to donate an unworn wedding dress to a charity shop.

Of course it was Rachael who helped me do that, too. She helped me with everything, starting at the end, at sunset the night Audrey died. Breaking the news to her sister. Canceling the wedding. Arranging the funeral and then being around, every step of the way, with Parker, who just days ago asked her to get in the car and drive to us at the beach, the way I know she'd drive to us anywhere. She has *become* the hygge in our lives. The coziness. The comfort. Against the "overhead lights," Rachael is our candlelight.

The more I put this together, the faster my heart beats. This is the woman with whom Parker and I have formed a placeholder family. The one who has been there from the very beginning, who *can't wait around for everything else to fall into place.*

And now I have taken her for granted for so long, she has scrambled together an international escape plan and is leaving. *While I do what? Fling open the door and usher her through?*

I look at my brother. A man who so often gets romance wrong. Someone who has famously blundered through a string of consecutive dalliances that have left him with nobody with whom to share his gleaming life at the top. Yet somehow he has seen straight through me. And he is absolutely clear. Despite the shuddering loss I've experienced—or maybe because of it—we could have fifty years . . .

48

Audrey

Explosive, he'd said. *Lit up the sky. Dangerous, impulsive, electric.* The protagonist in his film was all those things. And now he can't handle me?

The music that bursts from me now has an edge of rage. Red tones. Fiery staccato. Turbulent, clashing chords over which a pristine melody soars that's probably the best thing I've ever written, annoyingly, because it's emerging from furious, unbridled disappointment and, worse, jealousy.

What did he mean, "You've read the tabloids"? First, I would never! My source is April, and she ignores salacious gossip. *All my research is based on photographic evidence and statements from the verified accounts of people involved, Audrey. I've got you!*

So what's he saying, then? That I should believe that stuff? That I can't trust him, despite having been cajoled into exposing everything, because *Read the magazines, Audrey! He's Lothario-ing his way through the cast and crew of all the latest theatrical releases!*

I fold in on myself, head down on the lid of the piano, emotionally exhausted. I'd handed this man my whole story. He had stared at it, and at me, as if we were precious. He'd looked for all the world as if he was about to step up and be incredible, only to flee the room with every last secret. Even the stuff I've hidden from some of the people closest to me, because I couldn't bear to disappoint them!

My head is starting to pound. Something about Beau and the way we've been together the last few days convinced me he could take it. *Ugh, the rawness of how I acted on that clifftop!* It just makes me cringe now, because my addiction admission was chased almost immediately by this brooding backtracking, which tells me everything I need to know. I *have* scared him off. I was too much. I've literally run him out of this room.

Dragging myself upright again, I cycle through a steadying breath, press record on my phone, and start playing. Having fought my way back here, I can't discard my creativity *again.* Not for some emotionally volatile, A-list cowboy with a Sydney penthouse and a story about writer's block that might not even be true!

So it all bursts out of me. Everything, all at once, as I bash the keys, trying to expunge my distress, pushing through regurgitated shame, eventually sifting my way through to some mellow chords while I go all Drew Barrymore with myself about it: *I am worthy of love. Even the worst parts of me. Fraser would never have abandoned me like that! I deserve better!*

I'm about four soundscapes into this personal music therapy session when the door bangs open again and I lift my fingers off the keyboard right in the middle of a climactic line. He's back. Disassembled. I pull myself to my feet as he crosses the floor and I back into the piano, jangled notes clanging as my body leans against the keyboard, his expression all regret and desire and *everything* I just conveyed in my frantic composition.

"What were you just playing?" he utters in a low tone.

I won't tell him it was us, burning up on impact. A dangerous tornado that's going to rip through my heart, upend my life, and come out through my fingers in a composition I know I'm going to be absolutely thrilled with. "It was nothing," I say. "Just a vague attempt to—"

"There was nothing vague about that. It was explicit." He traps my gaze in a way that I can't evade and don't want to. "And don't take this the wrong way, because I mean it with respect. But I don't think that music was about your husband."

My heart throbs, exposed. That music was so far from being about Fraser, I am consumed in equal parts by the unfolding of intense captivation and by remorse. And yet I'm desperate to play it again. Over and over. I can barely breathe with how much I want this electric new sound in my life.

"I think I know what's wrong with the screenplay." He's pacing the room now. "My character needs to have suffered. Properly suffered. She needs to have been to hell and back." He stares at me: deep suffering represented.

"But the character you had was all glittering perfection. Wouldn't she make a more attractive lead?"

"No," he growls, frustrated. Hands raking through dark hair.

"Don't we go to movies to *escape* our lives—"

He frowns at me. "She needs to be flawed. I don't mean adorably quirky. I'm talking major flaws, Audrey."

Major flaws? If this is some newfangled chat-up strategy, it needs serious work.

"I want her heart on her sleeve," he says, the line echoing through the room's acoustics as he moves closer to me. "All her open wounds exposed and so red raw it hurts to look." His eyes run along the lines of my forearm as he speaks, gaze burning along my skin, settling gently inside my wrist, despite the fierceness in his tone.

"Is this really what you want, Beau? A majorly flawed, broken woman with exposed wounds, who's been to hell and back?

It sounds like a storm you'd want to outrun. I thought you wanted a supernova."

He drops his arms to his sides. "Out*run*?"

"Your former muse lit up the sky," I remind him. "She burnt bright and exploded on impact. You're describing a woman who might accidentally smolder if she tripped in a pile of kindling and her phone fell from her pocket at just the wrong angle so the glass caught the blazing sun."

He smiles at this, eyes sparkling. "The writer in me wants to hear you say that again."

"You can't charm me into wordplay." *He absolutely could. I would fold, instantly.* "We're having a serious conversation."

He holds up both his hands and wipes off the smile, or tries to.

"A flawed character could work," I press on. "But even with 'major flaws,' surely she's not a *total* flop. I mean, doesn't she scrape herself up off the floor every once in a while and do something at least mildly impressive?"

"Audrey—"

I pull him down onto the piano stool with me, discovering, too late, that it's really not built for duets. Cue awkward reshuffling—mine, not his—as I attempt not to press myself against his *entire* side.

"I'm sensing you have some notes for me, Hepburn."

My posture straightens, clarity dawning on my key message. "I would not want to be defined by my suffering. Or by my addiction. I am so much more than those two things." I badly need him to understand this point, and I deliver the information like an orator—my tone unambiguously strong.

He doesn't argue. Doesn't speak, actually. *Does he agree with me or not?* My hands are shaking and here I go again, hurtling into an awkward silence as I say, "Nor would I want to turn myself inside out and show someone everything only for that person to storm out and humiliate me because they cannot seem to handle my messy plotline . . ."

Glory, when did this workshop upgrade itself from fiction to reality?

"I mean, if I was this character. And if you were my . . . Well, if you were the—"

How do I switch myself off?

"I think the technical term you're searching for is 'hero.'"

The room sucks in its breath, piano strings taut, moment of truth having blundered across the floor. Beau repositions his body on the stool now, easily finding the room for both of us that seemed missing just moments ago.

"The hero won't know what has hit him, Audrey."

"Obviously I'm not suggesting—"

"He won't deserve her. He won't trust himself around her. She'll be all the things I've said, fused with this hidden strength and creativity and sex appeal that's just . . . *flammable*—"

With his thigh touching the length of mine, hips, arms, shoulders, there is no hope that he doesn't feel the way I am trembling.

"Even in bright yellow Wellingtons . . ."

Is it possible to asphyxiate from a compliment?

He makes me look at him now, twisting me to face him, eyes piercing mine as he says, "The problem is that after she's told him her life story—the whole messy plotline in three acts—and he understands just how much she has at stake, his public life will bring her undone. Journalists will dig and pry, and they won't let up until they've fed like vampires on all her secrets. They'll take the precious life she's reclaiming and they'll blow it all up again—"

This isn't about not trusting him, I realize very belatedly. It's about not trusting *them*. He's not abandoning me; he's trying to protect me.

"And here's the real kicker," he adds before I can collect myself, pain really searing across his face now. "All along, no matter how far she opens her heart and how much music they make, there will never be a time, for the rest of their lives, when she's not still madly in love with someone else."

49

Fraser

"I need you to help me sift through Bumble," Rach announces while I mix her a cocktail.

She'd been so distressed on that ladder on the mountain, I doubt she even remembers me telling her I'd been taking her for granted. Every interaction with her now is confusing and fragile. Her rising sense of certainty and empowerment is being charged from my own rapidly depleting power bank. She even looks different. *Is it the clothes? Has she cut her hair?* I'm having unsettling flashbacks to the time Maggie had already made up her mind that our marriage was over and, having switched onto that different track, nothing could divert us back.

"I thought you were moving to Ireland," I say, passing Rach a margarita.

"I'm not moving away this week. I can have fun, can't I?"

Can she? It's her life. But suddenly the notion of Rachael "having fun" with individuals other than myself makes my insides buckle.

"Here I am. No partner. No kids. No prospects . . ."

"Need I remind you you're a kick-arse cybersecurity ninja? You do your own prospecting."

"No *romantic* prospects. I told you, Frase, I've got way too comfortable loafing around the house with you every week."

"I thought we were calling this 'place-holding.'"

She laughs.

"It's not like we sit around doing nothing," I argue. "Outdoor cinema. Cooking classes. Concerts. Galleries. Day trips . . ."

"Yes, and every time an eligible man sees me gallivanting with you on our endless quest to be the poster couple for *men and women can just be friends*, I lose another opportunity!"

Oh, Rachael McKenzie, we have well and truly lost that title. She might be able to accomplish "friends," but I seem to have dropped that ball. I fast-forward to her settling down with that faceless Irish bachelor—or any bachelor at all—and I'm already missing her. Not in the way you miss a friend. The way you lose a lover, languishing in their absence.

This woman has had complete control of her love life, or lack of it, ever since we met. She has kept herself away from relationships, citing no time, no interest, no viable prospects, no trust in the apps. She's been "picky" and "fussy" and "endlessly disappointed in men," and she's stayed deliberately, happily single. But now that she's flipped this on her own terms, she'll be unstoppable. She'll plunge into that dating pool, a late entry, and storm to victory. The top-shelf contender. She'll be inundated.

"Is this why you've forced me onto the apps?" I ask, having lost feeling in several limbs. "To make room for your own love life?"

She looks me square in the face. "No, Fraser. That's because you're too good a man to stay single. You're depriving some woman, and yourself, of future happiness. Have you had any matches?"

"None that feel right."

"None that are Audrey's twin, you mean? Don't tell me, you're waiting for some tormented creative who'll write songs about you . . ."

I thought I'd been avoiding everyone equally. But maybe

she's right. I've been waiting for someone to come along in the exact shape of the hole in my life.

"Lightning doesn't strike the same place twice, Frase."

"Actually, Rach—"

"Don't mansplain the science to me! I'm being poetic."

But lightning *can* strike the same place twice. In fact, it often does. If something is tall enough or isolated enough and it's made of a material that attracts lightning, it can be struck multiple times, even in the same thunderstorm.

I glance through the living room door at Audrey's piano, untouched since the day she died. Sometimes, I can almost hear the keys. If I close my eyes and focus hard enough, I imagine a faint vibration, as if her ghostly fingertips are trying to will the music back into my life.

When I look at Rach again, bright eyes, sapphire pendant sparkling, I can't help feeling a similar sensation. That invisible whisper of Audrey's encouragement. Some part of me *has* been waiting for that second bolt of lightning, someone so similar, she could almost walk straight into her shoes. It never occurred to me that the second bolt might be less about how alike that person was, and more about how close.

"What's wrong with you now?" Rachael asks. She's caught the way I'm looking at her. As if we've only just met and I'm seeing her for the first time. She stops chopping celery sticks and comes and stands beside me, peering into my face. "You look like you've seen a ghost."

She sweeps blond hair away from her forehead and folds the cuffs of her pale blue shirt. Then she reaches behind me and flicks on the oven like she lives here.

After that, she looks into my face again and frowns at me.

I glare back and smile.

Her eyes narrow.

It's like a tennis match, volleying facial expressions over the net, and when she shoves me along and plunges her hands into a sink of hot, soapy water, she says, "You're really getting to me lately, Fraser Miller," before placing her wet hand on my arm for emphasis.

"Trust me, it's mutual," I tell her, wiping my arm with a tea towel. She holds my gaze for just a moment longer than normal. Long enough to plant the hint of a question I haven't dared ask. Whatever major revelations I've been kicking around in my own brain about her recently, they haven't ventured far enough to envisage a scenario in which she feels remotely the same way. She's told me she's leaving. And moving practically as far as possible from here. Ten thousand miles. I looked it up.

She puts the glasses on the drying rack, wipes her hands on the tea towel, picks up the charcuterie board, and takes it to the other room. I stand here in her wake, her fragrance still in the air, staring at my own reflection in the kitchen window, shocked at the hope on my face.

This is Audrey's *best friend.* My own best friend. A woman Parker loves as if she's her own stepmum. And her current plan is to marry Seamus O'Grady and have a brood of Irish babies.

The only crack in that plan seems to be one slightly longer than usual, slightly irritated, ambiguous glance that my scientific mind has already categorized as an anomaly. Every logical fiber is screaming to listen to that science, to galvanize my heart and look further afield.

"What thorny issue are you wrestling with now, Professor Miller?" she says, scooping the cheese knife from the counter seconds later.

I'm not wrestling with anything. It's a proven fact. "I was thinking . . ." *Hoping.* "Sometimes all it takes is one microscopic anomaly to burn an existing framework to the ground."

50

Audrey

"Audrey?" a voice squeals in the corridor as I lock the rehearsal room after a second productive morning of writing alone. "AUDREY!"

A cyclonic teenager slams into my body, pushing me into the wall, making me drop everything. My heart bursts as I squeeze Parker to my chest, then push her to arm's length to take her in. "Look at you, Parks! You look incredible!"

How am I staring at her at eye level? When did that happen? I'm sick with how much I've missed of her life and just want to drink in every inch of her.

"Mum hates this whole fit." She shows it off proudly. Black jeans. At least three layered tops. Combat boots. "I *knew* you'd love it."

It's been far too long. Months, since we've seen each other. The secondary loss of this child from my life guts me every single day. I doubt there is any number of years of sobriety that Maggie would accept as sufficient to allow me back into her life again, unleashed.

I glance over her shoulder. Her uncle is waiting for her in the foyer, watching from the respectable distance I commanded yesterday, hands in pockets, frown on face.

"Mum doesn't understand my life at *all*," Parker is already confiding. "Not any of it. Not you. Not . . . *other things*."

We really can't be having this conversation. We're not meant to be unsupervised, let alone having an open rant about Maggie.

She takes out her phone and makes a call. My precious piece of Fraser. My connection to him, in human form. She is his DNA. His blood. Had he and I changed our minds and had a baby, she would have been my child's sibling—

"Mum? Can Audrey come to lunch if Uncle Josh is there?"

It's like being shocked by a defibrillator.

"Parker!" I move in close and talk into the phone: "Maggie, sorry! We just bumped into each other. I'm not involved! I can't really—"

She ends the call and squeals. "She said it's fine!"

But it's not fine! I wish Beau was still here—he would have been a good excuse—but he disappeared to work on his script. *And to give you time to think,* he said, *about risking this level of exposure.*

"Uncle Josh!" She runs down the corridor, and I can tell the precise moment she breaks the news, because he looks as impressed as I feel. Hardly surprising after I sent him packing yesterday.

I pick up the papers and the bag that I dropped and walk toward them, equal parts repelled and enthused.

"Mum said it's okay if Audrey comes, because you're here," she says to Josh, as if the whole family is fully abreast of the circumstances of my excommunication.

"Why wouldn't it be okay?" he asks, brows knitted. Perhaps Maggie did keep her promise.

"Long story," I answer. *This is excruciating.* "I don't think we need to get into it now, Parker. Where shall we eat?"

■ ■ ■

The one thing about having lunch with a thirteen-year-old is that you don't have to talk. We're at a sushi place near the university, and it's enormously overstimulating—the array of food choices, the loud music, the lunchtime rush, Parker's excited prattle, the constantly moving conveyor belt. *Josh.*

He's the anchor here. The only thing *not* moving. The thing I would focus on to get my bearings, like when you're in a car and they say to pick a point on the horizon, except traditionally when I focus on this man, my life falls apart.

He seems to have no such problem in reverse. I can feel his steady attention while I wrangle sushi and mineral water and Parker's peppered anecdotes and questions, with which I can barely keep up.

". . . And then I came out to Mum and she *freaked.* Hey, Audrey, when do you think Taylor will drop her next album? There was a rogue letter *M* in one of her Instagram posts. Like, right among all the emojis and stuff. Do you think that was a typo, or is it code for March?"

Josh and I exchange a glance. Did she just say she *came out*?

Emotion I can barely label floods my body. My face prickles with heat, and with a tremendous sense of having been absent during something so crucial. With Fraser absent, too. And Maggie *freaked*? Maggie, who is not only a loving mother but a trained and experienced psychiatrist.

"I don't understand," I say.

"About the emojis?"

"No, I get the Swiftie fan theories. It could mean May, couldn't it?"

The idea of my not being available to back her up with this just *kills* me. I am furious. At myself, and at what I did that caused her mum to enact this forced rift between us.

"I also told her I asked my friends to call me Bee, not Parker. She *lost* it! We had a huge fight—"

Words from the past echo in my head. *Fraser, why can't Audrey call our child by her proper name?*

"Then I stormed out and blocked her and stayed at a friend's place that night."

What's with her insistence on Bee? We named her Parker.

"So basically I hate her."

I wasn't meant to hear that conversation, years ago. I'd come downstairs as they were saying goodbye in the hall. *Maggie, they adore each other,* Fraser said softly. *It's just a name she made up because Parker is always buzzing around. Parker loves it. Let them have this one thing . . .*

One thing? Maggie said. *They've got music. And for Parker, that's everything!*

I look at Parker now and realize there could be a major gap in background information here. I'm sure Maggie could have handled this better, but I very much doubt her response was driven by what Parker assumes.

"Could your mum's response be more about your choice of name?" I ask. *More about me, in other words.*

"But that's been your nickname for me for years! You even called me that at Uncle Josh's concert, when I met you!" She looks at me, then puts her sushi down, understanding beginning to dawn.

"Sometimes we get things wrong, as adults," I explain, from bitter experience. I don't want to get into this in front of Josh, but who knows when I'll be allowed to see her again. "You know how much I messed up. I was responsible for you and I botched it. Badly."

I try to forget he's here. I will *not* look at him.

"Mum had a choice in how to act. You didn't. Addiction is a

mental health condition," she says, all progressive teen enlightenment and understanding. "It's a disease."

Right, so it's all on the table now.

"And you know who helped me through that?" I ask her.

Silence.

"No, you don't, because she never made a big deal of it. Your mum took me to the doctor. She arranged my first prescription, because I was too self-conscious to enter the pharmacy and ask. She helped me clean up the house. She checked in. She brought meals. She kept my privacy."

I flick a glance at Josh. He is gobsmacked.

"She wouldn't let me see you!" Parker protests, but her tone has lost some of its sting.

"Because she loves you. I bet it's killing her that she's let you down."

She twists a lock of her hair. It's cropped short, with an undercut.

"I love it like this!" I say, admiring it.

"You look different, too, Audrey. Do you have a secret boyfriend?"

The question gives me whiplash. I am not opening up about Beau in present company. The idea of even mentioning his name makes my nerve endings vibrate with alarm. And with something else. *And with everything.*

Beau was right. I am madly in love with Fraser. I always will be. But as for the rest of what he said—that I was strong and creative and talented and . . . *flammable*, even the way I appeared on Night One, like a dangerous swamp monster, wielding my vehicle against his—my whole body tingles at the thought . . .

"She *does*," Josh says, breaking into my thoughts, reading me right, the way he always did.

"Who is it?" Parker asks, leaning toward me.

"It's nobody," I answer, frowning at them both. "I've started composing again. That's why I'm here. To spend a few days writing music."

Her eyes are alight. "You can *do it*, Audrey! You can! You two are the whole reason I love music."

She holds out both her hands, palms up, inviting us each to take one. But the poignancy of the gesture is short-lived. As Josh and I reach for her, we seem to notice in unison the mirrored crisscrosses of raw red skin inside each of her wrists.

She sees her mistake instantly, lets us go, and tugs at her sleeves. And my heart cracks all over again.

"Parker, does your mum know about that?" I ask, gently, fragments coming to mind of her wearing long sleeves in summer, tugging at the cuffs, and that sense I'd had for so long that something was up.

"Please don't tell her." She's frantic now, her secret exposed.

All this time, I've been worried sick about the example I set. I've been so hard on myself for letting her down, and letting Fraser down, posthumously. He once explained, after we'd all had a particularly difficult day at home, that parenting was a constant exercise in trying to adjust our own warped perspective. We magnify our mistakes. We focus on the times we get it wrong, and never on the string of little triumphs that add up to a good job over a lifetime. But what if one mistake is so huge, we're cut from a child's life? How can I ever forgive that?

When I look at Josh, his eyes are glistening. Whatever else he's done wrong, there's purity in his love for Parker.

"What's this about?" I ask, and she shrugs. For a moment, I think she's not going to tell us, then the floodgates open.

"Everything is so shit," she says, hands shaking, starting to cry. "My friends whine about how hard life is and I just want to scream, *YOUR DAD DIDN'T DIE!* When it's Father's Day at school, the teachers bang on about the big breakfast as if I'm not even here, like I just have to suck up the whole thing and pretend it didn't happen to me. I never see you. Mum broke up with Rose's dad, so I never see her, either. You and Mum told me it wasn't my fault . . ." Now the sobs are free flowing, and she grabs both my hands and squeezes so tight it hurts. "It *was*, Audrey! Of course it was! And I *hate* my life without him. He loved me so hard!"

She's almost out of breath. "As for this?" She pulls her cuffs up again, showing us. "I felt too much. Then I felt *nothing*. And now I just want to feel *something* . . . This hurts just like everything else, but I'm in control of it."

There's a fresh round of tears while plastic plates of sushi trundle past and the three of us drown in unfamiliar waters.

"Audrey, *please* don't tell Mum. She'll hit the roof."

I glance at Josh for backup. Josh. The playboy uncle, who swans through New York, full of his own importance, and then blows in once a year with fancy gifts from Juilliard.

"Parker," he says. "Do you *want* to stop?"

She sniffs, and I pass her a tissue. "I don't know how."

"Don't worry about how. But do you want to?"

She takes a big breath, her tears calming, and nods.

"There's a way through this. It's not easy, but it exists."

Where is he getting this information? I try to steal a glance at his own wrist, but it's hidden behind the Rolex Oyster and a silver cuff link. *Why is he so dressed up?*

"Audrey isn't going to break your confidence," he says, "but if you can't tell your mum, I will have to. She needs to know."

Parker looks in despair from him—bad cop—to me.

"It will be okay. She'll know what to do. This is her job," I assure her.

I feel Fraser here now, circling the three of us, holding us up. Smoothing the way, as if this whole encounter, right when I'm needed, was meant to be. Because this—after all those lunches and lifts and cheering on the sidelines, all that help with homework and soothing her grazes and calming her nightmares—*this* feels more important than anything else. It feels like my motherhood moment.

"A very clever young woman told me mental health issues aren't a choice," I say. "And you know where she likely heard that? From her psychiatrist mum. Trust me, Parker, she was there for me in a big way. She'll be brilliant with this if you let her be. And . . ." I look at Josh. *God, how have we ended up in something together?* "Your uncle and I are here for you, too. I could come with you and help talk to her if you like?"

She's trying to hold herself together. Thirteen is a difficult age at the best of times, worse with the snowballing trauma she's lived through. And when she can't keep her tears at bay, she throws her arms around my neck. "I don't care what Mum thinks," she whispers. "She's wrong. You've always been a *wicked* stepmother."

"Keep me posted?" I ask Josh after we've dropped her back. I really didn't want a reason for us to keep in touch, but if there ever was one, this is it. Parker has Maggie. And, as much as I hate this, I feel like between us, Josh and I represent Fraser.

"It sounds like you've been through a lot," he says, his voice compassionate. I am not going to fill him in on any more of that. "You know you can always ask me for help. I'm not the enemy you think I am."

He is *exactly* the enemy I think he is. I shake my head and turn to go, but he grabs my arm.

"There's something else," he says, looking very much as though he doesn't want to elaborate. He checks the time. "I've got a meeting now, but can we find a time to talk?"

"Do we have to?" I know this man. He's always looking for a crack in the door to push through.

"Sully, I need to tell you why I really came back. And you're not going to like it."

51

Fraser

"I need to come clean about something," Josh admits, over a beer. "It's about Audrey."

Here we go. "We don't have to get into this," I say. I know how he feels. I've probably always known. But do I actually want to hear him voice it in so many words?

"It's not what you think," he says, downing several mouthfuls for courage. "I mean, it is. Obviously." He frowns into the glass. "Always."

Is he forgetting we aren't talking about some random woman here, but the one I almost married?

"That's not what I want to talk about, though," he clarifies. He may look polished in his designer suits and flashy accessories, but there's something desolate about the way he's propping himself up on the bar, as if the weight of what he's carrying is beyond his strength.

I tap my fingers on the countertop and check my watch. "Aren't we years beyond this?"

He shakes his head. "I wish we were. But this is about Ridges, and that summer."

I'm hit with an instant flash of anger.

"Josh, I know this story. He stole her piece. She confided in you. You promised you were in her corner. He bribed you with the recommendation for the Vienna position. You let your ego win. You two had a falling-out, and our mother has blamed Audrey ever since—"

"No, I'd already been offered that position in Austria."

Well, that makes no sense. *Why would he sell her out if he didn't need to?*

"She'd written this incredible piece. She was the outlier, not just in her own year but in our whole cohort. But she was plagued by this pressure cooker inside her head telling her she wasn't ready. She never believed in herself. Thought every success was a fluke. It made her an easy target."

"For you?"

He winces. "For Ridges!"

I let out a low breath. The way he's describing her rings so true, my chest clenches that he knew her this well, long before I did.

"So, what, you rode in on your white horse, intending to save her from her own impostor syndrome?"

"We were both on this trajectory. I could see it, even if she couldn't. We were going to crush the classical world."

"And you succeeded."

He rubs the back of his neck, mouth tight, and nods at the bartender to refill his glass. For the first time in over a decade, he looks miserable about his wild success.

"Fraser, when I confronted Ridges about her piece, I was on her side. But I'd barely mentioned her name before he reminded me of an incident a couple of years earlier. I'd been tutoring for one of his undergraduate courses. There was a . . . regrettable episode with an exchange student from Amsterdam. Entirely consensual, of course. Just probably not quite—"

"Ethical?" *How predictable.* My brother finding historic ways to disappoint me.

"The point is Ridges made it disappear. Said it saved him a load of paperwork as my supervisor. Totally understood how these things happened."

I bet he did.

"I was angry about what he did to Audrey. But he completely cut me off. Argued that if either of these things had come out . . . my indiscretion or his—"

"It would have been the academic equivalent of a murder-suicide?"

He nods.

"So it was blackmail. Not bribery like we'd all assumed?"

He looks gutted. "He only asked me to stall her a few days. That didn't seem so bad. I thought she'd still have an opportunity to argue her case—"

"After he'd taken advice from a crack legal team, fabricated evidence to prove she was wrong, and detailed a comprehensive gaslighting strategy?"

"Yeah, I know. I knew it then. Ironically, if I hadn't stalled her and he'd followed through on his threat to expose me, I probably would have received a discreet slap on the wrist and moved on. You know what the system is like."

"Why buckle to him, then?"

He looks me straight in the eye. "I was young. I'd just been appointed to the position in Vienna. I was so hungry for it all, I couldn't risk it. And she was so fucking talented, Fraser. I told myself this would be a blip. I was always so desperate to impress her, I couldn't bear the idea of her thinking badly of me if the story about the undergrad student came out. So I panicked."

I wish Audrey had known how scared both men had been. Scrambling to protect themselves in the wake of her genius, crushing her underfoot while they scuffled to victory.

"I had no idea she was going to take it the way she did. It was one piece. I'd spent all summer watching her churn out magnificent compositions, prolifically. I made the mistake of thinking she was unstoppable."

He could not have been more wrong. "Why are we talking about this now? You can't undo it."

He looks even more pained. "He never stopped. He teaches to this day, still pulling accolades for his 'original works'—stealing Audrey's at least taught him to be careful, but he constantly flirts with the line beyond which 'creative sampling' becomes thievery. I feel guilty every time he does it, because I knew all along and could have done something, and still haven't. So it's this enormous, retrospective monster of a backlist now—an entire body of other people's work. And I want to expose him, I really do, Fraser. I want to do it for Audrey. But I have so much further to fall now."

He pauses. Takes a breath. And when I look at his face, I know he's never going to follow through.

"Why are you really here, Josh?"

He makes sure I'm concentrating, glued to his final, agonizing point: "Because he's worked his way through the students at Australia's top tertiary institutions. And if someone doesn't step in and stop him, he's about to steal a whole lot of original compositions from a bunch of gifted high-schoolers at a summer music school."

52

Audrey

“Let me get this straight,” Sara says, all librarian vibes, dark hair in a bun, pushing glasses up her nose as she sits opposite me at a coffee shop near her place for breakfast. “You crashed into this guy, the Viper, on Thursday, less than a week ago? And you’ve already got the doom sparkle?”

I shake my head while swallowing a sip of my iced tea. “*Doom* sparkle? Is that what we’re calling it now?”

“Don’t you remember phoning me a couple of nights after Fraser’s funeral and telling me never to let you step *near* another man if I ever saw the ‘doom sparkle’ in your eyes?”

I don’t even remember the phone call. “Was I drunk?”

“That’s beside the point.”

“And what did you reply?” I don’t really need to ask. It would have been music to her ears. She’d have been all, *Yes, yes, good plan, Auds. Stay clear, I say.*

She puffs up. “I said you were my sister and I just wanted to see you happy.”

What kind of half answer is that? I cut the slice of carrot cake we’re sharing and pick up a piece with my fork. “So you agreed to stop me?” I’m recalling every previous conversation we’ve ever had about romance and all the times she’s warned me to stay safe, by avoiding entanglement like she does.

Sara softens in a way that makes me instantly suspicious. "Actually, Audrey, I said that I'd never, in more than forty years, seen someone as destroyed as you were over Fraser, which made me extrapolate that I'd never loved something or someone so hard that it could hurt this much to lose them. You broke apart. It made me realize I'd never properly lived—not full-out and recklessly in love the way you do."

I pause eating the carrot cake, mid-chew. Of all the conversations for alcohol to have erased.

"I knew you wouldn't remember this, but when you asked me to step in and stop you if you ever found happiness again, I promised you I would do no such thing."

I put down my fork.

"So to see you talk about Beau and look at me like this . . . after all the time we've watched you break, *willing* for the day when we'd see this expression in your eyes again—this *hope* . . ." Now she's crying. Actually crying. *My sister!* "I just think you have to risk this, Audrey. Risk everything for it."

This is the pep talk I was one hundred percent certain she was not going to deliver. I came here to be talked *out* of this.

"But he walks red carpets, Sara. He's in magazines." I scramble for my phone and pull up the screenshots of Harlow and Lucinda that April sent me. "He dates women like *this*!"

"And he cooked you breakfast after you crashed into his car, engineered some clifftop creative epiphany, jumped with you into the ocean, rescued you from drowning and sunburn, and dropped everything for a road trip with you."

"Yes, but—"

"Is that everything?"

No. I think of the gentle way he listened to my sobriety story and supported it, but Sara needs no further ammunition. "That's the gist."

"And that was just the first long weekend. What kind of sister would I be if I warned you off this?"

"He thinks I'm not strong enough to withstand the spotlight. He said journalists will uncover my history—the drinking—and there'll be all these headlines about him dating an alcoholic. He's scared it will kibosh the career I'm scrambling to get back. So now I'm imagining them latching on to the fact that I am currently of no fixed address and living in a camper and not realizing it was a deliberate bid for creative freedom."

"Write what you know," Sara says.

Why is she giving me writing advice at this crucial moment?

"You're writing a musical about being widowed. That experience drove you to alcohol, which took over your life until you pulled yourself out of it again. Write a song about that. Write a whole character arc! Put it in the show. Take control of the narrative. Then what can they possibly do to you?"

Sara works with numbers. She doesn't understand music or theater or creative writing. But she does understand risk. She strategizes risk every day, for enormous corporations. And she understands me.

"Imagine the good you could do, talking about this. You could help people. Instead of seeing Beau's public persona as a threat, think of it as a platform. Embrace it. Run toward it. You'll strip the journalists of their power."

My sister's role in my life is to keep me grounded. She's meant to dampen all my dreams to keep me safe.

She doesn't know it, but Sara's idea has injected an unexpected sense of purpose into my life that I think I've been missing for decades. It's not just music. It's storytelling.

"Also, Audrey, the fact that he has halted this conversation while you think about the potential impact on your life says a lot about him. He might be off rushing through his screenplay revisions, rewriting this film character, heavily inspired by *you*—but he's also giving you the space you need to figure this out. I have to respect the man."

What has gotten *into* her, rushing through this landscape, tearing down all the red flags?

"What you had with Fraser is more than most people get in a lifetime," she says, and I know she's talking about herself. "If you get a second chance at this, don't fuck it up."

If nothing else she said has penetrated, that last statement has smashed through what was left of my crumbling resistance. It's the first time in my life that I've ever heard my sister swear.

"Sara, this is a one-eighty spin on romantic advice. If I didn't know any better, I'd say you'd met someone!"

She picks up a piece of cake, holds it near her mouth, and smiles. "Can't have my little sister cornering the market on epic love stories, can I?"

I get in my car after a surprising breakfast and remember a similarly thought-provoking conversation I had with my now sponsor, Ali, in my kitchen that night after my first support meeting. We had a cup of tea at the table, two bottles safely in the recycling bin, the wine having been tipped down the sink in possibly the second-scariest moment of my life.

"You don't have to explain how you arrived here," she said. "I don't need to know. Not unless it's going to help you."

I was intrigued to figure out where the wheels had fallen off, having long blamed the way we swamped those drinks that first night after Fraser died. But one misjudged, completely understandable, reality-blocking binge in a crisis does not necessarily lead to this. It had to be deeper.

"I guess I should start at the end," I said. "The moment when I thought my life was over?"

"Start wherever feels best."

And I wondered, where does a story start and finish, really? I read something about world wars and how we never really know when they begin. It's often a gradual slide into conflict, the series of triggering events obvious only in retrospect.

"I'd chosen a *Pride and Prejudice* quote for the orders of service for our wedding," I told her. "You know that one where Elizabeth says, 'I cannot fix on the hour, or the spot, or the look, or the words, which laid the foundation . . . I was in the middle before I knew that I *had* begun'?" It's like that, this story. I think it really goes back to my twenties, when everything first went off the rails."

Ali pulled her chair in and sipped her tea, in that way that some people pull chairs and sip tea that just seems to open sacred space for quiet honesty. I'd run through the order of events. The doctoral program. The scandal. Josh's betrayal. The way I let it eat me alive. And a familiar disappointment had crawled up my frame as if its tentacles were grasping me from some underworld. A place where lapsed dreams lurk, endlessly hoping for revival that never comes.

"I had been molten glass back then, thrust in and out of a roaring furnace, scared I would cool and solidify before I'd been properly sculpted into the shape everyone wanted."

"You know, Audrey, glass can be melted and reformed over and over again. It's inherently recyclable. Even years later."

I reached for my wine. Surprised to find that it was tea. Forgetting who I was talking to, and the meeting we'd just left. Realizing for the first time that the roots of my addiction may have stretched further back than I thought and that perhaps it wasn't too late.

"We can hold injustice like a crutch," Ali said. "We can preserve failure as a theoretical concept. If you don't try, you can't lose."

"You mean, if I blamed my professor and my friend for wrecking my career—which they did temporarily—I was safe from wrecking it myself?"

"It must have been hard," Ali said.

"Oh, this is not the hard part," I answered, quickly. I wanted to rush out the rest of the story in case she thought I'd plunged myself into addiction over only that. Though that's not always how addiction works, either. You don't need something to have gone terribly wrong to find yourself trapped in it. I told her about the Zoom meeting. The silent phone on my desk that *haunts* me. The missed calls. The accident.

"Fraser left his meeting and ran to her, but when he was crossing the road outside the school . . . I know intellectually it was an accident. It wasn't my fault. It could just as easily have been me, if I had taken that call. But, Ali, I've never forgiven myself."

That's where the alcohol had come in. Via guilt. I wasn't helping myself get through. I was punishing my body. I was making things harder, destroying any chance to find even an atom of purity or happiness in the midst of all that loss. *Because underneath it all, I didn't deserve it.*

"It's the driver's fault," Ali said, simply. "Nobody else's."

I dismissed the argument for the hundredth time. "The campaign by the students to take down the plagiarizer just all sort of died off once they heard what had happened. They really needed me, and my music, to make it work. I've never followed up on our idea to bring Professor Ridges to justice. I'm too furious at myself for folding in the face of it when it first happened."

I was properly crying then, and I'm crying again now, pulling into the music school car park. Because this one loose end still plagues me and angers me and feels like it will forever stand in the face of my progress.

"Don't you see?" I said to Ali. "If I'd believed in myself and argued back when this first happened, Fraser would still be alive!"

That's when she frowned and said, "By that logic, couldn't it be equally true that if you'd faced up to it then, which, given what you've said, would have been an enormously difficult thing for a vulnerable young adult to do, your career might have taken a different path, perhaps even taken you overseas, and you might never have met him?"

But I dismissed that. We had our timeline. Surely he and I would have found our way to each other no matter which paths we'd taken, in every single version of events?

53

Fraser

Some widowed people go through everything. Emails. Messages. Google searches. Perhaps they're desperately seeking even more of the person they've lost. But I haven't touched Audrey's laptop since she died.

We might have been two days off getting married—what's yours is mine and mine is yours and all that—but we still had our own lives. We all put so much in writing these days, every message is part of a giant web of communication with friends and family, questions asked, secrets shared, support given. I never felt it was my place to go somewhere she didn't invite me.

They're not always big milestones. Having her computer on my lap is another first. Some of the hardest moments are these little ones. Touching something no human hands have touched since hers. Something once covered in her DNA. Long gone now.

The photo on the screen saver wrecks me, for starters. It's of the three of us on a holiday in Sydney, down near the Opera House with the Harbour Bridge and the water gleaming in the background. We'd picked up ice creams and wandered through the Royal Botanic Garden—such an innocent, happy little family, unaware of the detonation that lay ahead.

I don't think I'd ever felt so content as I had that weekend. So filled with anticipation for our future. We'd seen a show that night. Audrey had told us maybe she'd have a go at writing a musical again. She'd wanted to distance herself from the kind of music she'd made when she was younger, and her eyes burnt bright with ambition.

Her password is engraved in my head. I was forever encouraging her to choose something less hackable, but she claimed she couldn't remember anything else and she was sick of trying to change it only for the computer to say the new password can't be the old one.

It opens up like a time capsule of the final minutes before the accident. I'm looking at the last computer screen she ever saw. The notification that she'd left a Zoom meeting. Behind that, her email folder, now with three years of unread newsletters and promotions flittering into it, along with an internet window with her unnecessary number of open tabs—the florist, the venue, the photographer. It's as though she was poring over everything, imagining how it would unfold two days from then . . . seeing herself in that future, carrying a similar bouquet, dancing with me at the reception pictured on the venue's website.

I can't look at those pages. Or close them. It would be like closing the tabs on our dream.

She opened the email to her fellow students in a window of its own, so I click on that—all their names are there—and forward it to myself.

It was Rachael who had contacted one of them after the accident. One of their mutual acquaintances, who had asked the group, on my behalf, not to pursue this any longer. At least, not to pursue it as far as Audrey's music had been concerned. I knew that probably meant an end to the whole process. It was her music that had taken the worst hit. But it felt like agony, having anything to do with this then. I was so angry about all that was stolen from her, I couldn't go anywhere near it.

I close the laptop and put it back into the drawer near her piano. Back then this was about only Audrey. At the end of the day she was an adult. It was her fight. But now it's about my child. Someone just as talented, with the same amount to lose—but too young to protect herself. A kid who's already been through multiple traumatic events, with fragile mental health.

For the first time since Audrey died, I lift the piano's key lid. I run my fingers along the keys, not heavily enough to make a sound, wanting somehow to preserve Audrey's last notes, and rage roars to life beneath my grief.

"Dad?" Parker says, coming into the room and stopping still when she sees where I'm standing, this tiny concession to music opening a world of hope in her eyes.

I will not let Ridges *near* her. I've avoided music all this time, but I'd listen to every note that Audrey wrote and the entire catalog of modern classical music to find the evidence I need to bring that monster down. My brother mightn't have the fortitude to finish what Audrey started the day she died, even with his own niece's music in the firing line. But after all these years of pushing this away, I do.

54

Audrey

"So, nobody panic, but I've just received a message from a supermodel," I say to the Bookies on FaceTime.

"If you mean Harlow, she's not technically a *super*model in the strictest definition . . ." April clarifies.

"But for the purposes of dramatic effect, let's go with it," says Clair.

"Well, it turns out she's at least a triple threat. She's a model, she's playing the leading role in Beau's movie, and he's teaching her screenwriting. She said she's been workshopping the new character with him all week and they're having an emergency table read of the new direction in Sydney. And she wants me to come."

There's silence from my friends. A reverent silence, befitting the gravity of this development.

"A supermodel-slash-leading-actress-slash-writer has invited you to the table read of a movie script written by an Oscar-nominated screenwriter," Jess summarizes.

I nod.

"I would say stranger things have happened, but they never have," Rach adds, leaning into view on her couch beside me, Jasper asleep on her shoulder. When the email came in a few minutes ago, we both squealed and woke him up, and she's only just got the poor child settled again.

"Beau and I haven't spoken since a very charged conversation in the rehearsal room. I have been giving him space to write, like I'm a proper muse."

"Wait," Clair says. "What conversation?"

I've been avoiding it all week. Rach knows, but I need no encouragement from the other three, so I do my best to play it down. "He basically admitted he wants his new character to be sort of, well . . . There are some similarities."

Their eyes widen, each drawing their phone closer, amazed faces enlarged on my screen. Rach gets up and lowers Jasper into the pram in the corner so she can be properly present in this conversation.

She takes my phone and speaks to the others directly. "The executive summary is that he's given her space to think about being with him in the spotlight and he's gone off, all inspired by his crush, and has written her into a blockbuster." She places her hand on her heart with pride. "Our Audrey."

"Shut up!" I laugh and lean into the view again. "He didn't say for sure she was based on me."

"Just that she was some deeply suffering, flawed, creative woman who's sexy in Wellingtons and in love with someone else," Rach explains. "You're right. That could be anyone!"

"Flawed and sexy!" Clair chimes.

"The Wellingtons!" Jess repeats.

"My bet is that Harlow wants to pull together some grand Hollywood moment with you in the room, everyone watching—" April says, describing the exact circumstances of my worst nightmare!

"Then he confesses he's madly in love with you!" Jess goes on.

"Except he doesn't have to, of course, because it *shines* off the page!" Clair claps her hands in delight.

"Try not to get your heart broken, Auds. Jasper's teething,

and I don't think I've got it in me to add my best friend's A-list breakup to the sleepless nights . . ."

"I've been widowed, Rach. I'm hardly at risk of heartbreak after a week!"

"What, nobody in the world has ever fallen in love in a week?" Clair argues.

My own grandparents fell in love in a weekend. It's the stuff of family legend.

"What do I do? Just sit there like an unqualified impostor at this meeting he hasn't even invited me to?"

"Maybe she wants to surprise him, too? She's his wing-woman!" April says, strategizing.

"*Hello!* magazine said she was his secret on-again, off-again girlfriend," I remind them.

"And what did he tell you about the tabloids?" Rach asks.

April props her sunglasses on her head and looks serious. "Just don't run this by Sara, okay? I respect your sister, but we're at a critical moment in the arc of this love story and we don't want you spooked—"

She's talking about it like I'm a jittery animal, ready to bolt from headlights and plunge into a forest. "Oh, I've already spoken to Sara. She is unexpectedly obsessed with him! You all are!"

"*Sara's* onside? This must be worth chasing!" April says, beaming. "And we're not obsessed with *him* . . . I mean, *we are*, but we're more obsessed with *you*. This is your first real chance since Fraser died to be with someone incredible. You thought this person didn't exist. You were convinced nobody could ever measure up to him, and here you are, potentially with someone *remarkable* . . ."

Someone remarkable whom I haven't spoken to in days. Now that he's not in my vicinity, and with him working in that trailer with gorgeous Harlow, I can't help wondering if I made the whole thing up. *Poor Audrey. So starved for romance she's invented a famous boyfriend, like when she was ten and convinced herself Luke Perry would take her seriously.*

"The table read is in Sydney, at one o'clock. It should be over in time for me to fly back and get to Parker's concert. Either way, if I'm going, I need to leave *now* and book the only available flight on the way to the airport!"

"Oh, God, does Maggie know you're coming?" Rach asks. I'd conveniently left this part out, because it would have led to a conversation about Parker that I don't want to rush, plus an admission that I'd had sushi with Josh, and she'd have killed me.

"Can we just focus on one of my crises at a time? What if I turn up and Beau isn't thrilled? What if he's right—I *am* madly in love with Fraser and we can never find our way through that, and I'll flip out and run at the first paparazzi shot in the *Daily Mail*? What if I end up dealing with an even more shattered heart, and I can't ever recover from multiple emotional traumas—"

"What if you don't go, and you never see him again?" April asks, shutting me up, well and truly.

Never see him again?

It's swift, insightful wisdom, and utterly spot-on. Because the very idea takes the wind out of me.

"Remember, it's Fraser's life that ended," Rach prompts me, a gentle mic-drop message from a best friend in the midst of a bubbling exchange. "Not yours."

55

Fraser

"I'm doing the right thing, aren't I?"

Rachael and I are at my place, with the email to Audrey's former university peers open. She's beside me, feet up, looking over my shoulder, leaning against my hip and arm, and I can barely keep my train of thought. I don't understand how this woman has been in my life all these years without my ever going to pieces like this around her.

"We need to finish what she started," she says. "She'd want this. And after what Josh implied about the music school—we've got no choice."

We listen to the rough track that Audrey recorded when she was a student, and then again to the track from Ridges' album.

"It's exactly the same tune, right? I mean, it's unmistakable," Rach says.

I click on the link in the email to the cloud repository of the other students' music and we listen to the first sample. And the next. Over and over, there are unambiguous examples of Ridges outright copying his students' work. Just *lifting* it. It's abhorrent. And these are just the handful of people Audrey knew. He's been teaching for thirty years.

"I should never have stopped them from fighting this. It's not fair on any of them. It's only now that my own daughter is at risk that I'm doing something about it, like that evolutionary quirk that wires us to care more about tragedies closer to home."

Rach takes the laptop out of my hands. "What were you going to do, Frase? Focus on this from the depths of grief? You were parenting a devastated child. Teaching. Paying a mortgage. Battling your own demons. You couldn't have done one thing more at the time, and I won't hear another word about guilt."

She starts typing something on the keyboard, and I watch as she scrolls through, then leans closer, frowns, and uncrosses her legs. "God, look at this," she says, angling the screen. "How much research did Audrey do on this guy?"

She passes me the computer, open to the list of presenters at a conference a decade ago. There he is, presenting on the topic "Creative Sampling: A Critical Analysis of the Columbia Law School Library's Music Plagiarism Project."

I stare at her. "So he's an expert in his own crime?"

"Fraser, this is perfect. He steals students' music, but he's a leader in the field. They assume what he's doing must be within the realms of normal, because look at this—he's an international specialist on the topic, and what would they know? They're barely out of high school—*not even*, in Parker's case."

"Like when pyromaniacs turn firefighters. Or when police are corrupt."

Rachael is still scrolling and reading, shaking her head. "There are so many similar cases. Academics stealing students' ideas and publishing them in articles or book chapters. This one professor in the States stole his student's medical invention and sold it to a pharmaceutical company for millions!"

Anger stings. I'm enraged at the injustice, infuriated that Audrey never got the chance for justice when she'd been so driven for it, at the end.

"Let's see if the group wants to pick this up again. They deserve compensation, even if it's too late for Audrey."

"Shall I open an email?" Rachael props big plastic glasses on her nose as if she's ready to take dictation.

"Tell them I'm sorry I halted the case. If they're still keen to talk, we can make a time. Let them know I'm prepared to throw money at this for legal representation." Maybe Josh will pitch in to ease his guilt.

She starts typing while I switch the kettle on and watch her, vibrating with the excitement of having a new project together, watching her work, all her mannerisms so familiar—the way she pins her fringe behind her ear, where it never stays, the fact that her glasses prescription isn't quite right, so she's constantly nudging the sky-blue frames up and down her nose to bring the screen into focus. How she plays with Audrey's pendant while she thinks. All of it is as close as if we'd been living together for years, and when I imagine her on the other side of the world, it's just . . . well, it's impossible.

She snaps the lid of the laptop shut. "Right. That's done. Now I've got a favor to ask . . ." She leans beside the couch and retrieves her handbag as I bring her tea from the kitchen. Next thing she's pulling out a white envelope and a series of small photos of herself.

"My passport has expired," she explains, matter-of-factly. "I need you to be my guarantor."

I don't want to be her guarantor. Everything I've just felt—all the rage and anger and fury about Ridges—takes a back seat in the face of this new threat.

"Do you have a black pen?" She's looking up at me from the couch while I stand here helplessly, with her cup of tea in my hand.

"I think we need to do two, but maybe sign four while you're at it."

Does she not know what she's doing to me?

I put the tea on the coffee table and get a pen from the desk, sit down, and take the sheet of photos.

"They're not meant to be beautiful."

She's mistaken my expression for criticism. I turn them over and click the end of the pen. "What do I have to write?"

"This is a true photo of Rachael Elizabeth McKenzie. And sign your name."

As I do the first, my entire body seems to ache with the effort. It feels like I'm signing my life away.

My whole life.

"My God, Fraser, you're a *sloth*! What's the problem?"

I look at her sitting beside me, all bright-eyed with the promise of Ireland, lining up her ducks. And it strikes me, terribly belatedly, that I am not one of those ducks. Worse, I am almost certain that I used to be. And I can't let her go.

"Rach, before I sign this . . ." I put the pen down, a crystalline timeline of the next fifty years materializing, as fresh and glittering as it feels familiar. This is not an *instead of* situation. It's an *always was*. It's an *as well*. "Can we circle back to something?"

She's losing patience. Keen to get this done and submitted so she can get out of this holding pattern I've had her in and take charge of her destiny. "Circle back to what?"

I clear my throat and reveal my hand, scared I've left this far too late, knowing she has every right to reject me, but if I don't ask, I'll never know: "Can we revisit the bit when you were my fiancée?"

56

Audrey

Whenever I imagined attending a Hollywood-esque table read—*which was never*—it wasn't a forty-minute flight from home, and it definitely wasn't without having gone to a hairstylist beforehand. Yet here I am, in jeans and a simple green swing top, imitation Birkenstocks, and wild hair, having left it to air-dry this morning while I got sucked into my music.

I guess it's only an informal read and not a red-carpet event. Besides, Beau specifically told me he liked flawed women. *Majorly* flawed, and I assume he meant beyond the wiry incoming grays and frayed jeans and nerves. What I'm really doing is walking into this room with my heart exposed.

The table read is being held in an event room upstairs at a North Sydney bar near the producer's office. It's all reclaimed wood, exposed ducts, and copper pipes. Beau's in the corner by a window, leaning over a counter, concentrating on the script with a pen in his hand. Jeans. Dark shirt. Black-rimmed glasses even better in person than in my imagination.

My eyes are drawn to that incomplete compass tattoo peeking out from the fabric of his rolled-up sleeve. A reminder of his unpredictability. Watching him work, I feel a rising sense of protectiveness—I know how worried he's been, and I so badly want this to go well for him.

"Excuse me," someone says, bustling past. She's some sort of assistant, I think, and when she walks over to Beau and he looks up to talk to her, he catches me standing in the doorway. His genuine surprise kick-starts a wave of panic. It's clear Harlow invited me without checking first that he'd even want me here, and when he places a hand on the assistant's arm and signals to her that he just needs a minute, my old instinct—borrowed from pre-Fraser times—is to back out of this room and run.

"I'm sorry," I begin as he arrives in front of me, my whole body on edge. "Harlow invited me. I didn't know if you knew . . ."

"I didn't—"

"I can leave!" *I'm already leaving!* But he reaches for me, pulling me into a space near the door.

"I'm glad you're here."

"Are you?" I'm not fishing for compliments. Just reassurance.

"Hepburn, I've been a wreck."

That's good, right?

"How is it going? Have you rescued it?"

"The screenplay? I *think* it's good? Harlow has been a godsend. She's got an eye for a good story. It's been a bit of a joint effort the last few days. I didn't even get the chance to read the latest version before she printed it."

I cannot fathom being that hands-off.

"I've been worried about crashing your adult gap year," he admits. "You're just getting started. You don't need some man derailing you in front of a wall of camera flashes."

He is hardly "some man." The Bookies will argue over the semantics of this for days.

"Technically it was me who crashed into you," I correct him, and he looks as if he's replaying our first night in my Jeep in the rain. The way the storm lashed the soft-top, both of us drenched from the downpour as he placed his hand over mine on the wheel.

It's clear the reasons I might want to run from this have been bouncing in his brain for days, as they have been in mine. I have trust issues. Ridges. Josh. Fraser telling me we'd be married for fifty years and being so alive, and then so *gone*, so instantly . . .

"I'm worried about the chaos of my career," he goes on, voice gentle and earnest. "The headlines say I'm a serial heart-breaker, but I'm not, Audrey. Every relationship I've had has come undone despite me. I don't know if I can protect you from it all. I'd never forgive myself if—"

If what? If this failed and it drove me back into the arms of my liquid nemesis?

"Beau, surely we can talk this through? Not now, obviously. You're in the middle of—" I sweep my hand around the room at piles of paper, pens, coffee cups, and fruit platters as effortlessly attractive off-camera household names swan about in a way that April would rupture an internal organ over.

When he puts a hand on my arm, it thrills me to my core. *Thrills* me.

But then the door behind me opens, sending a brisk breeze up my spine, made cooler by the clouded expression on his face as he looks over my shoulder. And I feel like the wind has been knocked out of me. Without even turning around, I can guess who is standing there. Perhaps we've known each other only a few days, but we seem to be able to read each other's faces, and what I'm seeing here, writ large in the pain in his eyes, is not a serial heartbreaker at all. It's the heartbroken.

I follow his gaze, my body knowing to step back and make room for the unfolding, in front of my eyes, of a reunion as epic as the cinematographers would craft this scene. In his eyes, I see what he saw the other day in mine. *Still madly in love.* I imagine I can hear the thunder of the heartbeat beneath the lion on his chest, bearing her name. And I keep expecting one of them to say something, but neither does. They are just . . . spellbound.

Beau's arms fall to his sides, body language that's the very opposite of defensive. He is open. Willing. Trusting. Just seconds ago, that hand had been on my arm, and now it's reaching over for a one-handed hug, crushing her to his chest as if I'm not even here.

"What are you doing here?" I hear him whisper. The *you look amazing* is implied, as his eyes sweep over long, straight, lustrous blond hair, bright blue eyes behind designer glasses and a thick fringe. She is that extraordinary mix of cover-girl beautiful and creative intellectual, and I've never felt more underdressed, more underqualified, or more like an underdog.

"Lucinda, this is Audrey," he says, remembering I exist, at least. As she turns to look at me, head cocked as if she's sizing up her former fiancé's fictional future love interest, I imagine something passes across her face along the lines of . . . *Beau, this makes no sense.*

Instead, she just nods. Perhaps she's not seeing me as a rival at all. Probably thinks I'm the executive assistant, as she turns back to Beau, who looks as baffled by her presence here as he was by mine. "Sorry," she says, appearing authentically apologetic. "They were getting nervous."

Have the producers *called her in*?

I imagine his hurt just as proof of it lands in his eyes. I knew with just that one sighting of him across this room that he was back on top of his game. *Alive* with it. Confident in the way he was directing one of the actors, quietly reading a section of the script. Whatever work has transpired since I last saw him, it's good. But, seemingly without even consulting him, they panicked and brought in the Oscar-nominated writing partner. The woman who made him doubt his own talent. The one responsible for the look on his face now as the brawny, tattooed Viper tries not to crack in front of us both.

"I don't need help—"

"I'm sure it's fine!" she says. "Honestly. I believe in you, Beau! Always have. Let's workshop it?"

She pulls a marked-up copy of the script from a Louis Vuitton tote, and I'm crushed on his behalf. If she really believed he could handle this, and if the producers did, she wouldn't be here. I find myself nodding at him encouragingly, hoping he'll read my silent vote of confidence. The *Knock everyone's socks off.* The *Prove it!*

"Audrey! Nice to see you again!" Harlow says, leading lady and best supporting writer. She guides me to sit opposite Beau and Lucinda before she throws her script down and takes a seat on his other side. So now I'm staring at him, flanked by glamorous exes, questioning why the hell I thought this was a good idea.

The table read begins. And the further into the first act they go, the more invested everyone becomes in the emotion of the characters, the storyline, the stakes. Harlow is good. Even just reading the part. It's not only me becoming more enamored with her the more nuance she brings to the new main character. It's everyone.

That character is flawed in ways that I am not. She's vulnerable about things I haven't experienced. She's suffering, not with what I've been through, but with equally difficult, devastating things. Every so often, Beau glances at me, keen for my nonverbal feedback. He watches for my reaction whenever she's funny or hopeless or hopeful . . .

She is not *me*, and I am grateful for that, but I can see my influence all over her. Maybe I am his muse, after all. I try to convey *well done* as we exchange a discreet smile across the table, both of us delighted at how this seems to be going.

They reach the end of the first act, and the producer speaks up. "Take ten, but well done, everyone. Good work, Beau."

Lucinda puts her hand on his arm, perhaps ready to congratulate him on his success, but he barely registers her beside him.

Because he has turned the page . . . and suddenly the room tilts.

Panic shoots through his face as he devours that page, and the next. Then he picks up Harlow's script and compares the two. I watch as his shoulders slump and he sits back in the chair and covers his face, defeated. Finally, he looks at me, in obvious despair, then turns slowly and says, "Harlow, can I have a word?"

She looks excited. Buoyed no doubt by her impressive performance and how relieved everyone is that this movie is back on track. He stands up, the legs of the chair scraping across the wooden floor, takes her by the wrist, and pulls her out of the room with strong, purposeful strides, slamming the door in their wake.

I'm left sitting here alone, across from Lucinda, who is flicking through the script, too. After reading a page or so, she looks up at me through that perfect fringe and says, "I never knew he could write like this," which I assume is meant to carry some sort of subliminal message about the source of his inspiration.

This would all be awkward enough, but it's clear we have bigger problems, because the room falls silent as people realize, in the manner of dominoes, that there is an enormous row erupting outside. We hear only bits of it as Beau and Harlow compete with the noise from downstairs and the Sydney traffic outside the window.

Harlow's voice is heated. I'm sure everyone catches the words *drowning in writer's block* and *distracted for days*, because half the room looks in my direction.

Beau's voice is too low and muffled for me to understand through the closed door. Next Harlow is shrieking something about how this is the *pivotal scene for the entire film*, while Lucinda practically cranes her neck to see the exchange. And then her eyes flick back to me.

"What's wrong?" I ask.

She spins her annotated script around and pushes it across the table. "You tell me."

I slide it toward me and read through the scene that Beau and Harlow are raging over. It's clearly the powerful midpoint reversal in the plot. The part when the hero first really *sees* her. When she first lets him in. The part where she turns herself inside out and shows him everything.

"Okay, everyone," the producer calls, clapping her hands. "That's time. Someone drag them back in here, will you? Let's take it from the clifftop."

It's the part where she trusted him . . .

57

Fraser

Mention of our prior engagement was a leap, but if I don't pull out all the stops now, this woman is going to walk out of my life and leave. Not in the same way that Audrey did, but the impact is going to be devastating.

"How set are you on moving to Ireland?"

She frowns. "Fraser, what's this about?"

It's one of those critical moments when you know there will always be a *before* and an *after*. My next sentence has to clamber over my loyalty to Audrey just to make it out of my mouth, because what I'm proposing here is not some random fling. "I just wondered . . . whether there was any turn of events in which you might delay."

Rachael's sigh seems several years in the making. "Delay? What's that? The cousin of place-holding?"

I take the passport application from her hand, heart thumping, and place it on the coffee table. "I've got a custody agreement with Maggie that means I can't move from here until Parker is eighteen. I also couldn't take Parker with me. But there's an academic position at Trinity College in Dublin that would be a dream."

She looks at me blankly. "Don't be offended, Frase, but a big part of the attraction of Ireland was how far away it was from you, so I could start a new life. I wasn't imagining us taking our existing arrangement on the road—"

"I'm not talking about our existing relationship. I'm talking about a new life somewhere together. Away from memories here. No more waiting."

Now it's Rachael who looks nervous. Rach, who has ultimately knocked back every man she's dated since we met and whom I desperately want to impress now, if only I knew how.

Then suddenly, right when I need the insider intel, I remember a conversation I once had with Audrey. It was some late-night debrief across our pillows after Rachael had dumped yet another failed suitor: *They're all utterly hopeless, Fraser. Here's what men need to know if they're going to woo Rachael McKenzie. She wants a man who'd take a stand. Someone who'll* notice *her. And tell her. Make a grand speech, you know? Is that too much to ask?* Why *are men the way they are?*

I recall thinking, *Yes, that is a lot to ask.* I was exhausted at the idea, glad I'd already won Audrey over and would never have to put myself on the spot like that. Now here I am, face-to-face with Rachael's famed high standards, knowing I have to take the floor.

"The thing is, every time I approach our restaurant, I know you'll have ordered the veal scallopini," I begin. She looks confused at this diversion. "You'll have it with tap water, the 2021 pinot gris, and you won't want dessert. I won't want dessert, either, but I'll order the tiramisu, because you will have a few mouthfuls, regret you didn't order it, and I'll suggest you take the rest home in a container you'll have brought in your handbag—"

"Yes, because I know how much you hate food waste. Where is this going, Frase?"

I risk picking up her hand, and she allows it. "It gives me a thrill to make you happy in that one tiny, unimportant way. And in a thousand other tiny ways. And it's the same in reverse. When I walk in, there'll be a glass of red on the table waiting, and you'll have ordered the herbed bread and the vegetarian fettuccine, because you'll know I had a late class and a full afternoon of meetings and won't have eaten since noon. It's seamless."

This is nothing like the slow drag into the ocean with Maggie. It's nothing like the plunge into it with Audrey. It's as if we've been in the ocean, one way or another, all along.

"Rachael, somewhere in the last couple of years, this friendship has slipped into the territory of a relationship, in almost every way. Perhaps the reason I haven't been interested in dating is less to do with never wanting to replace Audrey. More to do with the fact that I don't need to. Because I'm with you."

She is staring at me, unable to speak.

"When you said you were going to move countries, every part of me railed against it. I'm not free to leave. Not yet. It eats me up that you might, and I'd be trapped here without you."

She's not even worrying about the tears falling down her face. Such a rare sight for this woman who holds it all in, nearly all the time.

"As for the idea of your baby, I meant I am here to help. Actually, I meant much more than what I said . . ."

With no warning, she clambers across me and moves right into my lap, hands on my shoulders, pulling us together as if we're starting the conception process right this second. She brings her lips onto mine. Soft and fierce. All fireworks and history and the agony of shared loss and tantalizing hope, as if we know every inch of each other already.

This feels like life starting again as floodgates open and the future rushes in.

"Does this go on the list of micro joys?" I ask her, when we finally pull apart. "You said we should chase them, remember?"

"Um, sorry, Fraser! Were you and I just present in the same kiss? There was nothing 'micro' about that."

Her lips are almost on mine again, when she stops, pulls back, and says, "Wait, are we okay with this?"

My fingers are threaded through her hair, thumb at the side of her face, desperate to pull her toward me. But I know where she's going here. It's the same place that I go every time I'm surprised by something good that would never have happened if Audrey hadn't died.

"You should be with her," she whispers, blinking back tears, her face a contradiction of happiness and desire and grief and guilt.

"I can't be."

"But if she were still here—"

"That is not how this works." I take her hand. "I've gone around and around on this. And I've concluded, very unscientifically, that it's probably best to commit to the universe we are occupying. To accept the reality we've been dealt."

I don't mean it to sound that way, as if she is second prize.

"And the one I've been gifted, in your case . . ."

She reaches for a tissue.

"Rach, somewhere in the middle of this hopeless mess, I don't know when, exactly, but I've fallen completely in love with you."

Now she is outright crying, and I pass her the entire tissue box.

"But don't *ever* think this is a sequel for me. This is a completely new, stand-alone story."

Her face softens, this reassurance providing profound relief.

"You're the main character." I don't know how many ways I can say it. "Rachael, this is one of your eight other lives. It's the one where it's meant to be you and me."

"Okay, okay, Beckham," she says. Her voice is softer now. "More than okay."

"Two things can be true, can't they?" I ask. "We can miss her—and love this?"

She nods. "I hope so! Because I can't *not* love you, Fraser Miller. Believe me, I have tried." She kisses me again, convincingly, delivering a trailer for the next fifty years, and I can't believe that I have been this unlucky, and this lucky, in one lifetime.

Afterward, she glances at the passport paperwork, playing with Audrey's pendant.

"Still hankering for Ireland?" I ask her. "Life Number Three?"

I pick up the remaining photo to certify, but she puts her hand on mine.

"Would Maggie approve a shorter holiday, do you think?" she asks, blue eyes sparkling with an idea. "Does Parker have a passport?"

"She does. And I'll talk to Maggie. But that reminds me, Rach, are you free tonight?"

"I don't know," she replies. "My stupid diary is full of placeholder events."

I laugh. "Can I take you to a concert?"

She smiles.

"With my ex-wife?"

58

Audrey

I cannot sit at this table and watch Harlow acting out one of the most intimate scenes from my own life. She'll probably clamber onto the table, pretending it's Beau's truck, and show us the bit where I gave him everything.

No notes, the script says. I mean, does he honestly have so little respect and so many tickets on himself he thought to include every single moment of that exchange?

I *storm* out. Beau follows me. Harlow tries to follow him, but he begs her to give us space and I am *breathless* with rage.

"I have some notes for *you*, Beau," I bite out. "The moment on that clifftop wasn't ours. It didn't belong to *us*. It wasn't yours, just to cheapen and give away to the world like this. It was *mine*."

Words from years ago storm in and meet my current situation, rotating like two giant weather systems, gathering force. *Josh, you know this is mine. How could you have sold me out like this?*

I imagine the clifftop scene playing out on the big screen, sweeping drone footage over the ocean . . . and the way I would *love* it if it wasn't lifted from my own life.

"Audrey, let me explain!"

"I know this feeling. I've felt it before. The plunging of shock when you realize someone has taken something *sacred*."

Staring at him, I am right back where I was at twenty-two,

reeling against the brazen thievery of the most personal part of my psyche. My music. He *knew* that, and now he's taken from me something even more layered and personal. The most vulnerable moment of my life. And shared it with twenty people in that room, with the intent to share it with *millions*.

"Were you going to take my music, too?" I scream. "Even knowing what you know? Is that why you recorded me in the rehearsal room?" My fury is galloping. I am appalled, not only at what he has done but at myself, for letting him in, giving him the chance. "You *knew* I'd been deeply betrayed in the past. You knew this was my hottest trigger point. You knew how much it took for me to open up to you about Fraser and this song. You saw me let my darkest emotion rip, in real time. And you sat there, watching me, doing an excellent impression of someone who really cared. I thought you were supporting me. Were you taking notes all along?"

He is speechless, unable to defend himself.

"I mean, what else happens in this movie, Beau?" I whisper now. "Does the protagonist become an alcoholic?" He sweeps me farther from the door, but I don't care who's hearing this. "Does she smash into his life drunk? I can't believe I let you convince me it was okay to—"

Where is this statement going? Okay to what? *Risk falling for him?*

I am sideswiped by my own realization. Devastated by it. Disappointed in myself that I could have allowed my already smashed heart to crack open again in front of someone, so fast, and let this much light flood in.

"Audrey, you have to listen!"

But that's not true. I don't have to do anything. I find myself stepping back from him, hands off, turning away, fleeing this place before he can hurt me any further.

And as I grab my bag and tear past him and down the stairs, faster and faster toward the curb, where I'll hail a cab, I start laying into myself. *What made you think you could slot into a world like Beau's?* This glittering red-carpet ride that he's on. I don't belong here, in the reflected spotlight of Oscar-nominated stardom. Of course it was all fake! That's his job! To tell stories! Maybe I do belong in the safety of the audience. Anonymously. Quietly. Where Professor Ridges told me to go because I had good ideas but they were never *enough.* Not without him. And now I have offered my stone-cold broken heart to someone who wasn't careful with the horrific path I've been thrown on. Someone who's rushed in, guns blazing, fireworks bursting, and trampled everything, hurling my heart at the wall.

I need to hold myself together. Once I slide into the cab's back seat, I try to center myself in the eye of this storm and in the protective stillness of the car.

"Airport?" the driver asks, and I nod.

Airport bar . . .

Breathe, Audrey.

I try phoning my sponsor, Ali, but the call goes to voicemail. Flashes of the impact of alcohol shoot through my body as if I've already taken several sips. The way it buzzes through your veins. The lifting of stress. The sense of it picking you up and carrying you away from the parts of life you don't feel strong enough to endure. In these crashing moments of even more loss, my mind is grappling for control over a body that is *screaming* for the short-term, solve-all balm for which it habitually wants to reach, even *years* on.

And I exhale, long and slow.

Inhale.

Exhale.

Don't let him take this, too, a voice whispers. I'm digging as deep as I've ever had to.

As buildings flash by and we drive through city streets, my imagination is filled with a maelstrom of hurt and harm and disappointment and betrayal, amber liquids and easy magic swirling through the images. *It would be so easy . . .*

I pick up my phone again. I could call Rach, but Jasper is teething. She hasn't slept in weeks. And I think this needs an expert. It's another clifftop, of sorts. But not the place where I let everything go and allow fresh strength to sweep through me as a result. A place from which it is too easy to slip, gravity pulling me into the surge, smashing me against rocks, dragging me into depths I don't have the strength to fight again. *It's like wrestling a monster.*

I dial a different number.

"Audrey?" Maggie says, when she picks up. "Listen, I already told Parker it's okay for you to come to her concert tonight."

Oh my God, it's only now that I remember the problems with Parker and how I've promised to be there, and wonder if Parker or Josh has spoken to her yet. Why did I phone *Maggie* of all people, when we've already got so much going on?

"I'm sorry for calling," I say, hearing the strain in my voice. "I just need to say I'm heading to the airport in Sydney. Now. I came here for . . ." I can't tell her I've been at a table read for a movie—she'd accuse me of intoxication!

"Is everything all right?"

I wait to catch my breath and my thoughts. I'd have to be crazy to divulge this to Maggie now, when I'm still hoping she'll let me back into Parker's life, but the fact is, I'm desperate. "I haven't had a single drop of alcohol in nearly two and a half years," I explain. "Not since my first AA meeting. But something happened today that really gutted me. I tried calling my sponsor. She didn't answer—"

"Okay, I'm glad you phoned." Her whole tone shifts to accommodate a conversation very different from the one she'd anticipated.

I sit back in the car and close my eyes.

"I'll stay on the line with you until this passes. It *will* pass, Audrey. You've triumphed over it repeatedly. Every single time. I can't tell you how impressed I've been."

If she's been that impressed, why can't I see her daughter?

"Can we talk about something else?" The cab flies onto the Harbour Bridge, and I try to focus on glimpses of the Opera House through steel girders. Strong sunlight flickers through the shadows as we rush past. It only makes me more anxious, and now I'm reminded of a time when I was standing down there with Fraser and Parker, the weekend we went wedding shopping. "Anything at all, Maggie . . ."

"I need to thank you for talking to Parker with Josh," she says, calmly. "She came home that night and confided in me about how she's been feeling and the self-harm. She said you convinced her to and told her about that time we went to the doctor together. You didn't have to go into all of that in front of Josh. I've kept your confidence."

"Some things are more important than my pride. I'm glad she came to you. Is she going to be okay?"

There's a long pause, during which I feel like she is carrying the world. Sometimes I forget what she lost when Fraser died. Her co-parent. The only person who loved Parker in quite the same way, who knew her from birth and was there for every first step. A person now glaringly absent from everything, without any clear label for her loss. Maggie isn't widowed, but as a sole parent, she might as well be. She's still shepherding a grief-stricken child through life and doing it all on her own.

"Audrey, I think I need you," she says, eventually. "In her life. In mine. I'm sorry I shut you out for this long."

Has she forgotten the purpose of this phone call, and the fact that I seem to be almost back to square one, furiously craving the substance that tore down my life for a time and put her daughter in harm's way?

"I've literally just called you to say I want a drink, Maggie."

"Yes, and you're not going to have one. Are you?"

I shut my eyes and listen to my body. Inhaling fortitude, exhaling anger and fear and grief. I picture myself arriving at the domestic terminal in Mascot, getting out of this cab, walking through security, straight past the bar to the coffee shop . . .

"No," I say. "I'm not going to drink."

"I can stay on this call until you board," she explains. "You'll only have to get through the flight itself, but I believe you can."

I imagine the flight attendants dragging the trolley up the aisle, little bottles rattling, within reach. I see myself ordering water. Maybe a chicken wrap. And I believe that Maggie and I have averted my current crisis together. *How do any adults get through their lives completely alone?*

"I've only ever wanted to support you with Parker," I tell her. "I know she and I have music, but I will never replace you, Maggie. I never could."

"Can I save a seat for you at the concert beside Josh and me?" she asks. "I don't want her looking for us in three different parts of the audience."

Much as I could do without seeing Josh after all this, I agree. Parker has enough going on. She needs a united front.

"I'd love that." It's as if, in one conversation, the tension in our entire relationship has ratcheted down several notches. As if we've been on opposing teams all this time and one of us has crossed sides. *Are you watching this, Fraser, wherever you are?*

"Do you want to call me from the other side of security?"

The airport is in sight now. “I think I’ll be okay.” That horrible, itchy static that was screaming for alcohol has dissolved, and I’ve got the music back in my head.

We end the call and I cue Fraser’s song. That invisible, powerful thread I’ve always felt between us. Grounded by what we had. Guided by it . . .

Except now the song also reminds me of Beau, and I can’t hear it without my brain layering the new sounds over the top.

What I must not do is let this latest betrayal harden me, or let this one tumultuous week close off my life. I must protect Parker, my music, and my sobriety over everything.

As I climb out of the cab and enter the airport terminal, there’s an incoming message from Josh.

Audrey, I really need to speak with you. Before tonight.

For *fuck’s* sake. There is nothing he could tell me at this point that would fix things between us. Men like Josh and Beau—the type who dazzle you with their creative admiration, luring you skyward—promise to keep monsters at bay.

Then they feed you to them.

Sully, this is bigger than you and me.

59

Fraser

Parker is self-harming.

Maggie's text brings my elation about Rachael crashing to the floor.

Self-harming? How did I not know?

Isn't it a parent's job to know? Have I been here, thinking about myself and Rachael, grappling with grief and joy and romantic potential while my child has been right beside us all, quietly sinking?

What does "self-harm" even mean? I'm jolted back to the times I plunged to my lowest, when my life was at risk, sick to my stomach that Parker could have reached anywhere *near* a place like that.

Fraser, it's not the same as you.

It's as if Maggie, professional as ever, has hurdled our divorce and remains inside my head to this day. I turn to Rachael and feel the apology that's written all over my face. It's not been five minutes, and I'm about to complicate her life already. I pass her my phone.

"Oh, God. I'm so sorry," she says. "But also, I know a little about this. It's a scary term, and it's serious. But it's often driven by a need to let out painful emotions. It can be an attempt to feel better. Not worse. Try to stay calm."

Calm? In these few moments I've already cycled through every mistake I've ever made as a parent. Could I have tried more to keep her mother and me together? Should I not have re-partnered with Audrey? If I hadn't re-partnered, we wouldn't have lost Audrey and gone through such an intense few years. Did I lose myself in my own grief? Neglect hers? Was she collateral damage to my own depression? And now my brain presents me with a reel filled with arguments over messy bedrooms or late essays, and I'm questioning every impatient word I've ever spoken.

She says it's the only way she can let out her guilt about the accident.

Parker's guilt? Rachael and I stare at Maggie's latest message and then at each other. I know exactly how heavy this guilt weighs. I cannot imagine a child carrying that around—all this time, in silence. I *ache* for her. Maggie and I went over and over the "it's not your fault" conversation when we broke up. *Have we not reinforced that about Audrey's accident?*

"It was Russian roulette who picked up the phone that day," I say to Rachael. "It could just as easily have been Maggie or me crossing that road. It never occurred to me that Parker would have felt it was her fault."

She takes my hand. "Fraser, listen to yourself. This is what you just told me. In that instant the cosmos would have downloaded a whole alternative future, but what's the sense in trying to imagine it? You can't ever know how things might have played out. Maybe Audrey would still be here. Maybe you'd be the one who would've gone—"

"And she might have handled everything so much better."

"Or she might not have. You can't know that. But Parker would have lost one of her parents!"

Did I miss something on the day of Audrey's death? It would be easy to do, swept along by the emergency. Maybe Parker messaged us and I didn't see it or respond, routine family communications knocked off course by the crisis.

She was supposed to stay with us that night, but Maggie made some excuse about the shift in our arrangements. Then Parker ended up at Maggie's parents' place. Maybe this is where it all fell to bits. Where she lost trust in the world, and in us. Because we made her believe everything was all right that night and then, just hours later, tore her world apart.

All this time, Parker must have replayed that afternoon and imagined a version of the day in which she hadn't raised an alarm. Hadn't been struggling. Hadn't gone to sick bay. Hadn't called us in early to pick her up. A world in which Audrey hadn't died trying.

"All I know is that good parents don't get a clear ride through. You can't protect kids from the harshness of the world. It's never about how we fall. Always about how we rise." Rachael takes my hand. "You and Maggie have got this, too, Fraser."

60

Audrey

Walking into the music school, I'm facing a new kind of miserable. This pain of losing Beau, a man I've known so fleetingly, is of course a loss that does not exist in the same universe as losing Fraser. I'm mourning the sense of possibility. The hope. And the breakneck few days I've just enjoyed, during which my heart roared to life again in a way that I hadn't known it could. Beau Davenport blazed across my path like a meteor, shifting me beyond a creative crisis that spanned years.

I'm not going to worry about the film. Surely it will be possible to have that scene written out. When he skated too close to his ex-girlfriend in writing, she had him upend the entire script. Talk about a repeat offender! And I'd assumed he was so creative! Perhaps it *had* been Lucinda who brought the flair. It's the whole Shakespeare and Bassano dynamic all over again.

Nearing the door to Llewellyn Hall, I'm hit with an unexpected sense of empowerment. Last time I was in this room with Josh, he was onstage. I was in the wings, barely breathing at the magnificence of his work, gutted by the canyon that more than a decade had carved between what should have been comparable careers. I'd been burning with professional disappointment.

Now I'm bursting with ideas. I was never the kind of

composer they tried to pigeonhole me to be. I don't want to be predictable. I want to take what I've been through and transform it into sounds that people can touch and taste. Something that transcends the fire of my own experience and flames into theirs. Music that might be technically clever and complex, but accessible. I want people to cry with relief because it means so much when they recognize their world in my pieces . . .

"Sully! I've been trying to reach you for days," Josh says in a whisper, sweeping up behind me, taking my arm, and pulling me away from my epiphany at the entrance to the hall, down the side corridor, and into a dark practice room, slamming the door behind us. There is a beat of silence in the dark, charged with urgency and regret and the familiarity of his scent, that throws me straight back to that hot summer in the studio, and I have to restrain myself from filling the quiet with tumbling thoughts on my recently inspired *where to next* compositionally. *He is no longer my sounding board.*

He switches on the light, looks at me as our eyes adjust, and says, "What the fuck happened to you?"

"What?"

"You look like hell. Mixed with hope. But listen, we haven't got time to unpack that."

It's like being run over by a truck.

"Ridges is here," he announces.

I forget everything else and go stone cold. "What do you mean he's *here*?"

"He's the patron of Parker's music school. He's flown in. He's going to be at tonight's concert."

I don't know what to say. I want to say *so much*. "But, Josh, the kids are all performing original compositions."

Now that I'm paying attention, he looks like he hasn't slept in days. Face drawn, dark circles—it's a far cry from that Manhattan chic he was flaunting when he first arrived.

"Sully, I've been in meetings all week with my lawyers." *Explains the cuff links.* "I want to do the right thing here. But there's a paper trail. It would come out that I was complicit in what he did to you, and that I've continued to ignore it for eighteen years, putting others at risk. They've strongly advised me not to get involved. I've got too much to lose, reputationally."

I was wrong when I thought he couldn't disappoint me any more. "What are you saying, Josh? You're going to protect yourself and offer up your *niece*?"

He looks at me, spent.

"Wow," I say, shaking my head. Is there a stage beyond "disappointed"? I feel like I've reached the end of human emotion. As if he's now put me through the full suite and wrung me out.

"I feel terrible, Sully. I love you both."

I stare at him as if he cannot possibly be serious. "You don't know the meaning of the word. When it comes to the crunch and you have the opportunity to do the right thing, you choose yourself. Every bloody time! It was bad enough you did this to me. It's *unforgivable* to do it to her."

"Please try to understand. I'm the artistic director of the—"

"I know. *We all know.* But more important, you're her uncle. You were my *friend.*"

If I thought he seemed torn before, it's nothing compared to how he looks now. As if I've thrown a grenade and it has scorched a hole right through his core.

"*You* could still do this," he suggests, quietly. And my blood boils. *He thinks I could do it because I've got nothing whatsoever to lose.*

"Let's see," I say. "I could stand up in that concert hall—a nobody. The former almost stepmum of one of the students. An alcoholic, no less! And I could make a scene. But I'd likely be escorted out."

"You are so much more than that—" He has properly wilted now, leaning against one of the room's acoustic panels, hardware on his leather jacket threatening to scratch the wood, and I wrench him away from it by the sleeve.

"On the other hand, Joshua Miller, artistic and music director of the New York fucking Philharmonic, could stand up and say exactly the same thing and it would raise all hell." Given his profile, it would make headlines around the world, but I'm not going to mention that.

He rubs his temples, as if my words have shot straight through them. He knows I'm right.

"Obviously, it would have made more sense for you to tackle this legally and civilly during the week—or any time in the last almost two decades—but unless you can hunt down Ridges right now and deal with it discreetly, we have less than ten minutes before your brilliant and innocent niece walks onto that stage, unaware that he is probably recording the performance, ready to rip off as many of their gifted creations as he can possibly get away with."

"I know, but—"

I open the door. "You have this one, vastly belated, spectacular opportunity to do the right thing, Josh! Don't let us all down *again*." And I sweep out of the room.

61

Fraser

By the time Rachael and I have arrived at the back of the concert hall, Parker is already onstage. She sees us, and I follow her gaze into the audience and to spare seats beside Maggie, Josh, and our parents. Given my brother's intended inaction, and the fact that I am determined to protect my daughter from Ridges, this is one event that's unlikely to go down the way Mum will want to retell it later.

Parker is in long sleeves, despite the warm evening. She's always in long sleeves lately, I realize with the benefit of hindsight and a pang of guilt. *You can notice only so much as a parent,* Maggie said during a quick phone call in the car on the way here. We're on the lookout all the time for subtle signs that something might be wrong. *Are they eating properly? Are they being bullied?* Murphy's Law says the one thing we didn't check for, injured arms, is the first place we should have investigated.

Audrey

Josh and I manage to fight our way through the parents milling about in the aisles and find Maggie and the rest of the family just before the lights go down. I squeeze her hand. She's not the hand-squeezing type; nevertheless, her other hand comes over mine in a moment of understood, silent solidarity.

Thanks for the call on the Harbour Bridge—

Thanks for rescuing things with Parker—

She's not even aware that another rescue is imminent. Josh is a cat on a hot tin roof beside me, glancing around the room, looking for Ridges. Looking also, perhaps, at his adoring audience, as whispers of the presence of a famed international conductor spread through the auditorium.

Fraser

With Parker's hand poised over the keyboard, I shoot a look at Josh and, beyond him, to the VIP seats.

"We're just going to let this happen?" I whisper, fuming.

He looks panicked. This is the older brother I admired for all the years we were growing up. The man who sold out Audrey, and who looks with every passing second as though he's about to sell out my daughter, too. All to protect his precious success.

Audrey

I taught her this. Taking this moment to collect her thoughts. Closing her eyes. Hearing the music in her head. Willing it from her imagination onto the keyboard. I can tell already, just by looking at the way she has stilled, and her presence, that she is about to channel this performance from elsewhere. She may be thirteen, and those long sleeves might be covering a deeper story, but in *this* moment, she is sheer confidence.

I nudge Josh. He has seconds left to stop this. Seconds to redeem himself.

Fraser

In the face of my brother's inertia, I prepare to take a stand myself. I put my hands on the armrests, ready to push myself to my feet, swoop in, and drag the prey from the predator.

But just as I get out of my seat, so does Parker. She moves away from the piano stool and takes the microphone from its stand, shaking.

"Sorry," she starts. "Actually, no. I'm not sorry. My mum taught me girls are always apologizing when they should be taking up more space. Let me start that again . . ."

Audrey

"Professor Ridges is here today," Parker begins, speaking into the mic. "He taught my stepmum at university, and she is also here."

Maggie and I exchange a glance. I shake my head to convey that I had no idea Parker was going to mention me, nor any idea where this is going.

"She's the one who inspired me to chase this dream. So, Professor, I guess I owe you, because you taught her."

There is a sickening round of applause. Parker only has half the story! It's like watching a train crash . . .

Fraser

"My stepmum passed away three years ago," she says, as Rach takes my hand discreetly. "She died still chasing her dream. In fact, she was killed on her way to help me, and I've spent three years trying to think of a way to—"

She looks right at Joshua now. He seems trapped in his seat, and in this tower that he's built, where he's climbed so high he's beyond the reach of his entire family.

"My uncle knew my stepmum at university. He saved tons of videos from their time composing and recording in the studio together and sent them to me soon after she died, so I'd feel like I still had her with me."

Audrey

"So, sorry for the last-minute programming change, but instead of playing my own composition today, I want to play you one of hers. Date-stamped eighteen years ago. Especially for you, Professor."

Fraser

Beamed on the screen is footage I've never seen of Audrey and Josh, laughing in the studio together, experimenting with chords and melodies, drinking coffee, and writing, before Audrey finally settles down to play. My heart pounds at visual evidence of what I've always known—that their creative bond was electric. Beside me, Josh has frozen.

Audrey

I know exactly the piece I'm about to play in the video. This was the moment I first played it for Josh. It's the moment I improvised it. He is staring at the screen, mouth slack, as if he can't believe he sent Parker this recording.

We watch as I play the opening lines, creative imagination sparked. I've never seen it from the outside in—my breathlessness. The flash of inspiration across my face. But a few lines in, Parker has edited the video. The music soars, but the visuals transition from me playing the piece for Josh to Ridges performing it at one of his acclaimed performances at the Sydney Opera House.

Fraser

There is a confused and increasingly horrified hush in the audience while the final notes reverberate, the acoustics delivering a slam dunk as Parker's editing lands on a still shot of Ridges' album cover, the track circled, his name credited.

"I *have* written an original composition this week," she says, looking straight at their patron, who looks on the verge of apoplexy. "But I am not playing it in front of you."

Audrey

The lights come up. There's an extraordinarily uncomfortable pause while Ridges, ashen, clambers to his feet with intent to remove himself from the auditorium, career in tatters.

"Professor Ridges, as I'm sure you know from the stacks of research you've done on this topic, plagiarism is a criminal offense," Parker continues as the people on either side of him block his exit from the aisle. "I was going to call the police ahead but didn't know if they'd listen to a thirteen-year-old girl, so if the security guards could just barricade the doors, maybe one of the five hundred adult witnesses in the room could make the call? Audrey?"

I stand up, Joshua sinking farther into his seat, and pull out my phone to make undoubtedly the most satisfying call of my life. Every adult rises to their feet after I've audibly requested police presence, and Ridges is escorted from the auditorium in disgrace, having to push himself through a unanimous standing ovation for the child who tore him down.

Our child. The one we are all so concerned about, whose welfare has kept us awake since the day she lost her dad. *Will she survive this loss? Is it going to ruin her life?* And here she is, clever, radiant, courageous—standing up for herself in a way that none of us could.

Fraser

"I think she'll be all right," Maggie says, turning to hug me, wiping tears from her eyes, actively sobbing, in public, in a way that she's never done. "Self-harm can be linked to a lack of control. But look how much control she just took back . . ."

"Maggie, just this once, forget you're a psychiatrist? Just be her mother. Isn't she *incredible*?"

Earlier tonight, I'd gone deep into a panic that life had been too much for Parker. That the divorce and losing Audrey had caused irrevocable damage. That the big picture of it all had ruined her. Now it seems the resilience she was forced into has done the opposite. It has emboldened her.

"Fraser, did you know about this?" Mum asks. "Did you, Josh?"

"I had a suspicion," Dad confesses, red-faced, looking at my brother. "I remember you mumbling something when you rolled in from a night out with the music faculty years ago, back when everyone thought Audrey was the problem."

"And you never said anything?" I ask him, freshly angered. *No, of course he didn't. Heaven forbid our father stand up for something.*

"Looking back, there's a lot I should have said . . ."

Mum has tears in her eyes. "It felt like you left me out on a ledge with the boys," she explains to Dad. "I did the best I could on my own."

Freshly terrified about the self-harm, I finally understand where she has been coming from all this time, and I pull her into my arms.

"I was scared to death one of you would fall," she whispers into my ear, holding me tighter than she ever has. "If it had been you, I believed you would fly."

"Parker Miller," the announcer begins, restarting the concert over an hour later, after an unprogrammed, extensive intermission during which it was decided the kids should still have their chance to perform. "Welcome back to the stage."

There's more applause, wilder than anything I've ever heard for Josh.

"I think you'll agree, this talented young woman deserves another moment in the sun."

The audience won't stop.

"Parker, on behalf of your fellow students and the parents, we would like to extend our deepest gratitude. You and your peers are some of this country's most talented emerging composers, songwriters, and performers. Also, clearly, some of the most vulnerable. What you did tonight took enormous courage. You've exposed someone in a position of power over you, knowing you risked your own path."

Josh can't look up.

"I'm sure that all institutions with which Professor Ridges has had an association will be asked to provide full cooperation in the unfolding investigation. We will keep parents updated in due course. But for now, Parker, you can safely play whatever you'd like."

The second her fingers strike the keyboard, three years of music avoidance simply evaporates. I'm entranced. She is so *alive* onstage—so light and hopeful and liberated—it barely seems possible she's wrestling such torment, or maybe that's exactly why she's expressing herself so beautifully.

And I have been blocking this at home, all this time. Not letting her play. Keeping her quiet. Protecting myself from reminders of Audrey. Pushing her to find other ways to let out her emotions.

Ironically, the way she's playing now seeps into my veins like it has been me bleeding out, and this tune is a transfusion. *This* is the music I mentioned in the eulogy. The music I longed to be able to listen for again. It's been the medicine, all along, and I've been avoiding it.

My thoughts are overrun by a second standing ovation. As I get to my feet with tears of pride streaming down my cheeks and she takes another bow, I can't wait to *lavish* her in music. I want to race home with her and throw open the lid of Audrey's piano—I want it to be *her* piano and for her to play it as much and as late and as loudly as she dares.

62

Audrey

"So, my friends and I have already decided we're writing a kick-arse composition together about what happened tonight," Parker says as we gather in the foyer after the concert. I'm not sure she appreciates the family complexity here, or that her uncle had his chance and blew it. "Like, to stick it in his face even more, you know? We're not going to let him get away with it. Full-blown social media takedown. It's already trending!"

That's what you get when you stage a public stunt in a room filled with clever teenagers. It's probably too late to warn them about interfering with the carriage of justice, but either way the man is undone.

"And you know what else?" she asks, glowing. "You know how you see those farewell concerts where music teachers retire and all their former students come back and everyone cries? What if we got, like, every student this guy stole from, including you, and put on a huge concert together to reclaim our music from him? We could raise money for something, like schools that don't have musical instruments . . ."

Maggie and I beam at the remarkable child we are collectively raising.

"Five minutes after this was revealed, you've come up with this plan?" I exclaim, throwing my arms around my stepdaughter.

She hugs me back, shrugs like it's just another day, and runs off again, and we look at her go, amazed at her talent and spirit and confidence.

"Audrey, she gets the music from you," Maggie says. It's a bit awkward, as her maestro uncle is standing here with music in his genes. Maggie glances at him, having joined the dots using her understanding of human behavior and tonight's dramatic unveiling of evidence, and adds, in the pointed and some might say mildly cutting tone that I've come to know and appreciate, "She gets her courage from Audrey, too."

My phone starts pinging. It's April in the group chat. She's linked one of the kids' viral reels from tonight—this one taken from the side of the stage, focused on our row in the audience. It pans along as Parker makes her speech, my face alight with pride. Maggie's, too. Then it lands on Josh—who is shriveled, stripped of every shred of self-importance.

"I.M.P.O.T.E.N.T. . . ."

She types it as a caption.

The definition of.

The crowds disperse and it's just me now, in the courtyard outside the music school, staring up at the building in the silence, trying to wrap my head around everything that's happened. I seem to drag heartbreak in my wake, my life filled with losses in every direction—my higher degree, Fraser, even the spark I'd felt for something new with Beau. But after tonight, thanks to Parker, for the first time I am not held back. *How could I be, with her taking the lead?*

She is back in my life. Music is back. In front of me now,

there's clear, open space, and the distant rumblings of the big future I was originally reaching for, before everything went wrong. Ideas are crowding into my brain—for music, for travel, for helping Parker pull together her composition and concert, although something tells me the kids can smash that together all by themselves.

I am *flooded* with the desire to stretch and climb and conquer. To cut ties with everything that's stopped me. I'm channeling me at twenty-two. Parker at thirteen. The real-life incarnation of the "I want" song in a musical. That one that sets up the narrative trajectory for the entire show: "Wouldn't It Be Loverly?," "I Have Confidence," "My Shot."

The drive back to the beach feels like the start again.

Is that what life is? A series of overlapping cycles—some years long, some just days. Each ending kicking off another beginning, new directions, fresh pages.

The first thing I notice after pulling into the Pretty Beach campground is Beau's RV, still parked there, along with his black Ram. My stomach sinks at the sight. I'd hoped to creep in and pack up my campsite quickly, extract my little trailer, and make an escape. I'd drive north to Queensland. Or perhaps south, down the New South Wales coastline into Victoria. Maybe I'd head for the Great Ocean Road. The freedom of being able to go anywhere for a while is intoxicating in the best possible sense of that word. I plan to spend the next few months drunk on life. Hungover from late nights stargazing, dreaming up fresh music in new places.

I take a deep breath—*just one more goodbye*—as I back up the Jeep, perfectly this time, and realize he is watching me from his doorway, hands in his pockets. Looking destroyed.

I shut off the engine. The door, which is always jammed, opens first go and easily. He must have fixed that during our road trip, along with the damage to the back of my camper since he returned, I notice now.

I climb out of the car and try to heave the trailer into place, having parked slightly short. He jumps down the step and comes over, picks up the tow hitch, pulls the trailer over, and settles it on the ball. Then he tightens the socket and checks the pin, shaking it to ensure it's all safely attached for my journey.

I push his hand off it, in the end. "I'm sure it's fine."

"Audrey, please hear me out?" he says, agony in his eyes. "Just give me five minutes before you go?"

The remorse seems real, at least. I stand there, hands on hips. Viperish myself.

"I need you to know I didn't write that scene. I had no idea it was even in the script. I would never have put it there."

I cross my arms. "Let me guess, technically your ex-fiancée wrote it? And she is, what? Psychic, as well as brilliant and stunning?"

I could have done without the last adjective. It adds a layer of jealousy to this conversation that detracts from the power of my case.

"I was as surprised as you were when she turned up. I didn't know she was even involved until she walked in yesterday afternoon. I haven't spoken to her in months." He'd done a convincing job of acting as if this part was at least true.

"Beau, how does she know the entire blow-by-blow scenario from the clifftop so perfectly?"

He seems heartsick over this. "She didn't hear it from me. I would protect you, and that whole experience, at any cost. I know how much that moment meant to you and how hurt you were to think I exploited it. You have to believe I would never have done this."

But he did do it. I cannot believe the man is standing here, lying to me, when the evidence is so blatantly undeniable.

"We are the only two people in the whole world who were there. How else has it wound up in the script?"

He's crushed.

"It nearly killed me when Fraser died. I almost drove myself into the grave, via the bottle, with grief. I vowed that I would never get close to someone else. Not like this. Ever again. Because it would be so easy for me to unravel."

He steps forward, his face lined with concern, but I step away from him, holding my hands up to stop him touching me.

"That day you spent writing music after Tathra? I spent it writing, too."

"You spent most of it washing your trailer," I counter. *Washing his trailer and caressing my shoulders with sunscreen.*

"You process your thoughts in music. I do it in words. I didn't write that scene. Not in the screenplay. But I hadn't been able to write for so long, and finally, having been with you, I *felt something*. I had one of those once-in-a-lifetime amazing experiences with someone who was worth writing home about."

Writing home?

"Beau, who is at home? Lucinda?"

"Nobody. It's an expression. I listened to the music pouring out of your RV and put pen to paper—just snippets of lines about you and how impressive you are, and how confused I was . . . Do you know how hard it is to compete with a man like Fraser?"

How can someone like *Beau* be insecure about a romantic rival? Particularly one who is dead!

"The journal was only ever meant for me," he explains.

"But even if what you're saying is true, it doesn't explain how she ended up in possession of this private source material, does it?"

He has the courtesy to look sheepish now. "Harlow's got a key to my RV."

Well, that's just great, isn't it? Because on top of the existing debacle, he appears to be admitting that tabloids don't *always* make things up. It's no surprise, of course, after that first night, when she waltzed in and opened that bottle of wine like she owned the place.

"She'd been helping me with the film admin. The mentoring had been going well. She wanted to try her hand at writing a scene herself, but I wouldn't let her. Not with this project."

I feel some tiny piece of anger dislodge and dissolve inside me, even though I still don't understand.

"I can only assume she came looking for me after you and I had left for Canberra, let herself in, and found the notebook I'd left on the bed."

"Does she have no respect for privacy?" I ask. I'm furious that she'd take something so desperately personal and do this.

"I didn't write your name in my notes. She must have read them, recognized the cinematic potential, and, when days passed and it didn't appear in the script—especially with so much riding on it all—sent the scene to Lucinda, who had already been called in. They were trying to rescue me from failure . . ."

What am I doing with this man? As annoying as all of this is, I can almost believe it makes sense. He's been nothing but kind and caring and thoughtful and compassionate since the second we met, and didn't I just decide only last night that I had cut ties with everything that's held me back all these years? My distrust of people included.

"Anyway, I want you to know I've written you out of the

story," he says firmly. "You don't have to worry anymore. And I had my lawyer draw up a new NDA and had everyone who was at that meeting yesterday sign it. I won't bother you from now on. You can keep going the way you are and write music and travel and expand your world again the way you wanted to at the start. But as far as I'm concerned, don't think about it for another second. All traces of you from my story have been completely erased. You can forget we even met."

He touches me on the arm, just once, offers a weak smile, and steps backward toward his trailer.

"Drive safely, Hepburn."

63

Fraser

"Right, hand over your phone," Jess says when the Bookies are all set up in the family room. "Let's go through this app and sort you out."

Sudden panic hits, because I think they are sick of my dilly-dallying and they intend to throw me at one of these matches for real. Rach and I haven't told them about us. We wanted to expand this friendship in private first, before turning the whole thing into a pep rally.

"I want Dad to delete the app," Parker says, so emphatically it silences the room.

She does?

She said at the coast it was okay with her if I dated. Maybe she's not ready after all. I can't even look at Rachael.

"But we went to all that trouble to make your dad sound attractive!" April explains, as if the exercise was unbearable.

"Yeah, and it obviously worked, because all these women kept messaging him the whole time we were camping! So cringe!" Parker mimics being sick, a gesture I detest, and I tell her to stop. "Dad is so uncool. He doesn't even listen to the top forty thousand, Rach said."

"Four thousand, I think I said."

"He doesn't listen to the top four million!" Parker replies.

“Too busy listening to everything you play,” I argue. “I’ve got a lot of catching up to do.”

Maggie found a psychologist who combines traditional approaches with music therapy, and Parker has already been finding the sessions helpful. She’s sitting at Audrey’s piano now, lid open, as it has been permanently since the concert. No more headphones. Endless music. And she’s rediscovered a whole lot of “new” tunes in Audrey’s old manuscript books, constantly filling our house with the sound of her, giving us “butterfly moments,” as if she is always here, in a way I’ll never be able to explain scientifically.

I look across the room at Rachael. Someone who is also always here, and who always has been, right from the start.

“Nobody on the app is going to work,” I say. “Parker’s right. We should delete it.”

“You mean no one on the app is Audrey,” Jess complains, groaning, echoing Rach’s earlier thoughts. “God, you are *so* predictable!”

Parker plays a dramatic few chords on the piano, lifts her hands theatrically, and says, “He means no one on the app is Rachael.”

The room falls silent. Rachael stares at Parker, then at me, while the others snap around to ensure they heard right.

“I’m sorry,” says Jess. “Did you just say nobody on the app is *Rachael*?”

“I said what I said,” Parker states, smiling.

“*Our* Rachael?” Jess wants to clarify. “Rachael Elizabeth McKenzie?”

“Well, duh,” says the resident teenager. “Where have you all been?”

“Parks is right,” Rachael says, from across the room. “You should delete the app. I told you it was a waste of time.”

"But I'm worried about Ava. A message flashed past just this morning again, begging to meet up. How will she carry on?"

Rach takes the phone from my hand and tosses it onto the couch. "Ava is really not my problem," she says, pulling me to my feet, taking me in her arms in front of the astonished Bookies. "My problem is that I hate camping."

"Oh, no!"

"I don't even like the beach."

I feign shock. "But the beach is my line of work, Rachael!"

"I thought you mapped climate models in a lab coat."

"Men always lie on the apps. I don't even own a lab coat."

I wrap my arms around her. It feels weird and new and right and beautiful to be doing this in front of everyone, and perfect, when she reaches her arm toward Parker, who joins our family circle.

"I wasn't going to invite you camping anyway," I confess, once the rest of them have gone home. "That's Parker's thing."

"I'll settle for the midnight talks," Rach says. "Isn't that what we put in the profile?"

"Some soppy thing. The profile was awful."

She leans back to put my face in focus. "Still worked. You were flooded with options!"

"And you were so irritated that night. I thought you were annoyed on Audrey's behalf!"

She laughs, threading her arms around my waist. "No-o. That was all me. I was furiously jealous." She moves her hands to my chest, as if I'm hers and we have the rest of our lives for this. "Are you *sure* Audrey would be okay with this? You and me?"

The answer to this one feels as clear as day. "Okay with it? It feels like she orchestrated it."

"I know you're a scientist, Fraser, and don't believe in this stuff, but do you think she's happy, wherever she is?"

"Look, the thing about science is that we don't know everything about how the universe works. The more we discover, the less we realize we understand. All I can tell you for sure is we definitively rule out—"

"Stop!" she says, plastering her hand over my mouth, laughing. "I'm not asking for a lecture, Dr. Miller, PhD. I'm asking *you*, Frase. Do *you* think she is happy?"

She takes her hand away, and I deliver the answer I've craved for more than three years, the one we both need, feeling its truth all the way to my bones. "I haven't a shadow of a doubt."

64

Two Years Later

Audrey

"Beau, I don't know about this dress."

Sitting on the sofa in his Sydney apartment, he looks up from his laptop, takes his glasses off, and assesses the sparkly gown. I wriggle uncomfortably, wishing it didn't hug my body, and feeling far more attracted to a night on the couch in sweats.

"The dress is perfect, Hepburn. I just don't know how you're going to walk in those shoes."

"I didn't bring anything else," I say, anxious that we're out of time now and I could break my neck and photographic evidence would end up in *The Sydney Morning Herald.*

"I was always partial to those Wellingtons," he says.

I laugh. "What did you really think when I ran into your truck? You played it so cool that night."

He puts the laptop aside and gets up. "Playing it cool was an act. When I met you, I remember thinking my whole line of work is about made-up stories. It's about trying to convince an audience that fake people exist. Most of the people I know are either making up fiction or acting it out, and then you crashed into my life . . ."

"Suffering, flawed . . ."

He frowns. "Will you ever let me forget that? I was trying to tell you what I loved about you!"

"Can we table this conversation for after the event?" I ask, conscious of the time.

He strips off his T-shirt for the shower, my eyes dropping to the familiar lion on his chest. I trace it with my fingertips, geography I know intimately now, right down to the new swirl in the mane covering the part that used to say *Lucinda*. Then I move to the compass on his arm.

"What's this?" I ask, confused.

He twists his arm to look at it. "That's a compass, Audrey. It's a device that shows the cardinal directions for navigation—"

"Am I losing my mind, or has it changed direction?"

He smiles. "I wondered how long it would take you to notice. I had the needle reoriented while I was in L.A."

Reoriented? Sounds painful!

"And these coordinates?" I trace the new string of numbers on his skin.

"Last time I had a woman's name tattooed, it didn't go well," he explains. "Thought I was fairly safe with a beach."

I feel my eyes widen. "*Our* beach?"

"The very same accident hot spot, yes."

I'm worried I'm going to mess up the professional makeup I had done this afternoon at April's insistence. He sees the tears forming and expertly snaps me out of it: "Look, we can't stand around all day while you admire my six-pack, Hepburn. Unhand me—or we'll be late for the premiere!"

Minutes later, we're out of the apartment, into an Uber, zipping around Darling Harbour, and climbing from the car onto the red carpet, camera flashes bursting in our faces. It's a situation to which Beau is well accustomed and to which I will never acclimatize, so he squeezes my hand for reassurance.

"Who are you wearing tonight, Audrey?" someone asks, with a microphone stuck in my face. I have no bloody idea. I borrowed it.

"She's wearing April's Wardrobe," Beau responds, deadpan, supervising the confused reporter while she jots down the words as if he's given her a hot tip on an up-and-coming designer. I slip my hand through his arm as we walk along the carpet, pausing to look up at Darling Harbour's Lyric Theatre, with an enormous flashing billboard that takes my breath away.

The next runaway Australian hit!

WIDOWED:
The Musical

"Wildly heartbreaking. Dazzlingly hopeful!" —Time Out
"Life-affirming in every note." —Who? Weekly

"Look at that, Hepburn. *Now* do you believe in yourself?"

I scoff. "You led me to believe the tabloids were full of trash!"

The screen flashes and the credits appear.

Music by Audrey Sullivan and Parker Miller
Book and lyrics by Audrey Sullivan and Beau Davenport

We gaze at the sign together, and I look at our names and say, *"Fortiores una."*

"Stronger as one," he agrees. "Any closer and we would have cycled through the entire welding process, right?"

I turn to face him. "You remember that? From when I crashed into your RAM? You were investigating the damage. I thought I'd try to lighten the mood. You didn't seem impressed—"

"Remember it? That was the second I fell for you! Well, that and the fascinating brag about your talent for spreadsheets."

I glance back at the billboard. "How did I ever attract a big-name, Oscar-winning screenwriter . . ."

"To this project," he asks, "or—"

I can't answer his question, because we're ushered inside and swept through a crowd and into the best seats in the darkened theater, where we meet Parker and Sara, with her new wife, Jodi, and my parents and Maggie, who's brought a date with her, Lachlan. He's a barista with a mop of shaggy sun-bleached hair. A younger man who surfs and writes poetry in a coupling with Maggie makes absolutely *no* sense, and I'm utterly mad for it.

The Bookies are here. Well, Jess and Clair, anyway. April talked her way into a role in the chorus.

Rach pushes herself forward, so proud of me she might burst. Ever my closest, most faithful friend, there hasn't been a step I've taken where she hasn't been by my side.

As I look at her, I just *know*. "Do you have something to tell me?" I ask. I've been desperate to know the outcome of the last cycle.

"Not tonight," she whispers, her face doing the talking the way it did when she first told me Jasper was on the way. "But yes."

So I'm already emotional as she takes my hand and we look at the stage. The red curtains are closed, and in white font projected across the folds are the words "In memory of Fraser Miller." For a moment, the sight steals the breath from my lungs. As the air in the theater moves the material gently and the light undulates, the letters of his name ripple, the way I've always pictured the two of us, our proximity ebbing and flowing through invisible folds in the fabric of time.

If Fraser was right the night he proposed, then I am here now, in this theater, watching a musical I would never have written had he not died, with a man I would never have met. And somewhere, perhaps in another dimension of this mysteriously tangled, incomprehensible universe, Fraser has written a new story, too.

I watch in endless, excited disbelief as characters born from my own imagination light up the stage, music swirling that I feared for so long that I'd lost. I remember the moment in the storm that first night at Pretty Beach, when it hit me that I wanted to live again. *Really* live. With trumpets and drums and disco balls and confetti cannons and brassy eleven-o'clock numbers—the whole sparkly, glittery extravaganza of it all!

And look at me now! Doing exactly that, my lap around this gorgeous country in Miss Bennet having produced this show, then led me home. To Beau. Struggling, despite how very much I loved Fraser, to imagine my life having played out in any other way.

At intermission, Beau takes Parker aside. "Need to talk to you later about a new script. The composer they've hired just isn't getting it, and I'd love your thoughts. Pay you for your time, of course. We'll draw up a contract."

She looks from him to me, eyes wide, secretly thrilled. Fifteen years old and already in demand! She's so like her uncle, at least in terms of her precocious talent, and I have one quick flash of the text message I haven't replied to—*Break a leg tonight, Sully*—before Parker reaches for my hand. She's in a bright red, showstopping, sleeveless dress, taking up space the way she deserves to, faded scars on show for the first time. And when she catches me looking at her arms, she says, "It's part of my story, Audrey. Sara told me to own my narrative!"

"You are my role model," I tell her. "I am *fiercely* proud of you."

"We are, too," Mum says, tears in her eyes. "*Always* choose music. Both of you."

As the lights dim for the second act, my heart is bursting for this little group. My family. My dearest friends. The daughter I adore. The man who has become an equal "love of my life."

I thought I'd have survivor's guilt, being this happy. It shouldn't be possible after a loss as shattering as mine. But Fraser took care of that the night he proposed.

Because somewhere else along the timeline, there's a version of him who's still alive. There's a version of us that's still together. There's a place that will always be ours and a song that will ring endlessly into the universe, where he'll be in every note that I'll ever play.

the end

and the start . . .

Acknowledgments

This book was released three months before the tenth anniversary of my husband's death. I've written it to commemorate that loss and celebrate our family's survival—our thriving—through a full decade without him.

Ever since Jeff died, I have wondered what would have happened if all of this had been the other way around. What if it had been me who died? How would he have handled the fallout? Would he have re-partnered? Shortly before he died, he'd been applying for an academic role in Ireland. Would the family have moved there from Australia? Everything would have been different . . . The main question was always *Would our little boy have been okay in either universe?*

This book is an attempt to answer those questions. I wanted to explore the different ways people manage loss. In real life, my choices resembled Fraser's more than Audrey's, but, in an alternate universe, I could so easily have been her. The story is also a reminder that, even when our lives take an unwanted turn, the path forward can still be full of music and light if we reach for it.

To my readers, thank you for letting me write my way through all of this. Your continued support of my career, your messages, and the sharing of your own stories in person and online have meant the world. We are in this together.

Enormous gratitude to my publishers and very patient editors: Cate Paterson and Sophie Bellotti at Allen & Unwin's

Atlantic Books in Australia; Zibby Owens, Anne Messitte, and Kathleen Harris at Zibby Publishing in the United States; and Sarah Hodgson and Rachel Imrie at Atlantic Books, Corvus in the UK. Thank you for taking a chance on an ambitious idea and for helping me tame it. To Diana, Gabriella, Sherri, Graça, Madeleine, and every person who has touched this book along the path to publication at all three publishing houses, it is a privilege working with you.

Chief among the dream-makers is my literary agent and friend Anjanette Fennell at Key People Literary Management, with whom I've been riding this roller coaster for well over a decade. Your endless encouragement and friendship is what keeps me in this career, and I couldn't fathom doing it without you.

To Kat Berney, my "alpha reader," who propels me through every draft; to Kerry Kohansky-Roberts, who made me believe this book had wings; and to the writers in my DMs—Kate Solly, Kerryn Mayne, Sandie Docker, Rachel Fox McLeod, Nina Campbell, Fionna Roberts, Vanessa Monaghan, and everyone in my Canberra writers' group—you can't know how vital your support has always been.

If you check the acknowledgments in every book I've ever written, along with the additions of Tom, Nathan, and baby Fred, you'll always see the same names of my family and closest friends. These are the long-haulers. The ones who've seen me through every challenge and every triumph and encouraged me to keep the faith when things felt impossibly uphill. To all of you, and you know exactly who you are, I send a depth of love that it feels impossible to articulate.

This book is for Sebastian. Our beautiful son. A kind, intelligent, funny, musical, compassionate teenager who I've learned would have been fine in either universe. Not because of anything his dad would have done differently, but because of who he has grown into as a person.

Seb, you are stronger and more resilient than you realize. You have faced some of the toughest challenges life can throw at a child and you continue to persevere in a way that would make Dad so immensely proud, as it does me. I adore you.

About the Author

Emma Grey is the author of seven books, including two international bestselling novels, *The Last Love Note* and *Pictures of You*, winner of the American Independent Publisher Book Award gold medal. Her adult and young adult novels have been translated internationally, optioned for film, and adapted for the stage. She lives in Canberra, Australia, surrounded by her three children, stepchildren, and grandchildren.

Scan for bonus content and book club resources: